DANSE MACABRE

CLOSE ENCOUNTERS WITH THE REAPER

EDITED BY

NANCY KILPATRICK

EDGE SCIENCE FICTION AND FANTASY PUBLISHING
AN IMPRINT OF HADES PUBLICATIONS, INC.
CALGARY

Edge Science Fiction and Fantasy Publishing
An Imprint of Hades Publications Inc.
P.O. Box 1714, Calgary, Alberta, T2P 2L7, Canada

Edited by Nancy Kilpatrick
Interior design by Janice Blaine

Interior art by Christopher Foster
Cover Illustration by John Kaiine

ISBN: 978-1-894063-96-8

EDGE Science Fiction and Fantasy Publishing and Hades Publications, Inc.
acknowledges the ongoing support of the Canada Council for the Arts and the
Alberta Foundation for the Arts for our publishing programme.

Library and Archives Canada Cataloguing in Publication

    Danse macabre : close encounters with the reaper / Nancy
Kilpatrick, editor.

Short stories.
Also issued in electronic format.
ISBN 978-1-894063-96-8
(e-book ISBN: 978-1-894063-97-5)

    1. Grim Reaper (Symbolic character)--Fiction. 2. Horror
tales, American. 3. Horror tales, Canadian (English). 4. Horror
tales. I. Kilpatrick, Nancy

PS648.H6D35 2012   813'.0873808351   C2012-902395-7

FIRST EDITION
(H-20120629)
Printed in Canada
www.edgewebsite.com

─TABLE OF CONTENTS─

—ACKNOWLEDGEMENTS—

Thanks... To the usual suspects, for keeping me relatively sane. To those who kindly sent me Danse Macabre images, some of which were new to me — much appreciated. To Christopher Foster of Factotum Graphics who did an extraordinary job of updating the lovely Holbein-inspired drop cap images. To Sasha Sergejewski for help with proofreading. To John Kaiine for his stunning artwork which graces the cover. To Brian Hades (yes, his real name) of EDGE Science Fiction & Fantasy Publishing for leaping yet again with faith in my direction; it's wonderfully refreshing to work with a publisher who throws caution to the wind and takes on a project solely because he trusts the editor. And finally, to the amazingly creative wordsmiths whose unique stories are included herein — you astonish me with your brilliance!

■ ■ ■

—INTRODUCTION—
By Nancy Kilpatrick

We, the living, have always exhibited a fascination with Death. We can't help ourselves. Death is, after all, one of our two most personal experiences, the other being Birth.

Back in the 14th century, when the world was in the grip of the Black Death, people were immersed in demise. From then until the 19th century, the plague was an on-again, off-again reality that, when most virulent, affected communities on a daily basis. The Black Plague decimated the population of Europe by approximately fifty per cent.

Whenever catastrophe strikes humanity, the arts always prove themselves invaluable. Through the metaphor of art, people come to terms with the inconceivable. Events that traumatize us individually and/or collectively evoke a need to make sense of what happened and the arts allow deeper connections to be made, aiding our ability to cope.

The Dance of Death (English); Danse Macabre (French); Totentanz (German); Danza Macabra (Italian); La Danza de la Muerte (Spanish); Dansa de la Mort (Catalan); Dans Macabru (Romanian); Dodendans (Dutch); Dança da Morta (Portuguese); these are but some of the names for what has been called 'plague art', visual artwork, sometimes accompanied by text, that grew out of the Medieval collective experience. Most commonly known as Danse Macabre, the visual aspect of this art depicts one or more skeletons — the formerly living — leading the dying from this earthly plane to another realm. These skeletons achieve this by inviting people to dance their way to the end of life, a rather charming approach to a date with mortality, if you think about it.

The initial Danse Macabre paintings appeared on the interior walls of *Le Cimetière des Innocents* in Paris in 1424 (artist unknown), accompanied by poetry. This was not a cemetery as we know them today but a fenced-in bone yard, where remains were tossed onto an ever-expanding pile. During the Black Plague, so many succumbed — the cause of the plague unknown at that time — that everyone knew someone who had capitulated to this disease: family, friends and neighbors, bakers, priests, Queens.

Danse Macabre took hold of the collective consciousness because in the midst of all this expiration, one truism emerged: Death comes to us all. No one is spared, from the beggar to the King, the merchant to the Pope. Death is the one great equalizer. And the bereaved can find some solace in that fact.

Early Danse Macabre art showed mostly males leaving this mortal coil, but soon artists were pencilling females into tableaux, for instance, milk maids, nuns, prostitutes, dowagers, mothers and their daughters. A wide spectrum of mortals were caught in a personal interaction with the Angel of Death, who was encouraging them to 'dance'. Meanwhile, the mortal was: stalling for time; attempting a bribe; pleading their case; hoping to trick the reaper grim, etc. And despite Welsh poet Dylan Thomas' warning that we should *not* go gently into death and his encouragement to rage against the dying of our light, the occasional person was shown dancing willingly.

Mortals in Danse Macabre artwork are, naturally, portrayed with emotion. Death, on the other hand, is usually seen as an impersonal skeleton, merely doing a job, neither just nor unjust. This artwork was taken as a *memento mori*: "Remember, you will die". The motif is a reminder that by being aware that Death waits in the wings until the music starts, Life should be viewed as precious, experienced vividly; each moment counts.

Knowledge of human anatomy was sketchy but became more sophisticated over the centuries. Earlier skeletons are barely recognizable as such. They appeared as hairy, fleshy, wrongly shaped, with crucial parts missing, and creatures that live in the earth added to their bones as special effects — it's a wonder some could stand, let alone play an instrument, which they sometimes did as accompaniment to the dance they were trying to entice mortals to! Many looked more like the skeletons of monkeys, rather than humans. But despite the primitive quality of the earliest artwork, it's surprising how often their bony skulls managed to hint at cuteness or cunning, cruelty or caginess, cynicism or chivalry. They could be laughing at us or weeping for us but the underlying sense is that Death has seen it all before, and will again.

The first Danse Macabre artwork from the 14th century did not survive when the Parisian cemetery was demolished (once science discovered germs and realized the dead should be burned or buried and not left out in the open). Those images were, though, reproduced in a book, woodcuts designed by Hans Holbein the Younger. This type of art was then recreated throughout Europe over the next 500 years, each country putting its singular spin on the final dance. Suffering the ravages of time, most of this special visual artwork has been destroyed, but some have survived. Manuscripts with original images or reproductions of existing images fared better than the actual art. But there are still approximately 50 pieces that can be found, the earliest dating from the mid-15th century.

Danse Macabre: Close Encounters with the Reaper sprang from my long-term interest in and appreciation of this primitive but poignant art. I have traveled to many countries, and some hard-to-get-to spots, hunting for what remains, treasuring these very human imaginings of what happens when we die.

The idea came to me to see if it was possible to translate the Danse Macabre concept from a visual art form to a literary art form. I wanted to edit an anthology that conveys two concepts through a series of stories presenting a range of interactions with the Grim Reaper. The first: that Death *is* the great equalizer. The second: what I believe is also imbedded in the artwork, but perhaps not so obviously — are human beings able to, as the artwork intimates, affect death? Physicists have discovered that certain sub-atomic particles are affected by the observer. Is it possible that Death, this evanescent reality of existence, regardless of the form taken and despite seeming dispassionate by nature, might in some way be influenced by us just as we are undoubtedly influenced by it?

The writers in this remarkable and unusual anthology 'got it'. They cranked their imaginations up a notch or two and envisioned tales which reflect a wide spectrum of humanity. There are fascinating interactions with Thanatos, outcomes not necessarily expected. These talented writers have managed to create powerful and very human tales that certainly are not all grim. It's a volume that tries to convey an existential dance with words, twirling readers through graceful twists and turns and clever and unexpected spins, with the hope of leaving you charmed by the *pas de deux*.

Death has and likely always will remain a mystery. But one thing mortals can be certain about: the Danse Macabre is a very personal dance, one it might be possible to manage with grace, style and perhaps even a few jaunty pirouettes.

Nancy Kilpatrick
Montreal, 2012

—DANSE MACABRE—

By Ian Emberson

Death came to me in a mini skirt
As skittish as a kitten,
And said: "I am come — for your final flirt,"
But added: "You don't seem smitten."

Says I: "Well — not in my wildest whim
Did I picture you looking like this,
I'd been told that you were a reaper grim
And behold — a saucy miss."

"Ah — many a one is like yourself
Surprised by my winning smile,
I have jokes and jests like a playful elf
And I know the way to beguile."

"But please — just pass me by with a nod
I've poems and plays unwritten,
There are footpaths I have never trod
As you say — I'm not much smitten."

"Oh hush my darling — and don't repine,"
And she gave a gracious prance,
Then she twined her fingers into mine
And whispered: "Shall we dance?"

Ian Emberson, writer and artist, was born at Hove in England in 1936, and is proud to have been christened by the poet Andrew Young. Ian has earned his living in both horticulture and librarianship, spending much of his working life as music librarian at Huddersfield Public Library. He has had twelve books published, and several one man art exhibitions. In addition to writing and painting, he enjoys walking and swimming. The idea for "Danse Macabre" came when he showed his wife Catherine an illustration in a biography of Petrarch, and she remarked: "That's death in a mini skirt."

THE
~SECRET ENGRAVINGS~
By Lisa Morton

Hans turned the corner and smelled death.

The odor, sudden and undeniable, cascaded his memory back to four years ago, to 1519, when his brother Ambrosius had succumbed to plague. He'd gone against the advice of physicians and friends to attend to Ambrosius, and the scent in his brother's final hours had been this same nauseating mix of rotten meat and metallic blood and sour fear sweat.

Hans was yanked back to the present as he saw a body being taken from a house down the alley. Two men, common laborers with thick rags wrapped around their faces, lugged a shrouded corpse into a waiting cart. As they heaved it onto the creaking boards, a foot fell loose, and Hans saw:

The toes were almost completely black.

Plague. Again, here in Basel.

One of the laborers glanced up and saw Hans staring. He stepped a few feet away from the dead man, glanced back once, and tugged down the improvised cloth mask. He was burly, with a long, unwashed beard and filthy peasant's garb, but his face and voice were surprisingly kind. "Best not come this way," he said.

"How far…?" Hans couldn't finish the question.

The man understood. "Only this house. He was a merchant, been traveling, just came back last week. I doubt it'll spread."

'*Doubt*'? *Precious little to put my mind at ease.* But Hans nodded and turned away.

He clutched his satchel tighter — it held the drawings for the prayer book, his latest commission, and as such was precious — and walked down another lane, unseeing.

The Great Mortality … here, again.

He'd been on his way to visit Hermann, the engraver who would complete the woodcuts that would allow the drawings to be printed; but now he found himself walking aimlessly, stunned.

After Ambrosius, Hans had lived in dread of encountering the plague again. Ambrosius, his beloved older brother, the one their father had believed would be a great artist. Ambrosius, who had his own studio while Hans Holbein the Younger was yet an apprentice to another artist; even if Hans was now accorded greater recognition than Ambrosius had ever been given, he knew the hole that his brother's gruesome death had left in his soul would never fill. He couldn't forget watching the buboes form under his sibling's arms, the black spots that spread up his face and limbs as he vomited blood. Four years later, not a day passed when he didn't see Ambrosius's dying face, or — earlier — that sought-after smile of approval. He spied his brother in statues, in paintings, in other men, in children.

And he saw his own death by plague in everything else. The thought terrified him; he'd seen what his brother had endured, and he couldn't imagine doing the same. The fevers, the bursting skin, the blood…

Hans finally looked up, realizing he'd wandered far away now from the engraver's neighborhood, and was near the house of his friend Erasmus. Hans had recently painted the great man, and they'd become friends as a result. Erasmus had read parts of his essay *The Praise of Folly* to Hans during the sittings, and Hans had come to admire the man for his wit and insight. He could use a precious dose of that today.

A few minutes later, the scholar was welcoming Hans into his study. Once seated before a warming hearth with a brandy ("good for all Four Humours," Erasmus assured him), surrounded by books and scrolls and writing desks and quills, only then did Hans finally begin to relax.

"Your fame is growing, young Hans," Erasmus told him, as he stood before the fire, his rugged face creased in pleasure. "I had reason to visit the Great Council Chamber in town hall today, and a traveler from Germany saw your mural and asked if it was the work of the Italian, Da Vinci. I was delighted to tell him that Basel has its own Da Vinci in the young Hans Holbein. He told me he would mark that name well."

Hans tried to smile, but wasn't entirely successful. Erasmus saw the attempt. "I fear you're not here for mere praise alone."

"No. I saw … plague. Plague has returned to Basel."

If Hans had expected some measure of panic or at least discomfort from his friend, he was surprised to see only a mild shrug. "Plague is always with us in some form or other. It's a constant companion. You of all people should know that, Hans — who was it but the artists who captured the *Dance of Death* when the Great Mortality first struck a century ago?"

Erasmus rummaged briefly through a shelf, then pulled down a large tooled and leather-bound copy of *Liber Chronicarum*, placed it in Hans's lap, and flipped through the parchment leaves until he came to an engraving that showed four skeletons, tufts of hair flying from their sere skulls, capering in a graveyard. Hans examined it briefly, then muttered, "It is the work of Michael Wolgemut. I could do better."

His friend laughed and clapped his shoulder. "Indeed you could, young genius."

Hans spent another hour with Erasmus, discussing art and civic politics and the gossip surrounding a local aristocrat, and by the time he left the sun was setting and his spirits had lifted. As he lingered in Erasmus's doorway, pulling his fur-trimmed cloak tighter against the cooling air, Erasmus told him, "Paint, Hans. It's what God meant you for, and it will ease your mind."

Hans nodded and left.

▪ ▪ ▪

He'd still been contemplative when he'd returned home. He ate dinner with his wife Elsbeth and their sons Franz and Philipp, then excused himself to the studio.

At first he wondered if he'd made a mistake; the studio had once belonged to his brother, whose spirit now seemed to infest every scrap of paper and brush and easel and ink bottle. Hans stoked the fire, shrugged out of his heavy outer garment, and tried to focus on his latest commission — an altarpiece design for the local church — but neither mind nor hand would bend to the task. Finally, he lowered his head to the worktable and closed his eyes, seeking simple oblivion.

Someone was with him, in the studio.

He didn't know how much time had passed, and he hadn't yet opened his eyes to confirm what his other senses screamed at him; a quickening terror clutched his heart. His eyes popped open, involuntarily.

A tall shadow stood on the far side of the room, draped in a black robe and cowl. "Good evening, Hans," it said, in a deep, somehow hollow voice.

Hans lifted his head, but he possessed no more strength. He opened his mouth, but couldn't form words.

"All will be made clear, my friend. Know for now that I mean you no harm." The visitor's basso tones sent shivers up his back.

"How…" Hans managed to look back at the studio's door, and saw that it was as he'd left it, bolted from within.

His guest stepped forward, and Hans saw the gleam of something white from within the folds of the cowl.

Is that—

"Yes, bone. What else would Death be made of?" Two skeleton-hands emerged from the sleeves, pushed back the cowl, and let Hans see his visitor's face … or rather, see the skull where a face should have been. There was nothing but ancient, polished bone, no shred of skin or hair or muscle or vein. Hans pushed away from his bench, and barely noticed when he fell to the floor.

His guest — Death — made a placating gesture. "You've nothing to fear from me, Hans Holbein the Younger."

"You're not here with … the plague?"

The skull moved back and forth. "Far from it. In fact, I'm here to offer you a way to *save* yourself from plague. I come to claim your services, not your life."

Panic started to abate, replaced by curiosity. "My … services…"

"Yes. A commission."

Hans blinked in surprise and drew himself up. "You want me to … work for you?"

"I do. What you told your friend Erasmus earlier…"

Hans went back in his memory, and he knew immediately — he knew how he'd damned himself.

I could do better.

"The old depictions of me, those ridiculous images of dancing and cavorting like some mad witch in the moonlight … they no longer please me. I consider you to be the finest artist of this age, and I want you to render me, as I am, every day. I want you to record me the way I truly am — not as some prancing fool, but as one who practices his trade with care and respect for the craft."

"*Respect*?" Hans gasped out, before he could stop himself. "You kill innocents—"

"No. I merely perform the tasks assigned me. There are greater authorities above me, Hans. If you have complaints with choices, you'll need to address those elsewhere. I only control the day-to-day practice, and I am not cruel, callous, or uncaring. I take pride in my work, as you do in yours."

Hans wanted to sneer. He wanted to stand and hurl epithets at this monster, call him a liar, a hypocrite, deluded, but...

What if he's right?

"So how would you—?"

"You will accompany me on some of my rounds. Neither of us will be visible to those I must take. You will observe, and record exactly what you see."

"And in return, you'll keep me safe from plague? My family as well?"

"Yes. And also..."

Death ran his fleshless fingers into Hans's leather satchel, and removed the small bundle of prayer book drawings. The sheets flew across the table, and Death leaned down to examine them closely. "These are lovely. They're too good for Hermann, you know."

Hans *did* know. Hermann's work was often slipshod, erasing the lovely details that made artwork live and breathe. "He's the best in Basel—"

"He's not. Seek out Hans Lützelburger."

"I know the name, but he's not in Basel."

Death turned to face him, and somehow he knew the smile was intentional this time. "He has only recently come here. He will be my other gift to you. Shall we begin tomorrow?"

Holbein swallowed ... and nodded.

❈ ❈ ❈

They began at a convent.

They'd flown like wind through Basel's crowded morning streets, and arrived unseen at Death's destination. Holbein felt like a voyeur, trespassing into the intimate inner realm of the brides of Christ, but when one initiate walked through him, he wondered which of them was really the ghost.

Death led him to a courtyard where the elderly abbess knelt in a small garden. Even from a distance, Holbein could hear her rattling breath, see her faltering limbs. She was halfway dead, but her will kept her clinging stubbornly to life.

Death waited a few moments, then stepped forward and gently touched the old woman's shoulder. She felt the tap, turned, and her mouth fell open in a silent shriek of protest. She tried to pull away, but Death clung to her habit's white scapular and pulled her to her feet. Holbein watched, fascinated, as her body fell to the earth of the courtyard while her spirit was led off by determined Death. In one of the arched doorways leading out to the courtyard, a young nun saw the fallen body of her superior and began to shout.

Holbein was too busy making preliminary sketches on a sheet of parchment to notice the grief that unfolded around him. He was surprised when he abruptly awoke, finding himself in his studio, alone, a half-finished sketch near his hands.

Death proved to be courteous, allowing Holbein enough time to completely finish one drawing before he reappeared. Hans began to look forward to the visits, fascinated by his patron's methods. He watched, invisible, as Death claimed a judge in the act of being bribed, a wealthy woman who felt the approach and dressed for the occasion, a peddler who tried in vain to flee to the next town, and a blind man who gratefully allowed himself to be led. He laughed when Death arrayed himself in the costume of a ragged peasant to claim a count; he allowed himself a measure of petty satisfaction when Death took a miser, and made the dead soul watch in helpless dismay as he also took money from a counting table. Each of these excursions ended with Holbein awakening in his studio, and intuiting that he was not yet permitted to see what came next for those called by Death.

Hans continued working on his other commissions, but he found himself always returning to his *Dance of Death*. He added his own touches to the drawings: He included an hourglass in many of them; he did complete new drawings, depicting his friend leading Adam and Eve out of Paradise, since they'd become part of his dominion. He drew a coat-of-arms for Death, and even an alphabet. He gave Death a sense of humor, although with subtler satire than earlier artists had provided.

He watched other citizens of his town die of plague. Not many — the sickness wasn't rampaging again, as it had in the past — and although the recognition left him uneasy, he had come to trust Death and knew he was safe. He took each new drawing to Hans Lützelburger, whose skill as an engraver surpassed his reputation. Holbein suspected that, if his *Dances of Death* were admired by future generations, it might be partly because of the brilliance of the engraver.

Then one day Death made him attend the taking of a child.

The boy was barely more than an infant, about the age and size of Hans's stepson Franz, his wife's son from her first marriage, which had ended when she was widowed. It was a poor family, living in a ramshackle cottage without windows, a badly-thatched roof, and no fire but a cooking pit in the middle of the floor. Death showed no compassion nor consideration as he took the little one by a single tiny wrist, leading it away from the body slumped on the floor, while the gaunt mother and older sister sobbed in a grief that Holbein had never seen, a grief born of a lifetime of desperation and loss. Holbein followed Death out of the cottage, and his face was still wet when his eyes snapped open to the familiar surroundings of his studio.

The beginnings of the drawing by his outstretched right hand repulsed him. But he didn't crumple it up or fling it into the fire. Instead he completed it.

He took it to Lützelburger, only to discover that the engraver had died in the week since Hans had last seen him. A terrible accident, involving a horse cart driven by a sot. The driver was in jail, and the engraver was dead.

Death came to Holbein that night. Hans was pacing in his studio, anticipating the visit. Still, his patron's first words surprised him: "I release you from our agreement, Hans. You have upheld your side of the bargain, and I'm very pleased with the work, which has re-inspired me."

"How could you take the child?"

The skull-head was unreadable, incapable of expressing emotion. "I've told you, I'm not the final authority—"

Hans cut him off, waving a hand in irritation. "Yes, yes, I know, I've heard all that. It's God's fault, is that it?"

Death hesitated, and Hans wondered if he'd finally provoked something that wasn't cold and rational. "Yes. Even I don't pretend to understand His wisdom."

"But doesn't it hurt you when it's a child, a babe, and the parents—"

"No, Hans, it does not."

Finally, Hans understood: He was dealing with a demi-god, a thing that was impossibly old and inhuman and with motives that nothing of flesh and blood could ever comprehend. And once again, he was frightened of Death.

"I leave you now, Hans, at least until we must meet again. I am grateful for your skill, although I suspect it may make us both famous, and you must admit — you will owe part of that to me."

Hans stood, frozen, as Death vanished again. Then he collapsed into a chair and poured himself a glass of ale that he hoped was big enough to make him as insensible as the drunkard who had killed Lützelburger.

■ ■ ■

After that, Basel lost its charms, and in the autumn of 1526, Hans fled to England, where he'd heard artists were often highly paid. He left Elsbeth and the children in Basel, and over the next decade found fame in the court of Henry VIII, where he became the King's Painter. He prospered to the point where he acquired a mistress and two new children. He still visited Elsbeth when he could, and made sure she and their children were well provided for.

The plague returned to London in 1543. Hans heard the news from friends in the Royal Court. It was only a small outbreak, but his anxiety rose like a black sun.

He was no longer protected.

On a cold night when fog covered London like grave dirt, Hans was returning from an audience with the King, who was inquiring again about the painting he'd commissioned from Hans in 1541, the one to commemorate the unification of the barbers' and surgeons' guilds. The painting was large, but size wasn't the issue; Holbein was, rather, simply bored by the subject. Of course he'd assured his royal employer that the work was progressing well, and would be completed soon.

Hans tried to negotiate his way through the fog, lighted windows providing little illumination until he'd nearly walked into them. He knew he was lost, and in fact he'd been walking for several minutes without even finding a shop or street sign. An overhead lamp revealed an intersection. He turned—

—and smelled plague.

He froze, panic starting to rise from his chest. The stench was nearly gagging him, and he staggered back as if physically assaulted by it. Then, from somewhere in the shrouded center of the lane, he heard:

"Hello, old friend."

No!

The black shape took form before him, hard white surfaces glinting within ebony folds, and Hans could only stare, immobile, sure that his time had arrived at last.

"You've come for me."

"Not yet, not that way. But I do come once again seeking your services. A new commission."

Hans felt exhausted at the mere idea. "We already showed you claiming victims from nearly forty different walks of life — what can be left?"

"Exactly, Hans. I, too, have again grown weary of the limitations imposed on me. And that is why I want something different from you: I want you to create entirely new works. This time, you will not accompany me on my rounds, but will work from your imagination, placing me in fresh situations."

"You want me…" Hans struggled to find the words. "You want me to show you…"

"The station of the victims won't be important this time, but the method of passing will."

"New ways to die … is that what you're saying?"

Death's jaws made a slight clacking sound as he nodded. "Precisely."

Hans shook his head. "No. It's ghastly."

"Why? I'm asking you to entertain me, to renew and reinvigorate me. Surely that's a more worthwhile goal for art than memorializing some pompous blowhard and a bunch of barbers?"

"I…" Hans had no answer, because Death was right, and Hans knew that was why *King Henry VIII Granting the Charter to the Barber-Surgeon's Company* had already gone on for two years. Over the last few years here in England, he'd become little more than a gifted technician, a highly paid and praised one, but not a true artist. And wasn't Death the ultimate critic? If he could win the praise of this patron for original works, it would surely (ironically) be his life's greatest achievement.

"Yes." The word escaped his mouth almost of its own volition.

The reeking scent vanished instantly. "I'm delighted, my friend. I'll visit with you next week to view your progress."

Hans wasn't surprised to find the fog lifting by the time he'd reached the end of the lane.

◼ ◼ ◼

Death became Hans Holbein's constant companion.

Hans began to notice new things about people, and about the world around them. He saw the potential for fatality in everything. A ship on the Thames could lose its rigging and hurl a sailor into the river's grimy depths. An urchin begging coins on a corner might be trod upon by a nobleman's horse, or perhaps fall victim to a far more outlandish accident — a bottle dropped from high overhead, an errant fist thrown by a bar brawler, a rare venomous spider inadvertently imported from a tropical region.

After his strolls, Hans returned to his studio and drew. For the first time in years, his work excited him. At the end of his first week, Death appeared by his side, and Hans wordlessly offered the initial piece: A man convulsing at a dinner table while a woman sat at the head, raising a glass in toast, having just successfully poisoned her husband; Death stood nearby bearing a tray, the attentive waiter.

"Superb, Hans, superb," Death muttered, stroking a bone-tip over the art, "but you can go *further*."

Hans could barely sleep that night, his mind aflame with lethal possibilities.

When Death appeared next, Hans handed him two more works, and Death stood speechless for several seconds before whispering one word: "Astonishing." The first of the drawings so praised showed a field of peasants in tattered rags torn apart by a wave of bullets from a giant gun mounted on a hill; Death held out strings of bullets to the mad gunner. The second new piece showed a man in a street being struck down by some sort of huge, horseless cart, a grotesque engine of destruction bellowing flame from its back.

Over the following weeks, Hans thought of little else but stranger and more horrible scenes of death. He drew on larger sheets, with bolder strokes. He drew scenes of soldiers enveloped in peculiar vapors on a battlefield, their mouths agape in their final dying breath, while Death stood above them, dangling long scarves that might have kept them safe. He drew a line of rail-thin, bent patients, all plainly dying as a wealthy doctor turned his back to them and accepted money from Death instead. He showed a priest gesticulating wildly from a pulpit, causing his flock to turn on each other in violence while Death stood behind him wearing a white miter. He drew a man of science holding an open box from which emanated a blinding whiteness that caused all those below it to fling up arms in useless attempts to shield themselves, while Death stood behind the scientist jotting notes in a book.

Death was ecstatic. He stared with empty sockets at each new drawing, lingering for minutes, stroking them lovingly. "Exquisite," he might murmur, or, "brilliant."

Hans knew it was his finest work. After Death had rendered approval, each new piece went into a large wooden box that he'd had designed and specially made; the top was ornately carved and gilt with Death's coat-of-arms from the first set of drawings. Hans had already completed the engravings on the first two drawings of this new set himself, having decided that no other could be entrusted to accurately cut the wood for his masterworks. Someday, when the engravings were completed and the books printed, the world would recognize his achievement as an engraver as well as an artist.

⬛ ⬛ ⬛

One afternoon, as Hans returned from another visit to Henry's court that had left him bored and annoyed and aching to return to what he considered his real work, he passed an inn and saw a ring of onlookers standing around outside, peering in anxiously. He spotted a man he knew in the crowd, an apprentice to a printer he sometimes dined with, and he asked the man what the commotion was about.

"Lady murdered her husband," the young apprentice said, nodding toward the building's front windows.

Hans found a gap in the crowd, bent down to peer in through a square of glass — and his breath caught at what he saw:

Two pikemen were questioning a woman who sat at the head of a table, a glass resting before her. A few feet away was a dead man slumped across his plate, still clutching an empty goblet in one hand.

It was an exact replica of the first new drawing Hans had given Death; the only element missing was Death himself, in the position of the waiter.

Hans stumbled backward in shock, carelessly bumping into others who cursed or cautioned him. He barely noticed when the apprentice laid a guiding hand on his arm. "Take care, there, sir, you don't want to hurt anyone."

"Too late for that!" Hans said, before turning to flee.

He staggered back to his studio, his thoughts racing past possibilities and deceptions: *It's a coincidence/Death put the image in my head and I didn't even realize it/perhaps I've gained some fortune-teller's ability...*

But only one explanation made sense: *Death copied my drawing!*

When he reached his studio, he bolted the door and raced to the box of drawings. He tore open the decorated lid, and reached to the bottom of the stack of drawings to pluck out the first.

A woman — no, *that* woman, who he'd just seen — poisoning a man. In that room. Even the glasses matched perfectly.

He slammed the drawing down, his motion causing some of the others to flutter aside. There was a woman being raped while Death kept her hands tied; there, a field of soldiers blown apart by some explosive, while Death stood a short distance away, one arm still upraised from the deadly missile he'd just hurled.

Hans leafed frantically through the drawings, realization growing like a cancer within him: He hadn't created entertainment for Death. Death had never intended to accept these works as art to restore his own flagging spirit.

No, this was an instructional guide. These were signposts pointing to the future. Hans Holbein the Younger had assembled a manual of coming murders. Death had lied to him when he'd told him he had no control over who he took and how; He *was* the final authority. He *was* God.

Hans collapsed onto a work bench, his hands tearing at his beard, at his expensive collar. *What have I done? Is it too late to undo it?*

He'd only finished a few of the woodcuts, and none had gone to the printer yet. He could simply burn them now, destroy them. Death had already seen them, true, had committed them to memory; but perhaps a memory as well-used as His was faulty, wouldn't retain details.

Hans stayed up throughout the night, turning over options and possibilities, and by morning he knew there was only one course of action. But first ... there was one final drawing to be made.

■ ■ ■

Death returned a few nights later and Hans was waiting for Him.

"What have you got for me this week, friend?"

Hans passed him the last drawing he'd made. Death looked at it, perplexed. "What is this?"

"You lied to me. You've lied to me from the start. There is no authority over You, and I was a fool to ever believe there was. There is only You."

Death stood silently before Hans. After a few seconds he glanced aside and noticed the wooden box full of drawings was missing from the table. "Where are the others?"

"Gone. I burned the entire box."

The skull head twisted back and Death trembled, the first real display of emotion Hans had ever seen from Him. "You *destroyed* them all?!"

Hans held his ground. "Yes."

"You know what this will mean for you?"

"I do."

"Look under your arm."

Hans could already feel the skin there swelling, as heat began to course through him. "There's no need."

"You are a fool!"

Smiling, Hans answered, "Not anymore."

With that, Death vanished.

■ ■ ■

Hans Holbein the Younger died two days later.

It was several more days before they found him; by then the blood had dried, but the smell hadn't abated. The messenger from the royal court and the neighbors who had battered down the door pulled back, nauseated. The young printer's apprentice had stopped by to visit Hans, and was there as the others were turning away.

"What's that he's got in his hands?"

The apprentice took a deep breath and stepped forward; he wanted to know what could have been so important to the great Hans Holbein that it was what he'd clung to as life had left him.

"Be mindful of the plague, lad," the messenger said. But the apprentice thought art was more important than death, and so he reached down and wrested the drawing from the master's stiff fingers.

The sheet of parchment had been splattered heavily by Hans's blood, as he'd coughed up his life, but the apprentice could just make out the image: It showed a man who looked very much like Hans Holbein in a room that was undoubtedly this studio, dying of plague, his face blackened, blood staining his bedclothes … but the man was smiling, at peace. Above the man's head was an hourglass, the upper compartment empty; from the side, a bony hand reached for the glass, but no more of Death was visible, a strange exclusion. At the bottom of the drawing was a Latin inscription. The apprentice had some familiarity with the language, and thought the words read: "Now I join Ambrosius."

He wondered who Ambrosius was.

"That's plague blood on that sheet, boy," muttered the neighbor. "Throw it on the fire."

The apprentice considered, then realized they were probably right. Who knew exactly how death passed from one man to another? Better not to take that chance.

He placed the drawing gently on the cold logs in the hearth, kindled a fire, whispered goodbye to the remarkable artist Hans Holbein the Younger, and left that chamber of death.

Lisa Morton is a screenwriter and four-time winner of the Bram Stoker Award. She is also the author of *The Halloween Encyclopedia*, and is one of the world's foremost authorities on Halloween. She lives in North Hollywood, California.

About the story she says: Earlier this year I worked on a lengthy non-fiction article about the work of Hans Holbein, and he became a minor obsession as a result. When I heard the premise of *Danse Macabre*, there was, then, no question that the story would be about Holbein.

—DEATH IN THE FAMILY—
By Morgan Dempsey

Death waits at the foot of everyone's bed. With each gasping breath he inches his way closer, trailing a bone finger against blankets of coarse wool or fine silk, until his icy hand rests against a warm cheek. Then there is silence.

Right now, at this bed, he stands on the opposite side of me, at the knee of Krysza, wife and mother of four. He studies the loose weave of the blanket trapping what warmth her body provides. I don't plan on letting him move closer.

Krysza will require only one leaf. She's not too badly off, just an illness that settled in her chest and refused to leave. Death was not close enough to warrant more. I muddle the leaf in a bowl with a clean stone. Water boils in a kettle over the fire.

"Her children are old enough, Dominik," Death says to me. "You could let her go."

My hand stops. Heniek, her husband, notices my stillness. "Sir?"

I want to tell Death off for what he said, but I don't need Heniek worrying after my sanity on top of everything else. One of the few gifts Death gave me was the ability to see him, even when no one else could. Ever thoughtful, my godfather. I ignore him. "Is the water ready?"

Heniek checks inside the pot. "Almost."

Death blinks out of sight, leaving behind a thin grey wisp in the shape of a man. It feathers apart in the shifting air, bringing the scent of freshly turned dirt. He reappears behind me, staring over my shoulder at the ruined leaf.

"This is a good way to pass," Death assures me. "Peaceful."

A log crumbles and the fire whispers with life.

Death shifts back against Krysza's bed, leans against the straw-packed mattress wrapped in a thin and threadbare cloth. He rests a hand against hers, and her fingers twitch. I hiss at him to stop.

"The water's ready." Heniek is hesitant. He worries this cure will not work, that he doesn't possess the kind of luck required for miracles.

I go to the fire and ladle boiling water over the muddled leaf. The stone bowl becomes warm in my hands so I set it on the table. She'll be fine in a few minutes.

My godfather sits on the bed. He straightens his waistcoat, black — all he wears is black — his jacket, cravat, everything, worn and ruined like the clothes of an exhumed corpse. His skin is pale, bloodless, and his top hat casts a shadow which hides his eyes.

"Mostly pain awaits her," he says to me. "Her lungs will bother her, especially in the cold. Many people don't have the opportunity to pass away like this, in bed, warm, surrounded by loved ones."

I sit beside Krysza, kicking at my godfather, but my foot passes through dusty smoke. He gives me a sad smile as I feed her the tea in small, slow sips. Heniek stands at the foot of the bed, his hands resting on Krysza's toes. He tenderly rubs his thumb along the arch of her foot.

Krysza stirs, and I step away, letting her husband rush to her side and take her hand. Her eyes open and she coughs weakly, but it's just the fading rattle of her illness.

I pack my things and leave before they can pin me down with gratitude and offers of payment. The sun is nearly set. Part of my walk will be in darkness. Hopefully the stars shine bright tonight. My breath clouds as I exhale.

Death appears at my side, mimicking a human walk, his feet inches from the ground. "You're a little too tenacious." He clucks his tongue, a dry, rasping sound. "Quality of life should matter more to you than quantity. Someday you'll listen to reason." Then he laughs, and asks, "Or are you trying to avoid the anger that comes when you fail?"

Healers aren't perfect, and I can't always get to the ill in time. Yet somehow, I am blamed for their passing. The curses that have been thrown at me would make even the best warrior check for his sword. "I don't know how you deal with it," I say.

The mocking smile fades from his face. "I hope one day you learn."

"You could let them live, you know," I point out, feeling sullen from the cold of the coming winter.

"I can't, actually." There's a waiver to Death's voice, a rasp of tired resignation. "I don't make the candles, you see. I merely help put them out."

The chilled air reaches through to my heart and I draw my coat tight around me, turning up the collar to cover my neck and ears. Partly to shut out the cold, partly to shut out my godfather. I pull a letter from the breast pocket of my coat before buttoning it up.

"Hoping for some kind words to warm you up?" Death was some yards ahead of me, then suddenly at my side, smelling of new graves. I hate that I know the scent.

I ignore him in favor of the letter, but it only encourages him.

"From that princess?" Death wafts up like the curl of smoke from a fire, hovering just over my shoulder. "My dearest Dominik," he simpers, reading the letter. "Just as my father's heart is weak with illness, my heart is weak for you." He huffs. His breath does not steam, despite the cold.

I fold the paper and cram it into my pocket. "You understand death very well, godfather, but you know nothing of life."

He appears in front of me, gliding backwards. "And you, as a healer, as my ambassador to the world, seem to know nothing of death." Lights of the distant town shine through him. "Are you so easily swayed by her title and her offer of marriage? You cling to this life too much, for someone who should know better."

"Isn't this what you promised my family?" I grip the letter in my pocket. "That I would have fame and wealth and standing? Why are you trying to turn me away from this?"

"As your godfather, I'm to teach you about life and death."

"Then stick to the half you're good at," I snap.

He shrugs, still floating just out of my reach. "I'm trying, but you mortals are stubborn."

The sun buries itself in the tree line, and the sky is a purple bruise deepening to black. Not enough stars to light my way, but I'm close enough to town that it doesn't matter.

"I'm ignoring you now," I tell him. It won't do any good, but I tell him anyway.

Death only now notices the coming darkness. He rests his hand over his chest, and a light grows within him, warm like a flame, glowing pulses fanning out in little threads, like blood from a beating heart. He appears at my side, feet settling into the dirt. Though he leaves no footprints, he makes the effort to walk with me.

"You have a big lesson to learn." The teasing, the snide mockery, the sneers, all have left his voice, only a tired weight remaining. "And a small amount of time to learn it in."

I stop dead in my tracks. "A small amount of time?"

He smiles that smile I hate, that smile of being the last to have to lay down his cards. "To me, all of you have a dreadfully small amount of time." He waves for me to keep walking by his side. "I wouldn't worry about it, if I were you."

"No," I say. "I suppose you wouldn't."

We continue on to the town in silence.

※ ※ ※

The walled city lies on a hill by a wide river, water curving around it on three sides. Death hasn't bothered me since I passed through the large gates, sitting wide open with only token guards protecting them. I reach for my papers as I enter, but they simply wave me through, suggesting an inn with particularly good beer. I thank them, and head for the castle.

The king should have been resting in some warm palace, but by the time he finally admitted to being ill it was too dangerous for him to make the long journey. So he remained month after month in a damp castle, his health withering away.

The princess, Anya, and I shared many letters in the months it took me to get here. The exchange started off formal, but that didn't last long. I place my hand over the stack of letters, bound in twine.

It takes a long time to convince the castle guard I need to see the king, and even longer to convince them he may need to see me. Only when Anya hears me arguing and steps in do they finally escort me to his bedchamber. As her father's illness worsened, she began ruling in his absence. She mentioned in the letters that she was managing a few things. It seems she was being modest.

As we walk, my hand accidentally brushes against Anya's. I mutter an apology and pull away, but she reaches out and tangles her fingers in mine. She keeps her face turned away from me, but I can see she is fighting tears.

I give her hand a small squeeze and whisper, "I wish we could have met under better circumstances."

Anya smiles tightly. "Perhaps you can make the circumstances better."

The king rests against a mound of pillows. His face is pale and drawn, eyes underscored in a charcoal grey and staring into nothingness. He takes in a stuttering breath, wet and sick, like a drowning man.

And Death stands at the head of his bed.

I stop in the doorway, staring, and my godfather holds my gaze. He shakes his head, no.

Anya tugs me into the room. She doesn't see him, none of them do, my godfather, all in black with hidden eyes staring down at their fading king. I release her hand to dig for my herbs and she goes to her father's side, sitting in a high-backed chair beside the bed. The chair is settled deep in the rugs around the king's bed. It has been there for some time.

Death steps behind Anya, a thread of smoke trailing from him over her father's body. He smiles down at her and places a hand on her shoulder. It goes through her, and she shivers.

I take out a fistful of leaves, nearly everything I have, and begin muddling them.

"You can't save him," my godfather says to me. "Or have you forgotten how this works?"

I haven't, of course. Death stands at the foot of the bed, I can heal. Death stands at the head of the bed, I must step back. He allows me to gather the herbs which grow at every entrance to his domain, he shows me who I can heal, and from there flows my fame and fortune. Thus far, I have not crossed him.

And how far have I gotten for that?

"Please," I ask one of the servants, "bring me boiling water?" He whispers to someone just outside the door and gives me a nod.

Death doesn't leave his station at the head of the bed. "Don't do it." He leans against the bedpost, a bit of dirt tumbles off his coat and bursts into dust, floating gently to the ground.

The water arrives quickly, and I pour it over the leaves, letting it sit for a few minutes. Anya stares at the brewing tea. A question sits on the edge of her lips, but she won't ask it.

"I know it seems just a simple tea," I say, "but it's a rare leaf."
I give her my best version of a reassuring smile, avoiding Death's
gaze. "Trust me."

"Dominik!" my godfather snaps. "You know the rules."

I walk to the bed, tea in hand, and Anya steps away, giving me
room. The king's breathing is thin, the sound of wind blowing
over reeds growing by the water. I place the cup against his lips.

Death leans over my shoulder. Cold air passes by my ear,
carrying with it the scent of dry clay. "Don't."

The tea hovers just at the king's mouth, ready to spill over.
My hand shakes, and I pull the cup away.

"Dominik?" Anya touches my elbow. "What's wrong?"

I thrust the cup into her hands and wave over the servants.
"Help me," I say, grabbing one of the bed posts. I point at the
other posts and shout, "Help me turn the bed!"

They hesitate, and Anya shouts, "Don't just stand there! Do
as he says!"

Everybody in the room rushes to the bed and grabs a post,
pulling as hard as they can. I don't know why I think this will
work. How could this ever work?

Death's face appears before mine. I can see his eyes. Red, angry,
and eternal. My legs give out and I fall back, releasing the bed.

"What are you doing?" He speaks with a thousand voices,
and I scramble away.

Everybody is so focused on turning the bed around that they
don't notice me, staring into nothing. My fear is suddenly swallowed by rage. "I love Anya," I hiss, "and I'm tired of travelling
the country, a new inn every night. I did that for *you*. But this?
This is for me."

They finish what I started, and Death is now at the foot of the
king's bed. He snarls at me, his mouth wider than any human's
mouth could ever open, teeth bared. I shut my eyes against it
and grab the cup from Anya's hand. The king's mouth drops
open and I give him the tea.

Death cries out in rage. The sound tears through me, and I
drop the cup to cover my ears. He attempts to strike me, but his
fist passes through me, leaving a trail of smoke smelling faintly
of brimstone. I'm frozen, unable to move. My godfather has never
lashed out at me before.

He draws in a deep breath, every tendril of dust and smoke
twisting back into his body. His eyes go dark, lost in shadow again.

"We're done." He turns his back to me. "Never use those herbs again."

"I'm sorry," I whisper, quietly, so no one else will hear. I want to point out how he was at the foot of the bed, so I didn't technically break our rule. But I know better. I know what I owe him. I wouldn't have been in this room if not for him. I could have more, but I could also have less.

Death stops for a moment, but does not turn around. When he speaks, there's such a sadness, such a weariness, an ache settles into my chest. "I hear that more times in one day than you will say it in your lifetime. I hear it enough to know you don't mean it. And by the time you do, it will be too late."

I climb back to my feet and watch him walk away. I try for another apology but it dies in my throat. It isn't that I fear he doesn't understand. He does understand, completely, and it weighs on him.

My godfather walks to a tall window. Thin, graying light streams in through the warped glass. "Do not cross me again." Threads of light pass through him and strike the floor. His face is once again shadowed, but thin lines gather at the corners of his mouth, giving the impression of a tired frown. "I will not be so lenient next time." And he vanishes, curls of dust fading away in the setting sun.

Anya takes my hand, and I turn to her. "Thank you." Her voice is marked with tears. She throws her arms around me and presses her lips to my cheek. Over her shoulder, I see the king is awake, his breathing no longer labored. "Thank you."

I return her embrace, thinking of what I've just gained, and what I've forever lost.

◼ ◼ ◼

Five years ago I married Anya and assumed some leadership, and still the disapproving half-glances of the courtiers follow me all the way back to my chambers. Knowing looks and whispers, which are not so quiet as they believe, have haunted my presence in court for the last seven years. The court's romantic affection for a peasant-turned-king had waned years ago.

Life was so much easier when I was just a healer, when my godfather showed me plainly who might live and who was certain to die. I know how to speak to a grieving family, how to help them accept what has come to pass. That does not help make me a king. Death is straightforward. Politics are fickle.

It's no secret Anya is the true ruler, and I am merely around because she has an inexplicable fondness for me. When I met her, she was enduring the trivialities of courtiers while her father lay ill, with a grace I could never manage. And now she lies sick in bed herself, a demon disease sitting on her chest and draining her of life. Her father is travelling here from the warmer climes he grew to prefer after his illness. Our child is in the other room, quarantined away. I have stayed by her side.

I sit and rest my hand over the bag of herbs strung around my neck. Perhaps I cannot use them, but they still provide some comfort. "I made another mistake today." She can't hear me, I know that. I feel for her pulse. It's soft and slow, but still, she lives. "I made a ruling on some petty land dispute and the courtiers were displeased."

I lay my head down next to her hand, and kiss her fingertips. The weight of the day slowly washes out of me, pouring onto the floor. I only notice I'm falling asleep when something wakes me — the scent of freshly-turned dirt.

My godfather is standing at the head of her bed.

The room is empty, for which I am grateful. I rise from my chair and tell him, "No!"

He shrugs, a gesture trapped between bitterness and apathy. "It's not for me to decide, Dominik, not really." He reaches to brush hair from Anya's face, but his hand passes through her. She gasps, a death rattle.

I've seen Death take people before. He rests a hand on their head, and they tremble. He told me that was the soul detaching from the body. Then he would take their hand in his, and their spirit would rise, leaving their spent body behind.

I've seen it many times before, but never someone I loved.

A nurse knocks on the door before entering with Anya's medicine and meal. On her tray rests a foul, chalky drink, a bit of plain toast, and a cup of hot water for tea. I run to her, and she mutters something about no, she'll get it, your highness. But it isn't the tray I'm after.

I snatch the hot water and empty the small pouch from around my neck, the last of the healing leaves.

Death appears at my side, and the scent of brimstone and burning wood flows from him. His face is even more drawn then when I last saw him, but he pushes down the fatigue. "What do you think you are doing?"

I send the nurse away, telling her to return in five minutes. Something will have happened by then. I'm just not certain what.

My godfather stares at the cup, watches the liquid grow dark as the leaves steep. "Have you forgotten what I told you?"

"I remember." My hands tremble. I tell myself it's only impatience. "I simply don't care."

"Oh?" He sneers at me. "You can't live without her? Is that it?"

"It's not that." The tea darkens. It's almost ready. Just a little bit longer. "I'd just rather not, given the choice."

"Do you remember why your father chose me to be your godfather, your spiritual guide?"

My father told me that story many times growing up. How proud he was, that God, Satan, and Death had all vied to be my godfather. How he turned God down, for the darkness that he let into the world. How he turned down Satan, for the deceit that flowed so readily from him. And he told me how he accepted Death's offer.

I give Anya the tea.

Death rises before me like a storm, his animal cry of fury knocking me to the floor. He is shaped like a man and fire and smoke and a burst of ravens taking flight, robed in crumbling ash. He stares at me, through me, and I see his eyes. Not the red fire of before, when I first crossed him to heal Anya's father, but the eyes he has in the final moments, the eyes the newly dead see. When he stares at me now, there is nothing, a black emptiness of an eternity alone and cold and unable to scream.

His voice is a cold nail drawn across hard stone.

"Because through me, all become equal."

I feel as though I'm falling. Then, I feel nothing at all.

⬛ ⬛ ⬛

The floor beneath my cheek is hard and cold. Packed dirt clings to my face and my clothes and I dust myself clean as I stand. I'm in a cave, in a small room lit with a thousand candles. The air is so still. I must be far underground.

"You're awake." Death used to greet me with kindness, but now there's only a frozen tightness when he speaks.

"Hello, godfather." I turn, expecting to see him, but I'm alone in the room. "Where are you?"

He steps out of the air and into being, and it's only an aching dread that stops me from asking if it's really him. In our domain, in the world of the living, he's a terrible specter, containing himself as best he can, but still always inviting a cold shiver. Here, he is different.

Death is still dressed in his usual funereal black, but clean and pressed, if a little worn, no longer inspiring the image of a freshly-dug corpse. The smell of earth, of fire and brimstone, all are gone, replaced by the sweet and musky smell of myrrh.

Most notably, however, his hat is gone, and for once, I see his true face.

He's middle-aged, and the age is wearing on him. His hair is brown, thin and pale, with streaks of white gathering at his temples. Lines run over his face, and there is a weight, a deep exhaustion from the years of his work running over him like water over a stone.

Death looks like a man who used to laugh, but sadness made him forget how.

I stare down at the hard floor, stomach tight with the child-like shame of being in terrible trouble, and knowing I deserve it. "I'm dead, aren't I?"

"Just about." His voice is a gentle whisper. He steps to one side and points at a candle, so short it can barely be called such, the flame guttering in a pool of wax. "This is your life. As you can see, there isn't much left."

The tiny flame stumbles on the wick, deep red where it should be bright yellow.

"What about Anya?"

Death nods to another candle. This one is tall, its flame burning bright and proud, with a thick column of wax yet to be spent. Another candle stands next to it, taller still, and I realize it's for our child. "I told you not to use the herb," he said. "I never told you it wouldn't work."

I stare at my candle. It's a wonder the flame hasn't gone out yet. "What if you use my flame to light another candle?" I ask him. "Or put it on top of one? Could that continue my life?"

"Well, it looks like you bypassed anger and have gone straight into bargaining." He sighs and leans against the cave wall. "At least I don't have to deal with you making a mess of things here with some childish tantrum." He sighs, and his hands, long and slender, cover his face. If it was anyone else I would suspect they were crying.

"I'm sorry," I whisper.

Death moves his hands from his face and looks at me with that knowing smile of his, but in full light, out of the shadows, his smile has a terror and a sympathy I haven't seen before. "I said you wouldn't mean it until it was too late."

I go to my candle and sit in front of it, my back to Death. "I'm supposed to blow it out, aren't I?" My words threaten the flame, the air from my lips tearing it from the wick, almost, not quite. I recall what he told me years ago. "You don't make the candles."

"I don't even put them out, actually. I just light them."

My wife and child are alive and healthy, many years ahead of them. Does she know I love her? Does our child? Did I tell them these things enough? Did I write to my parents recently? Would they remember me as a peasant who became king, or would they remember me as a man who loved and cherished his family?

And I realize, this is the gift my godfather was trying to give me, the lesson I was to learn. The deep awareness that he is always coming, and that there is nothing I can do but live the sort of life that would make him think twice before taking me. Shame that I only see it now. What I might have done, had I only listened.

He stops me before I can tell him once more that I'm sorry. "It's all right," he assures me, and for the first time I can see what my father saw, why he would choose Death as my godfather. The patience, the balance, the deep sense of understanding and acceptance.

"I am sorry, though," I assure him. "You have a horrible burden. I wish I could have helped you." I take a deep breath and give one last thought to Anya.

But before I can blow out the candle, Death cups his hands over the flame.

He moves the candle out of my reach and stares down at it, deep in thought. "Do you mean that?"

A response leaps to my lips, but I pause to give it real thought. Was that something I said in my last moment, to appease my own guilt? He wears his disappointment in himself plainly, and it's clear to see how this task exhausts him. I helped many people live, but I also watched as many died, their families screaming at me, cursing my name, spitting at me for letting their loved one slip away. And I only dealt with the souls that crossed my path. He dealt with everyone.

"Yes, I mean it." The pure honesty of my answer surprises me.

Death begins pacing the room, still holding my candle, muttering quietly, giving me a thoughtful glance every few moments. Earlier

I might have warned him to mind the flame, but a deep calm has settled within me. He can have all the time he needs.

Eventually he closes his eyes and gives a long sigh. All the tension escapes his body, leaving exhaustion behind. "You're much younger than I was when my godfather came for me." He smiles and my flame comes alive in his hands, his face washed in a clear yellow that transforms his tired lines into deep black scores. "Who knows, you might last longer than I did."

When I realize what he's saying, I step back as if struck. "You want me to ... take over?"

"Well not right away." Death slowly closes the distance between us, my flame in his hands growing with each step, burning bright like a cold star. "But that's the eventual goal."

My godfather holds out the flame for me to take. I expect to be burned, but it's cool to the touch. He tells me the choice is mine alone. "You can go to paradise, or you can spend the ages watching others pass, just as you have your whole life."

It's the cleanest white, soft and warm and dancing with life. He tells me it's a choice, but it isn't, not really, not when I hold life in my hands like this, so full and pure. I press the light to my chest, and it floods me with elation and sadness, hope and fear. I'm reminded of when I held my child for the first time. It's a weight, a burden, a joy, beautiful and heartbreaking.

I'm not sure how I remain standing. My head is light and my vision is smoke and stars, but slowly I come out of the haze. "All right." I rub at the new fire in my heart, the joy and ache settling deep. "I've learned what I can of life. What can you teach me of death?"

My godfather places his hand on my shoulder. "Why do you speak as if they're so different?"

॥ ॥ ॥

Morgan Dempsey is a writer and software engineer, currently living in Silicon Valley, California. Her fiction is available at Redstone Science Fiction, as well as another EDGE anthology titled *Broken Time Blues*. "Death in the Family" is a retelling of the classic folktale Godfather Death.

—BLUE-BLACK NIGHT—

By Timothy Reynolds

It was a cool Southern Utah evening and I was sitting on the front stoop of my rented trailer, strumming on my battered flat-top. I say 'battered', but even with worn strings, a missing pick guard and through-and-through bullet holes that have matching ones in the case from a long night in Buffalo, it was in a sight better shape than me. Granted, I have no bullet holes, but who needs them when you've got cancer?

"I want to learn a love song, Mark."

I looked up from the barre chord I was working on and nearly crapped my drawers. "Are you shi — *kidding* me?!" I was raised to not curse in front of a lady, especially a full-on beautiful one; even if that lady is Death. Yeah, that's what I said. Death is a woman, and she wanted me to teach her a love song.

"I'll pay you." She sat down next to me and vanilla drifted over to tickle my nose and tease me.

"No disrespect, miss, but money's not much use to me this late on." She knew what I meant. None of my friends or family would have had a clue because none of them knew the cancer was back. Matter of fact, none of them had seen me in at least six months; not since I stood up at Easter dinner and told them I was heading out the next day to tour with a buddy and his band. I was to be the show's MC, throwing out a little stand-up, a few song parodies, and keeping the boys out of all the small town jails waiting for 21st-century troubadours like us.

Of course there was no tour. There wasn't even a band. There was just my own Yamaha guitar, the Chevy and the wide-open state of Utah. And my tent, at least until I decided a few weeks ago to make my way up to St. George and spend what time I had left with a roof over my head.

So, like I said, Death is a woman, at least to me. She's a pretty, pony-tailed brunette with dark-green eyes and a little gap between her front teeth. She wears a well-loved, baggy, soft denim shirt with just enough buttons undone that her cleavage taunts me. Her jeans are tight enough so as to not hide her cute little butt and loose enough that she could spend three days in them on a saddled chestnut mare following trails wherever they lead without chaffing or burning. And she's wearing sneakers. Simple, no-logo, timeless, white sneakers.

"What payment would you accept? I can't cure you, though I can help a little with the pain."

"I can't."

"Can't what? Teach me a love song?"

"No, I can't take payment."

"I insist."

She was a stubborn one, Death was, but I was no rookie either. "You're hardly in a position to insist on anything."

"You *do* know who I am, don't you? The power I have?"

"I know exactly who you are. You've been standing just off to the side since I was a kid. With any face, in any shape, I'd know you."

"So then—"

"But I'm not taking payment. If you pay me, all you'll get is a song *about* love. If you just sit back and let me give you this one thing, then you'll get a love song, a song from my heart to yours."

She got real quiet for a moment, caught off guard most likely. It's nice to know that even Death can still be surprised.

"How do you know I've got a heart? I'm not exactly mortal, with blood coursing through my veins."

"A heart isn't about being a blood pump, and it doesn't matter whether you have one or not, because *I* do."

"Yes, you most certainly do." She gently placed her palm on my chest, over my heart. While she felt the rhythm of my life still beating, I noticed her long, slender fingers, her nails short, clean, and simple. She had good picker's hands, as my teacher used to say. Chord shapes would come easily to those fingers and picking would be sure and quick with practise.

"So, do you want to learn a song about love or do you want to learn a love song?"

"You'll teach me a love song?"

"I've been playing love songs for you for the past ten years or so, so I suppose it's time I teach you to play one yourself." I traverse-picked a simple G-C-D progression to punctuate my point, but she put a hand on the strings to still them.

"Back up a minute there. What do you mean, you've been playing love songs for me?"

"Just what I said. What's so tough to understand?"

"You're saying you love me?"

"Love you, in love with you — yes'm."

"You love *Death*?"

"Ever since the car accident. I saw you smile down at me lying on the shoulder of the I-65 and when you shook your head to say 'not yet', I was hooked."

"But—"

"You're in my dreams, waking and sleeping. You're first in my thoughts in the morning and last in them at night. Everywhere I go, every happy laugh I hear, every taste that touches my tongue, every sunset I watch, you're with me. Every perfect moment I want to share with you and every imperfect, painful moment I lean on the knowledge that you aren't far away."

"You're just in love with this form, this face."

"Is it *your* form? *Your* face?"

"One of the many."

"Then that's part of it. But there's your essence, what makes you unique. Your light."

"I'm *Death*, Mark. My essence is *death*. My light is darkness."

"Not to me."

She wasn't getting it. She didn't know that love sees none of those things.

"You're not afraid?" she asked.

"Of what? Dying? I'm fifty-one. I've had more time than many and less than others. Now, do you want to learn a love song or not?"

"There's nothing I would rather do more. What did you have in mind?"

I have over a hundred songs in my repertoire, and probably a third are love songs of one sort or another. Croce's *Time in a Bottle*? Chapin's *Taxi*? Or The King's *Fools Rush In*. "One of my own," I said. "One I wrote for you when I was finishing up chemo the last time."

"Blue-Black Night?!"

If I thought she'd lit up when she was feeling my heartbeat, then finding out I'd written *Blue-Black Night* for her made her go supernova. She glowed like there was no darkness left in the world, let alone the darkness that she carried with her.

"None other. Or would you prefer something more popular? Some Michael Bublé?"

"Your song, please."

"Yes, ma'am."

"Call me ... Jill."

What? No, I sure as Hell didn't see *that* coming. "Jill?"

"It's a twist on Giltinė, one of my many names."

After all these years I now had a name to go with the face. "Thanks."

I shifted my butt back to make room for her and patted the wood between my legs. Yeah, I know how rude that sounds, but it's what I did, literally. "Sit here, please." I swung the guitar out of the way so she could sit but she just looked over at me and raised one eyebrow.

"Are you sure? I can see just fine from here."

"If we had two guitars a side-by-side might do, though I'd go for a face-to-face, but this old Yammy is all we've got so this is how it has to be."

She didn't move.

"Look, Jill, you're the one who wants to learn a love song. You opened that can of worms that is my heart so let's get past it."

"But—"

"Are you afraid I'm going to try and take advantage of you? Just because my heart's full of you doesn't mean I'm going to be anything less than a gentleman."

"I don't feel fear, Mark." She scooted herself up and over my left leg until she was sitting on the wood stoop in the *V* between my open legs. She leaned left and spoke at me over her right shoulder. She kept leaning forward so only her thighs touched mine. "It's just that this wasn't what I had in mind when I asked you to teach me. To be honest, I was really just hoping you'd play one for me. I really needed to hear you play."

Damn. "Had a long day and you needed a break so you thought you'd come taunt the dying folkie?"

"No! That's not it at all! Well, yes it's been a long day, but that's the nature of what I do. No, I was at the Long Island Expressway yesterday and was just thinking about a musician I had to take a few years back."

"Harry."

"Harry. And thinking about him made me think of you and then I realized that what I needed was to hear a love song, maybe even learn to play one."

"So no one is dying right now because you're here for a guitar lesson? Wow."

"Not quite." She looked out into the yard and I followed where she was looking. There was a sleeping hound, a prowling tabby and two sparrows. The tabby was stopped in mid-step and the sparrows frozen in mid-air.

"Wow. You stopped time?"

"Something like that." She leaned back into me, slowly, but trusting me now, for some reason.

"How long have we got?"

"As long as it takes to teach me, Mark."

She twisted around and kissed me on my unshaven cheek. Her lips were cool, but not cold. It was nicer than it shoulda been. I swung the guitar around in front of her and she placed her hands where they were supposed to be. "We'll keep it pretty simple. Start with the easiest chords that'll get the job done and go from there." I put three finger tips down on the strings and strummed her a G chord. "This here's a G and pretty much the underlying chord to the whole song. Give it a try."

I shifted my fingers up a fret but kept the chord shape and pretty little Death copied my finger position almost exactly. I lifted my fingers and strummed her chord. It was a bit off. I adjusted her fingers a tad to get them back from the brass fret then pressed them down a bit harder. I strummed it again and it sounded a whole lot better. "You've got the perfect fingers for this."

Then she leaned back into me and we fit together like it was pre-ordained or destined or something like that. My heart pounded, my head swam and I was thinking that I'd just died and gone to Heaven. That wasn't the case, though. The birds were still frozen in the air and Death-who-was-also-Jill still sat in my arms, learning to play a love song. *My* love song to *her*. I took a deep breath and got back to the task at hand. I'd been waiting for Death's arrival for a long time but now that she was here, I wasn't ready to stop or give up. There was at least time for one more song.

"The chorus is the easiest part so let me just sing it for you. You watch my left hand so you can start associating chord changes with the lyrics."

"Okay." She whispered it like she was afraid to break the moment, so I stopped talking and started singing, softly, in her ear, like I'd imagined ever since I wrote the song for her.

> *It was a car wreck on the I-65,*
> *that made me stick around.*
> *It was the blue-black night and the light from her smile,*
> *That kept my feet from touching the ground.*
> *In the pouring rain, with the thunder growls*
> *I walked on into Huntsville.*
> *It was the blue-black night and the light from her smile*
> *That lights my way and always will.*

I let the last chord fade away. She took my picking hand in hers and kissed it.

"Thank you, Mark."

"It's just an old-fashioned love song."

"But you wrote it for me. I can honestly say that it's a first."

"Not true. There are plenty of songs about you, about Death."

"They're usually about obsession with Death or fear of Death or taunting Death with the immortality of Youth. Never a love song."

"Then I suppose it behoves me to teach it to you."

"*That* would be the highlight of my eon."

❖ ❖ ❖

I have no idea whatsoever how long we sat on that stoop like lovers, close and intimate, teaching and learning and making the stolen time our own. I felt more alive than I had in a long, long time. I suppose that's why I considered writing it all down in an old leather-bound journal I picked up in Sedona my last time through. Why? Beats me. Some nod to the immortality I didn't think I cared about? I've got a few other more personal thoughts in there, mostly about the cancer stuff that I just can't talk about to anybody. Some day someone'll read it, or it'll end up in a box, ignored. Either way, I won't care 'cause I'll be gone. Immortality is for, well, Immortals.

Jill stood, stretched the kinks out of her back, then turned and kissed me firmly on the lips.

"Time to go?" I knew it was, but I had to ask.

She took my hands and pulled me to my feet. "Shall we sing while we walk?"

"Whatever your little heart desires, missy."

Then Death linked her arm through mine and we sang our love song as we strolled off into the blue-black night.

Calgary writer, photographer (& occasional musician) **Timothy Reynolds** was inspired by the late Harry Chapin's song "I Wanna Learn a Love Song" and took a break from writing his latest novel to write "Blue-Black Night" especially for *Danse Macabre*. He says that as with many of his works, it combines a touch of the bizarre nestled within the normal, wrapped around some tiny segment of his own life.

~LA SENORA BLANCA~

By Lucy Taylor

The bleat of a train whistle greeted the couple's advance along the tracks, the jittering of the timber ties traveling up through the soles of their shoes, making their ankles wobble, their knees quake. In the distance, an owl mourned, crickets clacking in the tall weeds surrounding the tracks. No houses, no lights way out here. Just the *Estrella del Norte* headed south from Queretaro to Mexico City, right on time at 6:47 p.m.

Naldo lifted Lupe's hand to his mouth and kissed her fingers. "The train's coming, my love, are you ready?"

"Ready, Naldo."

"*La Santa Muerte*, she's keeping her promise."

"I can't wait to meet her, *mi amor*."

They sounded like nervous young lovers, but they were old now, curled and fragile as two brittle brown leaves nudged along one last time by the breeze. Lupe tottered unsteadily, pendulous breasts flopping under her loose blouse, grey-streaked hair tumbling over the knobs of her spine. Naldo clasped her hand, guiding her over the tracks in the twilight. He was squat and sinewy, with bowed legs and a flamboyant, devilishly curling mustache that flared out on both sides of his square, pitbull jaw. A knife scar pebbled the flesh at the side of his neck and faded tattoos, souvenirs from numerous incarcerations, festooned his biceps and forearms.

"She's almost here, Naldo!"

The *Estrella del Norte* blasted around the curve up ahead and roared toward them at sixty miles per hour, lights blinding, disorienting, and the engineer must have spotted them, because bells suddenly clanged and the train commenced a terrible cats-in-heat keening. The engineer was giving the brakes all he had, but it wasn't enough. Naldo had explained to Lupe that, at the speed the train was traveling when it took the curve, the engineer would need at least a mile to stop.

Not that either Naldo or Lupe wanted to be spared. They'd planned their suicide years before, when Naldo had just gotten out of Mexico City's Prisión de Oriente and Lupe was being treated for a virulent cancer that nested in her uterus like a malefic fetus. They'd vowed they would survive into old age and then face death together.

"It's been a good life," Lupe said.

"The best, *mi amor!*"

"No regrets?"

"No regrets."

Adrenalin rocked Lupe's heart and she shuddered — not just with fear, but with pride and love and a terrible resolve. She looked at Naldo and mouthed *Te amo* and leaned over to kiss him—

—as the tracks buckled and rollercoastered into the starless black sky and the *brujah*-screech of the whistle rent the world as red rain spattered the front of the train.

* * *

Lupe awoke with a howl on her lips, eyes darting wildly. Something was wrong. It wasn't the dream that had wakened her. Something else.

In the room next to hers, Luisa Sentavo, a buxom former librarian, huffed and moaned in her sleep. From across the hall came the contralto rumble of Olive Pattala's snores and Vicente Montoya's drugged mumbling. Most of the residents of Sierra House Nursing Home slept like logs. Flora Espinoza, the night nurse, dispensed sleep aids as if they were Tums, but Lupe squirreled hers away in her cheek. She wasn't one of those old people longing to fade away in her sleep. She wanted her death to be memorable.

From outside came a soft scuffling sound like panther claws on the linoleum floor or the rattle of chicken bones around the neck of a *curandera*. A broomstick-thin shadow bent to the door of Lupe's room, peered in and then withdrew, leaving behind a heady cascade of rich odors — cigar smoke and rum and something else, the rank, pungent tang of decay.

The banging of blood in Lupe's chest rose so violently that she was afraid Espinoza would hear it all the way to the nurse's station, but in spite of her fear, she slipped out of bed and mousecrept to the door.

Her first impression was of a roiling black thunderhead that filled the corridor and dimmed the sallow glow of the fluorescent ceiling lights. She heard a hollow tapping and saw in stark relief the outline of vertebrae snaking against an inky cloak, vivid as veins in a winter-blasted leaf.

Lupe bit the inside of her cheek and reeled backward, so stunned by the sight that she feared her heart might crack apart on her ribs like a cheap earthen vase.

Prowling the hall was *La Santa Muerte* — known to her devotees as *La Senora Blanca* — regal and terrible in a hooded black cloak, heavy rings on her skeletal fingers. The stew of odors Lupe had smelled before wreathed her mottled cranium like a widow's veil.

Holy Death, in all her glory, come to call.

Watching Death stalk the corridor, creeping door to door with cat burglar stealth, Lupe felt poleaxed with horror and awe. At the same time, her natural curiosity flared perilously high and she was beset with a rash desire to confront Death and pose questions. She opened her mouth, but her voice failed. She realized she was drenched in sweat and shivering. After so many years of praying to her image, to encounter Death — *La Senora Blanca* herself — was overwhelming.

Vividly, she recalled the first time Naldo had brought her to *La Santa Muerte's* shrine in Tepita, the most dangerous, crime-ridden barrio in Mexico City. Naldo had just completed a four year stretch for robbery and had come out of prison a man in love, transformed with adoration for Holy Death, the most beloved and venerated saint in Prisión de Oriente.

Lupe had gazed up in awe at the six-foot statue draped in velvet robes and a bride's taffeta veil, wielding a scythe in one hand and a globe in the other. Death's skeletal mouth seemed to twist in a cruel grin, as though she relished the terror she inspired and took pleasure flaunting her power over all living things.

With utmost reverence, Naldo filled a shot glass from a pint of *Patrón*, *La Senora Blanca's* poison of choice, and placed it on the altar. From his pocket, he withdrew a pack of Marlboros and a fat joint, meticulously rolled, which he added to the offerings. "*La Flaca* isn't like the other saints," he said, calling *La Santa Muerte* by one of her many nicknames — the Skinny One. "She doesn't judge the poor people, the criminals, the *putanas*. She understands us best. *La Flaca* also appreciates the finer things. If we come to her respectfully and bring her gifts, she always answers our prayers."

"Always, Naldo?"

"Always."

Lupe had brought gifts, too: a red rose and white candles bearing images of *La Santa Muerte's* frightful countenance. She laid them on the altar and said a prayer: *Keep Naldo safe. Let us grow old together. When the time comes, let us die together, too.*

It was the memory of that prayer, heartfelt and fervently uttered, that restored Lupe's voice and snapped her out of her fear trance.

"*Senora, Senora,*" she called.

Death halted mid-stride and twisted around with a click-clacking of phalanges. An inch of limp ash dangled from the *Cohiba* gripped in her teeth. Lupe could sense her disbelief and outrage. No one challenged *La Senora Blanca*. No one had the temerity to question Death.

Yet Lupe was a tough old bird who had lived almost ninety years, many of them in poverty and peril, so she blurted out, "Remember my husband Naldo, who was killed by drug dealers? He was a little man with a big mustache and an even bigger heart. Ever since he got out of prison, he was your devoted servant. Yet he was murdered eighteen years ago. Why did he die in such a terrible way?"

The silence that followed reverberated like a hail of bullets from an *arma automática*. Lupe clutched the doorframe, legs liquid with fear. What had she done?

Death said nothing, but regarded Lupe as if she were a half-crushed insect she was about to put out of its misery.

Lupe wanted to scuttle back to her bed, but the thought of Naldo's bullet-ridden body, stretched out on a slab at the Mexico City morgue, gave her courage.

"Please, Holy Death, what happened? Why didn't you protect him?"

La Flaca's gleaming cranium rotated to fix on the shriveled little woman who addressed her so boldly. Her limbs and torso were utterly still, but the tiny bones in her extremities crunched. The jeweled rings on her finger bones tocked together in agitation.

"Get lost," rasped *La Flaca*, her sepulcher voice somber and cold as the black of her pitiless eye sockets. Lupe heard the words as a thin hissing that burrowed its way into her flesh, the sound itself dry as broom straws sweeping a cement floor or a rattlesnake gliding through parched grass. "Be grateful I didn't come here for you tonight."

Smoke from the fat *Cohiba* snaked out of her eye sockets as Flora Espinoza passed by, studying a chart on a clipboard and drawing Death's attention. Espinoza was a pasty, fortyish woman with neatly bunned hair, marshmallowy arms, and dull eyes that sometimes, unexpectedly, grew twinkly as though with secret, subterranean mirth. She had a lovely singing voice, rich with consoling, and often serenaded residents of Sierra House who were ill or distressed.

Death turned to stalk after Espinoza.

"*Please, Santa Muerte*, wait!" Lupe cried.

She fumbled in the bodice of her nightgown and plucked out a tattered prayer card that portrayed Death as a magnificent, bejeweled queen, her bones draped in a royal blue robe studded with gems. The card was torn and faded from handling and the bottom half bore rusty stains.

"This was in Naldo's pocket when he died — look, you can see his blood! Tell me why he had to die when he had just found you in prison a few years earlier? Naldo was devoted to you and brought you expensive gifts. He'd given up the criminal life, he was no trouble to anyone. And what about *me*, left to grow old alone and rot in this place, which is nothing but a prison for old people! We were going to grow old together. When the time came, we were going to ride the *Estrella del Norte*."

Death seemed to find this last remark uproarious. From her throat trilled a pinging xylophone sound that might have been a laugh. "Kissing the train — you call that a plan? That's a death for fools! *Idiotas* like you and your husband imagine the train's like a one-night stand — wham, bam, and it's over!" She lunged at Lupe and gave a guillotine snap of her jaws. "They don't see the ones I turn away — like chopped down trees, all stumps. Mashed flat as a tortilla from the waist down or scalped alive when their hair tangles in the undercarriage. A fast and pain-free death, my knobby ass!"

She made a shooing gesture and strode up the hall to the room of Sylvia LaGuerta, an ancient, emphysema-stricken crone who, in her day, had dealt a mean hand of blackjack at the casino in Monterrey. Death peered into the room and, while her fleshless visage was incapable of real expression, Lupe heard her finger bones begin to agitate and her teeth grind together. The tip of her *Cohiba* flared and smoke began to puff from its ash. Death was displeased, and her fury altered the quality of the air, making it clammy and corpse-cold.

La Flaca stood at the foot of Sylvia LaGuerta's bed as though she were a vigil-keeping mother waiting for LaGuerta's eyes to open or her hand to twitch. But even Lupe, spying from the doorway, could tell that Sylvia, the *real* Sylvia, was long gone and that what remained was of no more consequence than a junked car on the towing lot.

Meanwhile, Death fretted beside the bed in mute pique, clicking her fingerbones together as though keeping time to an infernal song.

Lupe inched her way to Death's side and whispered, "About my question, Holy Death…"

La Flaca snapped her mandible and said, "Persistent pest, aren't you? I'll come again tomorrow night. Then we shall see."

▩ ▩ ▩

"Lupe, something dreadful's happened."

Lupe was watching a morning talk show featuring people who'd had sex change operations discussing their lovemaking techniques when Nurse Espinoza charged into her room, looking distressed and frazzled. She cut off the TV, pulled a chair up next to Lupe's and sat down with a woebegone sigh. She looked close to tears, and Lupe wanted to comfort her, but it was difficult — Espinoza scorned *La Santa Muerte*, insisting that she wasn't a saint at all, but the fabrication of the ignorant and misguided, undoubtedly leading the lot of them to damnation.

Lupe tried to be forgiving, though, having heard that Espinoza's own mother, with whom she was very close, had died less than a year ago.

"Oh, Lupe," said Espinoza, dabbing at her eyes with a tissue. "Sylvia passed away last night."

"I know," said Lupe sadly.

A small frown line appeared in the pale flesh of Espinoza's brow. "What do you mean?"

Lupe knew that Espinoza would think she was one of those old people lost in a fog of dementia if she talked of seeing *La Senora Blanca* go into Sylvia's room and tower over her bed, so she said quickly, "It was in a dream. I saw a great white sailing ship, like a magnificent swan, sailing across the ocean. Jesus was at the helm, the Virgin Mary by his right hand and Sylvia kneeling at His side."

Lupe had to fight not to giggle at the banality of the image, a version of which she had once seen painted on a china plate in a Mexico City souvenir shop, but Espinoza's eyes flooded with tears and she nodded, *yes, yes,* as though she'd seen such a ship herself and talked with Skipper Jesus. Lupe looked away and rolled her eyes.

"It's for the best, you know," said Espinoza. "Sylvia suffered dreadfully with emphysema. She was fortunate to have an easy death." She plumped the pillows behind Lupe's back and squeezed her hand. "Would that we all could go so peacefully."

To hell with peace, thought Lupe. *I want to know why La Flaca let Naldo die.*

■ ■ ■

Munching fried potatoes at the evening meal, Lupe shot furtive glances around the room, wondering who *La Flaca* was going to take next. Would it be eighty-nine-year old Guzman Torres, who lost a leg in the Great War and liked to brag that he'd lived through three marriages and two airplane crashes? Or eighty-year-old Bertie Angelina, who carried on long, rambling conversations with her dead brother and sometimes screamed out "Call 066!" — the emergency number — for no apparent reason? Or maybe Vincente Montoya or Olive Patalla or even prissy little Luisa Sentavo with her nose stuck in a book all day and then moaning and groaning all night. Or maybe, Lupe thought, *she* was the one Death was coming for.

Later, she lay awake, alert and listening. Around two a.m., she heard Espinoza singing softly in another room, the sound so melodious and comforting that she almost drifted off to sleep, but jerked awake when the telltale odor of cigar smoke reached her nostrils.

Creeping into the corridor, she saw Espinoza leave Bertie Angelina's room, sighing and typing out a text message on her phone. Espinoza ambled toward the rec room, where Lupe knew the portly nurse often passed the wee hours playing Internet poker or watching heartwarming rescue stories on the Animal Planet. She didn't see what Lupe saw — the black-robed skeleton puffing on a cigar just outside Bertie's door, her skull head metronoming side to side as she moved with lithe, insectile grace into Bertie's room.

When Lupe tiptoed in behind *La Flaca* and saw what was on the bed, her heart wilted like a drought-stricken *camelia*.

Her old friend lay with mouth agape and sightless eyes bugged out, as though she'd watched *La Santa Muerte* come for her and died purely from fright. Her arms were outside the covers, hands clenched into claws. Even in death, she appeared to be trying to fight her way free of some terrible assault.

Lupe gave a little gasp, and *La Flaca's* head jerked up. She opened her jaw in a feral grin and snapped her teeth so viciously she almost bit her cigar in half.

"You again!"

"Holy Death," said Lupe, bowing low to show her deep respect and reverence, "if you would only talk to me a minute about how my husband died—"

Fast as a swung machete, Death lunged across the room, seized Lupe by the back of her nightgown, and hoisted her high. Lupe's bare feet paddled the air, the breath left her lungs in a whoosh. The prayer card she kept tucked in her bra shook loose and fell to the floor.

"What do you care why your old man died?" hissed *La Flaca*. "He's worm food now, there's no bringing him back. I'm a one-way door, don't you get it?"

"But what about all that Naldo did to show you his affection and respect?" Lupe exclaimed, her fear squelched by indignation. "What about the statue of you he carved with his own hands?"

"Ah, yes, the statue, I do remember that," *La Flaca* said, baring the toothy semblance of a smile. "Before he brought it to the shrine, he packed the nostrils full of snow. It was a thoughtful gesture."

"He did much more than plug your nose with cocaine. He also built you a shrine."

Death's mouth split wide with lethal mirth — she might have been hooting with laughter or braying with rage. "Don't talk to me about shrines! The only shrines I give a shit about are the bodies I leave behind. Every time you see a rotting corpse, a cadaver laid out on a pallet, that's another shrine to me. Remember that, Guadalupe Mendoza-Delgado."

Lupe gasped. "You know my name?"

"What do you think, that this whole dying business isn't organized? I know everybody's name, I know the names of your papa's bastard children and your *puta* of a grandmama's johns." She shook Lupe so hard that her head bobbled and her eyes bulged. "Beside, ungrateful *pendeja*, your name was on my ledger a long time ago — you're luckier than you know just to be sucking air."

"Then why wasn't I the one who died?" demanded Lupe. "Why Naldo?"

La Flaca ground her teeth. The cold silence of gravestones in the *Panteón de Delores* radiated from the black depths of her ancient eye sockets. "You are a bitch, a *cabrona*," she said, "and your man made a foolish bargain." She impaled Lupe with a meatgrinder stare. "Now get back to bed, and if you wake up, consider yourself lucky."

◼ ◼ ◼

Lupe fled back to her room and burrowed under the covers. Soon after, she heard footsteps and held her breath, but it was only Espinoza, come in to check on her. And though Lupe pretended to be asleep, the nurse must have sensed her distress, for she began to sing a soulful lullaby, part mother's love and part lament, that made Lupe think of times gone by and filled her with bittersweet longing.

She fell into a fretful sleep and dreamed about that terrible day when Naldo stormed into their little house, bloodied and shaking with rage.

Lupe was trembling, too. But before she could tell him her own dreadful news, he began to curse and shout, "*Mierde*, but a frightful thing has happened!" For a flustered instant, she thought he was talking about her test results, but then he went on, "The government sent soldiers with bulldozers this morning and tore down *La Santa Muerte's* shrine. The people who'd come to worship tried to stop them, but they beat us back. Everything's gone! The beautiful robes and the holy statues, the paintings and icons have all been carted off to the dump! They say we are a cult of criminals and devil worshipers."

Lupe, overwhelmed by this surfeit of sorrow, began to weep and Naldo, not understanding that she was crying for herself, began to reassure her.

"Never mind, *mi amor*. I'll build a new shrine, you'll see. I'll make it bigger and more beautiful than ever."

He talked and talked, working himself up, until finally Lupe interrupted to tell him about her visit to the clinic and the cancer the doctor had found nesting in her womb. After that, he was silent for a long time, and then he cried.

All through that summer, Naldo worked alongside others in the *barrio* to build the new shrine. A few so-called upstanding folks chipped in, but mostly it was the outcasts, Gloriana the prostitute who stood in the alleyway all night selling her used-up flesh, the gangs and the drug addicts, the alcoholics, cab drivers and *policia*, fringe people whose lives were fraught with danger and risk, people who needed protection.

Lupe had lived that summer in mortal fear, but Death — whose fearsome image leered down from every wall in their house, whose face even stared out at her from across her husband's tattooed chest when he was mounting her, — never came.

▧ ▧ ▧

"Look what I found in Bertie's room," Nurse Espinoza said. She held up Lupe's slippers, one in each hand, as if they were week-old kittens. Her eyes were smiling but her mouth was crimped tight as a fist. "These are your slippers, aren't they?"

It was early morning and Bertie's body had just been wheeled out on a gurney by two white-clad attendants. Along the hall, the residents of Sierra House crept warily out of their rooms to watch the sorrowful passage. Olive Pattala pinched Bertie's toes to make sure she was really dead, and Guzman Torres lifted up a corner of the sheet with one palsied hand and gave Bertie a smile and little three-fingered wave. The same silent question played on all of their faces, a mix of dread and expectation — when does my turn come? Will I be next?

Having had little sleep the night before, Lupe had been dozing when Espinoza came in. Now she sat up, rubbed her eyes and squinted at the slippers as though she'd never seen them before. "They must be Bertie's."

Espinoza looked peeved, a teacher disappointed by a bright pupil's inadequate response. "But Lupe, these slippers are size six. Bertie's feet were big as barges. Your feet are like a doll's."

Lupe said, "I thought I heard Bertie cry out and went to see if she needed help. I must have left my slippers."

"And what did you see when you went into Bertie's room? Whatever it was, you can tell me."

"There was nothing to see. Only poor Bertie, looking like she'd been scared out of her wits when she died."

Espinoza's eyebrows lifted like elevators.

"How frightening it must have been for you to walk in and find her dead. Not only did you jump right out of your bedroom slippers, but you left behind this ugly thing as well."

From her pocket Espinoza whisked out Lupe's prayer card, which she flourished like a poker champ producing a winning Ace. She held the card up between two fingers, as though it were dipped in filth.

"*La Santa Muerte* wouldn't be pleased to hear you call her ugly," Lupe said.

"Death is no saint, and you're risking your immortal soul to worship such wickedness. I'm going to burn this, Lupe. It's an evil thing that can only bring you harm."

"But that was Naldo's!" Lupe cried.

For an instant, she glimpsed that tiny spark that sometimes flared up like an unvoiced scream in Espinoza's eyes, but then it vanished. Espinoza sighed forlornly and looked at Lupe with tenderness and sadness. "Haven't we had enough death around here, Lupe? For God's sake, let's pray there isn't anymore."

❈ ❈ ❈

Too exhausted to keep her vigil that night, Lupe sank into a stuporous sleep and dreamed a young and virile Naldo suddenly thrust himself atop her.

She smiled and opened herself to him, but his urgency proved overpowering. Brutally, he held her down, smothering her face with hot, asphyxiating kisses. She began to kick and claw, trying to make him understand that she was suffocating.

You're crushing me, mi amore. Stop, please! I can't breathe!

But the reckless assault grew more merciless. A blow jerked her face to the side, her nostrils were pinched shut — she flailed out— *Naldo, no, don't do this!* —as his strength punched the air from her lungs. Lightning webbed behind her eyes, and a chain-saw chewed at the back of her brain.

Then it ended.

There was only silence and glacial cold, and Lupe thought she had died.

The pillow smashed into her face grew feather light and dropped to the floor. Gasping, her head spinning, she made out Espinoza's face, ashen and stupefied, trying desperately to free herself from the skeletal fingers that gripped her biceps so tightly they opened bloody punctures in the flesh.

"*Cabrona*!" Death rasped, rocking Espinoza side to side the way someone would shake a milk carton. "You go around snuffing people out like bugs and I let it go, because what's one more dead body here and there when I've got billions waiting. But then you make the same mistake as all the other psychos. When you decide who lives, who dies, you feel immortal. You imagine as long as you're in control of other peoples' dying, your number's never coming up!"

Espinoza's tongue planked and her eyeballs bled. Lupe could see her puffed-out cheeks working frantically to dislodge the object in her mouth, a wadded prayer card that suddenly began to blacken and curl at the edges. There came a branding iron sizzle of flesh as the nurse's face blazed a furious scarlet.

"Your *mamacita* called it right the day you murdered her," *La Flaca* said. "You are indeed a stupid *puta* and up to no fucking good!"

With a snort of disdain, she dropped Espinoza, whose body slithered to the floor in a burnt and boneless heap. Death lit a fresh cigar and tipped the ash into Espinoza's open mouth. She turned to Lupe, who was crouched in terror by the bed. "Still want to worship at my altar, *cabrona*?"

Lupe got to her feet on creaking knees. This time her question came out a whisper that was barely audible. "You said Naldo made a poor bargain. Tell me what you meant."

Death leaned so close that Lupe could look directly into her gaping, empty sockets — their fierce indifference to all human plight a stark reminder of her power. "Remember when cancer infested your belly and the doctors said you would soon die? What happened?"

"The cancer went away," said Lupe. "The doctors said it was a miracle, but I knew it was you, *Santa Muerte*, who cured me."

"You see?" said Death. "That's why you are a *cabrona*, I gave you back your life and still you bitch. It wasn't your paltry prayers that saved you, it was your husband's. He pestered me night and day to spare you. But don't be a stupid *zorra* about these types of transactions. Your life still came with a price attached."

Lupe absorbed this like a blow. "Naldo paid for my life with his?"

"Nothing's fucking free. The world is commerce, nothing else."

"But I was the one afraid of death," said Lupe, "not Naldo. That's why he promised me we'd die together."

"Tough luck, old woman. You got left behind." She gathered her cape around her. As it swirled and eddied about her ancient bones, Lupe saw time's passage stitched into the fabric, the rise and fall of city-states and nations, the scourge of plagues and mass exterminations, a vast and undulating tapestry of deaths past and deaths to come woven into the folds of *La Flaca's* robe.

Entranced by the terror and beauty of Death's garment, she reached out to touch the hem.

"Please, *Santa Muerte*. Don't leave me. Before you go … one dance."

The black pits in *La Flaca's* skull glowed, and she grew preternaturally still. "What a night! One *puta* tries to do my job, the other *cabrona's* so crazy she wants me to hang around for a *bachata*."

But then, after a moment, she took Lupe into her cold embrace and began to glide around the room, slowly at first, with a kind of stately measure befitting a last waltz, then picking up speed until they whirled and capered out into the hall, raising a draught of frosty air, like wind off the highest peaks in the Sierra Madres. The icy breeze roused Vincente Montoya, who yelled out for his long dead wife to go downstairs and turn up the thermostat. It blew the roses on Olive Pattala's dresser so fiercely that she would awaken the next morning, astonished to find her bed covered in scarlet petals, and it chilled the bare butts of Guzman Torres and Luisa Sentavo, who were happily fucking away as they did every night, oblivious to Death passing by close enough to observe their octogenarian ardor and add one of their names to her To Do list

Their wild *bachata* carried Lupe outside Sierra House and over the lawn, through dense woodlands and wild, weedy fields, down to the train tracks where Death spun to a stop and placed her spidery fingers against Lupe's heart, the grin on her face like that of a rigored corpse. *Tic toc, tic toc.*

Panting and gasping, Lupe stared into *La Flaca's* skull eyes. To her surprise, she saw not emptiness but all eternity, where universes were conceived and thrived and perished, only to be replaced by others in an endless cycle of creation and collapse.

From those twin voids, she heard her own voice and Naldo's echo and intertwine.

It's been a good life, hasn't it?

The best, mi amor.

A vibration began at her tailbone and lurched up her spine. She heard the blast of the train whistle and the scream of the brakes and in the midst of the bedlam that built in her head, she managed a smile of relief and gratitude.

Even eighteen years later, the *Estrella del Norte* was still right on time.

■ ■ ■

Lucy Taylor is the author of seven novels, including the Bram Stoker-award winning *The Safety of Unknown Cities*, and over a hundred short stories. Upcoming publications include stories in *Exotic Gothic 4* and *The Mammoth Book of Best of Best New Erotica*. She lives in Pismo Beach, CA and says about her story: "The idea for "La Senora Blanca" came to me after visiting my mother, who lives in an assisted living center in Richmond, VA. I could imagine Death capering along the silent hallways as terrified residents creep to their doorways to peer out."

~TOTENTANZ~

By Nancy Holder & Erin Underwood

A kiss for luck. The merest peck, a whisper against Drea's mouth, when Paul should have given it his all.

Cologne's bitter winter wind set her teeth to chattering as she read the directions to *Firme Köln* for the tenth time, but she still couldn't find *Endlose Gasse*. She needed this job beyond just needing employment. It felt like a last chance.

That's not true, she thought. *You're just having pre-wedding jitters.*

Complicating matters, Cologne's carnival season was in full swing as it neared the final Crazy Days and the residents of Altstadt — Old Town — were enjoying the celebration. Navigating the streets was an exercise in patience to avoid being swept away by festive packs of wildly dressed Carnival goers. In her severe black suit, hair pulled back, she kept stumbling on her new black heels. Her dancing shoes, actually, but they went well with her suit.

Paul's family had this weird tradition that the bride and groom had to dance a special waltz at their wedding reception. The music was played on a brass disc inside a music box that had been in the family for generations. Paul's mother would bring the box and the disc with her from Berlin. For now, they practiced to a digital recording of it. It seemed tuneless, with no cues to help a non-dancer remember the intricate steps.

Paul was astonished by her awkwardness. But she'd *told* him the night they'd met that she didn't dance. He'd been too busy sweeping her off her feet to listen.

"Triller, triller!" a young man sang on the street in heavily accented English. He was dressed like a dead Michael Jackson, white face, his nose painted to look like a triangle of bone.

His moonwalk was spectacular; Drea felt in her coat pocket for a coin for the little black cardboard coffin beside him, the lid open to reveal a scattering of change and a few bills. She tossed in two euro coins. Dead Michael Jackson saw them and cried, "Woo!"

A high-pitched scream followed on the end of his triumphant shout. Drea spun around just in time to see a little blonde-haired girl running backwards away from him, directly into the rush of oncoming traffic. The girl's right foot left the curb, and she began to tumble.

Without thinking, Drea dove after her, grabbing the hem of the girl's coat and yanking it hard with one hand and reaching up to cradle her head like a football with the other as they fell hard to the sidewalk.

A woman tore the terrified child from Drea's arms and shouted at the boy. Then the mother and daughter disappeared into the oblivious crowd, leaving Drea sprawled on the cement.

"You're welcome," Drea muttered, then smiled weakly as Michael Jackson held out his hand and hefted her to her feet.

"American," he said, and kissed her hard on the mouth, bowed, and moonwalked back to his little coffin. Then he danced past the coffin, gesturing for her to join in — no, to follow him — down the street. Feeling a little goofy, she did it anyway — people were always saying she was too nice — and he stopped beside a small brass plaque at the mouth of a nearby alley. He did a hip thrust and pointed at it.

Endlose Gasse. Endless Alley.

"How...?" she began.

He handed her the crumpled printout of her directions, which she must have dropped when she'd saved the little girl, and swept an elegant bow.

"*Danke,*" she said, taking the paper while fishing in her pocket for more change.

He waved her off, blew her a kiss, and danced away.

Dashing beneath the inconspicuous Roman arch, Drea hurried down the narrow alley that opened into a generous courtyard surrounded by some of the oldest buildings she had seen since arriving in Cologne. *Firme Köln* was the third door to her right, the building large, Gothic style, with ornate decorations that drew her eye up to a tapered black spire inlaid with alabaster designs.

The building looked every bit the "old money" accounting company that the headhunter had described. Of all the structures around the courtyard, *Firme Köln* was the grimmest, with its shadowed windows and a clinging sense of silence.

With five minutes to spare, Drea entered the lobby. A stale scent stirred in the air. The reception room was small and lit with dim incandescent sconces that cast dirty yellow light on the walls. The ceiling towered above, decorated with delicate plaster designs and a large renaissance-style mural of angels reaching down from Heaven.

The receptionist, a gray-haired woman who appeared to have been stuck in the Victorian era — chignon, high neck, no makeup — told her to sit down. Fifteen minutes later, Drea felt herself nodding off. After another half-hour, she wondered if she had gotten the time wrong.

It was nearly a full hour before the receptionist ushered her down a hall and into a room so dark she could barely see the elderly gentleman seated behind an enormous ebony desk. His skin was stretched tightly over his sharply-angled face. His hair was as white as the teenager's stage makeup, with matching eyebrows. Long, thin fingers were splayed over what appeared to be a black ledger book. He didn't shake her hand, as was German custom. Didn't introduce himself either — and she felt at a tremendous disadvantage, for she hadn't been able to find out his name.

He opened the ledger book with a flourish and ran his finger down a list of handwritten names on the yellowed page. Each name had a check mark beside it — except for hers, which was the last one on the page.

"*Fräulein Armstrong*," he said, gesturing for her to sit.

He wrote something in the ledger. "As you know, we are looking for someone who can update our office systems, someone with a background in technology. The world is running ahead of us, I fear." His smile didn't quite reach his eyes. He seemed … depressed.

"Well, maybe I can help you catch up," she ventured.

"Hmm, *ja*." He tapped her name. "I am concerned about your work experience since you have just graduated from university. But my secretary thinks I should talk to you, and I have long since learned to trust her instincts."

He leaned back in his chair and folded his arms. It was her cue. Her time to shine.

But her frustrations from the last couple of months came to a head, colliding with her hopes for getting employment in Cologne — hope that was slipping away again. It was obvious to her that he'd already decided she was wrong for the job. Why prolong the agony? "Um," she began, and she wanted to kick herself. To her horror, tears welled. Her friends always said she was too soft, too sweet. They said Paul had bulldozed her into moving to Germany. That she needed to work in an American firm for two years so she could take her CPA exam. But he'd wanted to be home. It had sounded so romantic.

Now, Paul was mad at her because she couldn't get a job; and she couldn't learn to dance his stupid family waltz; and she was blowing her interview.

"Well," he said, about to end it, and she reached down deep inside herself and took a breath.

"I'm an accountant," she reminded him. "Like you. There are credits and debits. They have to balance. That's the same in IT, as well. Everything can be reduced to binary. On, off. And we can integrate everything so that you can keep up with all the changes."

"Balance." He sighed. "It is yes, it is no. But now there is all the gray in the world. So many variables."

"But in the end, credits and debits," she said.

He blinked and looked at her. "That's ... true." He was quiet a moment. He seemed to be considering something. "But how do I know you're not a, how does one say in English ... a slacker? You've come to Germany for an adventure, and then you'll meet someone and off you'll go—"

"Oh, no," she replied. "I live here. We're getting m-married." She heard herself stumbling over the word.

"Ah, true love." His smile was wistful. "I have not had that good fortune."

Neither have I, she thought; to her horror, she also almost burst into tears again.

"So, first step taken," he said, and then he snapped the ledger book shut.

■ ■ ■

"*Das ist Scheisse*," Paul said, practically spitting the words at her. "Shit."

"Trial periods at new jobs are normal," she said. She was standing in their apartment holding a bottle of champagne and her cell phone. He was still at work.

"Not for *free*. Did you even bargain when he told you he wouldn't pay you a goddamned euro?"

No, she thought, and although she'd braced herself for this reaction, and practiced what she would say in response, everything was melting away in a sea of uncertainty. It *was* a little weird not to get at least something for showing up to work.

"I thought we could go out, to celebrate," she said instead. "It's carnival."

"We say *Karneval*," he corrected her with asperity. "I'll be late. *Someone* has to pay for this wedding."

He hung up. On her.

She stared at the phone as if it were a foreign object and sank down onto the couch. He was right; no, he was wrong; he was wrong to be so mean. She was desperate; no one was hiring, and at least she would have some precious job experience if it didn't work out, wouldn't she?

When Paul came home three hours later, a little drunk, he handed her some wilted flowers and took her in his arms. He told her how sorry he was, and explained that his office had gone out drinking together to team-build, that it was too late to take her to *Karneval* tonight; it was time for champagne and waltzes at home.

"Kiss me first," she said; and he laughed at her and brushed her mouth again the way he had that morning, just going through the motions. Then he held his arm out to the side and draped his other one very loosely across her upper back. She laid her hand in his and wrapped her arm around his waist.

Blearily, he hummed the godforsaken non-melody, and she shut her eyes in resignation. He dragged her around the living room like a marionette with broken strings, humming in her ear, too loudly. It all felt so random and weird.

"Oh, my God," he said in English, "you really can't dance."

Fuck you, she thought, and blanched, because she didn't talk like that and she certainly didn't think like that, not where Paul was concerned. But what she said was, "I know."

* * *

She couldn't dance, but she could streamline, coordinate, integrate. The next day on the job, she dazzled her boss, who was simply called Herr T. He sat beside her in her frigid dimly-lit office with its heavy antique furniture that cast long shadows about the room, and watched as she showed him what she had planned for *Firme Köln*. There was something different about him today. He seemed ... fuller, somehow. She'd thought his hair was all white, but there were streaks of blond in it.

She was very aware of him sitting so close, and she tried very hard to hide it. He was a million years old, for heaven's sake, and she was engaged.

"You see, we make records for each client," she told him, tapping on her laptop keyboard. She had brought it with her to work. "Then the accountant inputs the variables for each tax situation, and with these prompts, the computer accesses the appropriate programs, which you would lease."

"Tax situation," he said, smiling a little. "Paying what one owes."

"Yes," she said, a little confused.

"What one owes," he said again. He walked to the window and pulled aside heavy red velvet curtains, stirring the shadows and revealing the brightly lit streets crowded with revelers. She stood and followed him.

"Will you go out tonight?" she asked and he glanced at her, startled.

Then he pursed his lips in amusement and looked back at the window. She had the distinct impression that at first he'd thought she was inviting him out, then realized his mistake.

"Saturday night is the *Geisterzug*," Herr T. said. A faraway look clouded his face. "It is a sight to be seen."

"The *Ghost Parade*. I'll be sure to see it." She moved from the window. "Good night, Herr T."

"*Gute Nacht, Fräulein Armstrong*," he said, his bone white fingers still gripping the curtain.

* * *

As she left *Firme Köln*, Paul called her and said he would take the streetcar and meet her, to make up for the night before. They would celebrate Shrove Thursday together. Tonight was the Parody Parade, playing off the coming *Rosenmotag* — Rose Monday — parade. Instead of big fancy floats, tonight's festivities consisted of dancers and marching bands interspersed with deliberately cheesy, mock *floats* that consisted of carts pushed and dragged through the partying crowds that spilled out from the pubs, filling the streets. The Crazy Days were here.

She and Paul drank hot wine, and applauded as the Parody Prince dressed in rags and a silver crown encrusted with plastic jewels rode by on a cart pulled by a pair of button-eyed clowns with fiery red wigs, blue Lederhosen, and candy cane striped socks. Dancing behind him in perfect formation was his troupe of *Prinzengarde*. They wore colonial-looking uniforms, women in dresses, men in pants, all of them wearing *Dreispitz* — tricorne hats. Then came more floats, with the riders tossing candy and trinkets into the crowd.

Paul was getting drunk, yelling and nearly knocked over a little boy to grab a shiny necklace of silver beads. Drea was very cold, and tired, and she found herself thinking about her first day at the job, and how well she had done, but Paul had only asked a question or two about it, and moved on.

A float trundled past with an *oom-papa* band. Dancing the polka on the slow-moving cart was a man in a skeleton bodysuit and two men wearing Renaissance outfits-one a priest with his red robes, the other a noble in his red and gold doublet. Paul grabbed her and started dancing maniacally in little drunken circles.

"Polka, Drea!" he shouted.

He whirled her in a wild circle with a series of hops. She stumbled on the slippery sidewalk, flailing and sliding, crashing into people, most of whom just laughed.

"Paul, please stop!" she said, as she tried to extricate herself from his tight bear hug.

"She can't dance!" he cried. "She can't make money! But she sure can fuck!"

"Paul!" she cried, humiliated. "Stop!"

"Oh, you fuck so great." He mashed his lips against hers, darting the tip of his tongue like a snake against her teeth. "Let's go home now. I want to fuck my American."

"Oh, my *God*," she said, turning her head and ignoring the chill that crept down her spine. "You're drunk."

But she knew he was speaking from his heart. She remembered the first time they'd slept together. It had been a long time for her, and they hadn't done much sleeping. He was dashing and funny and he obviously liked her a lot. The sex had been great because she'd been so happy. She'd felt special in his arms. He hadn't noticed that it hadn't been all that great for a while now.

He grabbed her head and kissed her again. She jerked away, almost tumbling to her knees, and hurried the seven blocks to the streetcar stop. She covered her mouth with her hand to keep from crying or screaming or both as the brilliantly illuminated city roared past.

She passed a hotel, and thought about checking in. She thought about going to the airport and flying back to Boston.

But if she left, she left in defeat. And maybe it was just nerves for Paul, too. Maybe he was as afraid as she was. That they were, in essence, dancing the same dance.

■ ■ ■

Paul came home even drunker, and passed out in the middle of apologizing. Drea slept on the couch but she didn't think he knew, because he was still asleep when she left. Smiling grimly, she let him oversleep. He might have the only paying job between them, but by light of day, she had somewhere else to go.

At work, she began to write up a technical document for Herr T. Paul called, apologized, promised he would never treat her so crudely again. To reward him, when lunchtime rolled around, she put on the horrible black pumps — her dancing shoes — and queued her iPod to play the quirky waltz. She would conquer it, by God, and everyone would applaud at the reception, and it would all be good.

Closing her eyes, she imagined Paul in her arms, and her feet were less clumsy, her movements more fluid than when he whirled her around like a puppet.

When she opened her eyes, she found Herr T. standing in a dark corner, watching. He looked even younger, and when he saw that she had spotted him, he smiled faintly.

"I was just practicing," she said, blushing.

"No one should dance alone." Herr T. moved closer, holding his hand out to her. "If I may?"

Drea stepped into his arms.

"When you move, move from your heart. That is where the dance begins," he said. He hummed the notes of a different waltz, something very strange, and together they glided, and she was almost graceful. His hand was cold without warming from her touch as they spun about the room, their shadows following them across the floor.

Herr T. seemed even more youthful while they danced, tall and strong, actually, and painfully cold. She reached up to touch his face and he stopped humming, and the dance ended on his breath.

This is what I thought it would be like, she thought.

Her fingers laced through his hair, pulling his head down to hers until their lips met. The air in her lungs froze; she struggled for breath, desperate for oxygen but not wanting the moment to end, not ever. Even as she clung to him, Herr T. pushed her away with such force that she crashed into the wall.

"What am I doing?" Drea cried. But he remained silent, withdrawing into the shadows as if he'd disappeared into thin air.

Drea grabbed her things and ran.

▩ ▩ ▩

"I can't believe you lost a job that wasn't even paying you. How do you do that?" Paul said. He stomped through the crowd of people who marched along with the *Geisterzug*.

It was a spectacle. Dancers were dressed in black gowns and white face paint with hollowed out eyes. Others wore rags and glow-in-the dark makeup. Mixed in were people in gauze shrouds; others held sticks that dangled skeletons from gossamer thin string; and others who carried drums and struck the solemn beat of the death march.

A bone-white full moon shone above, casting light upon the dancing shadows. Drea looked around, half expecting Dead Michael Jackson to moonwalk out of the crowd.

"Are you listening?" Paul said. He grabbed her wrist and spun her around to face him. He was a handsome man, but a grim and ugly look distorted his face.

She didn't tell him that she hadn't lost the job. She hadn't even quit it. She had simply decided not to go back. No one from *Firme Köln* had called, not even Herr T. And why should he?

But she'd thought he might. She'd hoped he would.

"Paul, it was for the best," she said. "I promise I'll find a paying job."

Paul snorted. "For the best? How are you going to find a job that pays when you can't even keep one that doesn't?" He smirked. "You think you'll live for free after we get married, is that it?"

And suddenly she thought, *I won't live at all. I'll die if I marry you. I'll be buried alive.*

She stepped away from Paul, finding herself in the flow of the Ghost Parade, surrounded by tall bony figures in black that looked strangely familiar. They were graceful and silent — except for the sound of their beating drums and the clicking bones of the skeletons that dangled from their sticks.

Goosebumps prickled Drea's skin, and she moved her feet in an unthinking succession of steps as she danced through the *Geisterzug* in a perfect waltz. Figures capered after her for a few seconds, as if she were the leader of the parade; their silhouettes were thrown against brick, plaster, and steel, and she stopped inches away from Paul, who watched her in shock.

"Drea," he said touching her face. "You *can* dance as well as you fuck."

She knocked his hand away, and then turned, stalking off toward the streetcar.

◼ ◼ ◼

They glared at each other from either side of the aisle of the streetcar. The lights flickered as the streetcar snaked through the city, casting Paul in ghoulish light. He looked devilish.

"It just seems strange that you can dance all of a sudden," he said after a while. "*Denkst du, das ist lustig?* Are you having a joke at my expense?"

"No." Drea stood and walked toward the far end of the streetcar. Paul followed after her. She tripped, stumbling, barely grabbing onto one of the metal poles in time to break her fall.

"There's the Drea I know. Two left feet. No balance at all," he said, laughing. The lights flickered again casting the train in darkness. "Let's dance, baby."

He pulled her against him as the lights flickered back on, and they spun in a circle with Paul humming the weird little waltz. She couldn't do it. Wouldn't.

He looked at her bleary-eyed. "You don't want to dance? Maybe you want other things?"

He grabbed her ass and pressed against her. The lights flickered on, off, and as she stared past him, she saw a white face looking in at them through the window. Dead Michael Jackson's face! That was impossible!

At the same time, the streetcar lurched, throwing Drea and Paul to the floor. A whine shrieked high-pitched and wild, like the little girl who had nearly fallen off the curb. The terrible sound of metal scraping and crumpling pierced the night as the streetcar tilted to the left, sending passengers flying, tumbling into the aisle, onto each other. Sparks filled the darkness, creating grotesque orange shadows throughout the car as it buckled and rolled to a stop.

People all around Drea were crying and screaming, begging for help. Dazed, she lay on something soft, comfortable in spite of the pain that lanced her side.

The dim emergency lights flickered on, giving her just enough light to see that the car was on its side. Passengers were covered with blood, some sobbing and scrambling over other people, others lay very still.

Drea struggled to sit up and something — no, *someone* — beneath her groaned.

"Paul!" she cried, rolling off him.

His legs were bent, and half of a metal handrail pierced his abdomen, pinning him to the door. There was blood everywhere. She scooped up his neck, cradling it, forcing down sheer panic.

"I'll get help," she said.

"*Fräulein Armstrong*," said a voice, as a gentle — but cold — hand gripped her shoulder. Everything around them froze; all the screaming stilled.

It was Herr T. And his blond hair curled around a face that was vibrant and young.

Dead Michael Jackson stood slightly behind him and peered over his shoulder.

"Herr T! Are you hurt?" she asked.

"Only by your absence," he said, "but in a terrible coincidence, I can no longer stay away from you." He gazed at her, and despite her terror, she saw the longing there, the sadness. "I had an account to balance tonight," he said, nodding toward Paul, who stared up at him in horror.

Beside Herr T., Dead Michael Jackson held up the two euros she had put in his coffin that first morning. "To pay the ferryman."

"*Nein. Nein, bitte!*" Paul said, groaning. His head lolled. "Help me, Drea. Help!" He coughed; blood spurted from his lips over Drea's fingers as he struggled for breath.

Then, as the German teenager moonwalked *through* the frozen figures of the other passengers, Herr T's face vanished into the hooded cloak he now wore that hid his features in shadow. The cloak enveloped him, and in his hand he held a scythe. The skin on his hand melted, and skeletal fingers gripped the wood.

Drea couldn't speak. She told herself she was going into shock. She wasn't seeing the things that she was seeing.

"Just as you did not see what a lecherous bully your *fiancé* is," Herr T said. He swept a courtly bow. "I am *Tod*. Death to you. And it is very unfortunate that you have danced with me." He smiled sadly at her. "And that I, after all these millennia, have fallen in love with someone so … temporary."

She just kept staring, even as he knelt down next to her and Paul. He rested a finger on Paul's forehead. Her *fiancé* was suddenly cold to the touch, almost icy.

Herr T got to his feet. He held the scythe like a staff, looking down at the two of them like an executioner taking their measure.

"No," she pleaded. "Let us live."

"*Your* account is not being debited," he said. "You saw me check my ledger when you came into my office. That little girl was due to be hit by a Mercedes Benz, but you saved her. I thought to take you then, at the interview, to balance things out. But I found I could not." She sensed that in the darkness beneath the hood, his eyes gazed at her, and he held out his free hand, made of bone. "I was drawn to you even then."

And I to you, she thought, holding Paul's head as he panted and writhed.

Dead Michael Jackson crouched beside Paul, holding up the coins to show to Death, as if waiting to be given the word to perform his task.

"Don't hurt him," she begged Death. "Please."

"My job is not to inflict pain," he replied. "It is to kill." He wrapped both his hands around the scythe. Dead Michael Jackson leaned over Paul and pressed the coins onto his open eyes.

"*Tun Sie das nicht! Lieber Gott, bitte nicht!*" Paul cried, limply batting at the teenager. His hands went through the young man and he grabbed onto Drea. His face was pasty, and his lips were turning blue. "*Nehmen Sie sie, wenn Sie sie möchten.* All you need is *someone*, right?"

"*Take me?*" she said stunned, repeating Paul's words. Drea looked down at him, her face burning as if slapped. He didn't look at her, keeping his unblinking gaze squarely on Herr T.

"I need to balance my book, yes," Death said. "But I would never take you, Drea. I will set you free."

"Oh, God, no. She's got nothing to live for anyway," Paul babbled.

"You have everything to live for," Death said quietly to Drea. "Soon you will see that. And this soulless creature—" he gestured toward Paul, "—will be a footnote in your very long and happy life."

"What happened to the little girl?" she asked.

From beneath his hood the faint glimmer of teeth shown through as Death smiled at Dead Michael Jackson. "This one balanced the account. He died of a drug overdose shortly after he led me to you. And you see? He is fine."

"*Nein,*" Paul begged. "*Nein, bitte.*"

Letting go of Paul, she placed both her hands over Death's two bony hands on the scythe. Michael Jackson watched them, then looked back down at Paul.

"I danced with you," she whispered. "I danced *beautifully.*"

Death averted his head. "A breach of etiquette. A blunder." He sighed. "There is so much gray now. People on life support, demises avoided for decades." He turned back to her. "And there is you."

The hood bobbed as he lowered his head, almost as if she were the one with the scythe, and not he.

"If he is spared, he will have scars and will not dance again. He will not even be able to walk," he said.

"Oh, God," Paul whispered. "Drea, tell him not to do that."

"Life has its price, but it is not up to me," Herr T said to Drea. "It is up to you."

Though he had heckled and bullied her, Drea found herself pitying Paul. Maybe such a life would make him kinder.

"Yes, his afterlife will be better for it," Death concurred, as if he was reading her mind.

Drea put her hands on either side of the hood and drew it away. Herr T smiled at her, handsome and young. The icy feel of Death's skin warmed against hers.

"What you're saying is that you can take me instead," she said, searching his face. "Paul is right. As long as the books are balanced ... credit, debit."

He tried to look away, and she held his face between her palms. "You need me at the firm."

"I need you." His smile was tentative, then radiant.

"Then ... hire me."

"Very well," he said, throwing back his head and laughing, lifting her to her feet.

Grinning, Dead Michael Jackson put his euros in his pocket and stood.

"What about me?" Paul shouted.

Together, Death and Drea walked off the streetcar, leaving the sounds of breaking glass behind them as rescue crews invaded the twisted cars. Through the falling snow, the *Geisterzug* appeared, everyone dancing, swaying in a mummers' ballet.

A single scream echoed through the night. For a moment she thought the sound resembled the ringing echo of her name. Then Herr T took Drea in his arms, both of them smiling as they waltzed into the shadows of *Köln Karneval*.

❖ ❖ ❖

Nancy Holder is a New York Times best-selling and multiple Bram Stoker Award-winning author, and a short story, essay, and comic book writer She is the author of the Wicked, Crusade, and Wolf Springs Chronicles series. *Vanquished*, in the Crusade series, is out now; *Hot Blooded*, the second book in the Wolf Springs Chronicles, will be out soon. She has written a lot of tie-in material for "universes" such as *Buffy the Vampire Slayer*, *Smallville*, and many others, and recently won her fifth Bram Stoker Award for the young adult horror, *The Screaming Season*. She lives in San Diego.

❖ ❖ ❖

Erin Underwood is a writer, columnist, and blogger. She has a degree in creative writing and literature from the Harvard University Extension School and an MFA in Creative Writing from the University of Southern Maine's Stonecoast MFA program. For her, the seed from which "Totentanz" grew was rooted in the question: How would Death adjust to modern times? What would that mean for him, for us? Erin lives in Marblehead, Massachusetts with her husband.

~OUT OF THE SUN~
By Gabriel Boutros

Two riders were approaching.

They came from the east, out of the desert. The rising sun had begun to creep over the horizon and it cast their shadows far ahead of them like tentacles. Even at such a distance and with the sun at their backs, the miners realized who these riders were, and each man felt a chill pierce his soul.

For the taller of the two riders was certainly Death sitting arrogantly astride his black charger. Beside him, riding jauntily on a pony so small it could have been a donkey, and with his dangling feet almost dragging in the sand, was the Joker.

They always rode together, Death and the Joker. The former rarely spoke, performing his tasks with a grim professionalism that many might have mistaken for indifference if it weren't for what was at stake. As for the latter, he was in many ways the crueler of the pair. His greatest joy was to tease and mock the people they sought out, giving them false hope that their time had not yet come.

The miners were seven, surely a lucky number they had told themselves the previous night when they gathered around the campfire, some of them still bandaging their injuries. They had hoped to delay the arrival of these travelers, if not postpone it indefinitely, but neither their medicine nor their superstitions were strong enough. Every man gulped down his own fears and looked surreptitiously at his comrades so that none could accuse him of casting an evil eye.

Each man hoped that it was not his time, that the danger might yet pass. Each quietly prayed that another might be taken instead. There was always someone else who deserved it more, maybe for cheating at cards or for not attending mass when the priests passed through the camp. None would ever admit to wishing ill on a fellow miner, although at a time like this such wishes lay in all seven hearts.

The eldest among the miners coughed, covering his mouth, and then coughed again. He spat out a thick black stream of phlegm, his weakened body trembling. He looked around him and saw the others turn their eyes away, some of them ashamedly, for a hint of hopefulness had come to their faces. He straightened his back and walked wordlessly to his tent. He closed the flap behind him to hide the fear he felt because he was old and had breathed the poisoned air of the mines longer than anyone else. Yet hadn't he moved quickly when the alarm had sounded? He felt that his bravery should count for something, but doubted that his opinion in such matters held much weight.

Behind his back a few of the others nodded meaningfully, the old man's ill health a portent that they might not be the ones taken after-all. One man sat down and began to stir the fire in preparation for his breakfast, suddenly remembering how hungry he was. Those who watched him took confidence from his actions, the fate of the eldest seemingly settled in their minds.

The youngest among the miners, however, turned to look at the tent into which the old man had disappeared. He still felt fear for himself, but the possibility of losing the old man filled him with sadness. He said nothing to the others, though, the throbbing pain in his head making it difficult for him to speak or to move.

The riders were almost at the camp now, and the wind that had blown heavily during the night suddenly died down. The birds that lived in this arid land, and who loved to flit about and sing in the cool of each dawn, were nowhere to be seen or heard. The clop-clop sound of the horses' hooves drowned out the buzzing of the cicadas, and it was many days before their song was heard again.

Despite their brief moment of confidence, none of the miners would turn to look at the new arrivals. The one who had stirred the fire fiddled with a frying pan for a bit, but couldn't make up his mind whether to break any eggs into it or to put it back down.

One miner stood up, deciding to take off his hat in greeting, but try as he might he could not raise his eyes above the leather-booted feet that rested in stirrups on each side of the black horse. He looked at his compatriots for encouragement but found none, each man busying himself, adjusting a bloody bandage or examining some stone or other on the ground that he had never noticed before. Finally the miner put his worn hat back on his head and slid down into a cross-legged position, deciding that greetings were probably not appropriate at this time.

It was then that the Joker, who had been eyeing the miners with a mischievous grin, jumped down from the back of his pony. The animal was so short that the Joker was the same height standing as he was when sitting upon it. Perhaps it was this realization that struck him as ridiculous, for he let out a piercing peal of laughter which froze the six men in their places. A sad and hopeless moan soon followed from inside the old man's tent, clearly audible to everyone's ears, although none of the other miners reacted to it.

Instead, their eyes turned for the first time to the Joker, and he stared back at them with an exaggeratedly stunned expression. From where each man stood they could see that the Joker was of average height, except to those for whom he seemed quite tall, or others who found him short. His hat, the pointy kind which may have been flopping down over one or both ears, or standing straight up depending on one's point of view, was all yellow, and all red, and all blue, and a mix of all the colors they could think of. His expression was like that of a naughty child, or a demented madman, or maybe even a playful clown, taking into account each man's state of mind.

After a moment the Joker put a finger to his painted lips, and with his other hand pulled out of a deep pocket what looked like a shiny marble, although it may have been a spinning top or even a piece of broken glass. He held this hand up for a moment and gently bounced the object in his palm, drawing the curiosity of the miners. He stepped lightly forward, his shoes hardly disturbing the sand around him, and brought his hand closer so that each man could see what he balanced there.

When all the men had looked upon it for several seconds, and it had brought the smiles of happy memories to each one's face, the Joker stepped toward the tent into which the old man had retreated. Another soft moan was heard coming from the tent, for the old man must have seen the Joker approaching, or maybe he had simply felt the air inside the tent grow cold.

The Joker turned back at this sound and looked to the dark figure with whom he had ridden in. None of the six miners dared to follow his gaze. Each preferred looking at the many-colored face that smiled before them. The men instinctively felt that this was a friendly visage, one they didn't mind seeing this early morning. They were happy to ignore the fact that the Joker was travelling companion to a much more lethal being. That harsh truth was something they would whisper about later, over cold beers from the village canteen to which they would certainly be treated after the recent events.

The Joker moved then with no warning, swiftly disappearing into the old man's tent and taking his shiny bauble with him, to the chagrin of the miners who had so enjoyed looking at it. Seconds later another moan issued from the tent, but it was cut off by the Joker's high-pitched laugh. This time the laugh went on much longer than the Joker's earlier shriek. It rose and descended in waves, and in its brief lulls the miners could hear the Joker take a deep breath before letting loose again.

After a minute or two of this it occurred to the man who still held the frying pan that for the Joker to laugh this loud and this long the situation must truly be humorous. And so this man began to giggle softly, earning a look of rebuke from one of his colleagues, and then to giggle even louder. Then the man who had thought to greet the riders also began to snicker, and in a moment both men were laughing heartily.

As their laughter rose louder, so did the Joker's, challenging them to keep up and inviting the others to join in. Soon all six miners were roaring with laughter. They laughed where they stood; they laughed where they sat. One laughed so hard he rolled in the dirt, slamming his fists into the ground, forgetting about any injuries he may have suffered the night before, such was his mirth. Tears poured from the eyes of all the men at the unexpected humor of the occasion, leaving wet trails in their dirt-caked cheeks.

The one who rolled on the ground came close to the black horse upon which the grim figure of Death sat. The horse was well trained and although it stamped its hooves in warning, it did not step on the man. This did not cause him to interrupt his laughter. He merely rolled in a different direction, making sure that he never looked up at the face of the horse's master.

And so the six miners laughed, feeling good to be still alive and to be allowed, even encouraged, to enjoy themselves like this. They did not notice that the sound of laughter from inside the tent eventually subsided. They did not see the Joker step out through the flap, with the old man at his side, looking forlorn. None noticed the Joker lean over and whisper in the old man's ear, nor the old man responding with a sigh of such despondence that it would have brought more sensitive men to tears.

And none of the six miners saw the old man point timidly at the man who'd long since dropped his frying pan, but who now stood laughing as he leaned against the outhouse wall. The old man quickly lowered his damning finger as if ashamed of his action, but the gesture was not to be undone. The Joker stepped nimbly over the miner who was lying face down in the dirt, gasping for breath while still laughing uncontrollably. He approached the man leaning against the outhouse and tapped him lightly on the shoulder, bringing the man's laughter to an instant halt.

This man tried to smile, then tried to laugh again, but the effort was obviously painful. The happy expression in his eyes was replaced by one of confusion. Was their enjoyment to end so soon? He saw that the other men were still laughing, and that none were looking in his direction except for the old man who could only shrug guiltily when their eyes met.

The Joker, wearing a smile of unnatural glee, took the man by the shoulder and turned him to face the rider on the black horse. At once the man's throat constricted as he found himself looking into the blood-red eyes of Death. Death's face showed neither joy nor anger at the man's appearance before him. The miner fell, grabbing at his shirt collar, but loosening it would not allow him to breathe more easily.

The Joker quickly returned to the old man and whispered into his ear again. The old man shook his head, but this merely caused the Joker to whisper more urgently. The old man shrugged once more, powerless in the face of Death as all men are, and pointed this time at a fat miner who was sitting laughing by himself. This drew a loud guffaw from the Joker, who slapped his hands together merrily, inciting the remaining miners to even greater gales of laughter.

But before moving away from the old man the Joker looked back at him expectantly, his eyes twinkling in a way which made the old man think of far-away stars and circuses and insanity as he lifted his finger again, a tremor running through his arm. He hesitated at the youngest of the crew, a lad of fifteen who'd come to work there after his father had died in an earlier accident at the mine. The boy was laughing with all his heart, his happiness making him forget the gravity of his wounds. The old man jerked his finger away, his expression clouded by fear and uncertainty, and quickly pointed down at the man who was rolling on the ground.

The Joker's smile disappeared for a moment, and he hesitated, displaying a rare ambivalence. Finally he shrugged just like the old man had done before and moved to the fat miner, lifting him up by his collar as if the man were nothing but a doll. The Joker dragged the fat miner to where the third man lay on the ground, laughing so hard it was a wonder he could breathe at all. Looking back at the old man with a leer that may have been mischievous, or maybe wasn't there at all, the Joker let his hand hover over the man on the ground. The old man took a moment to think, then nodded and shrugged once more, sending the Joker into paroxysms of delight, jumping and slapping his thigh as he laughed.

Finally the Joker grasped these two men and turned them to face Death, who sat unmoved on his horse. Both men fell in front of him, gasping for breath through clenched windpipes. The Joker stood briefly at attention before Death, his sarcastic expression mocking the seriousness of their work. He then removed his hat and bowed so low to the ground that his yellow forelock touched the dirt. He straightened wearing his widest smile. He kicked lightly at the man who'd been unexpectedly chosen then looked questioningly up at Death. Death's lips twitched slightly as if he wanted to smile, and the Joker leaped with delight, landing nimbly upon his patient pony.

The two riders recommenced their journey, heading west with neither a word nor a backward glance at those they were leaving behind. Their newly-minted travelling companions, those three unfortunate miners, rose and shuffled after the two horsemen. Their eyes were clouded and their faces purple from their inability to breathe, all three faces expressing surprise and disappointment at their fate.

As the travelers rode off with the three following, the remaining miners slowly stopped laughing. They looked toward the old man but said nothing, because what had happened was obvious to all. The boy of fifteen shivered as if an icy hand had run down his spine, but he smiled at the old man who shrugged modestly in return.

All four men stood and watched the departing group until it began growing small and blurry in the distance. For a brief moment the three men on foot became indistinct, as if surrounded by the shadows of many others, then all the travelers disappeared. The surviving miners blinked and rubbed their eyes, their thoughts turning now to their cuts and bruises, and their good fortune.

The old man thought that maybe he'd go to mass the next time the priest came out this way. He crossed himself, feeling a sudden need for confession.

As for the fifteen year old, he went to his sleeping bag and pulled out a small pencil and a piece of paper. He would finally write to his mother as she'd begged him to do. He would tell her of the tragic accident that had occurred, and of the brave old man who'd saved his life at great personal risk, when the boy had feared he'd never see sunlight again.

The wind began to howl, blowing sand into his eyes and carrying a high-pitched screech that sounded like the Joker's distant laughter. The boy paused before beginning his letter, shivering, wondering how long it would be before the riders returned to the camp.

■ ■ ■

Gabriel Boutros is a defence attorney in Montreal, where he lives with his wife and two sons, and occasionally dabbles in creative writing. His one previously-published story, "I Drive", appeared in *Carte Blanche*, an on-line literary review. He is a lifelong fan of Jimi Hendrix and has listened to *All Along the Watchtower* hundreds of times. Once, on a long night-time drive, he listened to the song's closing words and decided that somehow he had to incorporate this foreboding image into a story. "Two riders were approaching, and the wind begins to howl…"

—PRESSED BUTTERFLIES—

By Lorne Dixon

Surrounded by her three weeping Aunts, Chelsea Braybrooke waited in the darkened parlor for Dr. Wainsworth's nurse to summon her to her Momma's beside. When the nurse came, Chelsea took her hand, aware that the steel-tipped riding boots she wore tapped against the hardwood floor as her aunts burst into a fresh chorus of hysterical sobs.

The hallway was a dark tunnel leading to a fiercely bright rectangle at the end. Her mother's bedroom seemed unnaturally bright, too intense, as penetrating to a sustained stare as the rays of the sun. Her eyes dropped to the floor.

Entering, Chelsea's vision warmed to the light; dozens of lit candles cast out all shadows. She'd never seen this room so glowing, even in the day. She walked past the house staff, all dressed in garments as dark as their skin, past Reverend Prescott and a wary-faced seminary protégé standing beside a nurse with heavy eyes. All turned their heads away from her. In the center of the chamber, her father sat in a sturdy wooden high-backed chair, his eyes swollen into withered pink slits. Behind a wheat-hued lace curtain, Momma lay on her side at the edge of the master bed, unmoving, both arms cradled against the breast of her nightgown, as rigid as the talons of a dead crow. Her face, always radiant and beautiful, was now blank and expressionless, anonymous and unremarkable, the face of any of the Scourge's thousand victims.

Sidling up to her mother, she pulled back the lace, and wound it around the canopy post. Unobstructed, her mother's face was worse than from a distance: yellowed and weathered, she looked older by far than anyone else in Old Saybrook, even the black-smith's uncle, who was rumored on the schoolyard to be one hundred years old. She wasn't quite gone, although it would have been easy to mistake her for having passed; a dim vitality still danced in her eyes, fading but resistant. She cracked open her mouth to speak but at first only sour breath escaped. Then, a second attempt, only marginally more successful, but imbued with a whisper, too quiet for any but Chelsea to hear.

"...my angel..."

Mother didn't die then. No, that came later, during the blackest hour of morning, before sunlight but after the stars faded from the night sky. Chelsea knew it happened when one of the nurses slid a leather-bound Bible under her bedroom door. Between chapters, the holy book contained her mother's collection of pressed butterflies, painted by hand to resemble angels in flowing robes. All, that is, except for the enormous black moth pressed between the final page and the back cover. He was untouched. Over his dried, spread corpse her mother had written HE WHO FELL in her daintiest handwriting.

That was how Chelsea inherited a book full of dead angels.

* * *

Chelsea found a holocaust in her stepmother's garden, mouths open in eternal gasps, wings curled and edged in black, killed by the tobacco spray that kept the roses red and tulips yellow. She plucked them carefully out of their flower petal deathbeds, wrapped them in scented tissue paper, and gently carried them to her room in tiny jewelry box caskets. She would leave them to repose on the windowsill, to lie in state and wait for invisible mourners to visit at midnight. Then, the next morning, she would open the leather bound Bible and place each fragile body between the last page of one gospel and the first of the next, and then press the covers closed with a firm hand.

By late October, she only had collected half the angels she needed to fill her mother's Bible. Winter crept closer. She knew that a coming morning would bring frost and then the angels would disappear until winter ended. It would take too long for the butterflies to return in Spring, just too long for a frail, sickly girl. As she carefully slipped the latest orange and yellow body between *Ecclesiastes* and The *Song Of Solomon*, Chelsea made up her mind that she could not wait for the seasons to turn to finish her collection. She would need to find the nests where the angels slept and collect the rest all at once. She would harvest them from their beds.

To do this, she needed a perfect disguise. Too many times before she had been forced to dress, eat breakfast, and sulk away to the schoolhouse. The disguise would have to be better than any she had built before. Chelsea stared into her oval mirror and practiced. She curled her bottom lip just a little and squinted slightly. Then she coughed and sneezed. The cough was good, candid and raw, almost like a small dog's bark. The sneeze was not as convincing. She spent most of the night working on it as she lay in bed, listening with an orchestra conductor's keen ear to her nose's inhalations, quivers, and sudden releases. She did not sleep until she felt confident that the sneeze could compete with the symptom of any genuine illness.

◼ ◼ ◼

Morning came and the argument followed. They were in the hallway, just outside her bedroom doorway, her father's stern, concerned voice and her stepmother's annoyed chatter. She sputtered as she spoke, her words punctuated with vicious little pauses and deep breaths. They were discussing Chelsea's health, just as they had since Dr. Wainsworth had revealed his diagnosis.

Her father came in, kissed her forehead, told her to feel better and that he loved her, and left. Her stepmother stood in the doorway and barely let him pass. She stared at Chelsea on her bed for a moment, then blinked hard and shook her head.

Chelsea waited in bed, eyes shut to simulate sleep whenever her stepmother looked in on her, anxious to get her day started. Just before noon she heard feet descend the staircase and the front door open. She ran to the window and watched her stepmother rush into an unfamiliar coach and drive down the banyan-lined drive to the front gates.

She was free! She fished the previous day's clothes out of the corner laundry hamper and wiggled into them. Thrusting her mother's Bible under one arm, she sprinted out of her room, through the hallway, down the stairs, and out through the rear patio. Her butterfly net and an empty killing jar waited on the verandah's black cobblestone floor. She collected them up and dashed across the yard, sidestepping the stone bird table, the hummingbird feeders, and the frog pond.

At the edge of the yard she swung open the wrought iron gate that blocked the path to her stepmother's garden. She could not run anymore; she had been in trouble enough times to know that her heavy shoes would tear up the moss beds. She would walk carefully, stepping only on dry soil and not the patches of green, or when there was no other path, lightly on the frilly liverwort leaves.

The path ended at two large wintersweet shrubs that book-ended the garden's entrance. Stepping across the threshold, Chelsea was greeted by the purr of bumblebees busy with their endless gardening. She could already see a pair of angels flying above a line of vibrant Eastern Coneflowers. They were orange and yellow and brown, the same as the flowers, but marked with dots of black on the center of their wings. Chelsea wondered if this was how Cain had been marked by God for slaying his brother. Those brothers had been working in a garden, too, when that first murder had sprung into Cain's mind.

She set down the Bible and the jar near a cluster of tall ferns and the fiddleheads growing in their shadows. She tiptoed, head low, up to Cain and Abel with the net hidden behind her back. They didn't seem to notice her approach, their attention locked on the flowers beneath them as they flitted overhead in strange circles.

Chelsea paused for just a moment and watched the holy messengers play. She felt a passing tinge of guilt and worry, unsure whether she had the right to capture Cain and Abel and add them to the book. But then she remembered her mother curled up on her bed, eyes moist and red, pleading for the angels to come and save her. They never came with a goblet of sacerdotal elixir to heal her failing body. They let her die, choosing instead to play in the gardens.

She sprang — quick and precise — and caught both angels in one deft swoop, then twisted the handle so their narrow black legs would tangle in the netting. She brought them over to the jar and unscrewed the lid. Reaching inside the net, she took Abel by one wing and moved him to the jar. He flapped and writhed but the fight was futile. Then she repeated the process with Cain. Inside the closed jar, they both settled at the bottom and waited for asphyxia.

Chelsea wondered why Abel had been marked too.

As she set the jar down, she heard a crackling voice drift over to her from beyond the line of sunflowers at the edge of the garden. "Now, what's with all this rustling about over there?"

The voice reminded her of her grandfather, ancient and soothing. Chelsea slowly moved towards it, through a maze of budding Cherokee rose bushes and planter-bushels of bitterroot. She parted two thick sunflower stalks like a curtain and stepped beyond. An old man sat on an overturned watering bucket. The suit he wore matched his faded and wrinkled face but his blue eyes were bright and clear.

"I don't think you're supposed to be here," she said with a skeptical little swagger in her words. She put her free hand on her hip. "Who are you?"

He chuckled and ran a calloused hand over his unshaven cheek. "Y'know, I have a lot of acquaintances all over these lands and they all call me different names."

"Play names?" She asked.

"I suppose y'could say." He tilted his head playfully and pointed at her with his small finger. "I guess it's really up to you. Under what name would you like to know me?"

Chelsea shook her head. "I don't know you. How would I know what to call you?"

"Fair enough." She watched his forearms flex as he leaned forward, elbows on knees, and rested his chin on his knuckles. Though aged, his body was still muscular. "Why don't you just call me Pops?"

Pops extended a hand. Rather than shake it, Chelsea stepped back and crossed her legs. "What are you doing in our garden?"

"Just passing through." He dropped his hand and straightened out his cocked head. "Your next question, I guess, is where am I heading? It seems like I used to have some kind of plan, some kind of destination. But that was a long time ago. Things change, you know?"

She nodded vigorously. "Things *do* change. This is my stepmother's flower garden now but there used to be apple trees here. This was my mother's orchard."

His eyes squinted. "And which do you like better, all these pretty flowers or your Momma's apple trees?"

"The apple trees," she answered immediately.

"I would imagine so." Pops grinned. Then the jar in Chelsea's hand caught his attention. "And what are you doing out here today?"

Chelsea glanced down at the jar and her two prisoners. She blushed. "I guess I pretended to be sick today so I wouldn't have to go to school. It's easy, you know, 'cause I'm *always* sick. Got what my Mom had. But I had to come out here today and catch the rest of the angels."

"The angels, huh?" He pointed to the jar. "Can't barely see them so far off. Any chance you can bring them closer so I can see?"

She handed him the jar but did not step forward.

Pops studied them for a long moment before exhaling with a practiced whistle. "Just wanted to make sure they weren't anyone I know. This one guy here, he kind of reminds me of a fellow I knew a lifetime ago."

He handed back the jar and stared at her for a moment. Then he sucked his lips into his mouth and released them with a smacking sound. "There's a little stone house at the back of the garden."

Chelsea's eyes dropped to the ground. "I know."

"What is that little house?" he asked.

She took a moment to respond. "It's where Momma's buried."

"I knew that." He pushed off the bucket and stood up. His knees cracked as he stretched out. "Just wanted to see if you'd tell me. You go visit her much?"

She shook her head. "I don't like to look at it."

"I think you should come and see." He motioned to her as he began to walk towards the southern edge of the garden.

She reluctantly followed. As much as she hated her mother's grave site and the memories it would unleash, there was something obscene about a stranger trespassing there alone. They passed a row of hollyhock stalks, their proud pink flowers so reminiscent of trumpets, watching over a few shaggy Pepperidge bushes. Half buried in a shelf of Ivy Leaf Toadflax, her mother's tomb jutted out of the earth at an awkward angle, the sharp peak of its roof pointing towards the tree line.

"Look here." He pulled aside a patch of tall reeds beyond the garden's edge and moved aside. She cautiously peered inside. A frail sapling grew out of the rich brown soil.

"I think," he said from behind her, "that there will be apple trees here again. Soon."

They spent the rest of the afternoon hunting angels, Pops pointing them out and Chelsea catching them in her net. With the jar filled, she counted nineteen captives, enough to bookmark *Song of Solomon* through *The Gospel According To St. Matthew*, the first book of the New Testament.

As the sun began to sink under the tree line, Chelsea guessed that her stepmother would return home soon. She thanked Pops for his help and ran back to the house, proud of her bountiful harvest.

◙ ◙ ◙

The next morning Chelsea didn't have to fake coughing fits, they came naturally, some powerful enough to send bouts of dizziness through her head, some speckling her saliva with blood. She felt light-headed and a bitter taste lingered in her mouth. Removing a thermometer from under her tongue, her father tried to hide his worry behind a queasy smile and kissed her forehead. Then he wandered into the hall and started to argue with her stepmother.

"But what if this time is *the* time?"

"I promise to send for Dr. Wainsworth if anything—"

"—I could never forgive myself if I wasn't—"

In the end, her father relented and left for work. Chelsea pretended to sleep and listened to her stepmother move around downstairs. She heard her prepare a cup of tea, give orders to the house staff, and then answer the door at noon. Chelsea tumbled out of bed and rushed to the window. She watched her stepmother and a tall, handsome man step into the same coach as the day before. As the door closed, they embraced. The horses began to trot.

Chelsea dressed, fetched her net and a fresh jar, and headed out to the garden. She stopped at the gate to catch her breath. Normally the run from the house would have been easy but today her lungs felt heavy and it was difficult to breathe. She bent over, put her hands on her knees, and let out a string of crackling coughs. Wiping her nose, she called out, "Pops? You here, Pops?"

The garden seemed empty. There were no buzzing bees circling the tulips or birds chirping from the low limbs of the Ashe juniper trees. The ground was dry, but the garden looked as if it had been battered by a ferocious downpour. The flower heads were bowed. The bushes had shucked off much of their foliage.

Chelsea wandered to the back but found her stepmother's watering bucket empty. Disappointed, she scanned the garden for angels but didn't spot any. Perhaps they saw the garden dying and fled, just as they had avoided her mother in her final hours. Or maybe they had even caused the flowers to wither. She dropped the jar and net and plopped down on the bucket.

"You look like a overripe plum three days into a drought."

She twisted and watched Pops push through the crisp bur-reeds that stood guard on the perimeter of her mother's tomb. She felt a smile tickle its way onto her face. "Were you hiding back there?"

"No." Pops steered himself over the marshy ground with a knotty wooden stick. His face looked older than it had yesterday, more weathered and tired, like the garden. "I'm never very far away. I don't ever hide, though some people pretend they don't see me coming."

"Well, *I* was *looking* for you!" Chelsea said.

His lips curled back as he smiled, opening a window where she could see two rows of flat, rotten teeth. "And now that you've found me, am I what you expected?"

Chelsea looked away. "I don't see any angels."

He nodded. "You've got to call them is all."

"How do you call an angel?" She stood up slowly. She eyed him suspiciously again, like when they first met. Her mother had tried to call the angels, had desperately pleaded for them, but they never came.

Pops extended two fingers on both of his hands and stretched them high into the air, forming the outline of a wide cone around his head. Then he clapped them together quickly. Chelsea watched in amazement as a large yellow angel fluttered out of hiding inside a tent of drooping eucalyptus leaves. It glided over to Pops and landed on the tip of his crossed fingers.

She giggled.

Pop's hand quickly darted out and seized the angel. It struggled between his fingers as he brought it over to Chelsea. She opened the jar. He dropped it inside. "How many more do you need?"

She frowned. "Twenty-six."

"Then you had better get started." He grinned, the corners of his mouth stretched wider, waves of bulging wrinkles filling his cheeks. He motioned for her to follow his lead.

She raised both arms over her head as he had, but then sneezed violently and wobbled in place. Putting a hand to her nose, she dragged a red splotch across her face. She lowered her arms and began to cry. The she felt his hands snake around her wrists from behind and pull them over her head. Tears streaked through the blood on her face. She extended her fingers and clapped them together in time with her sobs.

Dozens of angels burst out of the dark brown hollows and shadowy nooks of the garden and danced in the air. They were black and white, red and blue, amber and gray. Her tears stopped as she watched them with hypnotized eyes. She released a gentle, uncontrolled giggle. He released her hands. She clapped faster and louder. More angels burst out from beneath drooping leaves and tangles of briar weed. The air was alive with beating wings.

Pops laughed and the deep, rolling sound turned her giggles into rollicking laughter of her own. He knelt down beside her and ran a hand through her hair. "I think you might need more jars."

■ ■ ■

The next day morning Chelsea was unable to get out of bed. A fever burned inside her. When she tried to pull herself upright, dizziness forced her back down. Pain shot through her with every coughing fit and each sneeze caused her to clench her fists in agony.

Her father stayed with her all day, hovering over her bed and bringing her cool washcloths and tall glasses of cucumber-and-lemon water. Dr. Wainsworth visited but spoke very little. She overheard him apologize to her father for not being able to do enough. "Make her comfortable."

Father started crying before the front door closed and didn't stop until he finally retired to his own bed. It was a long day full of rumblings in her head, hot flashes, fitful coughs, and the horrible warmth of her fever.

That night she strained to hear the hushed voices that crept down the hall from the master bedroom.

"—heard him, nothing that we can do—"

"—but a hospital, maybe, could—"

"—think she'd be more comfortable in a hospital bed?"

She reached across her bed and dragged the Bible off her dresser. She and Pops had caught twenty-five angels the day before. Only one empty space remained, between *The General Epistle Of Jude* and *The Revelation Of St. John The Divine*. They would have to catch one more after the fever passed.

She pulled the Bible to her chest and curled around it. She closed her eyes and hoped she would fall asleep quickly. Her head didn't hurt when she slept.

■ ■ ■

The tiniest sound woke her, just a slight fluttering of wings hovering overhead. Her eyes adjusted slowly. When the haze cleared, she saw a black-winged angel dancing just above her head. She reached up for it but it flew higher. She watched it circle just out of her reach.

Chelsea sat up and reached out but again it evaded her hands. *This one is much cleverer than the others*, she thought, and that thought made her realize that her head was clear. The fever had passed. She ran a hand over her forehead, expecting it to be covered in sweat like all of the times before, but her skin was dry.

"You won't catch this one so easy."

She turned and saw Pops standing in the doorway. If he had looked older on the second day of their hunt, he now looked positively ancient. He pointed to the angel with his walking stick.

"What are you doing in my house?" she asked him.

He waved away the question. "What are you still doing here in bed, lazybones? We have an angel to catch tonight, don't we?"

"Maybe," she pouted, "we should wait 'til morning."

Pops shook his head. "The first frost will be on the ground tomorrow morning. There won't be any more days to play sick and chase angels. It has to be tonight."

"But—"

Pops stepped away from the doorway and disappeared into the shadows of the hallway. "Don't worry, you won't be out long."

The angel flew to the door and hovered there. Chelsea rolled out of bed. It kept just out of her reach, leading her into the hallway. She glanced over at her clothes hamper, but when the angel started down the hall she abandoned the idea of getting dressed and followed it instead. She couldn't see where Pops had gone.

She tiptoed down the stairs, careful to avoid the ones that creaked. She was surprised to see a candle burning in the kitchen as she reached the first floor landing. Peeking inside, she saw her father sitting at the table, hands covering his face, and her stepmother standing over him, long fingered hands kneading his shoulders. He shrugged her off and dropped one hand to the tabletop and Chelsea got a clear view of his red face. Her father was sobbing.

"Quickly now," Pops called from the open back door.

Chelsea stepped into the kitchen. She wanted to console her father, to tell him that whatever was wrong would be right soon enough, to tell him all the things he told her each time she was sick or lonely or upset.

But then she saw her stepmother's face, as cold as steel in January and beaming impatience. That look froze Chelsea mid-step. She backed up and headed for the rear door instead.

The cold night air blew against her cheeks and whispered nonsense into her ears. She followed the angel to the garden but found her feet paralyzed by what she saw. The flowers were all dead, stems and vines lining the soil like ten thousand dead snakes. In their place a half dozen fully-grown apple trees stood, fruit dangling from their branches. Pops stood under the closest, reached up, and plucked an apple. "It could only be one or the other, an orchard or a garden. Do you understand?"

She nodded.

He polished the apple with a scrap of cloth and offered it to Chelsea. She took it, inspected its bright red skin for a moment, and then took a bite. It was sweet and ripe and reminded her of her mother's late June apple pies. "This is a strange night."

"They always are." Pops pointed with his walking stick. The black angel was dancing, happily inspecting the apples, making its way to the southern edge of the orchid. Chelsea followed it until she saw where it was heading and then she slowed to a stop and dropped the fruit.

Her mother's tomb door was open and the angel flew inside. Standing only feet from the doorway, Chelsea felt a gust of cold wind burrow into her pores and chill the muscles and bones beneath. She stared past the marble door into the dark and felt her mother's death again, felt the hollow dread build in her gut, felt horrible numbness shiver down her body. She began to tremble.

Pop's hands dropped down onto her shoulders and gripped her tightly. Her head rolled back and she saw his face beaming down at her, now not much more than a pickled and dried death mask, ashen skin pulled tight to a grinning skull. She screamed and he roared in laughter, laughter made up of a billion whispered unanswered prayers melded together and blended with the death cries of entire generations.

He pushed her forward, up three marble steps, and into the tomb's doorway. She reached out with both hands to resist being pushed inside, but the marble was as slick as glass and her hands slid away. Pops gave her a final shove and she tumbled inside to the floor alongside her mother's concrete-encased casket. She pulled herself up, her mind and mouth screaming, and scrambled to her feet.

Pops began to close the heavy marble door. She rushed forward, but the floor was slippery and she fell. With his free hand Pops tossed her Bible into the tomb. It landed at her fingertips. As the door closed, the dim light vanished, but before it did, Chelsea saw that words were etched into the walls. She read only a single line before the darkness became absolute.

I am Alpha and Omega, the first and the last—

She knew those words; words ascribed to the Lord and recorded by John the Divine in his Book Of Revelation. She was surrounded by the final book of the Bible. Crying the last of her tears, she prayed for the angels to save her, to release her from her mother's tomb and the words on the walls.

A grinding sound filled her ears and musty, unearthed air teased her nose. The walls were closing in on both sides of her. As they pressed in, she heard her mother's whisper once again, "...my angel..."

She raised both trembling arms over her head and clapped.

But the only angels that heard were the dead butterflies pressed in a book at her feet.

■ ■ ■

Lorne Dixon lives and writes off an exit of I-78 in residential New Jersey. He grew up on a diet of yellow-spined paperbacks, black-and-white monster movies, and the thunder lizard backbeat of rock-n-roll. His novels include *Eternal Unrest, The Lifeless*, and *Snarl*. His short fiction has appeared in four volumes of Cutting Block Press' *Horror Library* series, *Darkness on the Edge* (PS Press), *Metahumans Vs. the Undead* (Coscom), as well as many other anthologies and magazines. He says that "Pressed Butterlies" is intended as a meditation on the positive and negative magnetism of death, both in practical terms and conceptually, during childhood.

—MATRYOSHKA—
By Sabrina Furminger

There was no cloth for the coarse wooden table. Bronislava balanced the cup and saucer in her hands and stared down at the bare tabletop as if seeing it for the first time. She didn't own a tablecloth, and she hadn't thought to procure one for the occasion. A tablecloth was a luxury few in the village could afford — and an obscene frivolity when there was little food to place upon it.

For a moment, Bronislava's cheeks flushed hot as fire. *The table is too rough for this china.* She spotted a few drops of dried blood from the last time Dmitri had arrived home drunk and bleeding from his knuckles. The blood had soaked into the grooves of the tabletop and no amount of scrubbing would remove the stain. She sighed and surveyed her dwelling: the dirt floor; the coal stove; the tarpaper walls; the flimsy door; the single window through which streamed the cold afternoon sun; the table and two chairs; the cradle. Here her eyes lingered. *I must set a good table for Matryoshka.* She mustered her courage for the hundredth time that day and resumed her task with steely determination.

This was the first time Bronislava had handled the precious cups and saucers since Mama had died. The china was white and brittle and paper thin, like human bone that had been worn away by the ages. *Delicate like Mama.* Even now, as Bronislava prepared to place the first cup and saucer on the table, she could hear her mother's voice speaking to her out of the past, explaining once again how the two cups and two saucers had been given to her grandfather by a travelling Chinaman who'd hawked strange ointments and gunpowder in village squares. "Your Didi drank vodka from these cups every day until he died," her mother would say breathlessly as she'd inspect the china for cracks and chips. "They hold his soul." The memory brought a sneer to Bronislava's lips. *Such drivel. Mama was spineless and sentimental.* She shivered and the cup and saucer shook in suddenly unsteady hands. *No, no. I am stronger than Mama ever was.*

Within a few minutes, the second cup and saucer had been placed at the seat beside the head of the table, and Bronislava stepped back to admire her handiwork. The cups and saucers from faraway lands seemed out of place in a peasant's hovel — especially conspicuous on Bronislava's blood-stained tabletop. *Will this offering be enough to sway Matryoshka?* Outside, a group of children played loudly in the snow. Bronislava marveled at their carefree laughter. *They laugh as if there is no famine, no death. Viktor will live to laugh with such abandon.* The kettle whistled from its perch atop the coal stove. *Matryoshka is close. I can feel her. I must prepare the tea.*

Despite the scarcity of food in the village, Bronislava had procured tea and bread and pickles for the occasion. She had stolen every morsel. The act could have landed her in a *gulag*, and she would not have lasted long there. Only a few weeks had passed since she'd given birth, and her body was broken and tired. But she wanted the best table possible for Matryoshka, even if it meant stealing from hungry people. *Everyone is hungry, but Viktor's life depends upon this meal.*

Viktor stirred in his cradle, and at once Bronislava was hovering above him. Her son's skin was white and brittle and paper thin. *More delicate than any foreign teacups.* She caressed his clammy cheeks and resisted the urge to scoop him up and press him against her chest. *Let him sleep. Rest is best.* The midwife's words echoed in her ears. *"He is weak. Prepare yourself to lose him."*

And Bronislava had watched Dmitri prepare himself, refuse to hold his son, refuse to refer to him by his name, refuse to love him. She knew Dmitri was capable of love. Theirs was a love marriage, a rarity in the village. He was withholding his love from his own son. It would take all her love to save him from Matryoshka.

She pushed Dmitri out of her mind and carried the stolen food to the table. Outside, the children had fallen silent and Bronislava knew that Matryoshka would soon appear. She had awakened that morning knowing that Matryoshka would come for Viktor before nightfall. She tore the black bread into several large chunks and arranged it with the thick pickles on her single platter.

As Bronislava fussed with the food, she considered everything she'd ever heard about Matryoshka. There wasn't much. She had never laid eyes upon her. Few in the village spoke of her. Mama had been the exception. From Mama, Bronislava had learned many things about Matryoshka: that she was as old as time; that she accompanied the immature souls of stillborn babies and sickly infants into the light; that nothing could distract her from her course. Mama knew this, because Matryoshka had taken Bronislava's infant brother years before her own birth. "I tried desperately to stop her, Broni! I begged with all my might, but when she went to take his soul, I couldn't move or speak." *Again and again she told her pitiful story. Again and again her mother showed her weakness.* "She pressed her lips against his head, grinned like a cat, and left his tiny corpse behind."

I am stronger than Mama ever was.

"I have come for Viktor." The voice was dusty and ancient and gentle, almost a sigh. Bronislava had not heard the door open and close. She spun on her heels. A plump old woman with a toothy smile stood at the head of the table. She wore a long brown coat that touched the floor. A red *babushka* framed her pale wrinkled face. Bronislava had never seen such clear blue eyes.

"Please, sit down for tea." Bronislava hurried across the room and pulled out the chair for her guest. *Do not look at the baby. Do not speak his name.* She hoped her trembling voice did not betray her terror.

"Oh, you're too kind!" Matryoshka laughed gaily and settled onto the chair. "It's rare that I am received so warmly." She patted the seat beside her. "Sit down, dear. You look exhausted."

Bronislava hesitated and glanced again towards the cradle. *Don't be disarmed by her smile and her lovely words. She is not your Baba.* She forced a smile of her own to her lips and perched on the edge of the chair with her spine as straight as a pin.

"Please, eat." Bronislava lifted the platter from the coarse table-top and thrust it towards Matryoshka. "Pickles and bread. It's all I have."

"Lovely, lovely," Matryoshka chirped as she plucked a particularly large pickle off the platter and stuffed it into her mouth. Juice dribbled down her chin.

Bronislava felt the tension slide off her shoulders. *There's nothing to fear here. She's just an old lady.* "Would you like some tea, Matryoshka?" She filled her cup to the brim. "I'm sad to say I have no cream or sugar to offer you."

"No need to apologize, dear," Matryoshka said sweetly as she lifted the cup to her lips. "I'm sure it's lovely all the same." Suddenly Matryoshka gasped and returned the cup to its saucer. "My word!" She gazed down at the cup. "These are your mother's teacups!" Bronislava's blood turned to ice. "I would never forget such lovely china. She offered me tea and bread, just as you are now. Did she tell you that? If not, what a happy coincidence!"

At the mention of her mother, Bronislava stiffened. *This is the moment.* "We have much to discuss, Matryoshka," Bronislava began slowly as she rose to her feet. She could barely hear her voice over the rapid thudding of her heart. "I humbly ask that you leave my son here, to live a full life. Please."

Matryoshka dabbed each corner of her mouth with the sleeve of her coat and sighed. The smile vanished from her lips but remained in her eyes. "Your son is already an angel, child." Her words were calm and gentle. *She's said these words many times before, but I am different from all the other mothers.* "You must try to understand."

"There must be something," Bronislava replied forcefully. "He needs more time."

"You need not be afraid."

"There must be—"

"You look so much like your mother."

Bronislava felt a sudden rush of tears behind her eyes. Her confidence fell away from her. "You vile woman!" She cried out in anguish. "Viktor deserves his life!"

Now the smile disappeared from Matryoshka's blue eyes. She scowled. "You could be taking this time to kiss his head and wish him well." She rose from the chair. "Instead you shout and scream and raise a ruckus."

Breathe. All is not lost. Frantically Bronislava's eyes darted around the room for inspiration. They fell upon the cradle. "Is it because of Dmitri, because he's been so distant?" Bronislava choked on a sob. "He's only been like that because he is frightened, and—"

Matryoshka waved a hand dismissively in the air. "It isn't because of anything you or Dmitri did or didn't do, and really, if you knew what I know, you wouldn't be afraid. One day you'll understand."

"You must make exceptions!" Bronislava's plea was shrill and loud. *I sound like Mama.* She gripped the edge of the rough table, clamped her eyes shut and struggled to stem the flow of tears. *It isn't over yet.* "Please make an exception for Viktor," she said quietly as she opened her eyes and peered imploringly into Matryoshka's kindly face. "I will be a good mother."

"Child, you are a good mother — a very good mother. But I already made an exception once for your family, and your line is allowed only one." Matryoshka cast her gaze towards the cradle.

"I don't understand."

"You lived," Matryoshka continued as she slid across the room. Her feet were obscured by her long coat so whether or not she floated inches above the dirt or simply walked with grace was a mystery to Bronislava. "I let you live, and now your son must die."

Stymied and horrified, Bronislava gaped and reeled. *She's a demon! A monster! How foolish I was to think I could charm her with tea and pickles! I must block her path.* But Bronislava was unable to move. Her limbs were cold and leaden and locked in place by unseen forces.

"When I returned to your mother to take you — I had already taken your brother too, you remember — again your mother begged, but this time she was prepared to bargain. Such a strong woman. Each line is entitled to one exception — my goodness, he is beautiful!" She leaned over the cradle.

"You're lying!" Bronislava cried. "She would have told me. She would have—"

"She could not speak of the bargain if she'd wanted to, my child." Matryoshka gazed down into the cradle and stroked Viktor's cheek. He cooed. Now Bronislava's tongue was stilled by the unseen force, and her cries were locked inside her head. She watched helplessly as Matryoshka bent down and pressed her lips to Viktor's forehead. He wheezed once and fell silent, and Bronislava's heart shattered in her chest.

Now Matryoshka floated towards the door. For a moment she paused, turned back to face Bronislava, and smiled. But this time, Bronislava knew that the sweet smile on Matryoshka's face belonged to Viktor, and though robbed of mobility and speech, she called all her love to her eyes. *Go in peace, my son.*

Matryoshka nodded and passed through the closed door, and Bronislava was alone with the tiny corpse.

I knew I couldn't prevent this. Deep down, I knew all along. And Bronislava also knew that, as soon as she was able, she would smash Mama's teacups to bits, grip the biggest shard in her fingers, and drag the edge along her wrists until Mama's bargain was forfeited. *I am stronger than Mama ever was.*

■ ■ ■

Sabrina Furminger is a writer and essayist based in Vancouver, BC. Her speculative fiction has appeared in *Ricepaper Magazine, OCW Magazine,* and *Luna Station Quarterly*. In 2009, her historical coming-of-age tale *Powder Blue* was shortlisted in *FreeFall Magazine's* Prose & Poetry Contest. Sabrina published her first novel (a paranormal romance entitled *The Healer*) in 2011. She wrote "Matryoshka" after the birth of her daughter compelled her to examine the tumultuous relationship between life and death. Her collection of antique Matryoshka dolls provided further inspiration.

—FINGERNAILS—

By J. Y. T. Kennedy

Harald had hardly gotten a wink of sleep. The twenty two hours of midsummer daylight did not bother him at home, but staying in the city was another matter, and the guest-house window curtains were completely inadequate. The one time he managed to doze off, he was woken by an earth tremor. The hosts came up to reassure the German tourists in the room next to his, but assumed he was used to these things. Never mind that the farm where he lived was in a part of Iceland that actually wasn't on a fault line, where you could set a hairbrush down beside your bed without worrying that it would land in your face in the middle of the night.

He dragged himself outside far later than he had planned, and proceeded blearily along the streets of Reykjavik through the cold, drizzling rain. Everything was just as he remembered it from the last time he visited: the same rows of garishly painted houses spoiling the view of the mountains, the same pungent sea air, the same noisy cars. He stopped at a cafe, but turned around and left almost as soon as he got through the door. It was far too busy and instead of the *kleinur* or cake he was hoping for, the menu was all things like vegan lasagna and couscous salad.

When he finally reached the conference room, he almost turned around and went back out that door as well. The room was full of people, packed to the point where it would be hard to cross it without bumping into someone, and most of them were foreigners. He had known that would be the case, but knowing was not the same as actually being here. He found the chatter deafening and utterly incomprehensible. Could all of these people really be world record holders, he wondered, or were most of them just hangers-on? No one particularly unusual here: one might encounter a similar assortment of types in an airport. A couple of people wore sports uniforms; they might have been famous for all he knew. There was a young fellow with a huge mohawk, who must have had to turn his head sideways to get in the door. His ears were very large and peppered with studs. Four middle-aged women might have been identical quadruplets, although Harald was too far away to be certain.

His mosquito — the world's largest sculpture made entirely from twist ties — was suspended over one corner of the room. It was not in the position it had been in the night before. Somebody, who apparently had never observed an actual mosquito, had decided to tip it up so that it was presenting its proboscis horizontally like a knight's lance. He could not see any of his other sculptures; he supposed that they were still beneath the mosquito, but probably rearranged as well. He only hoped that nobody had damaged anything in the process. He made up his mind to find out immediately, or at least as soon as he could get across the room.

It looked as though it would be easier to go around the edge than through the middle. The walls all displayed poster-sized framed photographs accompanied by small informative plaques, forming a sort of world record hall of fame, and a stream of people was shuffling around viewing them. He shuffled along too, pressed between a troupe in matching purple T-shirts that had something written on them in Italian, and three Englishwomen with irritating, high-pitched voices. It was hot in here, but he did not want to take off his sweater: he would only end up carrying it, and would mess up his hair in the process. It was getting thin on top, and apt to stick out in odd directions if not carefully supervised.

The first picture was of a bearded lady, which made him think of his grandmother. Not that his grandmother had a beard, but he remembered her telling him how the gigantic wolf, *Fenrir*, had been bound by a magic cord made of things like women's beards and the sound of cats' footsteps, which have not existed in the world since. Or almost never: perhaps the existence of bearded ladies was a sign that *Fenrir* was working his way loose, and the end of the world was at hand. And the guest-house had featured a cat that made a remarkable amount of noise scampering about the hallways when people were trying to sleep. Now if rocks just started growing roots and ... he couldn't remember the rest, not that it mattered. As far as he could tell, the Norse gods were quietly succumbing to the indifference of the modern world, no apocalyptic battles required. For his own part, he had stopped believing in trolls and hidden folk at about the age of three, and had preferred stories about real things ever since.

The next picture was of a tightrope walker, and then there was a tiny man in old fashioned clothes, and so on in no particular order that Harald could determine. He took the time to read the names, although he knew many of them already. These were the sort of record holders that people remembered, not the kind that got their name put up on a webpage just for managing to think of some weekend stunt that nobody had bothered doing before. Freaks, either by accident or by choice. Like him.

He had worked on his sculptures in every free moment for the past fifteen years. He had dedicated his life to making up his mind to do something truly painstaking and difficult, and then doing it. Some of his sculptures had taken more than a year, working for hours each day. He put many hours in with the twist ties just figuring out ways of joining them together, and was particularly proud of interesting arrangements he had come up with that gave an effect similar to the knotwork on old Viking ships. The world record people didn't care about that sort of thing: it was all about being the first, or the biggest, or using the most pieces. But the people who actually saw his work remembered it. They told other people about it; some emailed him with questions or comments. A picture of one of his sculptures had been used for a book cover. You couldn't say that for the world's longest chain of drinking straws.

The first corner held a sculpture which towered almost to the ceiling, constructed from old typewriters. It was not one of his: he would never make anything so crude. With materials that large, the whole thing probably could have been welded together in a week. He did take the time to read the plaque, though, and discovered that the typewriters were supposed to form a model of DNA, being arranged in a double helix and each having their A, T, C, or G key stuck down. The result was more hideous than clever, but he still felt some sympathy with the creator: they both built things from what others discarded.

Just past the typewriter tower there was actually a bit of open space. As the people shuffled along, they all seemed to strike out from the wall as they came to the sculpture, and cut across the corner. The purple T-shirt people did the same, and he gratefully stepped out of the stream. With room to inhale at last, he was on the point of doing so with gusto when he noticed an unpleasant smell. For a moment he worried that it might be coming from him, but decided that was unlikely. He was fairly sure he had put on deodorant that morning; his clothes had been washed since being worn in the barn; he had not been sweating very much; and anyway he never usually noticed his own odor. Perhaps something had died inside one of the typewriters.

There was just one woman standing close by the wall here, looking at a picture of Lee Redmond when she held the world record for the longest fingernails. Lee's fingernails curved in extreme arcs in front of her, giving the impression that she stood inside a cage that she had grown from her own hands. As Harald considered this image he pursed his lips and, without thinking about it, made a small sympathetic humming noise.

The woman must have thought the noise was intended to get her attention because she turned to look at him. She had a very pale face, with eyelashes and brows so fair as to be almost invisible. Her lips were startlingly dark in contrast, purplish, as though all the blood in her head had decided to settle there. The color did not look like lipstick, although it might have been some sort of stain.

He was thoroughly flustered. He opened his mouth, poised to speak, but failed to think of anything to say. It seemed like at least five minutes before he finally managed, "I don't usually have anything to do with these sorts of things."

She continued to look at him, not replying. Somehow he had assumed she was Icelandic. Her black jacket and long black skirt reminded him of the traditional costumes that were sometimes brought out for tedious rural celebrations, except that hers bore no embroidery.

"Do you understand what I'm saying?" he asked, sticking to Icelandic. He had no interest in trying to communicate in any other language, and had done his best to forget the little bit of Danish and English he had been forced to take in school.

"I understand," she replied. "You would much rather be at home, working on your sculptures."

She had recognized him! He was surprised at just how flattered he was by that. He supposed he must be getting to the stage of life where it was a novelty to be of any interest to a woman. She was not exactly attractive, perhaps because of her unnerving way of staring, but she possessed an unusual elegance that intrigued him.

Before he had thought of a suitable reply, she said, "I don't often bother talking to people either." There was a flatness about the way she spoke, rather like that of a person who is too tired to put emotion into their voice. He wondered if it was some sort of Gothic affectation, to go with the black outfit.

"And is there something you would rather be working on too?"

"Actually, I do have a project of my own."

That explained how she had recognized him, then: a fellow hobbyist. He made up his mind to be gracious and encouraging. "Well, tell me about it. What is this project? How long have you been at it?"

"Oh, a very long time. I'm building a ship out of nails. Fingernails and toenails."

Harald had trouble picturing that. He assumed she meant the little crescent shaped trimmings from nails: slender, uneven things. Some sort of glue must be involved, and the nails would have to overlap each other in layers to get anything remotely sturdy. He glanced at his own fingernails, with their thick strips of white. His father, who milked a flock of horned shaggy-wooled sheep every morning, believed nails should always be trimmed close. Harald had developed the habit of being careless about trimming during his surly teenage years. And it was useful sometimes to have longer nails: they allowed a certain precision of gripping, of creasing, of separating small things from one another. They let you touch a thing without having to actually feel it against your flesh. "How big of a ship?" he asked.

"It will carry an army of giants."

"So you are a gamer!" He decided not to mention his opinion of the sort of hobbies in which most of the creative part — the conception — is already done for the hobbyist. He leaned towards gracious and encouraging. "But you are making this ship from scratch?"

"So to speak." A little smile quirked her lips as though he had made a joke.

"That is good. Very good. It might be worth claiming as a record once it is done, though you would probably want to leave out the giants." He had a feeling that he had actually heard of someone making a ship out of fingernails before, but even if it had been registered as a record, hers might be heavier or longer or something.

"I think it will be a while yet, but I see the end in sight," she said.

"So much the better. Anyone can climb a mole-hill without breaking a sweat. Always stick to your vision; don't compromise. Never compromise."

"I don't."

Harald could not think of any more encouraging things to say, which he supposed meant that he should let the conversation die. But instead he found himself asking, "Do you live in the city?"

"No, but I come here often."

"Visiting family?"

She hesitated a little, and then said. "I don't see much of my family."

"Neither do I, except for my father. We both live out on the old farm; everyone else moved away. I haven't seen my brother in six years."

"My brothers were just small when I saw them last." For the first time there was a definite emotion in her voice: a fierce bitterness which made Harald wish he had avoided the topic of families. He had a feeling that this woman's life story would turn out to be something ghastly, and he felt he had already said enough about his own family. His brother's last visit was still a sore point: he had gone on about coming all this way and they would hardly talk to him, as though their father had ever spared more than four words in a row for anyone without that many hooves.

"Do you have any pictures of your work?" he asked. On those occasions when he ended up discussing his work with other people, they usually asked him that. He had even gone to the trouble of putting a few snapshots on his phone that morning so he would seem prepared for a change, though in hindsight it was a bit redundant when he could just point to a corner of the room.

"Would you like to see it?" she asked.

"Yes, of course." That was an easy one. The conversation was back under control.

"You can look at it today, when you come back to my place."

Harald was very glad he was not drinking anything, because he was sure he would have sprayed it all over that black jacket. Was she propositioning him?

He was not even close to figuring out how to respond when she asked, "Do you ever feel as though you are half dead?"

That definitely did not sound flirtatious: he should have known better than to get his hopes up. But he still found himself scrambling for something intelligent to say. People had asked him before whether he didn't feel he was missing out on life by spending so much time on his hobbies. He had always dismissed the question. They did not understand the wonderful peace that he felt when he was engaged in his work, when the world seemed to go away, and time seemed to stand still. If he had been sure that was all she meant, he would simply have told her that if she felt that way she should do something else. And yet he got the impression that she did understand, that perhaps she understood too well. There were times when, if he was completely honest, he would finally look at the clock after being up half the night and feel as though he had not experienced anything at all ... as though he somehow wasn't really inside himself...

"Doesn't everyone?" he said.

"Some people feel too much alive," she said. There was no sympathy in her voice at all. "And some people are so hardened off that hardly anything touches them to the quick."

Her words made Harald think of how unbearable life had been when he was a boy, when he had felt everything so intensely. He supposed he must admit to being hardened now. But would he be any less hardened if he had spent his work years at some city job, putting his energy into things that meant nothing to him, and coming home to some flat just like every other flat in an apartment building just like every other apartment building? He thought not. Instead he might have lost that part of himself that still thrilled at the idea of a new challenge.

He did not try to express these thoughts out loud; they were too personal. Instead, he fell back on a speech of a sort he had made many times before. "It seems to me that people these days aren't so much hardened as hypnotized. They are so distracted by all their computer games and text messages and television shows, they never have an original thought."

She looked him right in the eye as he said this, and silently held the gaze for long enough afterwards that his own words began to strike him as pretentious and even ridiculous. Just how did you decide what was or was not an original thought anyway? He had no idea.

Finally she said, "Of all the distractions people have come up with, the only one that has ever struck me as more foolish than the others was the pursuit of fame."

Harald bumped his shoulder into the typewriter DNA thing, and realized that he had been unconsciously backing away from her. He felt suddenly off balance, and put his hand on one of the typewriter casings to steady himself.

The sculpture tipped. As he made a startled leap to one side, the sleeve of his sweater caught on one of those things which you press to go down a line. It made a noise like a little bell and the whole helical monstrosity changed direction, grazing his shoulder as it plunged toward the middle of the room. It struck the floor and the entire room felt as if it was shaking. Harald's feet slipped out from under him, dropping him onto his knees.

When he recovered his equilibrium, he discovered that the woman was sprawled on the floor with one foot caught beneath the sculpture, twisted to an unnatural angle. "I'm so sorry," he squeaked, not sure if she even heard him over all the voices in the room which had now risen in the commotion.

She pulled her skirt up. The stench hit Harald first, and then he saw her legs. They were gangrenous black, the flesh rotted and shrivelled against the bone. The foot of the caught leg had pulled apart at the knee, bones showing through on either side. There was no blood, only a foul dampness where the inner tissues had separated.

She grasped the foot and pulled it loose, lined the two parts of the leg up neatly, and then popped the knee back together. A pustulant ooze seeped out, coagulating over the joint.

Harald's stomach lurched toward his throat and he made a desperate effort to avoid retching, choking the cry which had started to escape his lips.

The woman looked at him, at first with the exact same unnerving calm as before. Then her lips curled back from her teeth, her head rocked backward, and she began to shake with laughter.

Harald lost the battle with his nausea; he had no chance of making it out of the room, but he managed to turn and propel himself into the corner in time. There was not much in his stomach, but for some time he could not seem to stop heaving up little drips of bile. He was in no hurry to turn around. He needed to get his head together first and come to grips with the fact that what he thought he had seen must actually have been some sort of hallucination. Right now, the stench was still in his nostrils, and the laughter continued to echo in his ears.

Suddenly he remembered where he had heard about a ship made of fingernails. It was from his grandmother's story, the one which he had been making light of just a little while before. *Naglfar*: that was the name of the ship. It belonged to *Hel*, who ruled over the dead, who was half immortal and half corpse. Since the first human beings walked the earth, she had been building *Naglfar* from the nails of the dead. She would be finished at the end of time, when she would take the ship to join her monstrous brethren — *Fenrir* and world-encircling serpent *Jormungandr* — in their war against the gods.

The story did not strike him as humorous now; against his will, it was taking on a horrible reality in his mind. He did not want to see that ship. He did not want to imagine how many nails had been added to it, one by one, generation after generation, from the bodies of people who had lived and died and been forgotten.

The whole room heaved around him, and not because anything else had fallen, or because his nausea was making him dizzy. This time there was no mistaking that it was something much bigger.

Harald tried to stand but failed. He pressed himself into the corner as the shaking grew stronger and the walls buckled. People were yelling and shrieking and he could make out that some were calling for help and others helpfully letting everyone know that it was an earthquake.

All around him panels and plaster came down, striking him, burying him. Frantically, he tried to fight his way upward against what piled on top of him, grasping and scraping. His lungs burned, and soon he could tell that he was only shifting a bit of loose debris beneath heavier things which were settling inexorably. But he refused to give up the struggle. Even though it would make no difference, even though nobody would remember, he was not going to compromise and give up the struggle. Even though he felt his fingernails being torn down to the quick.

J. Y. T. Kennedy writes mostly science fiction and fantasy, and has had one novel, *Dominion*, published by DragonMoon Press. She lives in Alberta, and keeps a few sheep but doesn't milk them. She has had a lifelong interest in myth, legend and folklore, and performs as a storyteller mostly as an excuse to revisit favorite old tales and learn new ones. She was struck by the idea of Hel as the ultimate obsessive hobbyist when listening to an audiobook of Norse myths with her children.

GHOST NOR BOGLE
~SHALT THOU FEAR~
By William Meikle

I heard the yell of pain outside in the yard. By the time I got to him, old lady Malcolm from next door was at his side. My friend Doug lay on the ground next to a still buzzing saw, curled up in a fetal position. The old lady bent over him and managed to pry his good hand away from the wound on his arm. She sucked through her teeth.

"How bad is it?" I asked.

"Bad enough. He needs to get to the hospital, and quick."

The old lady tried to stand and lift Doug at the same time. He was a dead weight. His eyes rolled up in their sockets, and when I took the weight off Ms. Malcolm he fainted in my arms. He had his injured arm wrapped in the folds of his jacket ... a jacket that was already soaked in blood, black in the shadows in the yard.

Mrs. Malcolm got in the back with Doug.

"Don't be waiting too long at any lights," she said. "Your pal need stitches ... lots of stitches."

I reversed out of the yard at top speed before doing a hand-brake turn onto the road. I went through the first junction at fifty and got faster after that. Lucky for us, the traffic was light.

The old lady kept up a constant stream of chat, interspersed with singing soft childhood songs while cradling Doug's head in her lap. For one verse in particular she raised her voice, the song echoing high and clear inside the car.

"Ghost nor bogle shalt thou fear,"
"Thou art to love and heaven so dear,"
"Naught of ill may come thee near,"
"My bonnie dearie."

I was afraid to look in the mirror. My own grandmother had sung those self-same words to me, every time I hurt, every night when she sang me to sleep. I hoped they comforted Doug as much as they did me.

When we got to a long straight stretch of road she leaned forward.

"I could do with a cigarette, if you've got one."

I didn't like the way my hands shook as I tried to light the cigarette, and in the end I handed the pack and lighter to her to do it for me.

"How's he doing?" I asked, as she handed a lit cigarette back over my shoulder.

"He's alive," she said.

That was all, but I heard the rest in her tone, the two unspoken words.

For now.

▪ ▪ ▪

I was doing nearly eighty when I saw the sign for the ER and I went over the speed bumps in the hospital drive still doing fifty … the car's suspension held up to it, but the old lady cursed long and loud in the back. I guessed she had known a few sailors in her time.

I hit the car park at thirty and came to a halt in a bay ten yards from the brightly-lit entrance.

"Help us. We've got a badly hurt man here!" I shouted as I opened the car door.

I'd seen the movies and television shows. I was expecting ER doctors and nurses to dash out to our aid, gurneys rattling, perfect teeth gleaming in the headlights. But there was no movement, either in the car park or in the well-lit hall behind the entrance doors.

"Help! Injured man here!" I shouted again as we manhandled Doug through the doors and into reception.

Two rows of waiting patients turned and stared blankly in our direction. Behind a heavily fortified reception area a matronly woman with a blue rinse perm looked me up and down.

"You'll live," she said to me. "Take a seat. There'll be a doctor free in a couple of hours." She dismissed me with a wave of her hand and went back to filling in forms in tiny, neat, capital letters.

"I'll just leave this one with you then," I said, and on cue Doug woke long enough to raise his arm and bring it down close to the ten-inch square hole in the reinforced glass that shielded her. Blood spurted in through the opening, a small red fountain that covered her, her desk and all the paperwork in front of her.

She shrieked.

"I'll have security onto you," she said to Doug.

"You'd better hurry then," the old lady said. "For I don't think he's hanging around for long."

Doug slumped against the screen, smearing more blood down the glass as he fell forward. His eyes rolled up in their sockets and I only just got a hand under his jaw before he smacked it on the desk.

Finally, the receptionist hit the panic button, and I was gratified to see that the doctors moved just as fast as the ones on television. What they lacked in expensive dentistry they made up for in speed. One minute we had Doug in our arms, the next he lay on a gurney. An ancient janitor wheeled a bucket over and started cleaning up the blood.

I made to follow the gurney, but the old lady grabbed my arm and pulled me over to a seat.

"I've been here before. They'll let us know how it's going when they've got time," she said. "Lots of people die who shouldn't, either out in the world or here in the hospital. It's just the way of things, and you'll have to get used to it if you grow old like me. There are folks in every corner of this building who are just waiting for death to claim them. Some of them might even go happily. But not this boy, and not this time. He's going to be fine."

And that's when I saw *him*.

He ghosted through the waiting room, a tall thin man dressed all in black, dark eyes sunk deep in a china-white face, cheekbones so sharp they could pass as razors. Nobody else looked at him … nobody registered his presence. He walked quickly across the reception area and stood over the gurney. He put a hand on Doug's chest.

"Hey!" I shouted.

Old Lady Malcolm grabbed my arm.

"You see him?"

I stood up fast. "What are you talking about? Of course I see him."

The doctors wheeled Doug away. The thin man walked alongside the gurney, his hand still on Doug.

"Hey!" I called again, and made to follow.

The old lady pulled me back down on the seat.

"No use son," she said sadly. "What will be will be."

"But that man—"

"No. Not a man," she said quietly.

That got my attention. I sat down beside her.

■ ■ ■

She sang, almost a whisper.

"Ghost nor bogle shalt thou fear,"

"Thou art to love and heaven so dear,"

"You know the song?" she said.

I nodded.

"He's not a ghost," she said matter of factly. "He's a bogle. In fact ... I think he's *the* Bogle."

Somebody had taken my life and twisted it. I had no reference points to hang onto, so I sat quietly and let her talk.

"Cancer. That's what took my man Tommy. Seventy years of god-fearing abstemious living ... and look what it got him. He found a lump under his left arm ... just a small thing, not any bigger than a pea. He wasn't even going to tell the doctor, but when I saw it, I knew what it was all right. The doctor hummed and hawed, and sent him for tests. They opened him up here in the hospital ... and shut him straight away again. It was downhill all the way from then.

She looked up at me, heavy tears filling the bottom half of her eyes.

"At the end all I could do was hold his hand and watch it eat him away. I spent more time here in the hospital than anywhere else, trying to make things easier for him. In the end, the drugs did the job better than I could, and he started to slip away. The nurses let me spend an hour with him alone.

"Only when I looked up, there were three of us in the room ... the Bogle was there. He bent over Tommy, and put a hand on his chest. Then he started to sing the song. When he finished, my Tommy passed on ... a smile on his face as if he'd heard a private joke."

It took a few seconds for the implications of what she'd said to hit me.

"He's Death? You're saying that he's some kind of personification? *The Grim Reaper?*"

She nodded, and reached once more for my arm, but I pushed her away.

"Doug!" I shouted, and ran down the corridor after my friend.

※ ※ ※

I found him in the ER. A doctor and two nurses worked frantically at him while the Bogle stood, silent, by the side of the gurney.

"We're losing him!" the doctor shouted.

The Bogle started to sing.

"Ghost nor bogle shalt thou fear,"

"Thou art to love and heaven so dear,"

"No!" I shouted, and ran into the room.

I grabbed the Bogle by the arm.

Time stopped.

※ ※ ※

Everything was quiet. The doctor leaned over Doug, motionless, stopped in the act of trying to tie off a sudden spurt of blood. One nurse stood, hand raised to change a plasma bag, while the other nurse was about to open a box of cotton swabs.

Nothing moved ... except for the Bogle.

He turned, and those dead black eyes stared at me.

"Are you offering a trade?" he said. His voice had a sing-song quality in a deep bass register that caused vibrations in the pit of my stomach.

"Yes ... no," I stuttered. "Maybe."

He turned back to Doug.

"He's mine tonight," he said. "Unless you have something better to offer."

"Something better?"

"Or equal?"

I looked at Doug, his arm a bloody ruin, his eyes open, staring unseeing at the ceiling. I remembered the old lady's words.

There are folks in every corner of this building who are just waiting for death to claim them. Some of them might even go happily.

"Take anybody else you want," I said. "Just let him live. Please. Let him live."

"That seems fair," the Bogle said.

He smiled at me, and I went cold.

I blinked.

The Bogle was gone.

Time started.

▨ ▨ ▨

One of the nurses bundled me out of the room unceremoniously. "Please. Let us do our job. We'll find you when there's any news."

I went back to reception and sat beside old lady Malcolm. I told her what happened in the ER and she looked worried, but said nothing. The experience already seemed dream-like, fading into unreality under the cold harsh neon in the reception area.

"Maybe it was just the stress," I said. "Some kind of psychotic episode?"

"Maybe," the old lady said, but she didn't look convinced. She fell quiet.

I sat and watched the night people pass through the casualty department. It was now well after one in the morning. The clubs threw drunk youths onto the street, and the drunk youths threw themselves onto each other. Over the next hour there was a constant stream of scalp wounds, busted heads, vomiting drunks, cursing drunks and bleeding drunks. Add to that friends of the wounded, enemies of the wounded and policemen bringing in both groups, and you had a recipe for disaster. I gained a grudging respect for the blue-rinsed receptionist ... she dealt with a level of abuse that would have had me in a fit of rage ... and she did it every night.

Much later a tired-looking doctor came out to speak to us.

"You can see him now," he said. "He lost a lot of blood and is very weak. He's been moved to the recovery room ... it's—"

"I know where it is," Mrs. Malcolm said, and she took me by the arm.

▨ ▨ ▨

When Mrs. Malcolm and I were let in to see him, Doug was sitting up in bed, but he looked barely alive. His skin was alabaster white, almost as pale as the bandage that swathed the full length of his arm. He managed a thin smile.

"Two hundred stitches," he said. "Remind me to be careful the next time."

I moved over to the bedside, and we had one of those awkward moments that happens between men when they have emotions but no way to let them show. I settled for holding his hand, trying not to let the tears come. He gripped my fingers tight.

"I'm okay," he said. "And the drugs have kicked in, so I feel no pain."

And that was when I calmed down enough to notice what was laid on the chair in the corner. The hospital had provided him with clean clothes for the journey home. The shirt alone would have been cause for comment. It was red and white, sewn with tassels and sequins that danced in the neon overheads. The last time I'd seen anybody wearing anything like it, he'd been sitting on a horse singing about his four-legged friend. That in itself was bad enough, but lying on top of that was an electric blue angora cardigan.

"Roy Rogers meets Ed Wood," I said, and the giggles began to well up.

"You should have seen what I turned down," he said. "It could have been Vampirella meets Trigger."

That started Doug off, and we were both laughing like school-boys who'd heard their first fart joke.

Old Lady Malcolm looked on bemused.

"Is this a private hilarity, or can anybody join in?"

"You need to know some *really* bad movies," Doug said.

"Oh, *Plan 9* isn't that bad," she said. "Have you seen *Cannibal Girls*?"

Then I made a big mistake.

"Oh? And I suppose you can link *Frankenstein* with *Tremors* in three?" I said.

She hardly thought about it.

"That's easy. Karloff to Nicholson to Bacon. Do you want the names of the films?"

Minutes later they were into stylistic similarities between Fulci and Romero, having lost me way behind when they moved on from Roger Corman.

I was trying to find a way into the conversation when I heard the singing.

"Ghost nor bogle shalt thou fear,"
"Thou art to love and heaven so dear,..."

I walked slowly out into the corridor.

Voices raised in song from every room. And in every room a black-clad figure stood over a patient, hands pressed on their chest.

The nearest one turned to me. It spoke, and my own voice echoed back. *"Take anybody you want,"* I said.

Mrs. Malcolm left Doug and came to my side.

"What have you done?" she said. "Oh my God. *What have you done?"*

The black-clad bogle smiled at me.

"Take anybody you want," it said.

There was no escape. Throughout the hospital, in every corridor, tall black clad figures went to and fro. And everywhere the chorus rang out.

"Ghost nor bogle shalt thou fear,"
"Thou art to love and heaven so dear,"
"Naught of ill may come thee near,"
"My bonnie dearie."

▨ ▨ ▨

William Meikle is a Scottish writer with ten novels published in the genre press and over 200 short story credits in thirteen countries. He is the author of the ongoing Midnight Eye series among others, and his work appears in a number of professional anthologies. This story came out of his time working in hospitals in Scotland, and seeing good people die.

—DEATH OVER EASY—

By Suzanne Church

I've always figured a heart attack would be my ticket to the next life. My arteries and I have differing opinions on the virtues of steaks, eggs, and bacon. So last Wednesday, at 11:00 am when Death waltzed into my diner, I grabbed my coat, which hung on the hook below my *Classic Cars* calendar, swallowed hard, and said, "So how does this work?"

"You take my order," he said.

My coat fell from my hand, making a soft thud as it hit the floor. "I get it. You like to play with your quarry before you eat it."

"I'd rather have eggs."

"Oh."

Death cleared his throat, sounding like he'd had one too many smokes in his lifetime, deathtime, or whatever. "I'll have three, over easy, with bacon and whole wheat toast," he said. "The sign says you're famous for your raspberry jelly."

"Ran out during the morning rush. How about grape?"

"Give me honey, instead. I've never acquired a taste for grape."

Now the situation could've gone a thousand ways at that point. I could've told him to go to hell, but I didn't want to give the guy any ideas. I could've insisted we cut to the chase, because I'm an impatient person and if I was going to die, I wanted to bite it before the lunch hour rush. But when the bastard settled into the booth like he owned the place, and flashed me the vilest, most crooked set of stained teeth I had ever seen, I decided to do what I do best.

Pulling my order pad from my apron, I said, "Number three, coming up. You want coffee?"

"Black. I'm lactose intolerant."

With a final look over my shoulder at my only customer, I retrieved my coat from the floor, hung it on the hook, and headed into the kitchen to make the dark dude his breakfast.

◼ ◼ ◼

Death finished the eggs and bacon, but left a half slice of toast. I warmed his coffee a couple of times, and still he lingered at the table, spending his time studying the picture of the *1965 Ford Fairlane* hanging on the wall above his booth. I must have glanced at my coat ten or more times, waiting for my cue to leave, but he didn't seem to be in any hurry.

When my assistant, Betty, arrived, she headed for the kitchen, donned her apron, and set about making fries for the lunch crowd.

"Anything else?" I asked Death.

"The bill."

"Can I get my coat, first?"

He placed his hand on my wrist. His flesh felt cold, not like ice, but cold enough to drive home his job description. As he moved, dust shook free of his grey trench coat and released the stench of attic must and lanolin. I wondered if I would ever get the smell off the vinyl booth seats.

"The cheque, please. I would like to be on my way."

"It's on the house."

Death stood, continuing to hold my wrist with his right hand, and reached in his coat pocket with his left. Bringing out a ten dollar bill, he said, "This ought to more than cover it."

I stared at the money, all the while praying for him to release my wrist from his shiver-grip. Finally, he did.

"See you next Wednesday." And with a tip of his fedora and a swish of his trench coat, he glided out of the diner looking more like a dancer than the ultimate equalizer. A trail of dust motes traced his path like monikers.

"Quite the stranger," Betty called from the kitchen. "You get his name?"

"Nope." I headed into the kitchen so I wouldn't have to yell and added, "Said he'd be back on Wednesday."

"From the look of him, I'd rather he stayed gone."

With a nod, I said, "Couldn't agree more."

◼ ◼ ◼

I arranged for the town lawyer, Cliff, to make up my will. Like any small town, just about everyone had slept with every eligible partner their own age, and Cliff and I were no exception. I'm sure he'd blabbed the news of my urgent-last-testament-request to anyone who would listen by the time he showed up at my door on Sunday morning.

While contemplating the fact that I likely had only three and a half days to live, assuming that Death showed up at eleven on Wednesday, the doorbell rang.

Suddenly the couch seemed more comfortable than it had ever felt before, but I forced myself out of it and headed for the door.

Of course, Cliff, feeling like he owned the place since he'd slept with me all of once back when we were in high school, had already let himself in. "Hey, Lizzie. Your papers are ready."

I caught up to him in the mud room, and pointed at his boots. "You *are* going to take those off, right?"

"That's how you greet friends who do you weekend favours?"

"Hello, Cliff. Nice to see you. Thanks for coming by on a Sunday, and no doubt charging me double."

"Nice." With a smirk, he held up a manila envelope chock full of paper goodness. "We need to talk before you sign."

"I figured."

He sidled past me, headed straight for the couch where he flopped down and pointed at the cushion beside him.

I stood next to him, arms crossed, picking at the skin on my elbow.

"Sit."

"I'll stand."

"*Sit!*"

I did.

"You've got the whole town in an uproar. It's not every day someone as young as you insists I rush a will in a couple of days."

With a glare, I said, "So much for lawyer-client privilege."

"Most of the scuttlebutt points to cancer. Big-ass tumors, and with the diner, you've got no health insurance, right?"

"You've got a big mouth."

"I'm concerned about you. We all are." He sat back, crossed his left leg over his right knee, and stretched his right arm along the back of the couch. His attention skipped from the steering wheel of my first car, hung over the mantle like the antlers from a hunting trip, to my throw rug with the pattern of a *1967 Mustang* grill.

"You've got a nice home here, Lizzie."

"Thanks." I pointed at the papers beside him. "I appreciate your concern for me, and your need to spread the word that I might be in trouble, might need some help. But I was counting on your *obligation* to keep my request confidential."

"You do realize," he said, his voice turning more serious than his usual over-confident bravado, "that confidentiality is moot once you're dead."

And so the elephant appeared.

Cliff stared at me. I stared back.

"So the rumor is cancer, huh?" I managed to ask.

He studied my face. "You're taking this awfully well. Better than I would." With a pause, he added, "Better than I *am*."

My voice softer, I admitted, "I don't think it's really sunk in, yet." I pointed at the papers again. "Can we get this over with, please?"

He switched to legal mode and started explaining. I checked my watch a few times, painfully aware of how much he was going to charge for this visit. At the same time, I'd likely be hanging with the Death dude before Cliff could send a bill. The diner was worth plenty. He'd find a way to retrieve his fees from my estate.

Clicking his pen, he pointed to the first sticky-arrow, and said, "Sign here."

I did.

Lather, rinse, repeat, more times than I wanted to count, with the occasional initials for good measure. Before my hand cramped, he clicked the pen closed, stuffed half the papers in the envelope and handed me the other half.

"Done." He extended his hand to shake. "Well, I hope this gives you some closure, love."

The *love* was a nice touch. I stared at his hand generating one of those awkward-silence-moments, but when I looked into his soft brown eyes, I wondered if maybe he was being sincere. "Thanks. For being so quick." *Not unlike high school.* The thought brought a genuine smile to my face, and I slid my hand into his for the shake.

His touch felt warm. Not sweaty, or creepy. Warm. Comforting. A human kind of connection that reminded me I was still very much alive. I probably held on for a little too long, causing another awkward silence.

Finally, he said, "I'll show myself out."

As he left, I watched his well formed ass saunter back and forth with his strides. With the self-reflection only the dying can truly muster, I wondered whether maybe Cliff had been more of a man than I'd given him credit for. That maybe he wasn't a regular in the diner because of the bacon.

Then the door closed and I felt truly alone.

◼ ◼ ◼

For the first time in seven years, I didn't go into the diner on Sunday. After learning of the town's cancer-gossip, I decided to load up on cholesterol, stacking heart attack's chances. I defrosted smoked salmon in cold water in the sink, and while the pot came to a boil for poached eggs, I made hollandaise sauce, with extra butter and enough yolks that I should've picked up a defibrillator with the groceries.

My stomach was about to explode after four servings. Leaving the kitchen in a state that would normally drive me to drink, I chewed a few antacids, grabbed my car keys, and headed for the garage, feeling a need for speed.

Death was sitting in the driver's seat, with the window rolled down.

I swallowed, waiting for him to speak.

He picked at his nails, and yes, *ew*, licked whatever he scraped out.

My arms crossed over my chest and I demanded, "You said Wednesday."

"Yes."

"It's Sunday."

"You had four Eggs Montreal."

I hung my head in shame, then added, "Don't you have your own wheels?"

"I've always wanted to visit Niagara Falls. The Canadian side, naturally, since the views are more panoramic from their vantage points. And road trips are always more pleasant with company. Do you have a valid passport?"

I nodded. The thought of Death driving my car gave me a thousand different kinds of creep. But he seemed comfortable, and I wasn't about to give him a reason to be angry with me. I figured, what the heck? Why not spend my last Sunday with the dark dude on a road trip where I could enjoy the scenery and pick the brains (if he had any in there) of a guy who had *literally* seen it all? Besides, I had intended to go for a drive, to feel the wind in my hair.

"Give me a minute."

"Take your time."

I returned with a bottle of water, my passport, and enough snacks for two. After the incident at the diner, I knew Death had an appetite, and I didn't want him sucking back all the beef jerky. When I stepped into the car, I expected it to stink like the booth had last Wednesday. This time, though, he smelled of old tires and blackened motor oil, as though he'd spent the last couple of days fixing all the cars in hell.

When I took my iPod out of my pocket, he blocked the USB port. "Driver picks the tunes," he said. From beneath his trench coat, he pulled out a CD, the kind you burn yourself, with the title, *Road Trip Mix* scribbled in red Sharpie across the top. "Do you have a GPS?" he asked.

I shook my head. "But I know the way."

"Lovely."

Death put my car in gear and before I could click the seatbelt into place, we were off.

◼ ◼ ◼

By the time we had crossed the border into Canada, I had heard enough 1980s hair bands for this plus a couple more lifetimes. Who knew Death had a thing for long-haired posers, distortion pedals, and Marshall stacks.

We found a fantastic parking space, directly across from the American Falls. "I don't think I've ever parked this close," I said.

Death yanked the parking brake, and shrugged. "It's a perk."

"Cool."

We slipped into the crowd and headed for one of the most recognizable railings from my childhood. The scrolls in the ironwork always reminded me of my grandparents. Nana had loved the falls and dragged me here on more than one summer vacation while my mother ran the diner. My favorite picture of Nana and Grandpa was of the two of them, standing in front of the railing, him wearing those plaid pants with the white belt that advertised his job as a real estate agent, her with her fine-as-a-wisp hair combed over, her white purse (to match his belt, of course) dangling from her arm, and her lips stained that deep pink-red she always wore on a bright, sunny day. I'm not sure what made them happier: being with each other, spending the day with me, or just the glory of a gorgeous day spent in misty gardens.

Death and I had lucked out with a perfect day of our own to gawk at nature's wonder. I inhaled a long, deep breath and tried to imagine what it must have felt like a few hundred years ago when the first white men, guided by the natives, saw the falls for the first time.

Turning my attention to my companion, if you could call him that, I watched Death as he studied the base of the American Falls.

"Penny for your thoughts," I said.

"I'm impressed."

"Wait 'til you stand at the brink of the Horseshoe Falls." I pointed towards the railing where a crowd of tourists jockeyed for positions at the edge.

Death lingered, grasping the railing like a bull rope. "Many die here each year. I understand now why they're drawn to the spectacle."

I leaned with my back to the railing, taking in the manicured gardens, the endless stream of cars circling for a place to park, the countless cameras strung around necks. Twice I opened my mouth to respond, then changed my mind. Like Death, I was mesmerized by the power of this place. Somehow, in his presence, I felt the need to be profound. Otherwise, my words would waste in the wind, adding to the ever-present mist.

"Are you tempting me?" I asked.

"I've penciled you in for Wednesday."

"Shouldn't a guy like you be, you know, busy? All the time?"

"My services aren't required *every* time."

"Let the minions do the work, huh?"

"Precisely."

"I rate face time with the big boss?"

I looked at him when he didn't answer right away. He gazed at the water, lost in thought, or his duties, or whatever ran through his rotting mind.

"Am I special?" I asked.

"Everyone is unique, extraordinary in their own way."

I laughed out loud, catching the attention of a cluster of tourists. "Death waxes philosophical," I said, quiet enough that only the two of us could hear. I pointed to a young girl, the only one from the group still staring at the two of us, as though we were built of fear. "You're scaring her," I said.

"It's you she fears."

Staring back at the girl, flashing my best smile, I tried not to look like a psychopath with a pocket full of candy and a heart full of wicked intentions. She grabbed the hand of the nearest adult, probably her father, but continued to stare at me.

"Does she know what you are?" I asked.

He shrugged. "Only those in my agenda see beyond my humble attire." Gesturing, he held open his trench coat, revealing khaki shorts with zippered pockets and a plain white T-shirt. "What did you see in me, back in the diner, so that you recognized me straight away?"

"I don't know, exactly. I just *knew*."

For a moment, my heart skipped, as though a flash of something dire, like fur or scales, was about to erupt from beneath that trench coat.

The moment passed.

With a tug on the sleeve of his coat, I said, "Come on," and dragged him toward the Horseshoe Falls.

By the time we had walked along the railing to the brink — the spot where the water rushes over the edge to smash onto the rocks below — my clothes hung heavy on me, sodden by the mist. During one trip here with my grandparents, we had seen a movie about a family whose boat capsized in the river above the falls. The father swam to shore, the son was tossed over the falls with only a life jacket to protect him and he miraculously lived. The daughter was yanked out of the river in the nick of time by tourists who were milling around right where Death and I stood now. The daughter's terror had felt so real to me, as though I had come within inches of being sucked over the edge to drop a zillion feet and break apart on the rocks below. Outside the theatre, on the way to our car, Nana and Grandpa had chatted about how real the experience had felt to them. All I could do was grip their hands, my Nana on my left and my Grandpa on my right, and try to swallow away the lump in my throat. For the first time in my nine years of life I realized that I could die, *would* die. That at any moment, I might close my eyes, fall asleep, and drift into oblivion. That day I had never felt so loved and yet also so alone. Almost three decades later, everyone I loved had died, and I had filled in their gaps with nothing but loneliness and eggs. It struck me as grimly funny that I was spending one of my last days with Death instead of with the living.

"The precipice, or the *brink* as you call it," he said, "is definitely worth the walk."

Jolting back to reality, I glanced up at Death. "Told you."

"You did."

I glanced around for the little girl, the one who had been more afraid of me than of my road-buddy, but the crowds were too thick to see her.

"You done?" I asked.

"Are you?"

I stuffed both my hands into my pockets, feeling cold shivers despite the warm day. "Yeah."

He tipped his hat, or at least pretended to, as he had left the fedora in my car. I felt as though something had changed between us, like we were either becoming friends or sizing each other up as enemies. For the first time since his visit last Wednesday I began to feel the weight of him, and the panic of time ticking louder than it had ever ticked before.

My thoughts veered towards Cliff, of his warm smile, firm grasp of his own worth, and wonderfully formed ass.

When my focus returned to reality, Death was almost at the car. As I sprinted to catch up, I took one last look over my shoulder at the falls. The tourist girl was standing at the railing, her back to her family and their picture-snapping. She crossed herself, made a series of scary hex-like gestures, and then spit in my direction.

⬛ ⬛ ⬛

Monday and Tuesday, I worked in the diner. My road-trip adventure lingered so strongly in my mind that I could not bring myself to deviate from my routine for fear of losing even a minute's worth of my remaining life.

I wondered how many people in my position, those granted a week to chew through items on their bucket list, would have chosen to spend their last moments doing what they had always done. Call it fear of living, maybe, since I hadn't really focused on adventure back when I thought I had all the time in the world. Or maybe I was simply clinging to the structure that made me feel safe.

Wearing my apron like a crown of thorns, I cooked burgers and fries, bacon, steak, and eggs, and convinced myself that Wednesday would never arrive.

Then, God damn it, Wednesday came.

I got to the diner at my usual 6:00 am, and Cliff was waiting by the door.

I smiled, before *and* after I looked him up and down. "Morning, counsellor."

"How are you?"

"Alive. You?"

"Same." He smiled back at me, like he knew what gutter my mind had been lying in. Or maybe he had followed my gaze and figured he was about to get lucky.

I shivered.

In anticipation.

Doing the math in my head, I figured I could spare a good fifteen minutes with him in the back office and still have the grill fired up for my early regulars.

He grabbed a menu and chose his usual booth near the door. As I headed to the back to wake the kitchen, I yelled over my shoulder, "Be right with you."

"Take your time."

I haven't much left. I turned back to look at him, truly *notice* him. He was much more handsome now than he had been as a teenager, especially since he grew a beard. More distinguished, as though being a professional had made him a better person. Maybe it had. How did I miss it? Where had I been?

I winked and wiggled my hips a little, then sauntered through the swinging door, hoping Cliff might get the hint.

With one hand reaching for my apron, I caught sight of Death, sitting on my prep counter.

My heart skipped. I grabbed at my chest.

"You don't have time for Cliff." He paused, and added, "Or to take his order."

"I thought I had until eleven?"

Death reached into his trench coat and pulled out a small, black, leather-bound notebook. After flipping to the spot where the cloth marker held the page, he simply said, "No."

I sagged onto the stool I kept near the kitchen phone. "One last fling?"

"No."

"Not even a kiss? A good, solid kiss can be even better than the actual carnal act?"

He ran his long, cold fingers down the open page in his notebook and shook his head.

Wondering what kinds of notes Death kept, I leaned in closer to have a look. My eyes began to water, as though they knew better than to allow me the chance to screw this pooch, or Cliff for that matter.

"Cliff!" I shouted through the order window. "I need you in the kitchen."

Without reacting to my cry for help, and without so much as a glance in my direction, Death opened the big walk-in fridge and stepped inside.

"Just a sec, Lizzie." Cliff called from the diner, sounding like a cross between confused and worried.

Death exited the fridge, carrying a full flat of eggs.

"Someone's hungry," I muttered under my breath.

The big guy held the flat with his left hand, balancing it like a pro, and with his right, he tipped his fedora at me. Then he dropped the eggs. All thirty of them splattered all over my floor. Everyone who's worked in a kitchen despises that sound.

Cliff's footsteps echoed on the tile. He was about to walk through the swinging door and flash me his handsome smile. All I wanted was to tell Death to come back tomorrow, or even in an hour, and give me one last chance to live instead of merely existing.

I didn't watch where I was stepping.

My shoe found the eggs and I flew through the air. My head hit the corner of the prep counter with a sickening crack-thud.

I closed my eyes tight against the pain because we all know that stuff hurts less when we can't see it. Funny thing about pain. Just when I thought it couldn't get any worse, that I couldn't take any more, that I was going to black out and it might be like falling asleep, and maybe I could see my mother again, and she would hug me, and I wouldn't even mention that time she borrowed my car and brought it back with a scratch on the driver's door, the pain intensified.

"Oh my God, Lizzie!"

Cliff was close. He sounded like he was in his own kind of despair. I wanted to look up to see if he was standing over me, staring with longing as though he was anticipating a morning romp, too, but I couldn't open my eyes.

He shouted into a phone. Ordered paramedics.

My eyes still wouldn't open. My skull felt as though it was on fire. I was in a kitchen, so maybe fire was involved.

Cliff's lips found mine. I tried to kiss him back, savor the moment, but he was pressing down, pushing air into me. Into my lungs.

No! I thought. *We're supposed to kiss.*

Then the smell blindsided me.

Not attics and lanolin, not motor oil and old tires. This time, Death stunk of the job, of sewage, rot, and decomposing bodies. He must have been right next to Cliff, trying to figure out whether or not I had stopped breathing so he could get on with his work day. Judging from Cliff's continued attempts to keep me alive, I guessed the good lawyer didn't realize Death was in the room.

Or maybe he *did*.

When Cliff switched from blowing air into my lungs to pumping my chest, I used the air he'd gifted me to say, "You're ... good..."

I needed another breath, if for no other reason than to scream out in pain, but Cliff was still pumping and counting to fifteen.

"Lizzie," Death whispered in my ear, full of comfort and pleasure, "open your eyes."

###

The pain ends. Blissful, joyous, fantabulous cessation of the crushed-skull-misery. I take in a breath. It doesn't feel the same, as though my lungs aren't part of the oxygen-equation any longer. Afraid to see what has happened to me, I slowly open my eyes.

Death stands over me, holding a set of car keys. Not mine, though. This set is the old-fashioned metal kind, no beeping car alarms or plastic fobs or computer chip technology in sight.

"Where's Cliff?" I say. Looking around, I'm not in the diner. I'm lying on the pavement beside a red *1967 Mustang* convertible.

"I guess I earned a ticket on the up-elevator, huh?" I say.

"The car is merely a means of transportation."

I shake my head. "A *67 Stang* is a hell of a lot more than a means of transportation."

He jingles the keys. "You'd best get going."

"Can I choose the destination?" I ask.

"It's your funeral."

A snort escapes me, right out my nose. For a moment, I wonder if Cliff saw my ungraceful reaction. Then I remember where I am. *What* I am. And sadness fills my insides.

He places the keys in my palm. I stare at them, then up at him, and ask, "How do I find my family?"

"The rules are different here. Finding love isn't about chance or destiny. It's a journey of conscious thought, of choices and consequences."

"You're waxing philosophic again," I say.

"And you're stalling." He points at the door. "Get in."

Moving with caution, I pull myself to standing, climb into the car, and put the key in the ignition. Still unsure as to which direction to take, I turn over the engine but it doesn't catch.

Again and again, I try to start the *Mustang*, growing more frustrated by the minute, though here time doesn't seem the same. Convinced I've flooded the engine, I push the pedal all the way down, close my eyes, and remember that photograph of my grandparents by the railing.

The engine starts. I give the gas pedal a few pumps, feeling the exhilaration of the horsepower under my control. When I look up, Death is gone. I am alone, stopped in the centre of a roundabout, with dozens of exits.

I recall a moment with my mother, on a night when her warm arms wrapped around me, tucking me in. I shift the car into gear and take the first exit that tugs at my soul.

▧ ▧ ▧

Originally from Toronto, **Suzanne Church** lives in Kitchener, Ontario with her two teenage sons. She is a 2011 and 2012 Aurora Award finalist for her short fiction. Her stories have appeared in *Cicada* and *On Spec*, and in several anthologies including *Tesseracts 13* and *14*. "Death Over Easy" is a scrambled combination of her love of greasy diner breakfasts and her fond remembrance of summer excursions with her grandparents.

⸺MR. GO AWAY⸺
By Brad Carson

Deputy Brian poked his head through the pine root fence that ran opposite their Ontario tobacco farm. "Bang! Ka-pow!" he shouted, aiming his colt .45 at Nasty Ned, the no-good bank-robber.

Trooper barked a bullet in return. Deputy Brian ducked as the shot splintered wood. "Missed me, ya ornery cuss! Take that. Bang! Bang! Bang," he said fanning his finger gun.

But Nasty Ned didn't die, didn't even stop coming. He poked his big fluffy head through the fence and gave Brian a face-full of wet tongue.

"Trooper, stop that!" Brian said. "You're supposed to be Nasty Ned. How can I shoot you when you do that? Awwgh. Get back over there and play right." Brian wiped his face and re-adjusted the silver deputy badge on the pocket of his cowboy shirt. "If Grandpa was still here, he'd show you how."

He stopped, tears filled his eyes. Marshal Grandpa had left the town to his deputy.

Trooper's tongue washed the tears away. Brian hugged him and then leapt up both guns blazing. "Bang! Bang!"

Nasty Ned dropped to the ground, paws out-stretched, pink tongue dangling, then he barked twice.

"Hey! I shot you first." Brian said. "You can't shoot me when you're dead. You have to wait a count of ten then you get up. One two..."

The lop-eared Lab mostly had the hang of playing cowboys. Of course, he couldn't shoot a finger gun, because he didn't have fingers and he couldn't count to ten ... well, because he didn't have fingers, but the old dog was a lot more fun to play with than his sister who made Brian sit through boring tea parties and never really got the hang of dying.

Trooper wasn't as good at dying as Grandpa, but then Grandpa wasn't playing anymore.

▨ ▨ ▨

Brian could hardly recall a time when Grandpa didn't have a cig hanging from the corner of his mouth or the makings in his hands.

"Why you smoke?" Brian asked one day.

"Be like a beef farmer not eating meat," Grandpa said, deftly rolling the tobacco-stuffed paper with wrinkled fingers and licking it shut.

"Mom says them thing's is gonna kill you."

"She tell you that?"

"I heard it through the stove-pipe in my room."

"Well, don't go believing everything you hear through stove-pipes." They stepped inside the kiln. Grandpa buried his arm in hanging tobacco that Brian's mom and the table gang had tied to sticks so it could cure. As usual, bits of flakes rained down on Brian, but he didn't mind.

Grandpa pulled out a golden leaf. "Feel how it's dry, but still got some bounce? That means it's in case. Ready to come out tomorrow." They stepped back outside and Grandpa adjusted the temperature. "Everything's going to die sometime. This tobacco, goes into the field a seedling, grows up then we put it in the kiln. The green goes out of it and it dries up and crumbles away"

"You gonna crumble away?" Brian asked.

Grandpa laughed. "Yeah, I suppose I am." The laughter got harsher and louder and turned into a wheezing that made Grandpa's eyes red. He held his chest just like the bad guys after a shoot-out, but still fished a red and white tipped match out of his vest.

Before he could strike it, a long, skinny arm in a dusty dark sleeve snaked in with a flame flickering from a burning finger.

The tall man wasn't wearing a black hat, but Brian knew a bad guy when he saw one and blew the finger out. "Go away, Mister. Leave my Grandpa alone."

The man's face got dark red, like Brian's mom just before she yelled, and he flicked up another fire, but this one was skinny and weak. He glared at Brian as if it was his fault and burst into a raging flame that wrapped up Grandpa and the tobacco kiln behind him.

"Go away!" Brian cried and blew on the fire as hard as he could.

Flames disappeared as if they'd never been.

Grandpa stared at Brian. "You okay? You look kind of funny."

"Did you see him?"

"See who?"

"A man. With a fire hand. He burned the kiln and..." But Grandpa wasn't burned up. Neither was the kiln.

"Is this a new game?" Grandpa asked.

"I don't know," Brian said. He brushed off a bit of ash thinking that it must have fallen from Grandpa's cig, until he noticed Grandpa was still holding the un-lit match.

He grabbed the cig in his grandpa's hand. His voice broke and tears rolled down his dusty cheeks. "Don't smoke anymore, okay? Just don't."

███

That night, his mom rousted him out of bed. "Brian, get dressed! One of the kilns is burning! Hurry! A stick of leaves must have fallen on top of the burners."

But Brian knew better, just as he knew which kiln it was before he saw the clouds of black smoke writhing around the inferno.

Brian looked around for Mr. Go Away.

Kiln fires didn't happen often, but when one did, it scared everyone. Neighbors arrived from miles around to help, with their kids in tow, aiming their car headlights at the burn, although there wasn't much they could do but huddle together and watch, waiting for a fire truck from town.

His dad and Grandpa and a couple of the other men got out the tractor and chains and pulled the fuel tank away before it could explode. Tar-paper smoke circled around them, like Injuns surrounding soldiers.

Grandpa inhaled an awful lot and afterwards couldn't seem to stop coughing.

The next morning his mom drove Grandpa to the hospital.

Brian ran down the laneway chasing the car, shouting and waving.

From the rear seat, Mr. Go Away waved back.

"...eight, nine, ten!"

Bark! Bark! Bark!

Deputy Brian dodged the bullets and ran for cover. Nasty Ned followed fast. Brian turned to get off a quick shot and saw the pick-up truck barreling around the curve in the gravel road, Mr. Go Away at the wheel.

Truck met dog with a too-real crunch. Trooper yelped. Brian screamed.

Trooper lay on his side. Not moving. Not breathing. Blood trickled out of the dog's nose and mouth.

Brian hugged him. "Get up, Trooper. I didn't even shoot you!" Tears blinded him, but he knew whose shadow stood over him.

Mr. Go Away reached for Trooper.

Just like he'd reached for Grandpa. "Go away!" Brian shouted. The next minute Mr. Go Away was further down the road.

"Get up, boy!" Brian pleaded.

A sharp whistle sliced the air.

And Trooper stood up.

Or at least *a* Trooper did. He took a few steps away, then a few back. He looked at Brian. The whistle sounded again, harsher. Trooper whimpered and ran toward Mr. Go Away.

"Trooper! Don't leave me!" Brian looked down at his dead dog. It wasn't right, wasn't fair. Grandpa, Trooper. No!

He pressed his face against Trooper's ear and with all the belief he could muster he whispered, "Ten."

Trooper's ear flicked, his legs kicked.

"Ten!" Brian shouted. "Ten! Ten! Ten!" The old dog licked Brian's laughing face, his tail thumping the ground.

Mr. Go Away roared over top of them, tall as a tree. His mouth opened wider than an empty barn and a huge sucking wind tried to rip Trooper out of Brian's arms.

"You, go away!" Brian shouted. He dug his fingers into the soft fur and held on as tight as he could, but felt Trooper slipping away from him.

"Need a hand, Deputy?" and Grandpa was there, a big, bright golden star, blazing on his chest. "I'll take care of Nasty Ned," he said, "You get that cayoot."

Deputy Brian stood up; his hands hovered above his guns.

A snaky arm snapped towards him, but he drew his pearl handled Colts like greased lightning and fired, screaming louder than the roaring wind, "Go away!"

Something streamed from deep inside and a bullet forged in the real world of play traced a shining path straight into the monster's howling mouth.

A bright light flashed. Mr. Go Away exploded.

Darkness thundered over Brian, knocking him down.

※ ※ ※

He awoke to a big wet tongue.

"I got him, Grandpa!" he jumped up shouting, "I got him!"

But there was no Grandpa. No Nasty Ned.

Only his dog Trooper, tongue lolling, tail thumping, drooling Trooper.

He looked down at his guns, and saw they were really only fingers, and his silver badge, well, that was just a piece of cardboard his mom had cut out and wrapped in foil.

But his cowboy shirt hung in tatters and he could feel a burn on his skin.

He knew he would never see Mr. Go Away again. And in a kind of grown up way which he hadn't felt before, he knew he would never, ever defeat him again.

He whistled for his dog and they went home.

※ ※ ※

Born and raised on a tobacco farm, (where he played cowboys), **Brad Carson** learned the craft of writing dialogue and the value of strong coffee while working in theatre. A 2009 finalist for an Aurora Award, he has sat beneath hundred year old oaks in Wistman's Woods in Dartmoor, and wandered Druid paths in Snowdonia. He currently resides with his writing partner Arlene Stinchcombe in Norfolk County where they listen to the trees whisper stories. One night while contemplating childhood loss, the veil shimmered; "Mr. Go Away" appeared and wouldn't go away until the tale was told.

—A SONG FOR DEATH—

By Angela Roberts

The song filled her like it always did when she sang for the dying, the notes infusing her skin with the tingle of their vibration. She closed her eyes and was no longer in the crowded hospital tent. She was bathed in the sunlight of the feast day when she first heard this song. The thin shaking hand that clutched at hers now became a strong firm hand, wanting to join her in the dance circle. The moans and soft sobbing turned into laughter. And through it all, the song poured from her throat, a song that spoke of happier times, before the *gripe pneumónica*, before the Great War.

The last of the woman's strength left her and she released Ana's hand. Ana opened her eyes and the dream was gone. She felt a pang of disappointment at viewing her stark surroundings. The dirty white canvas hospital tents were a blight on the venerable whitewashed walls and clay-slatted roofs of Leiria.

It seemed as if the whole of Portugal had come to this small rural town because they'd heard that there was a doctor. Young men in short coats and fishermen's breeches lay on military-style cots next to young women in wide dark skirts and white blouses, paisley kerchiefs binding their hair. Her husband had said that The Spanish Lady had come to Portugal. He had seen that term for the *gripe pneumónica* in the letters that continued to come to him from his British medical colleagues. It was an expression so bizarre to Ana that she had laughed when he tried to explain it in Portuguese.

The patients who came did not know that the doctor was dead. That he had departed only a few months before when the world-spanning epidemic returned in force. She had many of his letters to answer, when she could bring herself to do so.

She felt for the young woman's pulse as Ana's husband had taught her to do in those carefree days when it had been a lark, a love game between the two of them, feeling each other's heartbeats. That had been before he died coughing in her arms. Before he'd returned with the remnants of the Expeditionary Corps a haunted man who cried out in his dreams.

The woman was dead, a peaceful smile curling the corners of her lips. Ana had not even known her name.

"You should not sing with your mask off, Mistress Ana," said a soft stern voice above her.

Ana shrugged and pulled the sheet over the woman's face. She could at least say she had brought some comfort to her at the end.

A distant sound of mourning reached Ana's ears and she lifted the tent flap to see what the commotion was. A funeral cortege was passing, a small entourage escorting a plain wooden box on its way to the cemetery. Three women draped in black wailed and beat their chests. Most bystanders barely looked up as the group went through the square. Funerals had become so commonplace that the busiest men in town were the gravediggers and the priest. There were so few people not sick that the old and young had been forced to go out into the fields just to ensure the town had food.

"Some are calling you the angel of death," said the voice again.

Ana turned sharply to face the source of that voice. Sister Maria Graciete clasped her hands in front of her black-robed stomach, a white mask covering the lower half of her face so that, with her wimple, all one could see of her head were her eyes and the bridge of her nose. Even toiling eighteen hours a day in this tent could not prevent the nun from maintaining her impeccable composure.

"I tell them that is blasphemy, of course," the Sister continued.

"I do not care what they call me," said Ana. Blasphemy. *Do we not live in blasphemous times*, she could almost hear her husband say. *What kind of God would condone such death? Would take the young and strong, the pregnant?* Her beloved Ricardo had been a socialist, and when he spoke in that passionate voice of his, she supposed that she was too. Ana had not been educated enough to read his thick books, had never learned English and German as he had, but when he spoke of Marx and Lenin and Trotsky, it had all seemed right to her. She had shared his joy when he wrote to her from the trenches about the Bolshevik revolution, so far away yet seeming so close when he wrote of it, even if she had not understood all of its implications. It all seemed hollow now.

Ana reached up to replace her face mask and a cough erupted from her chest. Pain stung her lungs and throat. The back of her throat itched madly and she coughed again. And again, doubling over, her face swelling with the force of her coughs. She was dimly aware of Sister Maria thrusting a cup of water into her hands and lifting her hands to her lips.

The water drowned the cough. Ana straightened, her lungs still reflexively heaving, her face hot and red. She waved away Sister Maria's hovering concern, and replaced her mask.

"*Ay Jesus!*" Ana, surprised by the profanity escaping the prim nun's lips, looked down at the white mask.

The mask was spotted with bright red blood.

■ ■ ■

The cobblestone streets of the town were terribly silent at night. All public gatherings were forbidden because of the *gripe pneumónica*. The cafés were dark, the community hall shut and silent, the church closed off with a thick chain around the great brass door handles. Here and there a light shone in a window, but no voices broke the silence as Ana made her way towards the fountain in the town square.

The gas lamps lit the street in isolated circles of light only a few feet across. Between them lay pitch darkness. Ana hurried through the dark patches, feeling her way along the rough pockmarked walls. Every time she stepped through the boundary between light and dark, she felt that she was being watched.

She reached the town square and its fountain, the trickling of water into its basin the only sound. This was the best-lit place in the entire town, but to Ana's eyes, the light seemed to make more substantial shadows on the structures. She tread lightly on the cobblestones, uncomfortably aware of every footfall.

The fountain was older than the great stone church behind it. A statue of a woman elegantly poured water from a jug into the basin, a lamb reclining at her feet. The fine details of her face and dress had worn away with time, but one could still make out the serene curve of her lips as she gazed down into the water. Townsfolk had ringed the Lady with tiny lit candles and offerings of flowers, bread and fruit. The fountain had long ago been dedicated to the Virgin, but Ricardo had told her once that it belonged to a goddess much older and more powerful.

It mattered not who was listening, as long as someone was. Ana knelt at the edge of the basin and clasped her hands, resting her elbows on the stone edge. She still clutched the blood-stained mask in her fingers, the red livid against the white. She closed her eyes and tried to think of what to say. It had been so long since she'd prayed, not since before she was married, when her grandmother, iron-gray hair bound in a long braid, had insisted that her son's grown daughter join her in evening prayers. Ana remembered that braid and steel black-clad back more than she did the words she'd mumbled.

But she had come here for prayer. The words of the Hail Mary prayer surfaced in her memory, and she spoke them aloud, the proper phrasing hesitant at first then more confident as she remembered. Then she reached the last words, and was suddenly angry. "Sinners?" she exclaimed. "Do we not suffer enough? Is there not enough death? Enough sickness? Enough pain?"

The statue gazed down dispassionately at her. Ana grimaced and threw one of the candles into the water. It was unfair. Unfair that her Ricardo had died so soon after surviving the war. Unfair that the young and strong were being struck down in their prime. Unfair that she was powerless to help any of them. Unfair that she'd been left behind.

The dulcet notes of a guitar cut through the silence. Ana froze. Who would be playing a guitar at this time of night? The music was soft and mournful, a *Fado* song she recognized about a woman waiting for her fisherman husband lost at sea. Perplexed, she turned to look behind her.

A tall, slender man perched on the back of a stone bench, a guitar on his knee. He was dressed entirely in black from head to toe in a long-sleeved shirt and narrow trousers that only accentuated his thinness. A round wide-brimmed black hat hid his face from her view as he bent over his guitar. His feet were bare. But it was the entire image of him that drew her attention, as if the barefooted guitarist was a façade. She could not shake the impression that she could see something else beneath the man's skin, like the bones of a skeleton inside the flesh of his bare feet and hands.

He noticed her staring at him, and lifted his head to stare right back at her. His face was so gaunt that she could make out, even from relatively far away, the shape of his cheekbones and jaw. His eyes were dark, almost black, and they pierced her chest like daggers to the soul. He smiled and it was a ghastly smile, like the grin of a skull.

"Come closer, Ana," he said, his voice a whisper yet she heard it as clearly as if he had shouted.

Ana approached the strange figure, her feet seeming to move of their own accord. "How do you know my name?"

"I know everyone's names." He strummed absently on the guitar's strings as she tried to puzzle out his answer. Who was this man?

"I have a proposition for you, little Ana, little Angel of Death."

Ana frowned. "I don't understand."

His thin digits tickled the guitar's strings, not really playing, just pretending. "I heard you. All of it. You think death is unfair, yes? You feel powerless?"

Her flash of anger dissolved into confusion.

"What if I gave you a choice, then? I can be very fair when I wish. Would you make a choice?"

"Who are you?" Ana breathed.

His grin grew wider. "You know who I am."

A chill ran up her spine. That face. It was not just thin, it was fleshless. It was a skull. Those eyes, they were not just dark, they were pitch black holes, bright red pinpricks of light in their centers.

She turned to flee, but his hand shot out and grasped her wrist. "Do not prove yourself a coward, Ana. We both know you are not one. Look at me."

Ana turned, his words stinging her. "What choice?"

"Good." He released her. "I give you a choice, pretty Angel of Death. I will give you the lives of these people if you will sacrifice your own."

It took her a moment to find her voice. "And the town? The patients?"

The guitarist shrugged. "They will succumb as they would naturally."

"What is the choice? I am already sick."

"Yes, but the time of your death is in my power. Choose now, and I will spare your patients. They will live to a ripe old age. Choose life for yourself, and you will live to see grandchildren."

Ana crushed the blood-stained mask in her fist. What kind of choice was that? Herself or others? She knew what her Ricardo would have said.

She looked up, her jaw set. "If you know me, you know my answer."

He pressed one bony finger to his chin. "Yes?"

"Take me. Spare the others."

He regarded her a moment more, then nodded. "Very well. A bargain is struck."

He vanished. Ana looked all around her, but she could not see any trace of him. Then his voice reached her ears on the breeze.

"Prepare yourself. In one month's time, I will return for your life."

■ ■ ■

The next morning, Ana woke feeling no different than before. She spent the day at the hospital as usual, ministering to the sick and dying. She was a little dismayed at first when no change seemed evident in the patients' symptoms.

By midday, she was convinced that the entire encounter had been a dream.

Time passed quickly. Ana became absorbed in her work. It seemed that the stream of patients was never-ending. The government could not keep up with the people's needs. The President was murdered, news that seemed to come like a distant cry, removed as they were from the capital. To Ana, this was important only in how it affected her daily life. There were never enough clean bandages, never enough medicine, never enough pure water and nutritious food.

The moon waxed and waned and one night, not long before the end of the month, Ana chose to walk home from the hospital. It was not completely dark yet, the sky awash in the purples and oranges of twilight. She had been getting steadily sicker over the past week, but she felt a sudden refreshment that evening, like that burst of wellness one sometimes feels before dying. She refused to stay at the hospital, and no one tried very hard to stop her. There was no room. The patients seemed to live in a sort of limbo, neither improving nor worsening, merely waiting.

She had not gone far before a familiar figure stopped her short. He stood in the light of a gas-lamp, the wide brim of his hat casting a shadow over his face. A guitar hung lazily from his thin fingers as he leaned his black-clad frame against the lamp post.

He lifted his head and those glinting eyes bore into her. "Are you ready?" he asked quite softly.

All Ana had comfortably forgotten rushed back to her. Then her body took over where her mind was paralyzed and she turned and ran.

She did not even know where she was going. Her body and mind screamed only to be away, and so she ran. She could feel and hear her blood pumping in her ears and the steady rhythm of her feet on the cobblestones. The rest was a blur.

She suddenly found herself in the town square. Ana stumbled across the cobbles to the fountain, the adrenaline draining away and pain like a knife exploding in her chest. She coughed and wheezed, the weakness in her lungs catching up to her.

"You know you cannot run from me, Ana," said that same awful voice.

Her eyes opened wide as she saw him perched on the back of a stone bench like a vulture surveying a fresh kill. She coughed again, her throat burning too much to speak.

"Please..." was all she could manage.

"No, my dear little Angel, no. We made a deal, you and I." He hopped off the bench and walked up to her. His shoulders hunched for an instant under the gaze of the fountain's statue, but as quickly as the discomfort manifested, it was gone, and he gazed down at Ana, a slight smirk twisting his bloodless lips. "But I can be merciful."

He lifted her chin with one bony cold fingertip. "I give you this. In three days' time, I will come for you at nightfall. Do not hide. Do not run. Be ready."

And then he was gone.

███

Ana knew when Sister Maria Graciete looked up at her that the nun did not believe her story. Her expression was one of concerned disbelief, the corners of her mouth down-turned in worry and one eyebrow crooked in skepticism. Ana felt foolish when the Sister looked at her like that. Foolish for having come to the convent in disarray, for insisting to the doorkeeper that she be allowed to see the Sister, for blurting out the tale of bargaining with Death — for that was who she believed the skeletal singer must be — and for thinking that anyone could help her.

Sister Maria Graciete put down her tea cup and folded her hands in her lap. "Ana," she began, and Ana could see she was choosing her words carefully as if speaking to a frightened child, "you must not give in to superstition. Death does not visit us in the form of a man. Death is a state of being, not a person."

Ana wrung her hands, the chill of the man's presence still in the stiffness of her shoulders. "I *saw* him, Sister."

The nun laid a hand on her shoulder that was probably meant to be comforting. "I fear that the stress of your work at the hospital and…" she faltered at the mention of Ana's illness and it hung unspoken between them for a heavy moment. "You must rest, Ana. That is what you need. These are just the fancies of an overwrought mind."

"I am not mad!"

"I never said that."

"But you think it. I tell you, it happened!"

"Of course it happened, child," said a gravelly voice from the doorway. They looked up to see an ancient nun standing in the entrance to Sister Maria Graciete's room, her hands folded in front of her black gown.

"Lourdes—"

"Quiet!" the nun dismissed Sister Maria with a wave. "You young nuns, you think you know everything."

She bent down and eyed Ana. "Death will get what he wants, child. You must never bargain with him."

"What do I do?" asked Ana.

Sister Lourdes straightened. "Seek guidance from God."

"How?"

Sister Lourdes nodded as if she understood Ana's frustration. "There are three children in Fatima who have been visited by Our Lady. You can go speak to them; perhaps they can ask the Virgin to intercede."

Sister Maria Graciete frowned at Sister Lourdes. It seemed to Ana that the woman's expression throughout had been a perpetual frown, but every new word out of Sister Lourdes' mouth produced a nuance to her turned down lips. This time, it was exasperation that Ana saw. "Sister…"

The look that Sister Lourdes gave her fellow nun silenced anything she would have said. "I went with the bishop's delegation last year to see the miraculous children. Their vision was real."

Sister Maria Graciete nodded, chastened. Ana did not know what to think of Sister Lourdes' suggestion. Children in Fatima seeing the Virgin Mary? She recalled something about it. The news had caused a sensation throughout the country, even in the middle of the war. Ana had paid little attention to it at the time, preoccupied as she was by her husband's welfare at the front.

Sister Lourdes wrapped one thick arm around Ana's shoulders and drew her up and out of Sister Maria's cell. "Come. Let me write you a letter of introduction to the parish priest."

🖾 🖾 🖾

The ride by cart to Fatima took a good portion of the morning. Ana was not sure what she had expected to see when she arrived at the village. It was no more than a collection of cottages in hill country. Flocks of sheep and goats roamed the fields. But, as she approached the small stone chapel, she saw that the dirt roads were crowded by pilgrims kneeling in the dust.

The parish priest, a short, balding and pleasant Jesuit, received Ana warmly and read over the letter from Sister Lourdes. He sighed as he refolded the letter. While they walked, he said, "Sister Lourdes speaks for you, so I will take you to see the children. But I must warn you, the *gripe* has hit us hard of late."

Ana nodded. "I understand."

"Yes." He folded and refolded the letter until it was a quarter of its original size. "I am afraid little Jacinta and Francisco have fallen ill. Please do not take too much of their time."

"I ... Of course."

He showed her into a simple cottage. There were only two rooms that she could see — the kitchen with its wood stove, and a bedroom near the back. In the bedroom lay a boy and a girl no more than ten years old, and an older girl sat on a chair next to them crocheting. It was the older girl who spoke as they entered.

"Can I help you, Father?"

"Yes, Lucia. This is Ana. She has come to speak with you," replied the priest.

Before the girl could respond, the other girl opened her eyes and spoke. "Thank you, Father."

The priest nodded and left, a final warning look in his eyes as he passed Ana. She stared at the bedridden child, who must be Jacinta, and marveled at the maturity in her expression. Her brother lay dozing beside her.

Lucia gestured to another wooden chair next to the bed and Ana sat down. She struggled, now that she was here, to find a way to express her predicament that did not sound crazy. Sitting here, before these children, she felt foolish for even coming. And yet, there was a peace that surrounded the girls that seemed to contradict their youth.

In the end, it was Jacinta who spoke first. "You have come for help?"

Ana nodded.

"Help only our Lady can provide," chimed in Lucia.

Ana nodded again.

Then Jacinta coughed. It was a rough wet cough. Ana noted the redness of her eyes, the sallow look to her cheeks. The sleeping boy, Francisco, winced in pain in his sleep. These children, these little saints, looked like many of her patients. They had the *gripe pneumónica*.

Ana stood up. She could not stay. "I'm sorry. You cannot help me. No one can help me," she said as she stumbled out of the room. They were dying, she could see. If even these children, favored of the Virgin, were doomed, what was there for her?

No one followed Ana as she ran from the cottage all the way down to the village crossroads.

◙ ◙ ◙

It was a long while before Ana could get to sleep that night. She could not stop turning over and over what she had seen and heard, thoughts she was ashamed to have. She should have welcomed death. Had she not pined all this time for her Ricardo? Had she not walked as if in a fog, barely alive except for when she sang for the dying?

And yet a cold dread gripped her at the thought of fulfilling her bargain with Death. Perhaps it was because she was still amazed. Death, in the form of a man, had spoken to her, had singled her out.

When she finally did sleep, Ana dreamed deeply. She became conscious suddenly of standing in a vast field of waving grain. The sky above was a rich orange from the splendor of the setting sun. She ran a hand through the stalks of grain and marveled at the tingle in her fingertips.

"Ana." A voice, a familiar voice, called her name, once, twice, three times. It was behind her, around her, but she could not see the source. She felt no fear. The voice soothed her anxiety.

"Ana." She knew that voice. She was sure of it. It was a feminine voice, and seemed to combine all of the comforting female voices she had ever known: her mother, her grandmothers, her elder sister who had died of typhoid when she was quite young, even Sister Maria Graciete.

Ana was aware, even in her dream state, that if she tried to look, the apparition would disappear. She stayed as still as one could be in a dream, her fingers extended into the grain.

"Dearest Ana." The voice was a whisper next to her ear. "Do not despair. It is not your time."

Ana swallowed and hazarded a sideways glance. She could see a delicate hand and white-sleeved arm resting on her shoulder.

"I made a bargain. What can I do?"

"The only way you can break a bargain with Death is to move him to tears."

"But how?"

"You will know when the time comes." The hand released her. "I am always with you."

❧ ❧ ❧

Ana waited nervously in the square as night fell. She had brought her own offering to the Lady's statue, some freshly baked bread and a small lit candle. She had gone over her plan in her head. The most tragic song she could sing was a *Fado* song her mother had loved. She had wept every time Ana sang it.

It was not long after the moon rose that she felt a chill in the air. She looked up from contemplating the candle she'd laid at the fountain statue's feet. He was there, emerging from the shadows, clad in black and still lazily pulling a guitar behind him. Ana steeled herself as he approached. She could not show her fear. Not now.

There was a sort of expectant excitement in the way he stepped forward. "It is time," he said as he held out a long-fingered hand.

She shrank back as much as she could. "Wait! I have a new bargain for you. Will you hear it?"

He seemed to consider briefly. Then he shook his head. "No. I like the one we have made."

Ana reached out to grab his arm then stopped short of his sleeve, suddenly realizing what she was about to do. Her hand hovered between them. "Please, hear me. If you do not like it, refuse."

"Very well."

"I..." She willed herself to not stumble on her words. "I propose this. If I can move you to tears, you release me from my promise. And you leave me and this village alone."

"And how will you move *me* to tears?"

She straightened her back. Under his gaze, she had found herself instinctively cringing. "I will sing."

He laughed, a sound like cracking ice. "No."

"What is it? Afraid I will win?"

Death had been about to reach out to her again but stopped. "I am never afraid. Very well. If this is how you wish to spend your last moments, so be it."

Ana slumped in relief.

He went and sat on a nearby bench, crossing his arms over one bony knee. "But, if you fail, I take you *and* your village. Do you understand?"

His words hit her like a blow to the chest. What had she done? What had she been thinking?

Ana nodded hastily. She could not back down now. But for a brief moment, as he gestured for her to begin, she was not sure what to do next. She feared for a second that she would not be *able* to sing, but opened her mouth and breathed in.

The notes filled her and poured out of her as they always had, and she lost herself in the song. It was a tale of a woman, young like herself, whose husband was gone to war and had not returned. In the song, the woman waited and waited at the seaside, refusing to believe her husband was dead and would never return to her embrace. Ana felt the ocean wind beating at her tear-stained cheeks, felt the pang of loss in her chest resonate with her own, and her voice grew thick and rich with it.

After the first verse, she suddenly heard the strains of Death's guitar accompanying her. She opened her eyes and saw him bent over the guitar, his hat obscuring his face.

And then all around her, she had the sensation of no longer being alone. She sang and sang, the woman's plight becoming even more desperate, and around her, ghostly figures began to appear. Souls, attracted by her voice and Death's guitar. She recognized many of them; her mother, her sister. Men and women who had died in the hospital tent, people she had cared for until their demise. The young woman she'd sung to; the one whose name she had not known.

And Ricardo. Her beloved Ricardo, gazing at her with that proud smile she'd seen on their wedding day. She almost faltered when she saw him, but he nodded as their eyes met, and she knew. She knew that it was not her time.

Finally, there was no more song to sing, and she wept as the woman threw herself into the sea. Wept because she knew that was an unfair ending to the woman's tragic story.

Death stopped playing, and the souls of the dead dissipated into the mist. Ricardo was last, and he waved to Ana as he left, and Ana knew it was not a farewell forever. She would see him again. But not now.

Ana strode up to the bench where Death sat, hunched over his guitar.

Death lifted his head. A single translucent tear fell down his bony cheek and hung off his chin. A wave of relief passed through her as she reached out and caught it in her palm. It was colder than anything she had ever felt, so cold it burned. She nearly dropped it, but instead closed her fist around the droplet and said, "You have wept."

He was silent for a long moment then he rose from the bench, shaking out his lanky frame. "So I have. Very well, you have won our bargain, little Angel. You and your people will escape me."

Just before Death vanished, he added, "For now."

■ ■ ■

Angela Roberts has been writing stories ever since she learned to write, and her second grade teacher published her for the first time in her school's literary journal. By day, she edits video game texts; by night, she edits and writes for *The Gloaming Magazine*, an online SF magazine. She drew upon historical accounts of the Spanish Influenza pandemic and elements of her own Portuguese-Canadian heritage to weave together this story of a bargain with Death.

~THERAPY~

By Bev Vincent

Lying on a couch in this brightly appointed room, he feels safe. Here he can share the dark thoughts that plague him day and night. The therapist seems to understand. At least she makes sounds of encouragement in all the right places.

"I think we've talked enough about your work for now," the woman says. "We'll come back to it later. Let's focus more on you."

"There's not a lot to say."

"What's your earliest memory?"

"My mother. Father was very protective. We were kept on a short tether, never out of our mother's sight. She saw how we were being smothered."

"Sounds like she loved you very much."

"She was the one who set me free."

Her pencil tip scratches the surface of a yellow legal pad. The comforting sound makes him feel like she is paying attention. Taking him seriously. Previous therapists didn't take notes, merely recorded their conversations. He likes this better.

"You seem reluctant to discuss your father."

"I told you about the accident."

"Yes."

"What more would you have me say?"

"What's the first thing that comes to mind?"

"Blood."

"Yes."

"Blood everywhere. I didn't mean it."

"No."

"My mother gave me the blade as a present."

"She knew how you would use it."

Adrenaline courses through his veins. "You think so?" This idea never occurred to him before.

"Why else would she give it to you?"

"It was a gift."

"Yes."

"And you think...?"

"She set you free. What do you mean by that?"

He stops to think. He has uttered the phrase so often it's become ingrained in his nature. His mother was the one who set him free. "She gave me the blade."

"The one involved in the accident."

"Yes."

"The accident that killed your father."

"Yes."

"And after that you were free."

He sighs. The memory is unpleasant, even though it was forever ago. "Yes."

"Let's skip ahead. You were married."

"Yes."

"Had children."

"Yes."

"Tell me what happened to them."

"You know what happened."

"Tell me again. As if you've never told anyone before."

He points to the hourglass on the table near the couch, marking out the span of their time together. Grain by grain, the upper chamber empties of sand. When the last grain drops, it will be time to leave. "Nothing lasts forever. That's what the hourglass tells us. Time devours everything."

"It devoured your children."

"They died, yes."

"You were protective of them?"

"Like my father, I guess. I was afraid for them."

"For them ... or of them?"

"What does that mean?"

"Did you never worry that one of them might do to you—?"

He cuts her off. "That's crazy. What happened to my father was an accident."

"You didn't look at them and think, 'Blood everywhere'?"

"Never."

"Never?"

A deafening silence permeates the room. He imagines that he can hear each grain of sand sliding against the tapered glass as it falls to join those that have gone before.

"But they all died," the therapist says. Her voice is soft and tender. She understands him. He nods and knows it's enough. Knows that she is watching him and that she registers the gesture. "And your wife?"

"Her time came as well. Too early, our friends said over and over again. Struck down so young."

"Losing the children — that must have been devastating. For both of you."

He nods again. Some things are too difficult to put into words, even a simple confirmation of the pain they endured. He looks at the hourglass once more. Only a few minutes remain in their session. "What does it all mean, anyway?"

"What?"

"This life. This existence. People are born, grow old and die. Some watch their parents pass on before them. Others watch their children perish."

"Some see both."

"Yes."

"Must it have a meaning?"

He considers the question, but can't come up with a satisfactory answer. "If not, why must I do what I do?"

"It's part of the natural order."

"You're taking this very well. The last therapist I visited couldn't handle it. My history—"

"It's a tragic tale."

"It's my life."

"A life full of loss."

Suddenly he feels embarrassed. Self-indulgent. He's not the only one who has suffered great loss. "Your parents passed away recently."

Her voice hitches as she breathes in sharply. He can tell she wasn't expecting this. "First my father, last year. Then my mother, four months later. Once he was gone, she gave up. She didn't want to continue without him."

"I see that a lot."

"I was angry with her."

"Because you weren't important enough for her to want to go on living."

"Yes."

Fewer than a hundred grains of sand remain in the upper chamber. They always seem to drop faster when there are less of them.

"Our time is almost up," he says. The tables have turned between them. It's time to go back to work. Time — it's always about time.

"Yes."

He reaches down for his scythe, which has been resting on the floor beside the couch. Its blade is stained, first with the blood of his father and then with that of the billions of others who have followed.

"Are you ready? It will be quick. I promise."

"Yes."

He rises with the scythe in his right hand. With his left he picks up the hourglass. Together they watch the final three grains of sand tumble through the narrow channel to the lower chamber, almost in slow motion.

He closes the door gently behind him on the way out. When he looks at the blade, he imagines it is his father's blood he sees there.

❖ ❖ ❖

Bev Vincent is the author of the *Stephen King Illustrated Companion*, which was nominated for both the Bram Stoker Award and the Edgar Award, and *The Road to the Dark Tower*, nominated for a Stoker. He is a contributing editor with *Cemetery Dance* magazine and is the author of over sixty short stories, including appearances in *Tesseracts Thirteen*, *Evolve* and *Evolve 2*, *Ellery Queen's Mystery Magazine* and *The Blue Religion*. "Therapy" won the 2006 *Wee Small Hours flash fiction contest* at Hellnotes. com that invited writers to design a short tale that explains what makes the Grim Reaper so grim. The story appeared in electronic form on the *Hellnotes* website for two weeks. This is its first print version.

—ME AND LOU HANG OUT—
By Tom Piccirilli

I turn as a punk in a ski mask holding a .32 emerges from behind a '73 Chevelle. It's a nice car, almost fully restored, and I'm jealous as hell. I'm driving a Saturn with two hundred thousand miles on it and a transmission that coughs as loudly as my old man did before he died of lung cancer. I let out a ten thousand year old sigh.

I've got a mortgage company breathing hot murder down my neck, I've got my mother in a nursing home dying of Alzheimer's. When I visit, my ma looks at me and says, "Lou, my feet are cold, turn up the heat." Who's Lou? She doesn't know any Lou, she's never known any Lou. And worse, she's lost everything under both knees to diabetes. My ma, she doesn't even have feet to be cold. Somehow, that almost gets me laughing because if I don't laugh I'm going to bawl in front of her, and what man can stand to cry in front of his mother? Lou, whoever you are, turn up the heat.

I've got a third marriage on the skids and two daughters who never come around anymore. Sometimes I can barely remember their faces. I look through old photo albums and everyone seems to be a stranger. I occasionally recognize myself. Seeing myself always startles me and comes as a shock, like spotting someone who shouldn't be there.

"Hand over your wallet!" the mutt shouts. The .32 shakes in his hand.

I do it without hesitation, practically laughing in the kid's face. You can't even go to the mall without getting mugged anymore.

The mall, half the stores are shut. I need new underwear. I can't find a store that sells men's underwear. All of them, closed up. My wife, she's gonna be pissed. She washes my briefs and complains that they're falling apart. They are, but what am I gonna do?

I can see through his cotton wool eye-holes that he's got sweat in his eyelashes, hanging there like tears. I've got eighteen bucks in cash and three credit cards maxed out to over twenty grand. I'll never pay them off. I carry Visa around like ninety pounds of bricks on my back. I expect him to break his arm trying to lift my wallet. He can maybe get himself a hamburger with all I've got on me, so long as he screws the waitress on the tip.

He should only know how much worse it's going to get for him, the prick. He thinks he's driven to desperate measures now? Because he's got college loans to pay back, because he needs another hit of meth. Wait until the gray starts up in his beard, his hair bailing out like passengers on a sinking ocean liner. Shit, wait until he loses the job at the factory he's worked at for twenty-two years, and the bank loans go bad, the roof leaks, your dogs die. The angina claws at your chest, the knees buckle. The flagpole never flies past half-mast. Wait until you turn around to talk to your friends and realize you don't have any, you're on the long walk all on your own. They're dead or have moved out of state or were never there to begin with. You can name them all on your left hand but it would take you six weeks to list all your enemies. Toss a rock and you'll hit six people who hate you.

"The rest of it!" the punk screams. And it is a scream, a girlish shriek. He's already feeling the weight of what's going to happen to him next in the world. He understands what's coming. It would make anybody scream if they could see it beforehand. His lips are skinned back. Tip of his tongue darting.

I shrug and grimace at him. What rest? Like I'm hiding Krugerrands in my shoe.

I clean the change out of my back pockets. I toss it at his feet. Thirty-seven cents. No, thirty-eight. Live large, mutt. Live like it's your last day, your very last hour. Because twenty-five years from now you'll be wandering the streets at two in the morning.

And you know what you'll do? You hit the strip clubs hoping for some kind of relief, but the tight poopers and upturned tits only make it worse. You roll over to get some action from your wife and she huffs air like a broken carburetor.

Maybe the hardest thing to get used to is that your father never leaves you. He's been dead for twenty years but he's still there, in your head, listening in on every word you utter, watching every play you make. He comments and critiques. He wises off and gives you big shrugs. He shakes his head in disappointment, punches you on the shoulder. He's here now, telling me everything I've done wrong, everything I'm doing wrong, everything he thinks is going to go wrong in the next few seconds.

He says, "You're about to be shot in the head."

"I know," I tell him.

"It's a damn shame what the world has come to."

"Christ, isn't that the truth, dad."

"I'm not your father."

And he's right, it's not my old man at all. "Well, who the hell are you?"

"I'm Lou."

The kid says, "You rotten bastard!"

I take a step towards him. Maybe it's to give him a smack upside his head. Maybe to give him a hug. Maybe to grab my thirty-eight cents back. No one should steal a man's last thirty-eight cents, no matter how rough you've got it.

Then the mutt shoots me in the head.

Then there's nothing but a vicious sting on the far side of my skull. It's electrical, all my nerve-endings firing at once, everything inside letting go the way it lets go every time I'm on the phone with the bank or the hospital or the old folks' home. I want to shout. Where are my daughters? Where are my mother's feet? I want to ask the girls in the strip clubs, Why the fuck are you looking at me like that? I'm no different from the rest. I'm as disgusting and bangable and righteous as the next guy trying to tuck a buck in your g-string.

And I must be dead already because there's no sound. A bullet moves faster than the speed of sound. If you hear the shot you know you made it through. But I haven't. I haven't heard the shot, I haven't made it. And it makes me chuckle. At last, it's over. I've been waiting a long time, but I finally got here.

Then the sharp noise of gunfire makes the kid drop the .32. He lets out the kind of sound my father made on his death-bed, a deep choke in the back of his throat. He gags and backs away a step. He vomits on the change scattered at his feet and yanks the ski mask off, gasping. Good-looking kid except for the meth-mouth. If he puts the pipe away and cleans up his act he'll make it just fine in the world.

Lou says, "You're going to fall down now," but I'm already down, on my knees. The kid nearly backs over me with the rear left tire. I reach out and touch the bumper. It feels important that I make contact with the car, like I'm touching 1973. I'm sixteen again and life's all out in front of me. I've got a cute girl and a Mustang with a rusted out front quarter panel. I've got a job and pocket cash.

The tires squeal and the Chevelle sideswipes my Saturn as he hauls ass up the aisle.

That fuckin' little prick.

"Did you see that shit?" I ask Lou.

"I saw," he says.

"Did you take my mother's feet?"

"Yes," he tells me.

I'm still on my knees. Feels like I've always been on my knees. Blood is running through my hair and down my forehead. It catches in the wrinkle between my eyes that's as deep as a knife scar. It's a two-inch trench. The blood picks up speed, like there's rapids up ahead, and washes down my face.

I fall over next to the .32. So far as I can tell I'm still breathing. A crowd forms, all these faces like farm animals shouldering each other aside and practically going "Moo" at me. I'm a touch surprised that there's so many smiles. You'd think looking at spattered brains might ruin somebody's day. A couple of people snap pictures. A bunch more are on their cells, clucking away. Half of them are calling 911. The other half, they're talking with friends, giggling, tittering, chuckling, chittering.

One girl, maybe nineteen, all eyes and lips and hips, excited, "I'm looking at him right now, some old guy dead in the parking lot, I swear."

I give her the finger.

"He just shot me the bird, the fucker!"

Paramedics arrive and start doing their thing. They keep trying to rouse me, asking me questions, saying, "Sir? Stay with us, sir! 140 over 89. Are you allergic to penicillin?" I think, Penicillin? You think I got the clap? I think, 140 over 89? That isn't bad at all. Better than when I use the blood pressure cuff at the Safeway.

They hook me to machines, stab me with some needles, get me on the gurney, and stuff me in the ambulance. The girl makes sure that I see her giving me the finger back.

The driver doesn't know how to get out of the mall parking lot. He tries edging out onto Elm, but it's a one way going in the wrong direction. He thinks about crossing the median but he'll bottom out for sure. He circles back into the parking lot, passing the dispersing crowd. He heads up and down the aisles looking for an exit onto 2nd. When he finds it, he stomps the gas pedal so hard that all the shit on the ambulance shelves falls. One of the defibrillator paddles jerks loose and smacks me in my mangled noggin.

Lou's crouched on the floor, watching the scene. He's got a sorrowful, haunted expression seared into his features. It's not because of me. It's not because of anybody. He'd be beautiful with the soft looks and long golden hair except the lines of his face are filled with the dust of millennia. I recognize him now.

I want to ask him about the garden. I want to ask him about the desert. I want to know if he's got a list with all my sins written out in blood. I start ticking them off, but I get bored somewhere between number three and twelve thousand. Besides, we're rolling into the hospital now.

The emergency room docs are waiting. They wheel the gurney in and Lou rides along, sitting cross-legged on my chest. He reaches out and puts a hand to my cheek, tells me, "Don't be afraid."

I want to say, Are you kidding? Afraid? I'm done, man, I'm finally done. I want to laugh until I howl like a wolf at a blue moon. No more taxes, no more collection agencies, no more mutts ripping off my last nickel. No more ungrateful kids, no more nagging wife chasing me off the couch when I want to drink one beer and catch five minutes of the game. No more staring in the mirror going, Holy fuckall, what is happening, it's like some mutant staring back at me, some radioactive monkey with white fur and giant hanging nuts. No more, no more, my name has a red line through it, I've been scratched out. Who could ever possibly be afraid of this?

"They're going to take your head off," Lou says.

My head's pretty much already off. The surgeons are going hog wild on me. There's a fleet of them around the operating table. I keep waiting for someone to yell for a retractor, but nobody does. I wait to see a nurse sponge off a doctor's forehead, but nobody does.

Then it happens. I leave my body.

I want to say, Thank God, but maybe Lou will take it the wrong way. A little courtesy isn't too much to ask for considering he's been at my side the whole time. My phantom self hovers over the operating table, standing in mid-air and looking down at the surgeons using a buzz saw to take off my skull cap.

My eyelids are taped down but twitching. I can see the damage my brain has suffered. A .32 will do it to you up close.

I always thought brains were muscles, tight and tough, fibrous kind of tissue, but mine looks like runny eggs. The trajectory of the bullet has caused a channel to run along the right side, leaving my brain with a hinge-like flap. Maybe I'm not as dead as I thought, but I'm still hoping. I drift above the doctors and curse them for trying so damn hard. Like I need more nasty letters from the hospital for non-payment. I'm surprised the finance department lady isn't in the operating room asking me about my co-pay.

Christ isn't calling me. St. Peter hasn't opened to the proper page of his enormous book of life. I'm not in any kind of hell they taught us about in Catholic school. There's no loved ones here to greet me, no long bright tunnel to enter.

I try flying but it's a no go. I try to walk through the wall but I notice I'm tethered, a silver leash going from the back of my busted head on the table to the back of my head up here. I tug but I can't get a good enough grip.

Lou's floating with me. I don't feel any kind of a breeze but his hair is flowing around his shoulders like he's moving against a stiff wind.

"All right, Lou," I say. "What's the game?"

"I'm here to take away your pain."

"I thought you were supposed to punish bad boys like me."

"That's never been my duty."

"That's not what the big book says."

"It's a book of lies, written by madmen to give voice to an insane god."

"Lou! Blasphemy! No wonder you got sent to the furnace room."

"No, that's not where I was sent."

I can't help it, my heart goes out to him. He looks like he's been on the verge of weeping for maybe twenty thousand years, but he can't let a teardrop fall. It's all there, written there in the way he hangs his head. He's weary. He's at least as weary as I am. I figure, the two of us, we should go out for a beer together, have a few laughs. Except I'm tapped, and Lou, he doesn't have any pockets.

"So if you're not here to stick a pitchfork in me, then why are you here?" I ask.

"I'm your guide."

"Guide to where? I'm not dead yet."

"And I'll answer your questions."

"I just asked one. Guide to where?"

"Into the next phase."

"Next phase?"

"What lies beyond. The next world."

"Lou, just tell me there's a couch where I can sit in the dark without anybody hassling my ass."

"No, that's not what it's like."

"Fuck!"

I grab the tether again and pull with everything I've got. I try to snap the cord so I can just drift on up and up and up and screw anybody who tries to bring me back down. I tug and bring the cord up to my phantom teeth and bite down on that son of a bitching bastard thing but it won't break. On the table, my eyes pop open. A nurse has to restick the tape over them.

I give up and drop my leash. "Damn it."

So I hang there, Lou at my side, the two of us alone with our heavy thoughts, both of us looking like we want to cry. From time to time we brush shoulders. Occasionally he reaches out and puts a hand to my face. It's not the kind of thing I'm all that comfortable with, but I know he's just trying to show support, build a rapport, share the moment. Maybe it's part of the next phase.

The surgeons pop my skull cap back on. It makes a wet hollow sound. Bits of bone and brain are collected in shiny metal dishes all around. I wonder how many memories are gone. It seems like they ought to be pouring out of my ears across the floor. I ought to see myself on my wedding day, watching my kids being born, taking them to college, sitting with my mother at my old man's funeral, putting the dog down, flushing the fish, telling the Jehovahs to get the hell off my stoop. Somebody uses a staple gun to jam a few staples around my head. You'd think they might put some putty or rubber cement along the edges, some super glue. One good sneeze and the top of my skull is going flying.

They wrap my head up in a turban. They start stripping off their bloody gloves and yank off their masks. The leash loosens a little at the back of my head. I wrap it up around my shoulder like the garden hose in my yard. I'm drawn along as they wheel me out of the OR and into ICU. They hook me up to about five million bucks worth of noisy machinery. All I can think about is how I have no insurance. Three, four days of this, and my house is gone. For the sake of my wife, I try to will my heart to stop, but my body, it's stubborn, and somehow just keeps on going despite my efforts.

"When do we get this show on the road? Why aren't I dead yet?"

Lou puts a hand on my shoulder. "There's more for you to do."

"Like what?"

"I don't know."

"That's not much of an answer. You said you'd guide me."

"Yes, that's what I said."

"So what is this?"

"I simply don't know."

"Lou, tell me the truth ... are you just fucking with me now?"

"No. Our god requires greater service."

"No matter what you do, it's just never enough."

"No, it isn't."

My wife shows up in hysterics. She's wailing like crazy and already hyperventilating. She keeps this up and she'll be in a bed right beside me. I try to talk in her ear and tell her to calm down. Now's the time to be strong. Now's the time when she has to think about everything I tried to teach her about the bank accounts, dealing with the bills, how to dodge the collection agencies, how to transfer balances from one credit card to the other. None of it gets through. She sobs in a frenzy and throws herself against the foot of the bed. The nurses try to calm her down but it's no deal, she's got herself too worked up. A young doc with too much mousse in his stiff pointy hair has to give her a sedative. They prop her on the couch in the waiting room where she slumps over in a daze. Anybody watching would think I must be a hell of a guy for her to react like this. They don't know my wife.

The kids come rushing in about an hour later. My wife's still out of it, red-faced and weepy and only semi-conscious. My daughters have the courtesy of looking upset. They split up and one takes my left hand and one takes my right. They cry and call me daddy with a lot of affection in their voices. The sound of it is so shocking that I sort of jerk around on the end of the leash. For the first time I'm almost sad about what's happened.

A thread of blood has worked out from beneath the turban and is inching down the length of my nose. There's something about watching your blood creep that can really get to you. My youngest daughter wets a tissue with the jug of water on my night stand and dabs at my face until the blood is gone. It's a sweet moment, the kind I used to believe in. I glance at Lou and he's watching the scene intently, and there's somehow even more sadness in his expression now."Tell me your story, Lou."

He stares off through the window towards the sun. The burning sunlight is no less bright than the fiery glow coming off him. His mouth drapes open. His hand tightens into a fist and he brings it up to cover his heart. Then it opens again and he presses his hands together as if in prayer, but only for an instant, before he turns away. A sob that's been rattling around inside him since the birth of man tries to find its way out but he swallows it down again and again, like he's done since the garden. "I was the firstborn, beloved above all others, until my master decided I had no grace, and threw me aside."

"Rough deal."

"Yes."

"And the rest of the big book? Is any of it true?"

"A bit."

"Which part?"

"I'm not altogether certain."

"But you were there right from the beginning."

"Since before the beginning, yes. But I've been lied to as well."

I've got tubes up my ying-yang. I shit and piss into bags. My kids are embarrassed, listening to the sound, but not like I am. I couldn't even be left with a little dignity in my death. The nurse comes in and shoos the girls away. My wife is zoned out, stoned on the sedatives. My daughters stutter-walk their mother out of ICU to the chiming and beeping and shrieking whistles of machinery. The guy with brain cancer next door is flatlining. Docs and nurses come running. I want to say, "What's the point? Show some compassion." But they don't. They flip him this way and that way, jab needles in him, stick an air hose down his throat, and hit him with the paddles a few times.

Lou walks over and puts a hand to the man's chest. The machinery bloops a few times and all the lights go red. The guy with brain cancer heaves one last time, his final breath hanging in the air like toxic fumes. At least it's finally over for him.

"You do that for all of us?"

"Yes."

"Don't be so upset, you're just being kind."

"It rarely feels that way."

"You're too sensitive, Lou."

"Perhaps."

"Let me ask you though. Why'd you take my mother's feet?"

"I was told to."

"By who?"

"Our master."

The tether seems longer, looser. I try making a break for it. I zip through the hospital corridors, glancing at other poor bastards with their chests opened, heads opened, feet gone, arms gone, eyes gone, minds gone. Out of the whole bunch, Lou only touches one other person, a boy who was mowed down on his bicycle by a garbage truck. The docs and nurses go through the whole show again, the needles, the air hose, the paddles, the chest-thumping, but the boy is gone. It's a mercy.

I check my watch. My phantom wrist still has a phantom watch on it, the phantom hours spinning past. We wander some more. We head outside. There's a park next door. Children are playing, dogs are romping. I wonder what happened to the punk. They couldn't have caught him yet. He's probably still behind the wheel, with the hammer down. Flying down 495. He's got no gun now. Maybe I scared him straight, but I really doubt it.

I know how to kill time until somebody decides to send me on my way.

"I want my eighteen bucks back," I say.

"Take my hand," Lou tells me.

I do. We fly together. I can feel the power and misery within him. It would've been a lot easier for him if all he had to do was sit on a throne of bones, waxing his horns and watching lawyers, insurance salesmen, and IRS auditors burn in pits of sulfur. Who wouldn't dig that?

The mutt is in a hole in the wall bar off of Route 347. I know the place. I used to drink here, years ago, me and a couple of buddies when we got off work. Nice dark atmosphere, and the local hookers never pestered you too bad. He's deep into his fourth or fifth beer and orders another double whiskey. The bartender should know better than to serve a punk like this, but in this economy he's trying to grab whatever he can.

Kid's probably spent three times what he took off me. He's got a face on the verge of crying, the pain bleeding out of him. No different than Lou's, no different than mine.

"Can I talk to him?"

"No."

"Can you?"

"Yes."

"Tell him to quit now. Tell him to have a few laughs. Go make more friends. Get out and get laid. Tell him not to take everything so seriously. Life's too long to waste it worrying. Tell him ... tell him I forgive him, he should just let it go."

Lou wraps his arms around the mutt and hugs him close, whispering in his ear. The murmuring goes on and on, and I lean in trying to hear what's being said, but I can't make any of it out. The kid's skin is ashen and tight. I can almost recognize the language. The whisper is as old as mankind. It's inside of us, in our DNA, and has been since the first human wail was heard over the hills.

The mutt starts sucking air through his teeth. His nerves are snapping, one by one. I recognize the sound of it. On his barstool he leans away from Lou's lips but Lou follows, becoming more insistent. The kid mumbles and sobs in his beer. The bartender asks, "You okay?" But the mutt can't answer. He shudders once, twice, and again, then flops sideways off the stool and hits the floor, where he goes into convulsions. In twenty seconds his eyes roll up in his head, he shits himself, and he's dead.

The bartender comes around, takes one sniff, and goes, "Goddamn." He turns away to call 911.

"Lou! What the hell did you do?"

"As you asked."

"Then why did he croak?"

"He thought it was a lie. He thought everything I said was a lie. I spoke the great truth, and he was resolved so intently not to believe it that he couldn't live another moment."

"Aw shit! Lou, you've really got to work on your delivery."

And then I feel the leash loosen and fall away. Back in ICU, I'm dead too. The docs are jumping around like clowns with their syringes, and they're zapping my heart, but it's all as pointless as voting or spending time on your knees in church. Fuck the co-pay.

"It's time for the next phase," Lou says. "What lies beyond. We must now face our mad master."

"Is it going to be bad?"

"Worse than you can imagine."

But I think about it for a second and realize it won't be. I've already crawled on my belly across the cellars of hell. Lou doesn't know what it means to be human. To fight a daily war you can never win, lacking meaning, devoid of purpose. He thinks he's got the worst job in existence. He's never had to punch into a factory for thirty years straight. He doesn't understand how many people beg for him to show up and snatch them away.

I reach across the bar and grab the kid's beer. Maybe it's a phantom beer, maybe it's the real thing. It doesn't matter. I take a long pull from the mug and enjoy the cold taste of it running down my throat. Maybe this was all I needed in my life, more time in dark corners alone, dreaming my dreams, a chance to pretend that the fight was a good fight. Lou's watching me and I'm watching him. He holds out his hand and I drain the rest of the beer and take it.

■ ■ ■

Tom Piccirilli is the author of twenty novels including *Shadow Season*, *The Cold Spot*, *The Coldest Mile*, and *A Choir of Ill Children*. He's won two International Thriller Awards and four Bram Stoker Awards, as well as having been nominated for the Edgar, the World Fantasy Award, the Macavity, and Le Grand Prix de L'imagination.

—ELEGY FOR A CROW—
By Opal Edgar

As a person I'd never been a great conversationalist, as a crow it got mildly better as no one expected anything from me. I liked Japan for that; the bird was so common I was inconspicuous. Soaring over Nagoya, a few of the black birds started to join me, smelling the tenacious scent of corpses on my plumage. They swirled around me, in the crisp morning air, sometimes dipping into the organic bins of the neat city, and for just an instant, creating a mess. The mess never lasted; street sweepers were everywhere, popping from corner police stations and unbearably cute vans, ready to chase the birds with large arm movements and quickly order the myriads of bins.

I landed on the rim of the flammable pink recycling bin, between high rises from the seventies, an open car park and a decrepit corner store. The *kanjis* of the *combini* were written in neon paint. A happy frog creature with pink cheeks leapt from the side of the store in a colorful poster, advertising an incomprehensible product in a yellow box. For a second the man named Kanbu Matsuka hesitated, broom above his head. But he didn't dare shoo me away. The broom lowered as I stared him down with my beady sulfur eyes. He picked at the mask covering his mouth for a second, scratching his head as if a colleague had been there and needed the code to know how very unsettled he was. He crouched slowly in the industrial, clouded street and, pretending to gather the rubbish, he threw uneasy glances at me.

The crows landed one by one by the bins. One quickly found a piece of squid to pick at, before a bigger crow pecked it away.

Kanbu Matsuka had a heavy belly under his faded baseball t-shirt. He was in his forties and he lived alone with his clogged arteries in a small room above his sister's flat; thin paper wall discreetly sliding to separate the one which had done well from the child who had failed. She had two children and every Tuesday invited her brother for diner so he would eat more than just curry rice. Kanbu had been in love once, with a girl from his high school. Her high socks still remained his most fetished memory. But she'd chosen the boy who grew up to become an architect. She had moved with him to Osaka and Kanbu had met other women and remained alone. I could see it all flicker as motion pictures evaporating from his stomach. Most people didn't know the soul liked to coil itself in the stomach, pulling at all the blankets of emotions settling in there.

I could hear Kanbu's troubled breathing, blocked alveolus in his lungs, slow blood in his veins. Curry had never been his friend, but the spicy cubes were easy to prepare and it was better than eating white rice. His arms felt numb and the discomfort was starting to turn into pain. Kanbu Matsuka didn't know he was dying, that I was slowly pulling on his soul to dislodge it. Only when he felt the pain in his chest and his legs refused to carry him did he understand. But he didn't even have time to throw me one last glance. He toppled over as he was turning his head and two lawyers in the old building saw him. They had been talking quietly in the corridor, one had just gotten the job, she was nervous, her name was Hana Neiko. The other already had her head by the window and was calling out to Kanbu, except she didn't know his name. But they were too late to influence his life. I soared up storing the soul far down my throat as I escalated into the sky. My job was to make sure those souls all arrived safely to the netherworld. And I still had a long day, something big was calling at me north east of Nagoya, towards the small town of Owarisahi.

The crows of Nagoya left one by one as they felt the borders of their territory grow near. Other ones joined me and left in a soundless dance as I passed over their city. In Owarisahi there was a white crow, like an omen. It brushed against me and dove in the distance not joining the flock. At the border of the town there was a fountain where young women gathered, their feet and calves offered to tiny fish that ate dead cells and left soft skin. They were loud, barely muffling their laughs behind their hands as they talked about men. There were two fountains here, one for entertainment and one for water. The second communicated with the whole place's water main and fed into every house. The water then ran into other villages in a complicated system of pumps and filtering. One of the girls had the image of it clearly imprinted in her mind. She was not laughing with others, she didn't even have her feet in the water, she knew the time was counted for them all, she knew the fountain was poisoned and that hundreds would die. Her name was Yuki Dorimu and she had wanted to be a violinist. And that's all I saw. Suddenly she was not giving off any images of what her life was, suddenly I could only see her long almost blue hair and her soft skin. Her hair draped over her simple light chrysanthemum tunic. She was out of fashion and others barely noticed when she excused herself away. I didn't even hesitate to follow. I didn't even think about what I was meant to accomplish here, I simply trailed after her.

The inside of her house was as traditional as the exterior, wooden and minimalist. I lost sight of her as she walked past windowless walls. She reappeared for a few steps before vanishing up a staircase. I soared up, but the first room wasn't hers, it was dusty and the walls covered with boy-band posters. The window of the next room opened and there she was, settling at a small desk between a single shelf and a rolled up futon. I perched myself on her open window sill.

I hadn't been in love for so long that at first I didn't understand my fascination. I watched her delicate fingers pull a small journal out of a fabric bag. Her violin case rested neatly on a shelf, between vases of dried flowers, her year books from 2005 to 2008 and a photo of her and what could only be her sister in the country. It looked like a set created by someone who'd read too many romance novels, all so sickeningly perfect I could have nestled in my feathers and stared for eternity. As she took out a pink plastic pen, for the first time I felt her full gaze on me. There were specs of blue in her dark eyes; she was so very young, barely twenty. Yet, there was something simmering under the surface, something very familiar, but I couldn't place it. She smiled at me, a very sad smile, one of recognition, and I felt my heart beat in my chest. I hadn't felt my heart for such a long time I let out a small cry.

She had poisoned the whole city so as to find me, so that I would come to her. My conviction was so great I almost turned into a man. But I didn't dare. I didn't know what she thought, I was no good at talking. I hadn't a grand gift for her. I was only me. So I tip-tapped closer, almost through the window, and watched her open her journal. Partitions were glued on pages, between long passages of frenzied writing. She tapped the pen against her lips, which were a soft pink too. She poised her pen on a page and started to write, very slowly. The urge to know was too great. I flew in and landed on the edge of her futon. She folded the page before turning towards me.

"Is there anything I can get you?" Yuki Dorimu asked.

Her voice was soft and her Japanese so respectful my eyes fogged. Yet, she was rolling the paper slowly between her fingers into a tight cylinder, all the while looking at me. I crowed a lament of a cry, torn by my inadequacies. She was so lovely and what had I to offer? She had a small ribbon in her pocket and she used it to tie up her message.

"I'll do my best," She said.

She dropped the message on the window sill before moving to the door. I heard her going down the stairs and into a further room, and then the clutter of plates. I didn't even think about all the people that were meant to be dying right now, the hundreds here, the tens of thousands in the rest of the world. I clambered from shelf to shelf pecking at miniature books talking about me, a hidden collection of good luck charms and letters held in tight colorful ribbons. The ribbon frizzled after I snapped at them. All the letters came from her sister, Kasumi Dorimu. She had chosen to live in a remote collective. She was telling Yuki not to worry, she was happy away from the world. I wasn't interested in the sister. I pecked, planting my beak deep into stacks of partitions. Notes flew and I recognized the language of Mozart and Bach and Händel. She was too pure for the rawness of Beethoven. I finally skipped back to the window sill and unrolled the carefully prepared message.

On the paper was a single *kanji*. It was a long forgotten one only inscribed on dilapidated Shinto shrines. I thought it had been lost but for old priests who knew that gods and demons did die too. It was a name that had been given to me at some time and in some place of the world. It was believed to be a protective ward to keep me away. I smiled, an awkward gesture pulling the skin around my beak. She had placed a ward by every window and door of the house. She was intending to keep me away from the world.

Yuki Dorimu's steps were careful on the wooden floor, gracious, controlled, not letting a single creak out of the old boards. She held a platter with cold tea, a bowl of rice, a peach, a tall bottle of sake, and a burning incent stick in a holder. She kneeled and bowed before pushing the tray towards me. I didn't deserve so much servitude. I was a glorified slave at the mercy of every person whose moment it was to cross into the other world. Her posture reminded me of the times when people were scarified in my name, of those eras when I arrogantly fed off the flesh and the souls of the damned. It reminded me of my infant phase when I didn't know about freedom and I thought all existed for my benefit so that I could squish it through my chubby baby fingers and watch the lifeless sludge pour out. It reminded me of the moment I realized I would never know what happened behind the door I lead everything too, that terribly ironic moment I realized I was but a tool and that I was the only one barred from the ultimate truth about what occurred after Death.

I hopped onto the rim of the rice bowl. That was such a sweet gesture; feeding me like a spirit. It was such a shame I didn't eat. Yuki smelled of new books and apple blossoms. She had tied her hair with a blue ribbon. I hadn't known that femininity was still valued in the current society. I'd mourned its slow passing a few years ago as I'd seen the rise of global vulgarity. But she was so lovely, still on her knees, watching me watching her.

"I'm so sorry." she finally said.

I wanted to tell her she shouldn't be, that everything felt pleasant. But I was a crow and I'd forgotten how to interact with people. All I wanted was to stay with her, and her ribbons. As I flew above her head, her scent became intoxicating, and so very familiar. I knew that smell, or perhaps I'd always loved it. I landed next to the violin and carefully tapped it with my sharp beak. The case indented a little. I wasn't made to be delicate, just to break things, no matter how hard I tried not to.

In her hands the violin sang. Shubert's *Der Tod und das Mädchen* breathed into my ears, so appropriate and tragic. This was a piece composed for me, every musical word praising and fearing and cursing me. The sound rolled and rose into the room and out. Her long fingers danced. Hypnotic cords lulled me into a lethargic state letting the sky turn from day to night. Cocooned in my feathers, I watched my prisoner play for me. She was too young to realize a guard shares the jail of the captured, and that if I chose to be trapped so was she.

The front door had opened and closed a few times but Yuki hadn't moved and had continued playing. I felt her mother's presence, still resounding of the crowd she'd mingled with so as to bring back tonight's food. She was salivating in front of a square fruit. This was one of the first watermelons of the season; it had come all the way from Zentsuji, where they caged the fruits so that they would grow into the famed convenient shape. Her father came much later, thinking about the insufficient solar panels on the new electric car his team was designing. They had celebrated the birthday of the branch last week and his boss had congratulated them heartedly and he was ashamed. The project wasn't doing well enough. He would be going back tonight to work on it until he fell asleep in front of his computer, just as he had yesterday, and the day before, and the day before…

Yuki's mother slowly came up the stairs. From her mind's eye I could see the plate of watermelon slices she brought up. Yuki didn't hear her drop the plate and a heart-covered napkin by her door. Her mother was used to her staying in her room when she played. She looked at the door with longing before she sighed. She was afraid that Yuki would go join a sect like her sister, Kasumi. She was scared she might never see her older daughter again. Last time she had visited the commune, Kasumi had refused to come down to see her. Yuki's mother hadn't told that to anyone. She had felt ashamed and lost. She wondered what she had done wrong. Yuki's mother had woken up at 5:30 every morning of her life to prepare fresh bento lunches for her family. Each morning, she had shaped rice balls into birds and pigs and cats. She had opened the door to her daughters every night when they came back from school. She had cried secretly when her husband spent *Hanami,* and Christmas, and their birthdays at work instead of at home with his family. But she had planted a cherry tree in the garden when her daughters had been seven and nine so that he'd be with them when the first cherry blossoms appeared. She walked back down the stairs quickly when she heard her husband slide his shoes on.

It was three in the morning before Yuki stopped playing. Her mother had long gone to bed, discreetly walking by the door. Yuki hadn't eaten, her left hand was red, her arms were sore but she had played all day for me, keeping me from collecting the dead. Exhaustion was inscribed on her oval face and shining in her dark eyes. Sweat beaded along her hairline and trickled from the base of her neck as if she had a fever. Only then did I recognize her, as she weakly unrolled her futon. My wings had brushed past her once. She had been much smaller then, but to me it seemed like an instant ago. It had been that same year her mother had planted the cherry tree. Yuki had had meningitis and everyone thought she would die. But as I'd looked in her soul I had seen this wasn't it, not yet, there were things waiting to be accomplished first. So I'd continued my stroll and taken those whose time was over.

Yuki sat on a corner of her futon looking at her violin and painfully stretching her hand; perhaps she was an instrument too, made to amuse with violin and give company to a lonely Death.

"I am sorry," she said again.

I didn't want her to apologize. I was angry at myself. She had exerted herself for me and I hadn't even seen it, too busy wallowing in my thoughts. How could I be this selfish in my love? So I tweaked at her soul just enough for her to topple into a deep sleep. After all, sleep is but a little death. I watched her cheeks grow rosy and her chest rise and fall in rhythm to a dream only she could witness. I'd always wondered if it was love which blocked their thoughts to my vision or if it was their mystery which created my love. I sat perched on her little chair by her desk watching her beauty bloom in the tranquility. I wanted to be man so as to hold her against me and be lured into thinking I wasn't alone.

It was five in the morning when the front door opened again. The hand was hesitant, the steps were weak, the mind was lost. It was Kasumi, the sister, returning home. Her breath smelled acrid and her stomach screamed. She thought she would vomit again. The poison burned her insides. She had drunk two liters of it to no avail. When that hadn't worked she had been sent with others to pour more poison down the fountain. They had dutifully followed their *sensei's* orders so all would reach a better world. But they came back still standing and after attempting to breathe carbon monoxide and only getting headaches, they had resorted to more drastic measures. Kasumi had opened the veins of her wrists and fainted. They all had. When she'd woken up, she'd opened the veins on her ankles. Then she had cried. She wanted to go home and they let her. They all wanted to go home.

She was here now, stumbling up steps, leaving trails of blood on the dark wooden floor and the paper walls. She slid her door open, looking for comfort but not daring to go to her sister. She fell on her bed, convulsing and moaning, arms outstretched, face towards the pillow. She hadn't been home for a long time, but her room had stayed intact, her mother not daring to touch a thing. Kasumi cried as she remembered her last talk with her sister. She had told her water was sacred and would cleanse them all, her *sensei* would make sure it did. Yuki had been scared then. Yuki had spent the next month waiting from dawn to dusk next to the fountain with piles of books. They'd had to come at night, when she was too tired to stand guard. But Yuki hadn't been waiting for them, she had been waiting for me.

I looked at Yuki's small silhouette, reading in her clasped jaw her determination not just to stop the event but all future ones too, perhaps save all people from dying. It's only then I really felt all the souls calling on me, the ones starved or aged, or diseased, or suffocated, or shot, or burnt, or bleeding, or hit, all screaming in pain for release. But Yuki didn't want people to die. She'd tried to capture me so people wouldn't die, to keep me away. And this could be my gift to her, so that perhaps, just perhaps I would be worth her love. I jumped to the floor, tip-tapping forward so as to nestle close to her, feathers almost touching her hand.

In another room, Kasumi was thumping the side of her bed, unable to get any respite from the suffering. Her mother woke up soon after she'd arrived, but she was frightened of ghosts. She would never have admitted it, but she was afraid every morning, as she put her first foot down on the floor before stepping into obscurity. The banging sounded to her like a spirit and she stayed coiled in bed, eyes open, skin clammy, with visions of demons flickering through her head even though she tried to keep them away. At first she'd really thought it was all in her imagination, but as the minutes on the alarm clock flashed on and left, she realized this was reality. Heart beating, she snuggled her feet into tiny slippers before sliding her door open. Glancing carefully into the corridor, she took two large gulps of air before walking out. That's when she realized the noise came from her elder daughter's room. She was torn. Either her daughter was back or this was indeed a very bad sign. She tried to laugh it off: *stupid old woman*, she thought, *scared of things that don't exist*. But she didn't believe what she told herself; she was just trying to gather her courage. After long minutes of hesitation she slid the door slowly, inches at a time, holding her breath.

"Kasumi," she whispered, a sob in her voice.

She walked into her daughter's room, tears already streaming down her face. She was so happy her daughter had decided to come back, life could start over again. Things were never too late, Kasumi was only twenty-four. Today young ladies married late, sometimes even waiting to be in their thirties. Things would get better from now on. She hadn't seen the blood. Kasumi lifted her white, almost blue, bloodless face from the pillow. Her hair hung limp and her mouth was caked with grime. Her mother yelled, ancestral fear welling inside her and spurring out like carbonated water shaken and uncorked. Abruptly it stopped when she fainted.

Yuki jumped up, fear being contagious. She scanned the room quickly, panic growing until she laid eyes on me, so little, so insignificant, huddled next to her. There was too much white in her eyes and I saw shadows of doubt cross her mind. I could easily guess the questions going through her head; after all, she had brought Death into her house and trapped him there, or so she thought. But it was only a word. Nothing could trap me as I was already in a prison. She couldn't know I wanted only to please her.

I sat up, body growing into that of a man, black feathers turning into silken fabric. She quickly bowed down as I changed. My hair reached down my back in blond curls and my skin glowed. I had many shapes but this one was the least frightening to a young Japanese girl. Tentatively I took her hand. The gesture was slow; it had been so long since I'd moved in such a body. I had to think before I talked, unsure how to use my voice.

"Yuki Dorimu," I said, almost startling myself, "I will do as you please. I will not answer the call anymore, I will not take the souls to the netherworld. If that is your wish, I shall obey."

Her relief was almost palpable. I could see the muscles tensing in her throat. She gave a short nod unable to speak and suddenly she jumped into my arms.

"I am sorry I captured you. I am so sorry. Please do not hate me," she said.

Tears wet my collar, seeping through the silk, and they felt so good. The screams in my head from the tens of thousands which I'd meant to collect vanished in an instant. I'd never thought about not going where I was called before. I'd never thought that perhaps I could be free too. And for the second time that day I smiled.

"Your sister has returned," I said to her hair.

Yuki was still encircling me, arms around my torso. She looked up and into my eyes, her smile beautiful. My heart pumped once again and I had to show her my gift. Eyes sparkling, she held tight onto my hand. The warmth grew into me. I would have liked time to slow so that I could observe it all like I had when she'd been asleep, hypnotized by her breathing. My steps were unsure as I'd gotten unused to the balance of people. The weight and the lack of tail were odd. It really had been a very long time since I'd walked the earth as a human, almost a thousand years.

I slid the door slowly to show Yuki that her sister was still alive. She had saved her. Kasumi had gotten up and tried to carry their mother onto the bed, but she didn't have the strength. She cursed the day she had asked for a foreign bed because it was too high. There was only a little blood on her mother's cheeks and clothes, almost all of it had already poured out, a large quantity had pooled in the bed.

Kasumi's heart burned trying to pump something that was no longer there. She looked up at her sister, unable to talk because of the pain. Her eyes were now deep inside their sockets and her face and lips white as snow. Yuki screamed and fell to her knees. The warmth fled from my heart.

"Kasumi please forgive me. It is my fault. It is my entire fault, I didn't understand. I didn't want you to die. I didn't want anyone to die because of what you did." Yuki said.

Kasumi looked at her slowly, eyes unfocused. Her thoughts were incapacitated by her internal screams. Every part of her shrieked abuse, from the organs that had shut down because of blood and oxygen deprivation to those which lay corroded in poison. Two words did escape her lips.

"Kill me," she pleaded.

The horror imbedded in Yuki's face as she turned towards me froze my very bones. I'd wanted her to be happy, to see my gift to her, but I was a monster. Her fear smelled acidic and my body melted into that of a crow. This was not what she had wanted, but how could I have known? How could I have realized that she never expected pain to be apart from Death? I cowered for a second, under her shocked eyes. Yuki had given me freedom, but for her I was willing to give it up again.

I rose into the air, brushing past Kasumi and dragging the three souls with me. I heard bodies drop to the floor as I soared past. I didn't turn to watch. I concentrated on taking the rolled up paper Yuki had carefully placed on the window sill before slipping through the open window into the crisp morning air, and back into slavery.

◼ ◼ ◼

Opal Edgar was born in Australia, and grew up in France. She spends most of her time cramping words on tiny bits of paper she then has trouble deciphering. She has been published in *Aurora Wolf, Hungur Magazine* and in the anthologies *Detritus* and *Behind Locked Doors*. About this story she says, "I found a stranded baby crow in the park last spring, and during the few days I kept it at home I was reminded of how much I wanted one as a child so I could teach it to speak and perhaps so it could tell me its story."

—THE ANGEL OF DEATH—
By Lawrence Salani

Oh, Angel of Death, what sorrow in your touch; sorrow not for the departed but for those that mourn. Your harvest forever plentiful while we, who remain, forlornly await tomorrow as we watch the putrescent misery of your parting. We stand helpless in your cold shadow and pray may you be swift and do not linger, for like a pitiless tyrant you would have us implore your mercy as you gloat over our suffering. Indifferent and indiscriminate in your choosing, countless have fallen and followed you into the unknown darkness: the great, the wealthy, the beautiful, the young and old are but dust blown on the winds of Time into your nethermost abyss. What secrets you could whisper that only the dead may hear as, ignorantly, we observe the signs of your passing.

Like a sun's final burst as it dies, the life of an ant is extinguished by an unaware child while playing on a clear summer's day. And amidst the multitude of the dead in a vast, lonely graveyard, an ant struggled on a moss-covered tombstone, and life seemed futile and incomprehensible. The concrete angels stared blankly, frozen in a moment of perplexed wonder as they stand over the silent graves guarding the wilted flowers left by a mournful hand. As the shadows of evening lengthen, the greyness of twilight slowly thickens while the willows that grow amongst the tombstones rustle eerily in the evening breeze.

░ ░ ░

The thick, soft whiteness of the lilies that Nigel Truman placed on the grave before him glowed in the semi-darkness, their fragile beauty still radiant with life. The quiescent twilight had bought with it imagined movement around the weathered and crumbling gravestones. Night life moved ominously amongst the black shadows. Although never actually seen, creatures slithered and moaned behind the weathered and moss-covered sandstone slabs.

Suddenly, something huge moved in the tree branches above! The rustling of the foliage startled the lone figure into wakefulness. Quickly, he looked up in fear, but could see nothing in the darkened mass of leaves. The coldness of night began to engulf him, and, as Death spread its diseased wings over its dominion, darkness slowly enshrouded the earth.

Oh! Death, how deep your pangs are buried!

The memory of the unexpected tragedy was again an open wound. And as the blackness slowly surrounded him, memories cascaded into Nigel's mind like a waterfall of broken glass.

It had been nearly twenty years ago, yet while standing in the gathering darkness before the silent, weed-covered grave, he recalled the sound of the waves and the howl of the wind as memories of that accursed day returned.

The unusually high waves that the turbulent weather had produced pounded the weather-eroded coastline. As Nigel and his four companions walked towards the rocky shore, seagulls shrieked amidst the turmoil sounding like the cries of lost souls amidst the raging sea that swelled before them. Turbid clouds hung on the horizon heralding a storm, too far away to be of concern, so they decided to experience the fury of the ocean at close hand.

At the time, they were all attending the same college and were all friends, his closest companion being Paul. The mystery of Death was a subject frequently discussed amongst themselves, and Paul often stated that if he died before the rest, he would return and let them know what existed in the afterlife. They always laughed at his words for they were young with long lives ahead, and Death seemed unimaginable. That day was another adventure of fun and freedom, but little did they know the consequences of their imprudence as the five youths walked along the slippery, weed-covered boulders toward the pounding surf.

The rocky platform was situated beneath a cliff face accessible by way of a set of steps carved from the stone. In more favorable conditions, this was a favorite spot for fishermen, but today it was deserted. Incredible green waves broke against jagged rocks spraying foam high into the salty air, the sound of their force reverberated along the rock ledge. Advancing as close as they dared, they watched the mighty ocean as it surged before shattering angrily on the unyielding rocks. Unaware of the potent force of nature, they were all watching massive breakers forming in the distance when an unexpected wave, much larger than the others, smashed against the ledge. In that moment, Nigel looked up; it seemed as if the sky had been covered by a massive, green hand. Before any of them had time to realize what had happened, the mighty hand swatted them, leaving them like five tiny insects drenched and prone on the wet, slippery rocks.

Nigel regained his senses quickly and looked towards the churning water; Paul was being dragged over the ledge by the foam and caught in the turbulent ocean.

It was impossible to do anything; the force of the waves was too strong to attempt to assist him. The four youths could only stand at a safe distance, stunned, not knowing what to do as the waves continued to churn and break along the rocky shoreline.

It felt like a dream to Nigel, as if that moment in time had never existed.

Once they recovered from the initial shock, the full import of what had occurred was realized. Quickly, they telephoned for help but were advised that because of the chaotic weather conditions, nothing could be done until the storm passed. Later, emergency rescue patrols searched for a week, but Paul's body was never found. Eventually, the search was abandoned.

The following week was borne with grief by Paul's family and close friends. The pain in their eyes filled Nigel with anguish, and his weary days dragged by shrouded in sorrow. Death had swiftly taken its due and left its legacy. Disbelief filled him. Even while Paul's remembrance service was being arranged, he could not accept that his friend was gone.

Over the years, images of that tragic day became jumbled in his mind. Amidst those thoughts was a more painful knowledge — the tragedy could have been avoided.

On the day of Paul's remembrance ceremony, the sky was a beautiful, clear blue, and the calm sea disturbed only by a few gentle waves breaking along the rocky platform on which the small congregation had assembled. Twenty relatives and close friends had gathered to lay a wreath on the rocks where Paul had been tragically taken. A priest from the local church conducted a service to commemorate a life that had been taken so early. Seagulls squawked incessantly as they circled the group of mourners and the grieving parents were supported by their relatives and close friends. The priest's voice drifted lethargically over the lapping water as the group sadly stood around the wreath of flowers and reflected on the unfortunate loss.

The tide had commenced to come in; small waves had begun splashing over the rocks. It was then that Nigel noticed a large piece of driftwood floating in the distance. The ceremony continued uninterrupted but, as the shape drifted closer, other members of the group began to notice the object until all eyes were no longer on the priest but directed towards the ocean. The priest finally noticed that the crowd's attention was focused elsewhere and he, too, turned to where they were staring. Suddenly, a scream from one of the women echoed across the cliff face. Astonishment fell over the gathering, for the black object was not flotsam but a dead body. As the crowd stared in wonder, the body continued to drift towards the spot where they were gathered until it became lodged amongst the boulders below the rocky ledge. Its arms swayed backward and forward disturbingly amongst the lapping waves making it seem as if it were trying to climb out of the water and onto the rocks above. The horrified women turned away while some of the men descended and, beneath the raucous screeching of the gulls swooping from above, pulled the body from the slippery rocks.

The corpse was finally lifted onto the platform and the blueing, cold flesh made Nigel feel weak. But the greatest shock was reserved for when the body was turned over on its back. Paul's mother collapsed, and an agonized moan arose from her husband. The remainder of the gathering turned away in horror and revulsion; the badly mutilated body was Paul.

With an unbelieving look on his face, the priest blessed the body while someone from the crowd covered the face with a coat. The remainder of the gathering had filed hastily up the rocky staircase to summon assistance.

The vision of Paul's mother, clutching pitifully at the rusty, iron rail that lined the stairs while being supported by friends and relatives, flooded through Nigel's mind as he looked upon the lonely grave of his former companion.

Death, your blow was as a dagger through our hearts; must you now twist the blade to further the agony? What other abominations have you perpetrated to amuse your twisted wit while we wait in ignorance for your pleasure? You lead us back into the serene oblivion before life began, but what fate have you reserved for those who refuse to follow?

Absorbed by the memories of the past, Nigel was unaware of the darkness that had slowly thickened around him. The tombstone contrasted with the darkness; its cold, marble whiteness proclaimed its sterile message of remembrance to any who bothered to read it, for now, not even Paul's parents visited regularly.

His water-logged body had been quickly buried, but a peculiar atmosphere permeated the burial. Not many people had attended the interment and those that did attend left quickly when it was over, for there had been a strange chill in the air of the graveyard.

Looking down at the effulgent lilies that were on the grave before him, he watched their soft whiteness begin to turn brown and the long green stems wilt until only a shrivelled, decayed mass remained. Startled, he quickly glanced around the graveyard. Darkness surrounded him and fear washed through his body. The iron fences that sectioned off some of the graves seemed taller, the ornate arrow points twisted and swirled in the ghostly blackness. His body felt numb and his legs would not move. Things scuttled in the darkness and hid behind the tombstones, watching.

Something brushed the back of his neck sending a tingle through his body. He spun around to empty darkness. Scattered throughout the yard were the black silhouettes of the enormous trees that grew amongst the moonlit statues and gravestones. What resembled inhuman shapes seemed to form in the blackness.

A whisper drifted through the churchyard, an intangible sound that floated on the night and slid between the trees. Nigel listened but heard only a kind of incoherent babble in the distance that he strained to make sense of. These sepulchral voices mocked his sorrow, confirming that death is inevitable and, like countless before him, he would eventually succumb to the final caress.

Twisted, bare trees reached for the moon, their skeletal fingers desperate to grasp this ghostly light reflected from the dead orb, struggling to catch the last rays of life. The dead surrounded him, and it seemed as if he were the only living thing on the planet. The shadows moved, and the incessant babble continued, and it occurred to him that even in death there is no peace.

Tree branches moaned in the night breeze as Nigel slowly made his way through the darkened graveyard along the willow-lined path that led to the exit gates. The murmur of voices rose in volume until they overwhelmed him, a pandemonium of wild screams as if the pit of hell had been opened and the agonies of the damned filled the night sky. But, the second he stepped through the gates, the chaos stopped. A palpable silence engulfed him.

The darkness along the lonely back street was broken only by the murky street lighting. He looked at his watch, surprised at how quickly the time had passed.

Ahead, the street lights appeared to merge into the distant darkness, the perspective of the road seemed broken and distorted. A surreal, sickly feeling overcame him. The safety of the main road was an eternity away and he quickened his pace in an effort to reach the flashing yellow headlights.

But as he looked into the receding distance, he could see a dark silhouette approaching. Fear surged. The black form drifted in and out of sight as it passed street lamps and into shadow.

Nigel began to regret that he had not been aware of the lateness of the evening and of his pensive reflection on the past in the graveyard; this area was not safe after nightfall. As the figure drew closer, he saw it was a teenaged boy and, to his amazement, the boy who stopped on the other side of the road resembled Paul.

"Nigel!" cried the figure. "It's me. Don't you remember?"

Nigel stared in disbelief. "But you're dead. It's impossible," he finally said.

"No, I'm alive. Can't you see?"

"But I was at your funeral, all those years ago. How could you still be alive?"

"Come over here, I'll show you. There's no need to fear."

Sceptical at first, Nigel slowly walked across the road.

"Come with me Nigel, I want to show you something, the most beautiful thing that you will ever see."

"It's late, and I need to get home," replied Nigel, but the excitement at having seen his friend again, after all this time, made him procrastinate. Staring into Paul's eyes he felt suddenly warm inside, and his doubts and fears melted away. An intense need to see and to know overwhelmed him.

"What is it?" asked Nigel.

"It's an angel." Paul started walking again. "Come on, you won't regret it, it's absolutely beautiful."

They turned and began to walk in the direction in which Paul had been walking, and were gradually swallowed up by the darkness as they left the soft glow of the street light.

■ ■ ■

Darkness slowly faded into grey, as the early morning sun rose on the horizon. The welcome light of a new day shone on red brick roofs and buildings, and signs of life slowly began to emerge from the silent houses into the empty streets.

A lone passerby found Nigel's body lying on the footpath by the side of the road; he had been badly beaten and robbed of the small amount of money that was in his wallet. The area near the graveyard had always been notorious for being dangerous at night, and most people knew of the dangers of walking along the deserted and badly lit road.

As the first rays of sunlight shone on the motionless form on the side of the road, the foliage-laden trees whispered eerily, as their silhouettes swayed mockingly in the distant sunrise. Like sad memories, the dead leaves of autumn rustled along the empty roadway, seeking a place to decay and fade into the earth.

The angel of death sadly gazed over life and knew that its bounty would be great, for its emissaries were mighty and many. Spreading its diseased wings, its corrosive touch silently bled into the black shadows of the new morning.

What new terrors have you designed to amuse your twisted wit today?

❖ ❖ ❖

After having completed an associate diploma in fine arts, **Lawrence Salani** decided that writing would help spur his imagination. He has always been interested in horror stories since schooldays, favorite writers being H.P. Lovecraft, Clark Ashton Smith, and favorite artist/writers Austin Spare and William Blake. Horror and death are analogous. His published works include: "A Fragment of Yesterday" with *Eclecticism E-Zine* and "Summer Heat" in the anthology *Night Terrors*. About what led to this story, Lawrence says: The contemplation of demise, the realization that nothing is permanent, and the inevitability of death."

THE
—PHYSICIAN'S ASSISTANT—
By Dan Devine

"Who's that tall lad with you, Thomp?" wheezed old man Markey, squinting up from his pillow. Doctor Thompson pushed him back down, thankful for the man's fever-blurred vision.

"Just a boy from the college over in Highmeadow come to observe," the doc lied. "Now try not to speak, you need to conserve your strength."

Thomp studied the gray figure seated on the edge of Markey's bed. A breeze from the window stirred the curtains and brushed back its cowl, revealing the humorless grin of a face composed of only teeth and bone.

Death was not an uncommon companion for any doctor, but Thomp always resented his presence. The physician concentrated on mixing his medicines, refusing to give in to the prevailing sense of doom. Thomp had stolen people back from the spectre's grasp before and he wasn't about to give up Markey without a fight. The man was practically an uncle to him.

Fortunately, the sedative Thomp had administered took effect before the farmer could take further notice that anything was amiss.

Markey's infection was bad. There was only one treatment that might save the man, and it was probably just as likely to kill the old-timer as the bacteria that were multiplying in his blood. Death seemed to sense Thomp's doubt, and flashed its cold grin in his direction once more.

The doctor shivered and mustered his resolve.

Markey was well past his prime. He never should have been working in the field in the first place. It had been such a sense-less accident. Regardless, Thomp would do his best.

He pulled on his gloves and tied a thin mask before his face. Opening his satchel, he took a clear pouch and filled it from a cup of water beside the bed. Next, he withdrew a small amber vial from his bag and added just a few drops of acid to the pouch, causing the liquid within to boil with thick, frothy foam. Finally, he carefully removed the leaves of a purple-tinged herb from their paper wrappings and crushed them into the acidic solution to dissolve them.

Thomp dipped his scalpel into the mixture to coat it then heated it over a candle flame.

Pushing his seat closer to the bed, Thomp pulled back the blanket and made a careful cut into Markey's puss-swollen side before withdrawing the blade. Unexpectedly, Death leaned for-ward to take a closer look, causing the doctor to flinch and jab himself in his other hand, but he soon steadied himself and completed his work. Thomp only squeezed out a few small drops of the mixture from his pouch into this incision in the farmer's chest — any more would be dangerous — then he stitched the wound closed.

Over the next several hours, Thomp checked his patient's tem-perature and breathing repeatedly, forcing water past his uncon-scious lips often. At last, the fever began to break. He reviewed his work with a satisfied nod towards his silent companion.

"You won't have him today!" Thompson whispered sharply at the specter.

Death turned to stare at him with cold eyes for what seemed an eternity. "He is not the one that I have come for," pointing a long, bony finger at Thompson's hand.

Thomp followed its gesture and saw blood running from the thin cut made by the scalpel when had he flinched. He felt confused for a moment, then realized the blade must have punctured the pouch at the same time. A bit of the dangerous herbal concoction had leaked out onto his cut hand and he hadn't noticed. There was no way of telling how much of a dose he had already taken.

Thomp began to feel woozy.

"Come, doctor," said Death softly. "Let us dance. You have been a worthy opponent all of these years, but now your time has come."

And as Death reached out its skeletal hand and touched Thompson's wounded one, suddenly, beautiful, somber music filled the doctor's ears, like nothing of this world. The music affirmed the human struggle for life despite the inevitability of death, even as it validated his own existence, and he closed his eyes and sighed in peace.

■ ■ ■

Dan Devine is an aspiring science fiction and fantasy author who has been published numerous times online and in print. His first novel, *The Next Best Thing to Heroes,* is currently available on amazon.com, and its sequel is due out soon. Dan was inspired to write this story for the anthology by the idea of a physical Death present in our lives and the stress it would place on those who struggle against it in their daily routines.

AN APPOINTMENT
—IN THE VILLAGE BAZAAR—
By S S Hampton, Sr.

"We ain't in fuckin' Kansas no more," Sergeant First Class Robert 'Chief' Nottingham chuckled from behind his dark ballistic eyeglasses and a puff of sulfurous smelling cigarette smoke, as Sergeant Caleb Justus staggered up the steep trail. Caleb stopped when he saw the rolling, rocky landscape of a thin forest with broken and splintered trees. Visible beyond the trees was a ruined village nestled below a low gray rise littered with skeletal trees. A chill wind moaned across the rugged, haunting landscape.

Behind them, such a deep contrast to the land before them, the valley they emerged from was a lush garden of green grass, brush, and pine trees.

"No shit," Caleb, who usually didn't swear, gasped. Sweat mingled with the cold drizzle that fell from gray clouds and trickled down his face. The platoon spread out and eyed an ancient narrow trail that wound through the ruined trees to a wide, rutted path that led to the village.

As the soldiers slipped between the trees, Caleb thought they resembled unearthly creatures moving through a blighted medieval landscape; each wore a camouflaged Kevlar helmet, Individual Body Armor weighted down with heavy ammunition magazines, first aid kits and combat knives, and grayish-green Army Combat Uniforms with dark elbow and knee pads. Each also wore the trademark dark ballistic eyeglasses that hid the eyes and gave the impression of emotionless, less-than-human faces. They carried M4 Carbines with Close Combat Opticals, M249 Light Machine Guns, and M203s, a 40mm grenade launcher mounted under an M4.

He knew that in their minds, and in reality, they were the meanest SOBs in this valley, or any valley. He felt safe in their presence. It was a much needed feeling after almost being killed by an Improvised Explosive Device three days before.

"Don't know how much drawing you'll get done on a shitty day like this," Chief commented as he ground the cigarette under his boot heel.

"That's why I brought my Nikon." Caleb patted a black bag nestled against the side of his IBA and first aid kit. His drawing kit dangled against his right hip, just above his holstered 9mm pistol. "If I have to I'll take photos, maybe do some color pencil drawings, and when I'm back at my studio at Bagram, an oil painting or two from the best of the images."

Caleb knew he was an almost mythical species that people rarely encountered — a soldier officially called a Combat Artist. Being selected for the Army Combat Artist Program had been one of the two proudest moments of his life — the other was the birth of his newborn son, Mikey, to him and his girlfriend Lesley. That he was selected was testimony to years of struggle to develop his drawing and painting skills under the guidance of a strict mentor, an art teacher at a community college in Las Vegas, who worshipped the techniques of the Old Masters as the standard which all artists should struggle to achieve and by which he measured them against.

The soldiers emerged from the trees and spread out along the path with weapons at the ready. They studied the landscape and the village while Chief lifted his head slightly, as if sniffing the air.

"Stick close to Chief Nottingham," Caleb was told by his boss as he prepared to fly out by supply helicopter to Combat Outpost Fairfax. The square, cluttered COP, once a 19th century British police station, sat on a bluff overlooking a river deep in Taliban territory. It was manned, aptly enough, by two platoons of Virginia Army National Guard cavalry soldiers. "He's a tough son-of-a-bitch, and half Cheyenne. He can spot sign at 300 yards and smell the Taliban a mile away. In four tours he hasn't had anyone killed yet."

Like all Native Americans that Caleb met in the military, Nottingham was referred to by the stereotypical nickname of 'Chief' by his men, in recognition of his heritage.

After his arrival at the COP the husky, broad shouldered, dark faced NCO introduced Caleb to a small, taciturn soldier. "This is Corporal George Weaver," Chief said. "He'll watch over you while you do your artist thing."

The dark eyed soldier with a pale, sharply sculpted face gave Caleb a bleak smile. An uneasy tremor went through Caleb.

"Thanks, but I know how to take care of myself and fight."

"Yeah, well, that's fuckin' great. George will watch your back."

As Chief studied the terrain before them, Caleb looked over his shoulder. His bodyguard stood nearby, carbine held ready, his face shadowed by his Kevlar and his eyes hidden by the ballistic glasses.

"Is something wrong?" Caleb asked as he edged closer to Chief.

"Something don't feel quite right."

Caleb studied the village; most of the compound walls and homes were reduced to burned and scattered rubble, some of which lay across the rainy path that wound its way through the village. In the gray daylight and the thin, steady drizzle, everything had an eerie, otherworld feel about it.

Even the journey from Fairfax felt like a descent into a strange world. The wide path by the COP that doubled for a road turned into a narrow, dirt trail that wound along the bottom of rocky ridges until they reached the narrow, stony path that they climbed up to the high ground. The cold, misty rain only added to the bleakness.

"Let's go," Chief said in a quiet though deep voice. A few soldiers hurried to take point, others moved to the left and right to provide flank security, while a few hung back to secure the rear. "Keep a sharp eye out." He looked at Caleb and added, "There's something in the air. It's hard to explain. The village we're going to sits right on infiltration routes from Pakistan. You never know when you might run into a bunch of fuckin' Taliban."

Caleb tightened his grip on his M4 Carbine that hung by a shoulder sling across his chest and stomach. Taliban ambushes were always announced by a shouted, rhythmic *Allahu akbar*, 'God is great!', followed by gunfire. He wasn't sure Chief was such a highly regarded soldier due to being half Cheyenne, with all of the abilities that supposedly came with his heritage. He *was* sure that anyone who did four tours probably had a well-developed sixth sense that was essential to survival in a combat zone.

"How far to the village?"

Chief pointed at the rise. "When we reach the crest, we'll see the valley below. There's a river running through it. The village sits on the other side. Damned strange village. There's only a few compounds, mostly near the river, a few homes, but most of the villagers carved homes out of beehive-shaped rock mounds scattered along the slopes. Sometimes real windows and curtains, some stone walls, and there's stone stairs everywhere, even a few wrought iron railings for stairs. It's like these people are halfway between being underground dwellers and surface dwellers."

"It sounds interesting," Caleb said as they entered the ruined village. He swallowed uneasily as he saw a skull among the rubble of a collapsed wall; the gaping eye sockets stared at him as if marking his presence.

"We've been working on the village elders since we got here. They're starting to trust us, but not enough to give us intel on Taliban movements and locations of arms caches. Can't really blame them. We visit, go away, and at night the fuckin' Taliban show up. If they're unhappy with the villagers, they shoot a few."

"What happened here?"

"The Pennsylvania guys who were here last year set out a night ambush. They surprised the Taliban, but there were more of the bastards than expected. Fighting went on all night and helicopter gunships were called in. The village caught fire and all of the villagers, those that survived, left. Even abandoned their fields, poor as those were. That shit didn't exactly win us any friends."

Caleb felt a sudden chill go through him. He looked back and saw George a few steps behind him. Due to the ballistic glasses he couldn't tell if the soldier was staring at him or not.

The trail up the rise, past broken, splintered, and fallen trees, was far easier than the steep trail that they climbed from their valley. The soldiers paused at the crest.

Caleb studied the narrow trail that wound down the opposite slope into the valley. Both the valley and the village were dark as if drained of life, or shrouded in deep shadows not associated with the rain clouds.

Pointed rocky mounds were scattered along the river and climbed bare, brown slopes that led to nearby gray hills and mountains. Near the river were half a dozen traditional walled compounds with family dwellings inside; pale green fields were scattered along the water, over which a trio of narrow bridges crossed — one at each end of the village and one near the center. Behind the village that looked so empty of life, he made out trails that wound up the slopes.

Chief lit a cigarette. "The Taliban come down this valley, and use the trails in the high ground behind the village. I know there's arms caches hidden around here. Until we get these people to talk, we're just tourists on a fuckin' day hike."

Caleb drifted away when the squad leaders joined Chief. He wandered along the crest, snapping photos of the valley and village, and the soldiers. He raised the camera to snap a photo of his bodyguard but the soldier barely shook his head *no*.

"Okay," Caleb said, and shrugged.

Chief walked up, cigarette cupped protectively in his hand against the misty rain. "I'm leaving a squad and the weapons squad up here for observation. They've got a good view along this rise, the ground behind us, and the damned valley. That still leaves us platoon headquarters and two rifle squads. More than enough security for when we go into the village."

Chief puffed on the cigarette — and Caleb wrinkled his nose at the strange sulfurous smell — then lifted his head as if sniffing the air.

Caleb had a sudden feeling that he didn't want to go into the village.

"Sergeant," Caleb said, and George stepped between them.

"Is something wrong?" The pale soldier with hidden eyes asked in a low, measured voice as a hint of a smirk played at the corners of his mouth.

"Uh, no."

"Then let us not bother Sergeant Nottingham. He has a lot on his mind. I will walk beside you."

That was the last thing Caleb wanted. It was bad enough that George walked behind him where he couldn't see him, but now he walked beside Caleb, where he *could* see him. More, he finally realized he didn't care for George, and didn't trust him.

"Thanks," Caleb began, but George turned his pale face to him. A cold, fierce determination filled the air around them. The valley below faded into deeper shadows.

"Let us go, Sergeant," George suggested in a low, icy voice.

A tremor of fear raced through Caleb. It was a fear greater than when, taking part in a convoy security mission outside Bagram, the IED went off a split second after his gun truck passed by it. The IED could have torn through the up-armored door and shredded him.

"Who are you?"

George let out a dry chuckle. The sound was like brittle fall leaves tumbling across dry, wind-swept ground.

"I would have thought you had guessed by now."

"I don't understand."

"Yes you do."

"Quit speaking in riddles," Caleb hissed. "Who are you?"

"Your one true companion, your one true friend since your birth."

Caleb stared as George removed his ballistic glasses to reveal volcanic black obsidian eyes. His pale flesh was drawn so tightly across his face that he resembled a bleached skull. His thin eyebrows were no more than black slashes above the eyes. Caleb's tremor of fear became a savage earthquake.

"You!"

"Yes."

"It ... it can't be. You, you exist, but you don't walk and talk like us!"

"I beg to differ," Death replied as he touched Caleb's shoulder to urge him forward again. Even through the wet IBA and uniform, his touch was cold.

"This can't be," Caleb shook his head as he stumbled down the trail.

"But it is. Long story short, we have an appointment in the village bazaar below."

Death put his ballistic glasses back on.

"Why?"

"Why?" Death mocked Caleb's shocked tone. "Because it is time. Actually, your time was three days ago. Sometimes my, ah, assistants, do not perform as they should. One second was all that was needed for you to miss your scheduled appointment. Today, I am here to personally ensure that our appointment is kept."

Caleb stopped, but Death grasped the shoulder of his IBA and pulled him down the trail.

"But why? I'm only here for six months, then I go home. It can't be my time yet!"

"I suppose I could respond with something flowery like, why do the stars move in their course, or some such thing. It just is, Caleb. I do not know the answer any more than you do, but I know when it is time for someone, just like I knew when it was time for 6,000 of your fellow men and women in this Global War On Terrorism. Yours was three days ago."

"No!"

"Do not make a scene," Death sighed. Caleb looked around wildly, but the soldiers ignored them as if nothing out of the ordinary was occurring.

"But wait! What if this is a mistake?"

"This is not a mistake. And I have new assistants, very dedicated, and very afraid after they saw what I did to their predecessors. There are half a dozen assistants with AK-47s, and even a suicide bomber among them, all waiting for you, who will ensure that our appointment is kept today."

"WAIT!"

"Please do not make this any more difficult than it has to be."

"Chief!"

Death's dry chuckle echoed through the misty air.

The soldiers ignored Caleb's shout. He swung the butt of his carbine at Death's skull face. The folding stock whipped through empty air and he fell and rolled down the slope. Death followed at a leisurely pace.

"Caleb, Caleb, Caleb," Death said like a chiding parent.

"NO! SERGEANT NOTTINGHAM!"

A sarcastic smile accompanied Death's shrug. "Go ahead. Do your best."

"Sergeant Nottingham!"

"Yes?"

"Sergeant, I can't go into the village! I have to stay on the crest."

Chief frowned and gave him a suspicious look. The soldiers stopped and a few looked at Caleb from the corners of their eyes.

"Why?"

"I-I'll die if I go down there."

Chief lit a cigarette as a couple of soldiers snickered. "Are you having some sort of fuckin' artistic fit? How do you know you'll fuckin' die if you go down there?"

Caleb trembled and shook his head. "Sergeant, please, trust me on this!"

"We're almost to the river."

"Look, look. The slope on this side is bare. The guys up there can see me plain as day. I won't be in any danger if I turn back now."

Chief's eyes narrowed and he suddenly lifted his head and sniffed loudly. He looked around them, and then tilted his head as Death descended the slope toward them.

"You're not Corporal Weaver." It was a statement, not a question.

"True enough." Death smiled and removed his ballistic glasses. His obsidian eyes within his skull-like face glittered darkly.

Caleb saw the color drain from Chief's face. He looked at Caleb, the village, his soldiers, and back at Death.

"Who are you here for?"

A puzzled look filled Death's face. "You do not seem surprised to see me."

"You're a soldier's constant companion. Besides, my grand-father was a medicine man back on the reservation, and he told me stories about you. You're not some goddamn frightful apparition to me."

"Yes," Death nodded. "I remember your grandfather. A good and dignified man. If only all were so accepting of me." Death looked pointedly at Caleb.

Chief saw the look and glanced at Caleb. "You're here for him?"

"Yes. We missed our appointment three days ago. I am here to see that we keep our new appointment."

"You can't fuckin' have him."

Death raised his thin eyebrows in surprise. "What?"

Caleb blinked and, though he knew his fate hung in the balance, there was a desperate glimmer of hope that Chief might some-how save him.

"You can't have him," Chief said. "I've been goddamned lucky. I've seen 23 of my soldiers wounded, even crippled. But I've never lost a soldier, and I'm not going to fuckin' lose one now. Not when this may be my last tour because the war is winding down."

"That is not my concern. He is overdue."

"You're Death. You can release him, give him an extension of time. You have the power to do so, right?" Death frowned at Chief and Caleb. "Right?"

"Well, yes."

"Then do it. Give Sergeant Justus an extension of time because you have the fuckin' power to do it."

"Why should I do that?"

"Because you have the power to do it."

Death shook his head. "I cannot do that. I choose not to do that."

"What do you want that will encourage you to give a fuckin' extension?"

"Nothing that you, or this world, has."

"Of course there is. You just haven't recognized it."

An unfriendly and menace-filled frown crossed Death's skeletal face. "There is nothing that I desire that would make me want to grant Caleb an extension." He pointed with a pale hand at the village across the river. "We have an appointment this afternoon."

Chief tossed the cigarette aside and lit another. He studied Death, looked at the village, and at Caleb.

"You know, I loved my grandfather very much. I treasure the time we spent together. He told me stories about his grand-father who fought at the Little Big Horn. A small fight, really, compared to some Civil War battles. But a small fight that became a heroic myth to a young nation, and an important part of my tribal heritage."

"And?"

Chief smiled as he puffed on the cigarette. "He also shared with me some things before the fuckin' coming of Manifest Destiny."

"The point, Sergeant Nottingham."

"My grandfather taught me to make paint from natural materials, and he taught me how to paint on a buffalo hide robe, as our ancestors used to do." The obsidian eyes glittered impatiently. "Art hasn't been kind to you, especially since the Black Death in the Middle Ages. Mostly art depicts you as a worm-eaten corpse, a skeleton barely clothed in fleshy tatters, a scurvy hound from hell preying on a helpless mankind—"

"I *get* the idea."

"Sergeant Justus will do a portrait of you. A goddamn digni-fied portrait that will do you, no pun intended, justice."

Death's eyebrows rose with surprise and Caleb's mouth dropped open in equal surprise.

"Excuse me?" Death asked.

"What?" Caleb gasped.

Chief glared at Caleb, and turned back to Death. "A god-damned dignified portrait. As you know, Sergeant Justus is an Army Combat Artist. A damned good one from what I've been told. Only the very best artists become an Army Combat Artist."

Death shook his head in disbelief. "No."

"What have you got to lose?" Chief asked. "If you don't like the portrait, the two of you keep your appointment. If you like your portrait, you give him an extension of time." Death's eyebrows curled thoughtfully and Chief added again, "What have you got to lose?" He flicked his cigarette at Caleb who shook off his shocked stupor.

"Yes, I can do it! And, maybe, five or ten years or more in exchange?"

Chief rolled his eyes at Caleb. "He lives to a very ripe old age with his faculties intact. No tricks."

"He offered five or ten years."

"He's not much of a negotiator. In exchange for a fuckin' dignified portrait, he lives to a very ripe old age."

Death rubbed his jaw and chuckled. "All right. A dignified portrait that I like, that my assistants like, in exchange for living to a very ripe old age."

Caleb held a hand up like a school child. "I can't do anything in this rain."

"Be patient," Death replied as the clouds started to break up and shafts of bright sunlight peeked into the shadowed valley.

"Assistants?" Chief asked. As if in response, loud snorts and grunts came from the soldiers who stooped and swayed as if unused to standing erect. A few sniffed the air loudly, while others lumbered down to the river where they lapped up water like animals.

"Assistants. They will see to our security, though that's hardly necessary at the moment." He snapped his fingers and the once-soldiers loped and scurried in all directions to take up their positions. From the crest came long, drawn out howls that were neither animal nor human. The once-soldiers growled and howled in response.

"I see," Chief said, a horrified look on his face.

Death looked at Caleb. "And now, I'm at your service."

"Sergeant Nottingham?" Caleb said.

He walked with Chief to the edge of the tall reeds and trees that followed the gurgling river. "I don't know what to do, I mean, how to do it. I mean, a dignified portrait of something that scares the bejesus out of most people?"

"Okay, before the Black Death, Death was, just fuckin' Death. He was the lord of the underworld. People were afraid of him, yes, but not like today. He's a companion to those of us serving in the Profession of Arms. You're the fuckin' artist! What do you look for when you paint a portrait of someone?"

"Ah, the inner person. The outer person yes, but to paint something of the inner person, to bring that to the surface so that the viewer can see more than the physical shell."

"Okay, good. Death is fearsome, yes, but he's not some fair-weather friend and, damn him, he'll always be with you. And he's fuckin' strong. Nothing can overcome him. You follow my drift?"

"Yes, Sergeant," Caleb nodded, his mind racing frantically at a morning that took such a strange, haunting, twist.

"Then fuckin' paint or draw or whatever, as if your life depended on it, because it does."

As Caleb returned he felt the obsidian eyes boring into him, measuring him. He discarded his IBA, ACU blouse, and combat pack, and from his drawing kit dug out a small sketch pad and colored pencils. Death cleared his throat and Caleb looked up. "Yes?"

"Are you going to do a portrait of me using colored pencils and a small sketch pad?"

"I usually do sketches, maybe take a few photos, and then go back to my studio at Bagram to do the final, whether oil painting or charcoal or pastel. It could take weeks to complete. I'm used to working standing up with a tripod easel and canvas or a drawing board with Rives paper. Sometimes even a wood board."

"What is your favorite medium?"

"Ah, oil, charcoal, pastel."

Death shook his head impatiently. "Your favorite?"

"Oil."

"Then may I suggest we go straight to the means for accomplishing the final product?"

Caleb blinked as a tall wood tripod easel with a large canvas appeared before him. A paint stand appeared next, well stocked with brushes, tubes of oils, liquin to mix with the paints, a large jar of turpentine for the brushes, and a variety of graphite and charcoal pencils.

"Uh, thank you." Caleb took his time arranging everything. He had no idea how to accomplish a portrait of Death without resorting to a stereotypical image. Death folded his arms as Caleb arranged his paints for the third time. Chief lit his last cigarette and disgustedly crumpled the empty pack. Death sighed and produced a new pack.

Death cleared his throat loudly, impatiently.

"Right!" Caleb said as he flipped the canvas to a horizontal position and carefully sketched three boxes; a large center box and a narrow box on each side. "Triptych. The center image is the strongest, the foundation. The two side boxes emphasize something from the center, or emphasize something related to the center. The triptych was big during the Middle Ages, usually done on wood, and in churches."

"Fascinating," Death grumbled.

Caleb felt the warmth of the newly revealed sun on his face as the last of the rain clouds dissipated. A breeze, though cool because it was fall, flowed gently across the valley that echoed with low growls and an occasional howl.

"No," Caleb said decisively. "Give me an oak board instead, gessoed and sanded, same size as the canvas."

Death blinked in surprise, and an oak board replaced the canvas.

"I need a large rock for you to sit on." Death sat down on a large rock that appeared. "Sit erect, body facing the river, your face toward me. Place your carbine across your lap, your hands on the pistol grip and the barrel guard. Put your Kevlar on the ground. Perfect."

"This is such a simple pose," Death observed.

"At your feet I'm placing a Mycenaean figure-8 shield, a Greek hoplon, a Roman scutum, a round cornered rectangular Celtic shield, and a Crusader heater shield. An Eisenhower jacket from World War II, a flak vest from Korea and Vietnam, and an IBA from this war. The background, darker at the edges and lighter toward you as if you're lit by a spotlight, a chiaroscuro effect, will be a wall of prehistoric cave art."

"Please explain."

"Everything taken together, from the beginning of mankind's first effort at drawing and painting, represents you as a steady companion, especially to those of us who wear a uniform."

"And the side panels?"

"On the left panel, your hand a little above, reaching down toward a human hand that is being raised up from below to your hand. Sooner or later we all come your way. The ancients accepted you as a part of life, while today we're very afraid of you. The panel represents us reaching toward you while you extend a reassuring hand to us, rather than a skeletal or diseased hand grasping us."

"The right panel?"

"I'm reminded of the World War I slaughter at Flanders Field where so many soldiers now sleep. A wheat field lit by the golden rays of a peaceful morning sun hanging in a deep blue sky. Sooner or later we all cross over to sleep peacefully for eternity."

Death said, "The theory sounds good. We will see how well you accomplish the execution."

Caleb silently mixed paint and liquin, and for additional colors, mixed various paints to produce the desired result. He also mixed lighter and darker hues of the same colors; once the paints were mixed, he chose a graphite pencil to sketch the painting. He was grateful that his mentor tirelessly emphasized drawing skills as the basis for a well crafted painting.

The graphite hissed lightly across the wood as he worked quickly, sketching, and erasing as needed, as if in a race before the sun set. Or until Death lost his patience. Chief paced silently behind him, lighting one cigarette after another.

Then he started the actual painting. His mentor emphasized working on the entire painting at one time, as working piecemeal resulted in a piecemeal look. Besides, wet paint made the blending of edges, and the blending of different hues that gave a painting depth, much easier. Clearly defined edges and a lack of careful blending always drove his mentor up the wall.

He hadn't thought about it in such a long time, but he almost chuckled when he remembered how primitive his first efforts were. Sometimes he was ready to chuck the brushes and his paints. But he hung in because he wanted to be a painter. He didn't think he would be another Peter Paul Rubens, Claude Monet, Henri Matisse, or Edgar Degas, but he would give those accomplished masters a run for their money — and he did.

"Why oak?" Death asked.

Caleb paused. "Wood has a finite life, like us. Someday this painting will crumble into dust, just like us."

"Go back," Chief murmured. "That's a Cheyenne way of looking at death. Sooner or later we all go back to Mother Earth."

"I see."

Caleb sighed and looked at the village. Half a dozen assistants, Death had said, including a suicide bomber, were waiting for him. Where would they be hiding? Or would they pose as a villager with an AK-47 or a pistol hidden within their robes? Perhaps all they had were hand grenades with which they would shower him in a deadly volley.

As he stared at the village, Chief crossed his view, cigarette in hand, and pointed at the board.

Caleb returned to the painting with a fresh vengeance. He wanted to go home, he wanted to see his family, marry Lesley, and especially, cradle Mikey in his arms.

"Done," Caleb finally said as he plopped his paint brush into the jar of turpentine and rubbed his face with paint stained hands.

Death stirred as if awaking from a deep sleep. Chief stood next to him. The once-soldiers, grunting and sniffing, approached curiously.

Death examined the painting and stroked his jaw thoughtfully.

"It's an excellent portrait," Chief announced. Many of the once-soldiers kneeled before the board and lowered their heads as if before royalty. "A goddamned excellent portrait," Chief repeated in a stronger voice.

Caleb held his breath as he looked at Death from the corner of his eye. Death leaned forward for a closer look.

"Our appointment is cancelled." Death looked at Caleb. "I hope you enjoy your extreme old age. I also hope you will remember this day with some fondness, if only for meeting the greatest challenge of your young life."

Chief gave Caleb a hard congratulatory slap between the shoulders.

A sob escaped Caleb and abruptly he sat down on the still muddy ground. The warm sunlight and the caress of the gentle breeze never felt so good. He grinned and laughed from relief, though he cast a doubtful look at the silent village on the other side of the river.

"My assistants have already vacated the village." Death looked at Chief and added, "There are no Taliban around here today."

"Thank you," Caleb whispered.

"What will you do with this portrait?"

"My art teacher, actually my mentor for many years, owns a successful art gallery in Las Vegas, of all places. I know he'll love this portrait and will hang it in a place of honor."

Death gestured with his hand and the oak board and all of the painting accoutrements faded like a morning mist before the rising sun.

"You'll find everything waiting for you in your studio." A flicker of a smile played at Death's lips. "Until we meet again."

Death's form shimmered with fleeting shadows and a faint, ghostly whistle filled the air. "Oh shit!" Chief shouted, and shoved Caleb to the ground.

The earth shook as Death's darkly shimmering form silently exploded in a bright, smoky white flash, like an exploding white phosphorous shell.

"That was some fuckin' exit," Chief grumbled as he raised his muddy face.

"Amen to that," Caleb whispered with closed eyes as he savored the feel of warm sunlight and the gentle caress of the fall breeze on his face.

◼ ◼ ◼

S S Hampton, Sr. is a Choctaw from Oklahoma, a divorced grandfather to twelve grandchildren (one more on the way), and a published photographer and photojournalist. He is a veteran of Operations Noble Eagle and Iraqi Freedom. His fiction has appeared in *Horror Bound Magazine, Ruthie's Club, Lucrezia Magazine*, and *The Harrow*, among others, and in anthologies from Melange Books and Dark Opus Press. Forthcoming stories will be published by Ravenous Romance, MUSA Publishing, and MuseItUp Publishing. He lives in Las Vegas, Nevada. The inspiration for this story is his life-long interest in art, a college painting class he is enrolled in, and his service in the military.

—THE EXCLUSIVE—
By Edward M. Erdelac

Tom Cotter was no man to be trifled with. He had rustled Mexican steer along the border into a sizeable herd in his youth and had built himself an empire as one of the first outfits to drive cattle to the Missouri railheads, putting beef in the bellies of starving soldiers during the War Between The States. He owned a good chunk of New Mexico. He was a king among cattlemen. There were senators that doffed their hats to him, and he in turn did their dirty work on occasion, sending out his hired villains to execute foreclosures on land he didn't own, gunning down those who tried to resist. He had a beef contract with the local Indian reservation which he rarely fulfilled, yet the government money stuffed his war bag every month on schedule just the same.

Everybody knew this, but Barry Twiggs, editor-in-chief of *The Perryville Premonitor*, dared to print it, and often. He had been warned off in various ways by Cotter's men. They had burned down his office twice, hired a drunk to bust his knee with a stick of firewood, and shot his horse out from under him. He had expected another reprisal after the Sunday edition's front page headline linked Cotter to a prominent member of The Ord Gang, but not the one he got.

Now, as his flesh was scraped away by brambles and his bleeding wounds filled with grit, as he bounced along the ground through cactus patches, towed behind a galloping palomino by his ankle, he wished he'd taken a drinking colleague's advice and bought himself a .44.

Cotter had sent a group of masked men to answer Twiggs's latest 'libelous' attack on his person with axe handles and lariats. They had yanked him and his printing press out of the office, knocked him ass over teakettle, then dragged the both of them out of town.

The frictional burning all about his body was a blinding agony, but if he opened his mouth to scream he choked on dust kicked up by the horses. He could hear laughter above the noise of his body dragging, and the banging of his press as it tumbled behind the other rider's horse.

He tried to retreat into his mind, away from the nightmare engulfing him, but composing accusatory editorial rebuttals in his pain-wracked brain gave him no comfort. He doubted he would live to print another edition.

He took some comfort in thoughts of Junia, but then a stone dashed against his face and he was cast back into hellish reality.

When they stopped, he didn't know, nor did he know how long he lay there.

"He's still alive!"

"He don't look t'be. Lost enough hide to half-sole an elephant."

"Listen to him breathin'!"

"Cotter wants him dead."

"Shoot him."

"You shoot him."

"Tie him to his printin' machine and sink him in the river."

Laughter.

He felt them cut the latigo chord that had dug through his flesh until it was wrapped around the bare bone of his ankle. Then he was propped up, head lolling, something blocky and cold jutting into his back. They lashed him to it and he was lifted, horny fingers digging into his bleeding elbows and ragged ankles. He got a last look at the sun burning itself out in the high desert before he was heaved into a chilly darkness.

He struck the bottom. He hadn't had the presence of mind to catch a deep breath before they chucked him in. His lungs burned. He gritted his broken teeth and weakly strained against his fetters, but it was no use. He gulped water in place of air.

He panicked and bucked, but his broken bones and torn muscles wouldn't serve.

His eyes bulged as he looked around the dark river bottom for any kind of way out.

Then someone broke the bright surface of the water way above his head and came straight down at him like a diving duck. He had long dark hair like a woman's, but he was definitely a man, naked as a jaybird, the wavy watery light playing across his lean muscles.

Strong as he looked, how would he cut him loose? *I appreciate the effort, fella*, thought Twiggs, *but I'm done*.

His coulda-been savior drifted to a stop in front of him and inspected his bonds. That was when Twiggs noticed the long knife in his hand. Actually it was more like a sword; and not one of those cavalry sabers either, but the sort of thing you think of a Roman soldier having. In a few quick flashes, Twiggs was loose and floating. He felt the stranger's powerful arm encircle his chest and draw him up and out.

He lay on his belly on the riverbank trembling like a bass plucked out of its habitat. He waited for the stranger to help him up, to bear him to a horse or a wagon.

But the man only turned from Twiggs and stood staring at the setting sun, the sword propped on his shoulder.

He made no move to put any clothes on, and Twiggs saw no rig or horse nearby, nor even a pile of duds.

There was something odd about this man, to be sure. He was too dang perfect. The water didn't speckle or shine on his skin. By God, his hair wasn't even wet.

For that matter, neither was Twiggs's. He ran his hand over his own head, then his face, and came away with no blood. He didn't detect any of the wounds the cruel desert foliage had opened up on his body; he inspected his hands and feet as thoroughly as St. Thomas and found no marks anywhere. His left foot, from which they'd dragged him, should have been hanging by a scrap of flesh.

No pain, either. Not even the dull ache in between his shoulder blades he'd been working on for the past three years, or the permanent stiffness in the knee Cotter's paid drunkard had given him.

As the sun dipped behind the mountains, the naked stranger turned and regarded him with a pair of stark white eyes, devoid of iris or pigment.

Twiggs felt a sinking feeling in the pit of his stomach.

"Ready?" the man said.

His voice was deep and bespoke infinite tiredness.

"Almighty b'damned," Twiggs spluttered. "What in hell's goin' on here?" Although he well knew, or at least had a better than average inkling.

The naked man sighed and lifted the sword down off his shoulder. He advanced, the keen looking blade swinging idly in his hand.

"Whoa!" Twiggs stammered. "Hang on now. Alright. That was a stupid question. You're a busy man, and you must get that reaction a lot, I'd warrant."

The man stopped before him, but said nothing.

Twiggs let his eyes run up and down the imposing, weird figure before him. He grimaced a bit when he saw that below the waist, the man had been cut, apparently a long time ago, and not in the Jewish sense, unless the rabbi had been in the throes of the St. Vitus Dance and botched the job. He was like a master sculptor's statue, a perfect male specimen but for the lack of that vital organ that warranted the appellation, as if it'd been neatly chipped away by some prudish art critic. Twiggs's curiosity over this mutilation burned him more than had the ground from town to the river, but it was not something one began a conversation with.

"I know who you are, sure," said Twiggs, thinking quickly. "Do you know who I am?"

"I neither know nor care," said the stranger.

"Well sir, I'm a newspaper man. Barry Twiggs, of the Shreveport Twiggses. Founder and editor-in-chief of *The Perryville Premonitor*, with a circulation encompassing the better part of two counties in the territory of New Mexico."

He paused.

"Ah, incidentally, what do I call you?"

"What?" the stranger blinked, as if he had been caught half-listening.

"You must have a name. Death, that's just an official title, right?"

"Mr. Twiggs, what do you want?"

"A busy man, yes indeed. Well sir, as I said before, I'm a newspaper man. By a turn of fate in life I was a crusader, a voice for the people. But I never set out to be such. The whims of fortune do turn a man from his intended path though, do they not? When I came out west, I only meant for journalism to be a sideline to my real calling. I wanted to be a biographer, you see. At that time all the newspapers back east were filled with accounts of Wild Bill Hickok's shootout with Dave Tutt, the exploits of the James gang, etcetera. I came out here to find one of these shootists, these up-and-coming killers. I thought I could hitch my wagon to one, become a Buntline or a Nichols or a Beadle. You get a sense of the real man and then embellish the rest, live off the residuals. That was all I wanted."

He trailed off, watching a gibbous moon emerging in the darkening sky, then shook himself. Death hadn't the patience for reflection.

"To be brief, sir, I feel the stirring of my old calling. Here I sit, in front of the most famous killer extant, whose career trumps the tally of any gunman who ever lived — who ever will live, even. I doubt you're in the business of granting last requests. I should think a man in your line would hardly stop to palaver even, after a time. But I think sir, that you have a tale to tell. I'll bet you millions of folks ask you 'why' and 'how come' and 'where am I going' and the like, but not a one of them has asked to hear your story."

Death regarded the man. "You do realize you're dead, Mr. Twiggs?"

"Please, Barry. I figured that out, yessir."

"Then who do you intend to relate my tale to?"

"Why, if there's an afterlife, I'll regale my fellow souls with it."

"And what if there is nothing?"

"Well, you'll pardon me, but if you're here, I'll bet there's something."

Death nodded. "From here, you go to hell."

Twiggs stiffened.

"You'll be purged in fire for a time, until your iniquities and your earthly concerns are burned away. You won't care at all for your stories and your curiosity will be gone."

"And after my time's served?"

Death turned to look at the moon.

"My God," said Twiggs, settling down on a rock. "You don't know, do you?"

Death wheeled on him, and lifted the sword, angry.

"Wait," said Twiggs. "Tell me your story. If not for me, then for yourself. When's the last time anybody listened to you?"

Death seemed to hesitate, the sword poised to whistle down. It did not strike.

"Come on. I'm all ears. Let's start …. with your name. What's your name?"

"There is no deceiving me, Mr. Twiggs. In all the eons I have been Death, I have never been once cheated out of my task."

Well, so much for that. It had been in the back of Twiggs's mind of course, maybe to get that sword away from him somehow.

"No tricks," Twiggs said. "No parleys, no last minute entreaties."

Death lowered the sword again. He turned it in his hand and drove the point into the muddy bank.

"Samael was my name."

"Samael. Sam. There. That's a start. Pleased to meet you, Sam." Twiggs's tongue touched his lip. He knew, of course, that this was a useless gesture. He wasn't even in his body anymore. That bloodied and battered corpse of his was supper for fish at the bottom of the river. But whatever form he held for the moment anyway, soul or shade, it was still his own. He didn't like what Death (or Sam, it was easier to talk to him that way) had said about losing his curiosity and desires, but at least hell wasn't eternal.

"How did you get picked to be the Angel of Death?"

"It is not an honor I was selected for," said Sam. "It is a punishment."

"And you're the only one that does it? You don't have helpers?"

"I do not visit every mortal soul, so I think there must be others, but we have never met. I cannot perceive nor be perceived by anyone but the souls of the dying, those in transition."

"Not even other angels?"

"I exist outside of Creation."

It was like a prison, then. A prison that spanned the world and held one inmate.

"What'd you do to warrant this?"

"I fought in the Great Rebellion, under The Light Bearer."

"That really happened?"

"It did. We lost."

"Yeah I read about it. Why'd you and Lucifer rebel?"

"Lucifer had his own reasons. He was my friend, but I did not share his motivations."

"But you joined him."

"Doesn't every man who goes to war do so for his own reason?"

"Fair enough. What was yours?"

Sam looked at the moon again, then down at Twiggs. He sat down on the stone opposite him, and rested a hand on the pommel of his silver sword.

"A woman," Sam said.

"You mean a mortal woman?"

Sam nodded.

"I heard stories of that too. Never figured 'em for true. So who was this woman?"

"The first woman."

"You mean Eve."

"Eve was not the first woman. God crafted Eve from Adam's body to correct the mistake He made with Lilith."

"Lilith?"

"The first woman. Lilith was made from the earth as Adam was. She was his equal."

"Now that I hadn't heard. What was she like?"

For the first time, Sam allowed a thin smile to slide across his face.

"Spirited. She pulsed with life. Her body, her skin, flushed with it. She had red hair, like seraphic fire. Seeing her, I know now I ached to hold her. But I did not even know what the feeling meant as I looked upon her. The creation of man and woman was not a popular decision among the ministers of heaven. To many, encasing a pure spirit within a mortal shell that was bound to expire was a perversion. To others, the commandment that we angels serve these malformed children was outrageous."

"What about to you?"

"When I looked on Lilith, I saw the soft light that shone within her as if through a cloud. It was so precious and innocent. Long had I lived among spirits. I was used to the glory of the naked soul. Seeing it obscured in flesh and blood was exotic to me. I was old, and she was new."

"But why rebel?"

"Lucifer made promises to all the rebel factions, as all politicians necessarily must, to form a cause."

"He promised you Lilith."

"Do you think me a fool?" Sam asked, and there was no threat in his tone. It was an honest question, backed by misery. It deserved a direct answer.

"Yeah, I guess you were. But there've been bigger fools since."

"You speak plain, Mr. Twiggs. I appreciate that. Most would lie to me in the hope of prolonging their existence."

"I told you, it's Barry. And I have no illusions," Twiggs said. "What about Lilith? Did you two ever meet?"

"Indeed we did," Sam said. "After the Rebellion, we Fallen were cast into hell. Lucifer built his capitol, his throne, and many of the Fallen remained his servants. I wanted nothing further to do with them, so I wandered. I lingered at the edge of Eden, the Garden where Adam and Lilith were. I watched, and loved from the shadow of the East.

"I became a fixture at the outskirts of the Garden, and soon they noticed me. The man, Adam, would take Lilith by the hair and tell her I was not fit to look upon. Michael and the other angels had warned him about the Fallen. At first, she was obedient. But sometimes I would catch her watching me. When Adam took her away, she would look back until she was out of sight."

Twiggs detected a hint of vehemence every time Sam mentioned the progenitor's name. He didn't take offense.

"I take it you weren't an admirer of Adam."

"That brutish ape!" Sam said, a terrible anger flashing across his face. "Naming the beasts and birds as if they were his. And then...."

"What?"

"Lilith would go away from him. She would come to a far corner of the Garden, and we would speak."

"About what?"

"About the secrets of the universe, about God and the angels. She was like a child, hungry for anything I would teach her. She could learn nothing from the man. One day, he caught us speaking. He raged at her, 'till all his pitiful blood was in his face. He threw her down, tried to mount her like a dog, as he always did. She would not submit to him. She raised such a clamor that the angels came to see, and God too.

"I stood helpless at the boundary of the Garden as Adam accused her and demanded of his Creator a more facile mate. Demanded! As though he were owed. God questioned Lilith, and her only answer was to run. She ran from the Garden, into my arms. Out of that lush prison, I swept her into the air. We flew across the world, embracing again and again in a passion that made Creation quake."

"Pardon me," Twiggs interrupted. "But when you say you embracing, what you mean to say is, you .... ah .... copulated?"

Sam blinked. "What did you think I meant?"

"But ... how is that possible?"

"It would be hard for you to understand," Sam said. "Angels could never mimic mortal bodies because being spirit, we'd had no experience with mortal flesh. It was forbidden. The moment she embraced me however, I knew her and she knew me. We found a middle ground, so to speak, and so—"

"Yeah, that's not what I meant either. Uh ... how do I put this? Even in this middle ground, were you uh ... equipped to...?"

He gestured to Sam's lap, hoping it would be enough to get his point across.

Sam cocked his head, then seemed to follow his thought.

"You are getting ahead of the story."

"Sorry. I hope I didn't offend you."

"Where was I?"

"Copulating over Creation."

"Ah yes. The fruit of our passion seeded the earth with demons."

"Demons?"

"Yes. There were no demons before then, only fallen angels. The offspring of Lilith and I were the first. The first four were daughters. We named them Lilit, Agrat, Nehema, and Eisheth. They were born almost simultaneously, at great pain to Lilith. More, they were hideous."

"Never heard a father refer to his offspring like that before."

"They were," Sam reiterated. "Bestial. As demons they could control their aspect, but as infants they did not know how. Lilith was terrified by them. She thought them monsters, a curse from God. She ran from me."

"Left you with them?"

"Yes. These were new beings. I didn't even understand them. They matured almost overnight. They came to me, each of them, in the guise of my Lilith."

He paused, and fixed Twiggs with a meaningful glance. "For four nights I thought she had returned to me."

"I see where you're going here," Twiggs said soberly, reminded of the sin of Lot and his daughters. "How'd you find out it wasn't her?"

"God sent Michael the archangel to me and he revealed their treachery out in the wastes. My daughters fled, and Michael told me that Lilith and our offspring were filling the world with demons, and it couldn't be allowed to continue. I tried to fight him, but the Lord was with him. He cut me, as you see me, so I couldn't father others. Then I was bound over to be sentenced."

"To become the Angel of Death?"

"Yes."

"Did you ever see Lilith again?"

"Once. We were tried together with God our judge and the archangels our jury. In the time we had been away, Adam and Eve had been ousted from the Garden, thanks to Lucifer. Adam blamed Eve as usual, and wandered away from her. He found Lilith in the land of Nod. For a time they were together." He chuckled. "I suppose she saw the light again though, and left him. But I had taught her strange arts, and she begat demons with him too. Our coupling had made her something more than human. She was caught fleeing across the ocean, and bargained for her life. She allowed a hundred of her children to die every day, but retained the powers she had been given. She was made immortal, and I became psychopomp to the dying."

"So you can never meet again," Twiggs said.

"I remember the last time I saw her, before they sealed me in this prison. She was clothed in animal skins. I had never seen such a thing. She was a fierce, golden spirit twice-wrapped in death. So willful. She would have stared God in the face if that act wouldn't have burned her to nothingness. But she didn't even look at Michael as he passed sentence. She looked at me. And there were tears running from her eyes. The blood of the human soul."

They were quiet for a long time, Death and Twiggs. Death's thoughts were inscrutable, but Twiggs' were of Junia and the last time he'd seen her. It was the last time he would ever see her.

"For the first thousand years," Sam said, "I punished you mortals. I tore your souls from this earth and shook you like babes wakened in the night by enemy soldiers. I flung you into hell wailing. I laughed to see you scream. I concocted new perversities to inflict upon every soul I was called to claim, and each one I think plummeted into hell a little less sane than the last. I think I was insane myself. I have danced with the dying, swung them around and around to music only I could hear, only to cast them into the inferno on the last go 'round. I emptied my heart in hatred of you until I became a great scar. Then my sadism bored me, and I spoke little at all. All the crimes I committed were useless. No soul came to me dreading what I had done before. Each feared only the change I represented. Once I sat silently on the soul of a man for eight years, just to watch him gibber beneath me like an animal."

"Well," said Twiggs, "I'm glad you're past that period, anyway."

"In time," Sam went on, "I do not know how long, I became curious about humanity. I asked every soul about the world. I learned of man's wars, of the plagues that brought him to me in droves, of the progress and failures of his civilization. But soon that fanned the hatred in me again, because I could not see these things myself. From time to time I asked about Lilith and occasionally heard rumors, but no one knew of her. Sometimes, I forced the souls of young women to mimic her. It was never the same."

"Do you still hate us?"

"Not anymore. Learned men came to me and begged me to let them stay. They wanted to see their work bear fruit. Artists, poets, leaders. But this could never be. Only one soul at a time, and so I threw them out with the rest. Such a waste. I began to pity you your mortality."

"Do you still?"

"Now I envy it. As long as men are born, no one will ever come for me, Mr. Twiggs. You live your lives and pass into something else. I go on and on without change."

Twiggs sat quietly, ashamed at his earlier thoughts of betrayal. Could he do nothing to help this poor creature?

"Sam, what if I took your sword there and—?"

Sam shook his head. "It will not cut me." Then, after a moment, he put his hand over Twiggs's and smiled. "Thank you, though."

Twiggs shuddered. Death's touch was colder than the bottom of the river where he'd expired.

Sam rose and stretched his long limbs. The moon was gone leaving the sky above in total darkness, though the east was purpling with a deep blue spreading over the rim of the earth. Somewhere a bird sang in anticipation.

"That is all there is to tell," Sam said.

"It's a helluva story," Twiggs said. "Hope to tell it to someone else someday."

Sam's expression was flat, and Twiggs realized he'd been fishing. He thought he had him then.

"If you don't know what happens to me, how do you know about hell?"

"I was told to tell you at my sentencing. It's my only other duty. If it is a lie, I would not know."

"God is a vindictive sonofabitch, isn't he?" said Twiggs.

"I think He's forgotten me."

"I won't."

"You do not know that."

"What happens now?" Twiggs asked, fighting down that trembling again.

"Put your hand by the crown of your head. Up near the back," Sam suggested.

Twiggs did. There was something there. It felt like a strand of cobwebs between his fingers, but it was attached to his skull. No, that wasn't right. It was a part of him, coming out of his head. Touching it made him swoon. The world seemed to jar and bend around him, as if everything hung from that tether.

"What is it?" he whispered, afraid.

"It binds you to this world. My sword will cut it." He pulled the sword out of the earth. The blade was still clean and pure.

"Will it hurt?"

"I do not know."

Twiggs wiped his mouth with a shaking hand. He tried to stand up, failed, and stood again.

"Are you ready?" said Sam.

Twiggs looked at the river beneath which his corpse lay. He looked all around, taking in the dark desert, wishing he could see more, wishing the sun would hurry the horizon. A small tecolote swooped into its little roost, a hole in a saguaro. He wanted to take it all in, take it with him, but dawn was a long way off. He found the sight he lingered on most was somewhere behind his eyes.

"Can I tell you why I didn't hunt me up a shootist and make a name for myself in the dime novels, Sam?"

"It can't take long," said Sam, not unkindly, but firmly.

"It was a woman too. Her name was Junia. We loved each other from the get go. But her pa was a powerful man. He wouldn't let us be. Sent her abroad. Fixed her up with some rich swell. He wouldn't have me for a son-in-law, so I made myself his enemy. Went after him with everything I had. Dug up every murderous deed, every underhanded thing he'd ever done and held it up for everybody to see. Made it my life, digging in the dirt. Didn't even get me a grave. Women and fortune. They drive us down strange roads, don't they, Sam?"

"Yes."

"Will I remember her?"

"I do not know."

Then Twiggs felt a buildup deep inside him, something he'd been holding back. He wasn't the sort to panic, but here he was, sitting by the dark water, and it would be the last sight he ever saw in this world. It should've been a waterfall, or a sunny meadow, or children playing. Junia ought to be here, holding his hand, a wrinkled old liver-spotted hand with a band of gold on the finger. God, did he have to die alone? He thought about how he had played with his life in the past, put so many things off. Now he wanted it back. He wanted it all back. And it was drifting away quicker than the river over his bones.

"What is this? *A goddamned game*? Why do I have to die? What's *next*?" he spluttered, losing his composure. He put his face in his hands.

The Angel of Death waited patiently.

"I broke my promise. I'm sorry," he said after a minute.

"No matter."

"Well," sighed Twiggs, hugging himself, though his body was already gone. "I'm sorry for your troubles. And I do thank you for the exclusive."

"Thank you for listening, Barry."

It was good to hear his own name.

"Go on."

Sam raised the sword. His face was placid. He tried to show empathy, and perhaps he did feel it, but it was a bootless, comical gesture, a thing with no hope trying to give hope to one who had lost it.

In the moment the sword tilted back. Twiggs saw great black wings over Sam's shoulders, like a crow's.

There had been crows like that around the farm in Shreveport when he was a boy. They would perch on the fence posts and chase the sparrows through the willow trees. He pitched rocks up at those crows, feeling for the little birds. Once he'd killed one dead.

He closed his eyes.

The sword cut the air and parted the ethereal chord. Twiggs came apart like a stack of copy sheets in the wind, swirled on the etheric breeze, and went off into the dark.

Sam lay the sword across his shoulder and walked on down the river.

※ ※ ※

Edward M. Erdelac is the author of *Dubaku, The Crawlin' Chaos Blues*, and the acclaimed *Merkabah Rider* weird western series for Damnation Books (in which Samael, The Angel of Death, and his paramour Lilith both appear), *Red Sails* for Lyrical Press, and *Buff Tea* from Texas Review Press. A member of the HWA, his fiction has appeared in *Murky Depths Magazine, The Midnight Diner, The Trigger Reflex* from Pill Hill, and Comet Press' *DEADCORE* anthology. In 2009 he wrote, shot, and produced an independent film, *Meaner Than Hell*. He has also written for Starwars.com, and contributed an entry to *The Complete Star Wars Encyclopedia*.

FOR I MUST BE ABOUT
~MY FATHER'S WORK~
By Brian Hodge

He could pass for normal when he had to. Which was most of the time, actually. Family man, businessman, everyman, each of them one kind of mask or another. A man could hide a lot behind masks like that. Behind what everyone else expected to see. But whenever he walked into a place like this — the cold, stark hollow of this warehouse — gearing up to get down to work, the *true* work, then he could drop the masks and get real. No more family man, businessman, everyman. Now he was the Bagman. They saw him and just *knew*. Knew that at least one person who'd also walked into the place wouldn't be coming out alive.

Like this one. Casey MacKenna — his name was pretty much all the Bagman knew about him. His name, and that tonight was his last night on earth. Anything else was trivia.

"Aw God," was the first thing out of his mouth. "No…"

Guys like Casey, even if they'd never laid eyes on him before, they knew him the moment they saw him, because they knew *about* him. Knew about him the same as children know about bogeymen. His reputation preceded him the way a snot-colored sky preceded a hurricane. Thieves, thugs, hijackers, extortionists, and the rest, if they'd worked one of Ritchie Scanlon's crews long enough, then they knew. New guys, the punks just coming up, maybe they didn't, if their roots didn't run deep enough. They'd hear *Bagman* and think in small letters. They'd think some guy doing deliveries.

But no. It was *Bag* as in body bag.

"Aw, fuck me, no..."

He wasn't even pointing the gun yet, but Casey MacKenna remained planted in the same spot like he'd never known the meaning of the word *run*. That was the power of reputation. It sucked the breath from a guy's lungs and cut the nerves in his legs without the Bagman having to say a word.

"Jesus, Mary, and Joseph..."

Casey would've heard the stories. Heard them, retold them, keeping the legend alive. Like the time the Bagman had dumped a corpse by loading it in the trunk of an old car and driving to the scrapyard. While the car was dangling from the giant claw and the crane was swinging it toward the crusher, that's when you could hear the guy screaming and trying to pound his way out.

Or the time he'd tied an underboss to a post and turned loose the dogs he hadn't fed for a week. How he'd set up a camcorder on a tripod for that one. Because the boss who ordered it done wanted proof that it hadn't been quick, or neat, or clean.

Or the time he'd knocked an informant down with a baseball bat, then finished him off by stomping him with his size 18's, later explaining he couldn't use the bat anymore because he thought he'd torn his rotator cuff.

The stories were all like that, each one worse than the last, until you couldn't be sure what was true and what had grown in the telling, like the size of a fish. But they all *sounded* true, and that was all that mattered. He wanted them all to believe the worst — that Death walked among them — and they did. Even if they laughed during the telling. They'd laugh like they'd never heard anything so funny.

Casey too — the Bagman would've bet money on it. Casey too stupid to believe there could ever be the slightest chance that he himself could wind up on the bad side of one of these stories. That the same guys he thought were his friends might someday be sitting around the same table telling a new story with him at the center of it.

These would've been the same friends who'd gotten him here tonight. *We need to go to the warehouse to meet some other guys about a truckload of stolen office equipment* — whatever their story was.

Another story for why they had to duck out for a minute. Some guy complaining about low blood sugar, maybe, and that he had to go get a candy bar. *Be right back, Casey. You stay right here.*

"Holy Mary, mother of God, pray for us sinners now and at the hour of our death..."

This was the common denominator. They all got religion at the end. Still, you had to hand it to Casey MacKenna — he was *really* good at it. Jesus this, God that, have mercy, help me help me help me. He was a savant, Rain Man with prayers on his lips. Or maybe it was a Tourette's thing, everything he'd learned twenty years ago during confirmation classes now flying out of his mouth, and he couldn't stop it if he tried. Impressive, in its way. Snake handlers babbling in tongues couldn't make a bigger fuss.

"Okay," said the Bagman, finally. "I've got time. We can wait."

"Wait...?" Casey went blank, like he didn't realize what he'd been saying. "For what?"

"For God to come save you. Weren't you the one crying for that a few seconds ago? Well ... I've got time. So let's wait."

He checked his watch. Then put the gun in his left hand, his watch hand, and fiddled at his wrist with the right. Fingers so big it seemed impossible they could work such tiny knobs.

"'Pray for us now and at the hour of our death...?'" he repeated, as his watch made a sequence of beeps. "So an hour it is."

With that, he started the timer. 59:59. 59:58...

"God, Jesus, Mary, Saint Peter ... whoever wants to step in, they've got one hour. They come, then hey. Maybe it'll mean some changes for me too."

"Thank you," Casey whispered. "Thank you."

The Bagman snorted and kicked a rickety little crate over for him to sit on. "Let's see how much you're thanking me before the hour's up."

Then it was just the two of them looking at each other in the cold cavern chill of the warehouse, listening to the distant sounds of mice in the walls. The Bagman feeling that reassuring alter-ego presence that seemed just out of sight, just out of reach, at times like this, when he didn't need to hurry. Like living a dream, watching himself do things that normal people couldn't.

He wanted to sit, too, but wouldn't allow himself. He wasn't a man at times like this. He was a force of nature, and forces of nature never took a seat. It was part of the image.

Everything was, really. He looked like somebody had shaved a bear and put a human head on it. Then shaved most of the head, too, but left a goatee so people would know this wasn't completely an animal. Then — and this was the worst part — plucked out the eyes and left them in the sun for years before putting them back, until every last thing had faded from them. Everything human, everything mammal, everything reptile, until there was...

Nothing. Absolutely nothing there except the implacable wall of destiny.

A look like that didn't come naturally for most guys. They had to cultivate it. Him, though, it was there in his first school picture.

Casey sat up straighter under the harsh mercury lamps dangling from the rafters. A youngish guy, not *young* young, but in the neighborhood of thirty. A full head of sandy hair, looking like he spent some money on the cut. He probably didn't have much trouble with women. He just looked like the kind of guy who'd gotten by on natural, crooked-grin charm.

"How's, uh ... how's the rotator cuff?" he asked.

Incredible. "You heard about that, huh?"

"It seemed pretty funny at the time."

"Probably doesn't seem so funny now, does it?" He waited for Casey to shake his head. "If you know about that, you must know it didn't change anything. I just went to Plan B."

Which pretty much killed off that line of questioning, and they were back to looking at each other in silence. Or would've been if Casey hadn't started staring at the shiny worn concrete of the floor. And when it came, the Bagman was surprised it had taken this long:

"Why are they having you do this? What's this about?"

"What makes you think I know?" the Bagman said. "You take your garbage to the curb once a week. The guy that empties it in the back of the truck, has he ever once come and asked why you don't want it anymore?" He muscled aside reasons with a twitch of his shoulder. "I don't know why. I don't care. I didn't ask and Ritchie didn't tell me. You guys, you fuck up, and it's not even because you're too stupid not to, it's because you just don't give a shit."

Reasons were like picking a card from a deck. How *did* someone like Casey MacKenna end up here? Skimmed too much, fingers got too sticky, cock ended up in the wrong hole, tongue got loose in front of the wrong person, wrong department, wrong agency, or looked like it could've — pick a card, any card.

"You guys fuck up in so many ways that when you're finally called to account for it, you don't even know what it is you've done." He worked his tongue along the front of his teeth, then spat. "If you can't keep track of it, don't expect me to."

At least give Casey some credit for not trying to tell him there must've been some kind of mistake. That it wasn't supposed to be him. The things the Bagman had heard more times than he could count. The things he never listened to anymore. They were just sounds coming out of a mouth, the stuff before the screams and rasps and gurgles.

Casey MacKenna went back to praying, silently now — head bowed and lips moving, the whole nine yards. Easy to do here, and it wasn't purely the circumstances. The warehouse looked more like a church than a lot of actual churches did nowadays. Giant old brick monstrosity, a century old if it was a day, built back when people cared how something looked, when they took pride in it. It was about more than function with them then. It was about style, too. Huge arched doorways at the loading bays, skinny arched windows higher up to let in sunlight and moonlight — as good a place as any for a man to find out if he actually had a maker to meet.

The Bagman could feel the weight of the hour building. All those minutes accumulating on his wrist and rolling off onto Casey's shoulders, it was a wonder the kid could keep himself up off the floor.

"How's the time looking?" Casey asked.

He checked. "Thirty-four minutes."

"Gone? Or left?"

His face was a skull carved on a mountainside. "Thirty-four."

"What do you want?" Casey asked. "I can pay you." He had to know how much good this was going to do, but couldn't help himself. "If you don't want money there must be something else. Everybody wants something. Everybody wants something they haven't told anybody about. I can be the guy that gets it, or does it, or finds it, whatever it is. *What do you want?*"

"How about you shut the fuck up and quit boring me. I'd like that."

Casey shifted on his crate, moving like he weighed 600 pounds, 500 of it desperation.

"You don't know the first thing about me, or what I want," the Bagman said. Gun in his right hand, he started ticking off fingers on the left, one by one. "I've got a wife. Got a son. A daughter. Three things I care about. They're *all* I care about. That keeps it simple."

He'd always figured that guys like Casey, the yappy little beta-dogs, had it in their heads that he spent his off-hours in a cage somewhere, a cave, hibernating until he was needed. They couldn't connect their truth of him with the other side, the family man mask. They couldn't picture him tying shoelaces and grilling hamburgers in the summer.

Just like they couldn't relate to the terrible, tricky balance of it. The razor's edge he had to walk. Only the things you cared about could make you feel fear, and when you kept such a short list, they embodied all the fear in your world. And his family, they didn't have a clue what he did. No idea. But someday they'd find out. The families always did. Worlds would collide and they'd learn the truth and their lives would collapse. It was the only day he dreaded.

"If that's all you care about," Casey said, "then what's it matter if you let me go?"

"Four things, then. I give my word, I care about keeping it." His eyes narrowed at this loser and his sad attempts at an exit strategy. "You don't think I've heard all this before? Anything you can imagine, I've had it offered to me. Not just money. Some of you lowlifes, you're ready to give up your wives, your girlfriends, your sisters, your mothers. Some guys, their own little girls, even. They've got such sewers for minds they think a little girl is something I'd want." Sometimes he couldn't believe the world they lived in. "Those are the ones that really get me. They're the ones that make this almost fun."

Casey hunkered in thought for a moment, then said, in a glum voice, "Reminds me of a song. One of those creepy old folk songs, all death and shipwrecks, you know the kind? It's about some poor bastard waiting at the gallows." With a miles-away look in his eye, he sang. "'Hangman, hangman, wait a little while; I think I see my sister coming, riding many a mile...'"

Figured. Some things never changed. A song about a guy pimping out his sister.

"How's it end?" the Bagman asked. "It can't have been good."

"Nah." Casey shook his head. "The hangman, he pockets all the bribes from the guy's brother and his friends, fucks the guy's sister, then hangs him anyway. He's laughing while he does it."

The Bagman nodded. "Sure. It's what he does. What he is."

Casey squirmed, eyes like a trapped rabbit's, inching closer to the unraveling point. "I've got no chance here with you, do I?"

"With me? No, you never did. But it's not me that's the variable here. Your divine intervention, that's what we're waiting for."

"Go on, then! Kill me and be done with it, why don't you," Casey told him, sick of the waiting. "You've got nothing better to do than wait around here? Just get this over with!"

The Bagman checked his watch, calm as a man waiting for a train. "No. No, I said an hour, so that's what it's gonna be. What if, you know, God checked in a few seconds ago, thought He had time. 'That idiot there, he's got eighteen minutes to go, so first I'll drop by Tokyo, there's these people there that have only got two minutes left.' Then God comes back and finds out I've done you early. What am I supposed to tell Him then?"

Pleased with himself for that one. Maybe that's why he'd let MacKenna have an hour. It was better than TV. It was predictable enough that he knew the ending, but it was the getting there that had all the laughs.

"Do you believe in Him?" Casey asked. "God, I mean."

"I used to. They raised me to. They didn't live it, especially my old man. My dad, he was a real heavy-handed sonofabitch. But they raised me to." His mouth barely moved while he spoke, like the words didn't want to emerge. "Now? Now I don't guess I do."

"What changed?"

"Nothing. Nothing changed. Not a fucking thing." He scowled at his hands. Clean, nails trimmed neatly, with a milky sheen to them. To look at them, you'd never have any idea how much blood was on them. "I'm the best argument against God that I know. If there's a God, what good is He if he lets somebody like me walk around?"

There was a part of him that missed it, kind of: the time before he really knew who he was, what he could do, the things he could do and not feel, when he could still believe.

"You don't think I've heard the prayers before? Guys in your position? Half the ones who know it's coming and have the time, it's the same thing out of them. Same words, only the voices change. The other half, most of them look like they're trying to *remember* the words. I never saw one of them come close to getting an answer. Unless the answer's always no. And if it's always no, we're back to what good is He?" The Bagman heaved a thoughtful sigh. "So if I gotta believe in anything, I'd say I believe in the finality of situations. I believe in death."

And surely, by now, death had to believe in him, too. Two-way street, there.

"What's going to happen to me? After?" Casey asked. "What are you going to do with—?"

"There's not gonna be a funeral, if that's what you're getting at." He pointed toward one end of the warehouse, where a wide roll-up door hid in the shadows. "I've got a barrel of acid waiting."

That was it. That broke him, Casey going boneless, face beginning to contort with that snuffle-snort crying you'd see out of the picked-on kids on school playgrounds.

"I like to experiment with different ways of getting rid of bodies," he said. "Some guys, they never stop trying to come up with ways to make their car run smoother. Or make a hotter barbecue sauce. Me ... this is what I've got."

Casey slid off the crate, pooling to the floor and starting to sob. Getting to that puppet stage they did sometimes, like none of their joints were connected anymore. The longer it went on, the stronger the Bagman felt a conviction that once tonight's job was finished, he was going to have to drive around a good long time before he went home again. He took nothing home, ever. The last thing he wanted was to bring any residue of this shit past the front door. His wife, his son and daughter ... he only wanted to show them the good things in life. Never this side of it.

I shouldn't have done this, he thought, before he could squash it. *Shouldn't have done it this way. This was ... a cruel thing to do.*

Which had to be the most absurd thought ever to cross his mind. He'd fed a man alive to a pack of dogs and filmed it — that wasn't cruel? But that wasn't the same. Pain was just pain. It either stopped, or got so bad you couldn't feel it anymore. Or it went all the way and *everything* stopped. He'd never had a problem with any of it. It was just work, the kind of work that few could even tolerate, let alone make an art of it.

So why was this different?

He puzzled on it awhile, as he watched Casey struggle to his knees and plant his elbows on the crate and clasp his hands and tip his face to the skinny arched windows, seeking the night sky, the blackness and the cold light of autumn stars.

Maybe that was it: Pain was a transitory thing, but *this* was shoving a man's face straight into the void. Showing him how nothing and no one cared, making him wallow in the freezing truth of the emptiness at his end.

And then...? Just the damnedest thing. Casey's hands broke their clasp and he lowered his gaze and seemed to follow something across the floor. Nothing there, though. The Bagman prided himself on good night vision.

"I thought we were alone," Casey said, not much more than a whisper.

"We are," the Bagman said. "After another couple minutes, I'm gonna be *more* alone."

It didn't faze him, as Casey's gaze seemed to track something moving closer, out of the shadows and into the light. Casey glanced back at him, confused and something worse. "You don't see that?"

Of course he didn't. Just a lame try at mind games and desperate theatrics. Casey stared up at nothing, nothing coming closer, nothing standing in front of him now, and the immensity of the nothing pressing him to the floor again. Too bad it was his time to go. He would've had a great future as a senile old man.

"Fuck me, it's *real*...?" Casey quavered to the empty space in front of him, half-question, half-statement.

This was what he wanted his last words to be? Play-acting? Seemed like a wasted opportunity, but then, it *was* coming at the end of a wasted life.

Casey whirled toward him. "Can't you *see that*?" he shouted, eyes wide and full of things the Bagman had rarely seen in the eyes of the soon-to-be-dead. Terror, sure, but this time it reached into the territory of awe. "It's the hangman! From the song. The way I always pictured him."

Empty space. It couldn't be anything except empty space. Or maybe...

"Maybe it's Death," the Bagman said.

It wouldn't be the first time. He'd done a guy years ago who swore he'd seen Death waiting in the shadows, a painted lover beckoning like the Whore of Babylon. Another guy who swore there was a surgeon picking his teeth with a scalpel. He'd always figured it was just the hallucination that guys like them got instead of tunnels and white lights.

Casey glanced back at him as his fear turned inside-out, into a crazed hopeful grin. "Then I wonder which of us He's here for."

What a thing to say. Real, though? The Bagman wanted not to believe it. There was no reason to believe. He ordered himself not to. Yet … the doubt was there. The possibility. Like with the crew guys lower down the food chain furthering his legend, it was always easy to believe the worst.

And that smell gathering in the still, chilled air. Like earth and mold, fungus and rot. Was that his imagination too, this guy's delusions turning contagious—

Dee-dee-deet. Dee-dee-deet.

The Bagman let his watch cheep a couple more times, then jabbed the alarm off. With the next deep breath, the spell was broken. Damn right this had been wrong, all kinds of wrong.

"It's that time," he said.

He stepped forward, the gun leading the way, Casey MacKenna scrambling backwards in a jittery crabwalk. He scuttled one way, then another, away from the line of fire, sure, but half the time his gaze darted to the empty space at his side, and he didn't want to go that way, either, his panicked scrabble guided by the seen and unseen alike.

The Bagman fired once, twice, saw sparks fly off the concrete floor, missing by millimeters but still, *he was missing*, even though he was nearly on top of the guy. A third shot, and Casey dodged again, yelping in fright the whole time, and it was amazing — this was some real *Matrix* shit. The Bagman had never seen it, but heard it could get this way when life was on the line. He'd heard of people who'd survived a brush with death come away swearing that their senses were so heightened they could hear the lug nuts on a passing truck, swishing through the air.

He barreled forward, determined not to waste another bullet until he could pin this slippery asshole in one spot for half a second. Was that too much to ask for? Then, of all the stupid-lucky things, one of Casey's flailing feet caught him square on the knee. All that bulk was intimidating, but it worked against him now. The knee bent wrong with a white-hot pop and he knew he'd be limping for days. He pressed on anyway, lurching forward and stamping down with one cinderblock shoe to hold Casey in place, leaning hard across his collarbone and up onto his throat.

One more muzzle flash, then blood.

Pain, too, Jesus God, more searing pain — how he'd managed to do this, he'd never know, but half the end of his shoe was missing. Then, too, he'd heard of golfers missing six-inch putts.

The Bagman hopped away on one foot before he went down hard and clumsy on the concrete, smooth as glass by a century of wear. From this new vantage point, he watched Casey MacKenna choke and bleed out, all spasms and denial now, bits of shoe leather and bone chips sticking out of his neck, as breath and life spewed from the same ragged hole. He watched without blinking, until it was over.

Casey hadn't once looked the Bagman's way. Just one hand on his throat, the other raised, feebly trying to ward off ... something.

And total silence had never seemed so loud.

The Bagman pushed himself away, a few agonizing inches at a time, until he could rest his back against a pillar holding up the roof. He stared at the ugly mess of his shoe, at the mangled foot inside, at the smeared red trail he'd left behind. While there were probably men who could laugh at the situation, he wasn't one of them. Fuck the shoe, the foot too — mostly he was wondering how to explain it all away at home.

And at a time like this, how could he be so sleepy? Go with it, though. You needed a clear head to come up with the best lies, a clearer head than he had right now.

And in his dreams, they hated him. Reviled him and left him, and the sorrow was so great it made him want to kill them too, because that's what you did to stop the pain, you had to kill pain at the source, that's how this path had gotten started so many years ago—

He jolted awake in the night.

"Huh?" he asked It.

"*Get up,*" It said again.

He cracked open his eyes, struggled to focus. He could see It, clearly now, and It didn't look like any hangman, but still, he knew It when he saw It. He smelled the mildewed rustle of Its robes, the spiced miasma of Its breath. The touch of Its bones would freeze him to the core, like a flagpole in winter. Silly. Beyond silly ... stupid. But he was old school, they all said so, and so it made a kind of sense that, for him, Death would be too.

"Both of us," he said, with a disgusted glance at Casey MacKenna's carcass. "You came for both of us."

"Don't be a fool," It said, in a voice that was both rumble and rasp. *"Only the worst kind of fool would die of a stubbed toe."*

"What, then? What are you ... why...?"

His voice trailed off as he looked up at It, through It, solid one moment and translucent the next, but the smell of It never left his nostrils. Seemed like he'd always known that smell, even before he'd known what it meant, and he swore there were times he'd smelled it seeping from his own pores no matter how long he stayed in the shower. He breathed it in and it took him back, took him away, took him in and down and up again. The smell had always been a part of him, just as he'd always been a part of it.

"It's my work that you do," It said.

He thought of the trail of carnage he'd left behind, an astonishing body of work when you considered that it had all been done by hand, it had all been ... personal. Right. That was it. The personal touch. That was what distinguished him from generals and bomb-droppers. It was the personal touch, not numbers, that made legends.

Death was the ultimate in personal.

And if the thing before him could beam at all, It beamed with pride.

"Now do you understand?" It asked.

He thought he did. Yes. Yes, he was sure of it. God had a Son. The Devil too. If you believed in any of that. Except he didn't, or couldn't, not when all he could believe in was the finality of situations. And Death. He'd never doubted Death. It was the most constant thing he'd known. So who was to say that Death didn't have a lineage of sons that was older than time?

"Do. You. Understand?"

"I think so," he said. "Everything except ... why you've come."

"To tell you this: No man can serve two masters. You must choose."

At first he didn't comprehend. Or didn't want to. Anything but that. Again, he looked at the ugly mess of his shoe, the mangled foot inside, still no closer to coming up with a way of explaining them that would keep the peace under his own roof. The one place that he'd sworn he would never bring this side of life.

But had he ever really had that choice?

"No. Please." He'd never begged for anything in his life. "Please...?"

It looked at him with a father's infinite patience. *"You. Must. Choose."*

And like any father worthy of his namesakes, It stayed with him until he was strong, and ready to pick himself up again. A father like that, how could you begin to think of disappointing Him?

Family man, businessman, everyman, all of them one kind of mask or another. Masks that got so heavy sometimes, there were days he thought he couldn't move. That first mask especially, because it was real, the only one that counted.

He let it fall away again, this time falling so far it shattered. Then he headed for home, ready to resume his father's work, and hadn't felt this light in years.

▨ ▨ ▨

Brian Hodge is the award-winning author of ten novels of horror and crime/noir, over 100 short stories, novelettes, and novellas, and four full-length collections. His most recent collection, *Picking The Bones*, from 2011, was honored with a *Publishers Weekly* starred review. Of his story in *Danse Macabre*, he says, "This was inspired by an incident in the life of notorious mob killer Richard Kuklinski, who really did make a man await his murder to see if his prayers would be answered."

⚊THE DEATH OF DEATH⚊
By Tanith Lee

"Hang Death by the neck until it be alive."

From a graffito found in various though closely similar forms, at many places, and in countless tongues, throughout all the known and recorded ages.

◼ ◼ ◼

"I know who you are," said the girl with golden hair, sitting down across the table from him.

He looked as she had known he must. Despite, or because of the propaganda. He was very tall, very thin, though with a strong, broad frame. His hair was the color of moonless midnight lacking all glow. His eyes were the color of cold, pale iron.

He did not answer her.

No answer, from him, *was* her answer.

As she said, she knew him anyway.

"I've been following you for several years," she added.

Would he say he doubted this, that she was only twenty-three. He did not. No. Of course not.

"Since my mother died," she informed him, "in the '00's. I was twelve. That was in—" she named an obscure area in Europe. Simply by naming it she demonstrated that a girl of twelve years, (there) and with her only parent no longer living, would have had every chance to go off in pursuit of *him*, if no chance at all for most other possibilities.

She was noticing by then he did not wear black. Or scarlet, as she had sometimes seen him clothed in paintings. He wore grey. Casual clothes that might have come from any sloppy unrich closet or cupboard. Almost from any time, perhaps. He wore boots, too. the boots looked old and worn and she wondered if their divided carapace was actually built up from layers of plague pits, dulled battle-blood, cannon shot and nuclear fallout ... things like that. Maybe all his garments were, that was why they were grey, where — to start with — they *had* been jet and ebony, cramoisi and ruby and gold.

"I bought you a drink," she said, and pushed towards him the tall glass of iced back coffee with just a couple of shots in it— "The bar's nicest Jamaican rum," she elaborated. Would he drink it? Was he even *capable* of drinking anything?

Raising her own fairly similar glass (she had chosen coffee with rye), she drank a mouthful, to remind him it was what you did, when you walked about the world, pretending to pass for human.

Oddly, as she thought so, he did raise his tumbler. But only to sniff at the drink. His pale chiselled movie-star nostrils flared and relaxed.

She thought abruptly, *He looks the way I want him to, of course. He'll look like that for anyone, their own fantasy or special dread.* "Leave the pale horse outside, did you?" she inquired. "Hope you parked it carefully. They get fussed about that around here."

The day was hot and dry, and now the narrow bar windows showed an afternoon dying in a fine amber haze.

She must only wait. She must simply stay close.

If he rose to leave she must follow — even if he went to the men's room. Be patient. Be calm. Be *wide-awake*. Actually, just be *alive*.

He got up.

Could he read minds? Well, very likely, but then, she thought, maybe only the *obvious* bits — that was, things like panic or respect or kinky lust. Absent in her case, all three.

He had not tasted the drink, or she assumed he had not. The bar was going shadow-dim, the windows even brighter with sun-fall, that somehow failed to enter, only hammered hazily on the low-polarized glass: Let me in — let me in — let me get a drink. I'm dying, can't you see? Surreptitiously, and she had learned to be good at surreptitious, she bore his glass under the table-top and poured the liquid away on the floor. After all, she did not know how lethal it might be. If he had set his lips to it — even breathed on it perhaps — it might inadvertently prove fatal.

Then she too rose and went after him. He was just passing into the street when she reached him.

"You don't mind if I walk along with you?"

He said — nothing. He strode off, but not so fast she could not keep up.

What did *he* think? She was a Death-groupie? She was a suicide wannabe enjoying a misjudged preview?

Or did he *not* think? No, probably he did not think, as he did not drink, or blink, or jink or stink or dress in mink—

Shut up, Ilka, the cooler half of her mind told her.

She obeyed. Her mind's cooler half had propelled and protected her this far. Best keep in line.

◼ ◼ ◼

After her mother died and the town was burned, Ilka had managed, Cool-Mind-guided, to get out. She had for a while travelled over scorched earth, by ruins and through bitter forests, and then into a winter of mountains deep in snow. People died all around her, like the town, like her mother in the town from the sniper's non-selective bullet. At night, sometimes in the day, Ilka slept with a man, only five of them in all. They gave her food. The last one helped her on the snow, until his snow-cough killed him, too.

Getting across into a safer country was tricky, but accomplished. She had a smatter of the language. Then there was the stowaway boat, and further on the bigger boat with the woman in fur who wanted her for a pet during the voyage. From the woman, guided by the Cool Half, Ilka learned extra, useful knacks, and also the language of the other, larger landscape in which, three years along, she would end up. Half-Cool made, or would make Ilka very intelligent, and she was canny and quick anyway. Quick as a monkey some of them said, or a lizard, or — once — a magpie. All this time though, and from the moment the shot pierced her mother's brain, or possibly in fact from the *next* moment when her mother fell, a body, tenantless, on the ground, Ilka had been in pursuit of Death. It was that she wanted to find him, (him — or her) and ask Why? What for? Never When?, though. Never that. She was too young for that. Or else too much her *self*. She had not perhaps been really properly aware of this quest to begin with. Even in the mountains, when the last man, only nineteen, had died on her lap with her arms around him, and the others straggling on, leaving her since she had not immediately left him too, even then she did not consciously know that all the while, waking and sleeping, a part of her (not the hot half, or the Cool Half, rather some glinting, spinning fragment that fizzed between the two) *that* was staring in all directions to try to anticipate him, to spy him and rush over: *I know who you are.* But *Why* this slaughter? What *for*? Of course it was not until the actual remonstrating accusatory questions dulled and faded from her double mind, like mist from a cold/hot window, that Ilka came to believe she had the *chance* to find Death. To find him while *she* lived. And presently to find him when she was equipped with her own answer, no longer needing his. And obviously she had decided by then he was male. but she had her own logical and legitimate solipsism also, for that.. He was her opposite.

By the time she was nineteen going towards twenty, Ilka had managed to pay her way through some form of schooling, and she was working in the Laboratory, at B—- G—- Heights. Not, that was, as a technician, naturally. She was a cleaner. but this job demanded certain IQ credentials, and even though her then sleeping-patron, SL, had helped a little, her skills with language and people, and a kind of urbane, apparently humble diplomacy, sailed her in like a skater over creamy ice.

One year, seven months and thirteen days later she had — almost by accident — Half-Cool and Fate joining elegant forces — discovered the great and wondrous secret, and taken her chance.

Undetected, she had stayed on at the lab, to be safe, a further quarter year.

And then she pretended to a love-type boyfriend, and another, better job in the south. A little bored with her by then, SL was really sweet about it. He gave her five hundred in crisp notes, to 'help her' with her 'new start'.

She spent a day absorbing steak, chocolate, beer and whisky, bought some better clothes, abandoned her apartment and the entire northern seaboard. Now her quest was to be full-time, and she was in full awareness of it. She had, before, never given that quest over, so much went without saying. Asleep or awake, awake or asleep, combing her hair, showering, paying her rent, humping a guy or cleaning a bone-white lab, with the ink stamp of super security smeared on her wrist and her eye-print in the B—- G—- Heights personnel bank, still, she was the pursuer of, the searcher after, Death. Yet, it had become not only her part but part *of* her. And when she deserted that last life and was able to *become* what always she had *been* — then—

Then Ilka graduated. No longer a pursuer or searcher, not a watcher and spy. She sprang from the wings a Hunter, a Warrior. and the war was on, always had been. And the final battle would at any minute begin, black as a spent bullet, blood-red as a burning town. Pale as a horse.

■ ■ ■

They visited a lot of bars, Death and she.

Also shopping malls, the parks, the subway transit ... and streets, endless streets, and alleys with drunks lying there like badly packaged sausages. Once a dog barked at them. Ilka decided it had in fact barked only at her. Death was invisible to it. It was not the dog's Time to meet Death. It was *Ilka's* Time — but not to perform the usual scenario; Ilka was not dying. Only dying to be and do exactly what she was.

She kept up with him. She did not tire. She had a will of bronze, and a bladder of pure steel.

She had walked through burnt ruins and over mountains and into other lands. She had walked away from her mother's corpse. Oh, she could walk all right.

No dialogue. They did not exchange any talk.

The date from Hell, that was Death.

Inevitably.

Whenever they stopped, she bought herself, and him, a drink. An Orange Coke in the park, coffee or spirits or wine or beer in the bars, a Lime Slinker in one mall and a Strawberry-Milk at another. Each time when she carried the drinks over to where he had sat or leaned himself, he did not drink them. But he always sniffed at them, like a connoisseur with a rare Chablis.

He won't, she thought. *He understands and it's useless.*

No, said Half-Cool. *It isn't that.*

What then?

It isn't that. Just go on. You have enough about you to do this for hours. Trust. Continue.

■ ■ ■

She broke the silence and started to tell him about what had in fact happened at the lab. (Not about her life. That was irrelevant, to him.)

It had been a late shift. About 2 a.m., PFN appeared scowling, and went into Third Bay. Third Bay was where new commodities were stored, and where any film connected to them was run, after they had made an info movie of an experiment. They only did this when it had been a great success — or a terrible failure. Lower staff generally did not know this, but SL had let her in on the method much earlier, for his own reasons.

PFN, a rude and nervy bastard, told Ilka, then cleaning the corridor outside with the floor-buffer, to 'Fuck off'. So, subservient, unfazed and mute, off she fucked. But, it was unusual for persons of PFN's rank to come in out-of-hours. Aside from anything else, they hardly needed overtime pay. She sidled back a minute after and listened at the thick silver door, pretending she looked for some dropped pin or button — surreptitious and inquisitive had often paid dividends. She could hear the film-Dex active and murmuring, and then, faintly, a bark or cough, followed by a recorded exclamation—applause. The movie then stopped, and instead she heard PFN whining to himself, as if something had viciously hurt him. Words came out through tears or saliva. Her hearing was acute. She heard: "It works, it does. It does. I saw the damn thing at eleven tonight. It was playing, ate its food. Oh Christ, it works. Oh—" whined PFN— "*Robby*—"

And Half-Cool said into her listening quiet, *Hurry and back off; he's coming right out now.*

Ilka retreated again, and was in the other corridor with the buffer, down at the farthest end, when PFN hurried into view.

Seeing her this time he checked, and then scuttled up to her. Ilka got ready to defend herself verbally or physically. There was no security camera right here. But PFN said, "Sorry I snapped, okay? Been a tough night — reason I came in — left some notes behind. Hey, buy yourself a drink, yeah?" and passed her some cash worth about quarter of a cup of coffee. "Don't let on I came back, okay? Don't want us to get in trouble, yeah?"

"Sure," she said, and shyly, admiringly smiled.

When he had gone, she let herself into Third Bay. Her security clearance allowed her to do this — SL had seen to that. She had eye-pass to almost all the labs, though not everyone knew it. SL liked her, just once in a while, to get him the odd little bit or piece, nothing really missable, for there was always so much of everything. You did it as you cleaned. If you were careful and cute, the camera could never see. With her certainly it never had. And SL, with his communications with the darker open market outside, had been reasonably grateful. When she left there, months later, she was aware he was already grooming his next protégé thief.

Everything looked undisturbed in the Bay. But she worked her way to the Dex, which she knew very well how to activate. It was done as if by mistake, after which, fiddling as if puzzled by trying to turn it off, she could watch. She had only done this once before, to pick something up for SL. There had been no official come-back.

They used animals, the Laboratory, that went without saying. This had always disgusted her, annoyed her, but no more, obviously, than humanity's careless use and ill-treatment of its own species. In the movie the young dog was dead, lying there while they finished two or three swift tests to make sure it was.

And then one of the men in spotless white took up a plastic vial and tipped out of it a colorless, viscous liquid. Leaning over the dog he smoothed the fluid into its mouth, and stood back.

Ilka *knew* the dog was dead on the film. She had seen enough, not only at B—G, but out in the world. Its death being a definite, when the dog quivered, snorted, rolled over, stood up and shook itself, stared, panted, then wagged its tail and barked, Ilka needed a moment to reprocess her mental reaction. The lab guys by then were cheering, cheering and hugging the dog, giving it little wholesome treats, (unlike the poison they must have fed it previously) and that was when the movie flickered to an end.

"Whine — *whine* — it works — it does — I saw the damn thing at eleven — playing — food—

—Robby—"

Robby? who was that? Not that it mattered. The main theme was evident.

Perhaps after all *that* was the instant she became the Hunter, the Warrior — that one, rather than those months on, when she left the lab and SL to conclude the Chase and her personal war.

Having switched off the Dex with a non-comprehending and exasperated sigh — for the camera, Ilka completed the superficial cleaning she was giving Third Bay. During which, locating the storage port, she used her eye-pass to unlock it. She had cleaned the port before legitimately, but never when it was full, as now it was. At least thirty sealed vials were in there. Even staff at her level knew not to touch anything like that. Ilka tutted and dropped her brush and cloth. Bending to retrieve them, she whisked out the single already part-emptied vial. PFN had seemingly decanted it into something. Maybe he had authority to do that, or not. Or he had fooled the camera in some way, as she was now doing. No alarm responded to her theft, as it had not to his. It occurred to her, he might have deactivated the alarm, but, in the state he was, then forget to retrieve it.

And later, it transpired, the abducted vial was blamed solely on PFN.

She found out later who Robby was too, when she heard SL telling someone that PF was having time off with his husband. Robby was the husband of PFN. Robby had been very ill. Robby had been near death — dying. PFN was at his bedside in the hospital. And then — a miraculous remission. Not only total recovery, but a full cure. PFN himself did not come back to the lab. He and Robby vanished, no doubt over the border. No doubt a secret inquiry was conducted into this. She heard SL again, talking one night on his cell-phone (some dubious contact) with the special scramble-light on, but careless of her, apparently asleep in the bedroom. "Oh sure, it may not last, that cure, that life. Who knows? But it works *so far*. I told you about the dog? The dog seems set to last another twenty years. And I guess nobody'll go after PF. The powers here want to keep the whole thing quiet, you bet, too early to leak anything on this one. It's way too big. So I reckon the old queer will get away with it."

███

"It's named LAZ A.O.," Ilka said to Death. "I should have worked out immediately what that meant, but sometimes, in another language … certain letters together, I don't always follow. It's Lazarus, though. Like in the bible. The man Jesus Christ brought back to life from the dead. Odd they chose a religious name. If you go by religion, what they're doing — what they've *done* — is blasphemous. Lazarus: Alpha to Omega — the beginning and the end. But that's God. Or life itself. Or you, maybe. Maybe you."

They were in another park. Night was down and only a moon on a diet, thin as a cat's shed claw-case, thinner. A glaze of light powdered in over the walls, giving the trees a sketched shape, and him, showing him. This time she had brought them both a throw-away cup of water from the No-Pay fountain.

He raised the cup. But only, again, to sniff at the drink.

"I don't know," she said, rather dreamily now since she was growing suddenly tired, "whether you don't trust me, or whether you just never drink anything. But you've stayed with me, or let me stay with you. I always knew I'd find you. I always knew you were *able* to be found. Can't explain that. Faith, perhaps. Can I guess this has happened before, at least once, somehow — I wonder how, *then*? But the other way around, of course — I mean, you weren't Death then. You were mortal. Like me. And you too — you just *hunted* Death."

In the darklight he stood gazing away with his eyes like pale iron. Death had no expression.

"I think," she said, "you don't feel anything anymore. You don't *know* anything anymore. Is that it? You were and became and *are*, and by doing that you've stopped being or becoming. You exist, but you're not conscious of it. If I did ask you *why* you do what you do — why you kill — why you let or cause killing to happen — bullets, bombs, disease, old age — you couldn't tell me, could you? No, I think you couldn't. You just only *do* it. *Are* it. And you must be here, and all places. It's the law of balance. Oh, sure, B-stroke G -stroke have found a kind of cure, LAZ A.O. But in the end it'll be kept for the very very few. Or else it won't rally work. Or — I don't know. It — I mean LAZ itself — will decay. Only it's young now. Just at the start of *its* life. So then, this will work, I think. If Death kills life — then *Life* can kill death. And if the effect only lasts a little while — well then, a dog's life of twenty years would make a man or woman's life — of about one hundred. So there'll be that long before the dog dies, or Robby, or LAZ itself dies. Or before *you* come back to *life*."

Ilka moved up close to him.

She looked up into his handsome thoughtless face.

Both Cold-and-Hot mind stayed silent, letting her speak as she must. A unique vote of confidence. And he — he never moved.

"I've put a little in all your drinks. I've then had to dispose of it, pour it away — hopefully where no one will get it. I don't know what it might do to someone healthy. Maybe nothing at all. I mean LAZ, of course. That's what I mean. But to you, even if not to anyone else, inevitably — well. Let's see."

She stood on tiptoe and lifted her left hand, over which she had poured the dregs of LAZ A.O. Only this ultimate dose now remained. He made no resistance to her gentle fingers as they moved across his lower lip into his mouth. The mouth felt entirely ordinary; clean, good teeth, firm gums and smooth tongue. A mouth to kiss.

When she withdrew her fingers she knew she had done exactly the equivalent of what the man had done with the resuscitated dog. But now there would be one more thing *she* must do, unlike anything required during the experiment.

She had observed that Death breathed, slowly and evenly, only an illusion, perhaps, passing for human, or for that other reason she suspected — Death, once, had *been* human. Before him, there had been other Deaths, also conceivably human prior to their epiphany into Deathness. She would not, if successful, be the first. Even if previous murder weapons stayed obscure. She speculated, in some different form, LAZ A.O. had always existed. If it was all a balance, how not?

He leaned forward. His eyes were closing.

Ilka, strong and young and mad and wise and a fool, caught him in her arms like a lover. She held him, all his manlike weight, as strength and coordination ebbed from him. She covered his kissable mouth with hers, uncaring of the wonder-drug, which anyway she believed he must have absorbed totally. And into her mouth, her throat, her lungs, her bloodstream, scentless, and cool-cold as any mental cunning, his very last breath gushed, whirling and sinking, like a sea-wave of melted snow.

When that was over, she let go of him. Death fell at her feet, lay like a long-bladed shadow then, as a shadow would at sunrise, faded into nothingness.

Alone, as always she was but for the facets of her self, Ilka stood and pushed back from her face her coils of night-silvered golden hair.

Was she growing taller? Was she altering in any way? She had killed Death. Which meant she would become Death. Just as he must have done, and become, centuries ago. And soon, soon, if it were truly true, she would know without asking Why and for What. And after that she would not care. And then she could be free. Free forever as uncaringly she patrolled the world, not in scarlet or ebony, not riding on a pale horse, but unspeaking and unthinking, and grey as the dust of burning towns, or the dusk that comes between light and night, and is both of them, and neither.

■ ■ ■

Tanith Lee was born in London, England in 1947 and started writing at age nine. By her early 20's she had had children's books published, and also wrote three SF/Fantasy novels including *The Birthgrave.* In 1975 these were published by DAW Books of America. She hasn't stopped since, publishing almost 100 novels and collections, over 300 short stories, and also writing for BBC TV and Radio. She lives in Sussex with her husband, artist/writer John Kaiine, and two tuxedo cats. This story came from nowhere — they often do. The idea of Death can (strangely?) be very inspiring!

~SYMEON~
By Bill Zaget

The *El Condor* was heavy with scent of the cheap and not-so-cheap. Aftershave and perfume — decadent, but not half as alluring as the heady smell of decay.

Symeon smiled and slid to the perimeter of the dance floor. His dark eyes — those deep unblinking wishing wells that drew all the *turistas*, homeboys, woo-girls, and divorcées into his shadow realm — focused on the writhing crowd. A range of social dance, from random galumphing to whatever street-style was *au courant*.

So-you-think-you-can-dance. Ha. A hollow laugh, Symeon noted. He sighed deeply, and despite the deafening music, a large portion of the revelers paused to slowly turn in his direction for a moment … and then continued to *boogey on*.

Symeon much preferred the 70s. He looked back fondly on its line-dancing. He had even occasionally joined in; reminded him of centuries before, leading the aged and the infirm — from the peasantry, gentry, and clergy (even royalty) in a line…

A flat line, hah. Nope, still hollow. And no longer packing a scythe. Or was he conflating memory with artists' handiwork?

A few of the revelers — of various genders — caught his eye. *If they only knew.*

Symeon ambled to the bar to fuel his lust. He narrowed his gaze to the banks of video screens at one end. One was mutely broadcasting the news. A read-out appeared across the bottom of the screen: "…yet another inexplicable fire — the eighth in as many weeks. Presumed dead is its lone occupant, an Hispanic woman…"

The bartender, stubbled and shirtless, leaned towards him and mouthed the usual something. Symeon shook his head and backed away, still watching the monitor. No longer sexed-up. *Fuck. What a way to kill a mood. Way to kill. Ha. Whatever.*

※ ※ ※

Her name had been ... Chiquita — at least that's what he filed her as in the deep recesses of his ancient noggin. *A Latina who could do such things with my banana — insert a chorus of hollow laughter here.* He had sidled up beside her and instantly sensed what she was looking for. He appeared ape-like in a white T-shirt, hirsute and stocky with a slashing smile.

"Ohhh, *papi,*" she had said. It was all that needed saying.

Sizzle-hot passion ended with the conflagration. He had slipped out before the sirens started blaring.

※ ※ ※

Symeon left the *El Condor* and dragged on a *Sobranie* en route to what he called his *El Hovel.*

Reflections of himself puffed away to various shitholes around the world. Here on the outskirts of Reno, and on the way to a *cortiço* in Rio, a sixth floor walk-up in Brooklyn, a garret in Prague, a mud hut in Darfur...

Shithole, he mused. *Reminds me* ... and here he twisted his gaze upward for effect.

Shit-For-Brains, Head-Honcho — God, how You do me in. I've been the good little soldier. Ad nauseum. To what end? Endless. And don't give me that old caveat about being careful what you ask for. And making my bed and now must lie in it, for fuck's sake. Lying — You must be good at it by now as that no-goodnik ex-angel of Yours.

Symeon kicked a beer can out of the way. It clattered into the street.

Little did I know.

I had fantasized, as one does, when I was merely mortal. I prayed for a long life. Okay, for immortality. Eternal youth and all that jazz. There was I, on bended knees in my rough woolen leggings — or was it a toga, or ... screw it; can't remember anymore. And You — a veritable God of Irony, it seems — granted my fervent wish. But with a twist, of course. Life ever-lasting, yes, but grimly so: Your servant here on Earth, not spreading any good word or giving hope to those in need, but as The Big D. And so I slew those whose time had come, with a tender touch, or swinging a metaphysical blade as a warrior does, or snuffing coldly as one does an insignificant candle wick. But no more!

Where's my celestial pink slip? Down-size The Firm; I'm more than ready. Gold pocket-watch me into Oblivion.

Symeon's rant was met with the usual silence. Not simply the absence of a response, but a silence that was palpable, with an indescribable density and texture that pressed against him and calmed him for a moment's grace. Symeon stubbed the *Sobranie* out in his palm. The stench of burning flesh was exhilarating. Of course, the skin healed over within seconds, but for those few seconds he felt almost human again. Half-memories peeked out, winked... *Is that a face?* And then were gone. Buried once again. *Shite.*

I need a vacation — like that's going to happen. Too bad the job isn't unionized.

The only union Symeon was able to effect these days was coitus. Things could've been worse. *They are.*

❂ ❂ ❂

It came to him the year before, during one of those precious moments of half-humanness. He had just done his reaper-thing with victims of a tsunami. Some mangled flotsam had surged towards him, and he allowed the debris to lacerate his body. In that moment of ecstatic pain, he felt something ancient — a fleeting remnant of, of ... being loved.

Was I? Did I?

Symeon then decided only the pursuit of love — or a reasonable facsimile — would be his salvation and act as a counterweight to the grimmer aspects of his job description. But where to pursue? Eschewing the more obvious and tawdry hunting grounds, he had settled on a visit to an art museum — the Tate in London. As it happened, the gallery had opened a new exhibit — The Mortal Image: Memento Mori in the Northern Renaissance. *How fitting.* Not one of the major exhibits, it took up a couple of smaller rooms in the building. A guard was quietly snoozing on a chair, just inside the entrance to the first room. Symeon browsed the numerous woodcuts and panels by Albrecht Dürer and members of his *atelier.* It amused him — those images of Death as a skull, as a skeleton. On those rare occasions that Symeon viewed him-self in a mirror, all that was reflected was a smudgy swirl, a slow-motion spiraling of shadow, twisting outwards, so that countless incarnations of himself took corporeal form across the globe and carried out his ghastly duties. *That's me — a smudge, a scourge.* Symeon caught himself sighing and snapped out of such gloomy thoughts.

The gallery emptied out of onlookers, but in the far corner of the second room, a lone figure stood in front of a smallish painting. Mere inches from it, a woman seemed to be mumbling something. A quick look-around: the guard was still napping by the entrance. The woman wasn't wearing a Bluetooth device, so her comments must have been either a product of schizophrenia or ... *or what?*

Symeon delved deep— *Nope, not schizoid. Good.* And yet...

"Must be so lonely," she whispered.

Perplexing. She seemed to be muttering to one of the subjects in the picture.

"Mr. Bones."

Taken aback, Symeon wondered if she was addressing him. After all, this painting, by Baldung, depicted Eve, the Serpent, and Death. There, the gloriously naked First Woman grasped an apple in one hand and, with the other, lightly fondled the phallic tail of you-know-who. And Adam was here transformed into a figure of Death, reaching from behind a tree to tightly clutch her arm. This First Man, Once-Human, now... *I hear ya, pal.*

Symeon advanced and took on the appearance of someone to the woman's liking: ascetic, monkish even, but with an edge — lanky, with a goatee and ear piercings, and with crystalline blue eyes that belied the somewhat melancholic look.

"Are you speaking to me?"

She turned with a jerk of her head. "What?"

"Were you speaking to me?" He watched her take his new image in.

"Uh ... no. To my Mr. Bones here."

"Still — my name is ... Osman. And the origin of Os is—"

"Bone, from the Latin — how bizarre. And wonderful."

She's no stupe. Promising. "There are more skeletal Misters hereabouts than that one."

"True. Baldung here gives us a slightly more fleshy version. Sensual, even."

Symeon's baby-blues met her greens. A fecund pause, accompanied by subtle smiles.

Bingo.

"Well, Mr. Os-man, I'm Sharon."

"The origin of which is...?"

"Umm... Share and share alike?"

Another pause, pierced by this Sharon with an unlikely guffaw. Symeon was delighted by the woman's smarts, coupled with a certain earthiness. His eyes swept across and down the curves of her body, the auburn curls framing her face, the ample peek-a-boo of her cleavage, the smooth leggyness below the hem of her linen skirt.

It wasn't long before he had convinced her to join him for coffee. A safe and un-sleazy start. *How normal. Wonderful. Human.*

Even while sipping his latte, various versions of himself continued to draw people into the hereafter: the forest ranger in the Poconos, the Benedictine nun in Argenteuil, the Taliban insurgent bleeding out on the streets of Kandahar *(I wonder if 72 virgins will give him welcome in Paradise)* and countless others.

Conversation turned to art and literature. And more. Sharon admitted her fascination with Death.

"I see."

"All that power — not flashy or anything. Quiet-like."

Symeon drank in Sharon's steady gaze, and despite a mounting giddiness somewhere within him, he decided to be the veritable eye of the storm. Quiet-like. He nodded sagely and smiled. Not that he had faith in anything providential, but all this — the Tate, the Baldung, the latte — seemed to suggest that "Osman" and Sharon were meant to be.

"And something sexy about it, even," she whispered, with a sly smile.

Nodding. "And fear?"

"Some of that too. I mean, I'm not fearless. I reckon I'm as fucked up as anyone else." And here she let loose another hearty laugh.

Symeon had wanted to wed and bed her on the spot in Starbucks, but he composed himself and took the gentlemanly route. He walked her home, and at the door he sweetly kissed her on the cheek. *Ol' dog me, learning new tricks and becoming a young pup again — halleluiah!*

He was mildly surprised when Sharon tugged him into her flat and planted a not-so-sweet kiss on his lips. There and then, he had vowed to withhold all his services. He shook a mental fist at the heavens— *Do your own dirty work for a change, Shit-Head.*

Symeon felt the insistent press of her tongue and allowed it to penetrate and squirm inside his mouth. Reciprocating, he made a further spontaneous vow — a change of vocation; no longer would he reap grimness, but L-O-V-E. He savored Sharon's life force, the fullness of it, and imagined his darkness being dissolved by her glow. The two of them...

Glowing.

In her bedroom, they strip-teased themselves into a state of nakedness. He was right pleased when her eyes flicked below his waist and widened.

"Quite the os, man."

They bellowed joyfully and leapt at one another, in a ravaging kiss. Her full breasts cushioned against him, his raging erection pressed against her belly. They fell upon the bed, glued to one another. Leap-frogging any foreplay, Symeon snaked inside her to the root. He heard her moan and joined her in a sensual duet, as love was superseded by S-E-X.

And before he knew it, he started to pour all his longing, needing, withholding into her. Her groan intensified and became a cry in pain.

Am I too much for her?

Not just pain. All the diseases and afflictions — all that had brought humankind to the brink of death; Symeon's act of shuffling them off their mortal coil and cleansing them to become spiritually whole again for their voyage to ... somewhere, while absorbing all their infirmities — had now filled Sharon up. Symeon quickly withdrew from inside her. Too late.

Her eyes widened in wild panic as she lifted a palsied hand to her face. Her once-creamy complexion mottled with open lesions. She attempted to speak through cankered lips, but could only emit a high-pitched wheeze and glottal clicks. Some portions of her flesh blistered; others encrusted and reddened from a frenzied bout of scratching. His bride-to-be reached out to him with a necrotic claw.

She's turning into a lobster.

Indecision was entirely foreign to Symeon. He wanted to help — *no*, to sob — *no*, to run. He was at once repulsed and entranced. Symeon simply watched.

Sharon began puking up blood as she slowly slid to the floor and started convulsing. Gripped with fever, she threw her head from side to side.

She's burning up.

A smell of feces filled the air. Sharon mouthed an apology.

I have done this to her.

Lowering his gaze, Symeon focused on her genitalia. Minutes earlier, it had been aesthetically perfect and gifted in the way it tightly wrapped about his bloated cock. Now, it appeared a labial maw, puffed out and inflamed. The lips gaped open. Symeon wasn't sure, but her insides seemed to be melting from the heat.

He might not have had a heart, but he discovered he wasn't entirely heartless, and it was breaking at the sight and sound and smell of his lover — the whole suppurating, scabbing, hemorrhaging, rotting hell of her.

Is that smoke?

Her mouth dropped open and let loose a deafening scream as flame ignited all her hairy bits.

Glowing.

Nothing to be done, Symeon backed off and, letting his ascetic, monkish, lanky aspect fall away, he rose upwards in a slow swirl of dusky smog.

Sharon — or this monstrous vessel she had become — could no longer withhold all the disease that riddled her body from within. Flaring in a blinding burst, Symeon's new-found love blew apart. Far-flung clumps were but blackened husks, which disintegrated into nothingness before his eyeless vigil.

Symeon wafted from that initial conflagration to his council flat in the Isle of Dogs. Congealing into a sludgy form, he hid beneath the bed he had never slept in and shook for days. Throughout the world tremors were felt — low-Richter quakes — which drew concern from scientists. This began to amuse Symeon, as the horror of what had taken place in Sharon's flat abated. Amusement was soon replaced with a growing anger, an anger that stewed for almost a year.

Thou Arseholiness! You must've foreseen what would happen. And You allowed it. Do You get some insane pleasure, testing my allegiance with Your divine brand of irony? It's tearing me apart. Like the beauteous Sharon. Well, my allegiance is fucked. So the hell with visiting only those "whose time has come." I'll choose the time, whether it's theirs or not. Two can play this godly game.

And so in weeks following, Symeon chose a mad hybrid means of revenge.

Am I now mad?

Thus did he impregnate pick-ups of every shade and gender with his combustive jism — from gym bunnies in South Beach to Russian hookers in Istanbul. The authorities and media began to take notice of these sudden infernos popping up in almost every nation.

Symeon read and listened to their comments. There were two camps of thought: the obvious bugaboo of terrorism... *Hey, I'm Os-man bin Laden!* ...and of course that great old standby — an approaching Apocalypse. *Nary a horseman in sight — just l'il ol' me.*

And li'l ol' he took pleasure in humanity's paranoia and fear and — he hoped — his silent Employer's irritation.

■ ■ ■

Symeon continued on his way back to his *El Hovel* in Reno. He much preferred walking in human form to floating in a vaporous state. It made him feel closer to ... something. *Don't know what I feel anymore. Something... Nothing.*

He now regretted his earlier retreat from sating his incendiary lust at the *El Condor*. He took a hard left from his usual route and turned down a dark side street he had heard about. Cars slid slowly along in dim light and lingered as teen-aged males sauntered over and leaned through open windows for a chat. Symeon's next conquest — and victim — was propped against a wall, with hands squeezed into tight white denim. A boy, all gangly, but fit and perhaps all of sixteen, his face was pale and smooth beyond belief. *Perfectamundo.* Crowned by a ragged mop of blondness, he was like an angelic beacon to Symeon. *Glowing.*

Now appearing broad-shouldered and middle-aged in a smart Armani suit, Symeon nodded in his direction. The lad nodded back, but then almost-shyly cast his eyes down at the pavement. *How quaint.* Symeon mentally licked his chops as he approached the boy. The kid looked up again, and for a moment it was as if another face was superimposed on his — rounder, with high cheek bones and a curly fringe of dark hair flopped over one eye. A face vaguely familiar to Symeon, yet not. Mysterious lips parted and mouthed a silent *help me.* And then — gone.

The blond boy's eyes were suddenly filled with fear. He skittered away from Symeon and huddled with a couple of his young comrades. Had Symeon's guise as a wealthy john dropped for a moment in the confusion and scared the be-jesus out of his young prey?

Now mad?

But not gone for long. Everywhere Symeon looked, every face was superimposed with that of ... *whom*? It was like a dream one cannot quite remember — not that Symeon ever dreamt, but now all the human flotsam and jetsam on this side street of sex and commerce seemed to lacerate his senses: the john in the rusty Toyota, the pimpled male prostitute smoking weed in a doorway, the gold-jangling drug dealer, they all wore the same androgynous visage that seemed to be haunting him.

And that plea for help — *what's that all about? Never happened before* — yet it drew Symeon, tugged at him like some gravitational force, pulling him to ... somewhere in the 20th *arrondissement* in Paris...

Off the early morning hustle-and-bustle of the *Boulevard de Ménilmontant*, Symeon found the epicenter of his inexplicable hallucination. *The Cimetière du Père Lachaise* was just a hop-skip-and-a-float from where he stood. He could still smell the subtle odor of decay in the air as he approached a small house along *Passage de la Folie-Regnault*. He peeked through the window and could make out the silhouette of someone sitting on a sofa. Symeon tried to sense what role he should assume this time, but his facility in this regard seemed to get mired in the multifold layers of the occupant's psyche. *What the hell* ... he decided to appear in a classic *gendarme's* uniform, replete with kepi and half-cape. The front door was unlocked, and he quietly entered the house.

Classical music was playing and the room was filled with the heavy aroma of incense. Several candles, burning low, surrounded the sofa and the person sitting there. A number of pill bottles were lying about, one whose contents had spilled out on a pedestal table beside her. Or him. It was hard to tell in the flickering candlelight, but Symeon recognized the high cheekbones, the dark curly fringe of hair — the face of the one playing peek-a-boo with him for the last several months. A face he might have known so, so long ago. And loved. *Could this be?* He tried to speak, but no words would come out.

"Are you meant to be my hero, *monsieur*?"

Symeon found his voice at last. "Are you in need of one?" he ventured. *Mademoiselle, monsieur?*

He/she giggled weakly. "A woman is always in need. This woman, at least."

Ah, mademoiselle, then.

"A few minutes later, and..." Her hand gestured to the pile of pills. "But I am such a coward."

"In this case, cowardice was the right choice, *mademoiselle*." Symeon did not sense that her time had come — this was not why he was here. *Then why?* His powers seemed to have gone totally askew.

"My life..." and here the woman hesitated. Nothing followed. There was such a sadness in her eyes.

Symeon supposed her personal history was likely an overwhelming parade of emotional disaster. A torrent of disappointment and grief. Mahler was playing in the background. He watched, as one candle, not much more than a pool of lumpy wax, guttered and died out.

"Have we met before, *monsieur*?"

Symeon found her looking at him intently.

Part of him was massively confused by all this. Part of him wanted to shout a joyous "Yes!" *Could this be the one?* The lost love of his human youth? Maybe she was a descendant. Maybe he was just imagining it all. Maybe it was all a tsunami of coincidence. *Too many maybes by far.*

"You seem so familiar to me, and ... kind."

"I ... don't know, *mademoiselle*."

"Well, perhaps in another life." Another weak and endearing giggle.

How could this be? Only the Big Guy and his minions could effect such abracadabra.

"You must think I am a lunatic, my heroic friend."

"I have known lunatics." He didn't know why he said that.

The young woman found this funny and began to laugh. Symeon joined in the laughter. He wanted to keep her laughing, keep her from harm's way, from others and from herself. He had several millennia's worth of jokes he could regale her with and extend her life — her time with him — not extinguish it. He told her a few from his repertoire, and it was clear that her mood was lifting. She swept the pills off the table; they scattered across the parquet floor. A Viennese waltz was now playing. She stood up with a radiant smile and began to sway to the music.

Symeon did not know what to do. *What the fuck* — he took her hand and placed it on his waist, his hand grasping hers. She smiled shyly as they began, absurdly, to waltz. The pills crunched as they danced, which brought further gales of laughter. When the jollity finally subsided, they stood still, staring unblinking into each other's eyes as Strauss came to a stirring finish.

Symeon felt humbled in her presence; he wasn't worthy. He wanted to fall to his knees and beg forgiveness. Waves of guilt crashed against him for his recent murder spree. *Yes, murder ... What have I done?* His cheeks were wet with tears, and he touched his face, uncomprehending. Tears were streaming down his dance partner's face as well. She dabbed at them with her fingers and touched Symeon's lips with her wetness.

He yearned to plant her with mad kisses and make love to her for days on end, pour his whole being... *NO!* Of course, he could not. He could never pass along the contagion seething within him. The fire. To her, or anyone anymore. He could never have her — whether she was his lost lover, now regained, or just the object of his ardent longing. And the pain of knowing this was crushing him.

She cupped her hands around his cheeks. Perhaps, he thought, one kiss, and then goodbye. Their lips sought each other out, and ... Symeon could no longer tell where he was — or when. The insistent press of human flesh held them together face-to-face for seconds, minutes, hours — he knew not how long, as the rest of him lost, or seemed to lose shape and integrity. He was a viscous member of the *gendarmerie*. He was a monkish *papi* in Armani. He was a raging stew of infection and disorder.

Puccini was now blaring through the speakers. So close to her, he stared through crossed eyes, took in doubly her beauty, the depth of her, and like a veil that had just been lifted — or a shroud — Symeon felt he was truly seeing her for the first time.

He could now hear her thoughts — or thought he did. A calm echoing voice resounded within him, saying, "Know that you are loved," and "I am your replacement." Her visage clouded over and dissolved.

Symeon could no longer hear the music — or anything, for that matter — as he was enveloped by a familiar silence. A silence that spiralled outwards, like a final twist of irony, through all time zones, engulfing all the reflections, all the Symeons. It felt like a warm embrace — no, a caustic penetration — no, a peaceful sleep. A slap in the face.

No.

It is all and none of that, he mused, as he was absorbed into a great and final Everything and Nothingness.

▨ ▨ ▨

Bill Zaget is an actor and writer. His very first story, "Renfield or, Dining at the Bughouse", was published in the Ace Science Fiction anthology, *Dracula in London*, 2001. "Zombies on the Down-Low" was published in 2009 by Ravenous Romance in the anthology *Beach Boys*. "Symeon" gave him the opportunity to work through his trenchant fear of death and irony — to no avail, but it did result in an ironic tale about Death. Bill has a couple of novels on the back burner and says one of these days he's "gotta fix that stove."

OLD MAN
~WITH A BLADE~

By Brian Lumley

It was Edinburgh in the summer but could as easily have been any city or place anywhere at any time, in any season since time began.

The old man with the blade, that long, curving ever sharp blade, was on the lookout, as usual, for fresh — or maybe not so fresh — victims. They had it coming eventually; but the way he looked at it they had done it and *were* doing it to themselves! Victims of their own stupidity ... but in an equal number of cases victims of their genes; for as often as not, that was where it started.

Take for instance the old boy in the wheelchair pushed by his haggard-looking wife. A classic case of who would go first: him with his Alzheimer's — prompting him to stick his fingers in electric sockets, because he couldn't remember what they were — or her worn down by the weight of caring for him, whose problem was in his genes, inherited from his father who in turn had got it from *his* father ... and so on. But both of them eventually, if not just yet.

The old man's curved blade tingled with a life of its own; its owner sensed it lusting after the lives of others — even of this harmless pair — but not yet. He leaned toward them anyway as they passed him by on the pavement, sniffing at them to make sure he wasn't mistaken. He wasn't, which in its way was disappointing; better them than some young couple. But then again it wasn't his lot to discriminate.

The street was as good as empty; on this early Sunday morning most folks were still abed or only just stirring. But there were, of course, those who were driven to be up and about. Like that middle-aged man who had just come out of the tobacconist's shop, already tearing the film from his pack of cigarettes, and then the silver foil, his hand trembling where it groped in his pocket for his lighter.

The old man with the shining blade stepped closer, smelled the smoke from that first long drag, heard the addict's sigh of relief ... and also the cough welling up from the diseased lung of which, for the moment, the smoker wasn't aware. But he would be, oh he would be! As the curved blade tingled again, a little more determinedly now, the old man nodded to himself, thinking, "We'll give him a year, my faithful friend, or perhaps a little less." And he patted the long handle of his blade.

A little farther down the street, a bearded derelict wrapped in a torn blanket mumbled to himself where he lay in a shop doorway. Sucking the last few drops of wine from a brown bottle in a paper bag, he flopped back into a shady corner and waved a fluttery greeting to no one in particular. Gray vomit had hardened to crusts on his blue-veined naked feet.

"Ah!" said the old man with the tingling, sentient seeming blade, also to no one in particular. And lifting the blade from the leather saddle on his shoulder, he reached into the doorway and touched the derelict's dirty neck. With his eyes closed and flesh numb, the bum saw and felt nothing at all ... but then he wouldn't have anyway. And:

"Next winter," said the old man, as he strode on along the street. "We'll see you again next winter."

Disease, drugs, drink, and occasionally accidents. And the absolute harvest of war, naturally. And always the old man with his shining blade: always Death, of course. He moved on.

The city was beginning to come awake now, daylight brightening. The old man wasn't especially fond of daylight: he suffered it but it didn't really fit the image of one who preferred to have things happen in the dark of night. However — and once again — it wasn't in his power to discriminate...

There was a fancy wine bar with an ornate varnished mahogany façade, opaque, small paned bull's-eye windows, and a hanging sign above the recessed, arched-over double doors that read simply: "B.J.'s." As the old man with the blade drew level with the doors they opened; a girl, beautiful, darkly gypsyish, with eyes that shone in the shaded doorway, ushered a young man into the daylight. She leaned forward to kiss him, a temporary farewell, left him on the street and closed the doors on him.

There was something about the young man. He blinked in the morning sunlight and lifted a hand to shade his pale face, his eyes that seemed a little distant, dazed and disoriented. The old man thought it possible that he knew that look: he believed he'd seen its like before: often, on the faces of men who were lost or bent on suicide!

And yet ... there was something else about this particular young man, so the old man with the scythe leaned closer, sniffing out the other's origins, essence, nature, destiny. But then a singular thing: just for a moment he thought he saw the young man's faraway eyes focus and look back at him! And more, it was as if the young man knew him, as if they were old friends!

Indeed they *were* old friends!

The scythe no longer tingled but shivered, and its master, the oldest man of all, shivered with it and jerked away, quickening his silent steps along the still mainly empty street. Ah, he knew this one now, remembered him for all the work he'd done for him; knew also that he would never be required to accommodate him. Oh, his time would come eventually — well, possibly — but not now and not in this world. That was not this one's destiny. But there were other old men with blades, a great many of them, in all the many worlds where life had taken root.

One of them would accommodate this one — this Necroscope *, this Harry Keogh — well, eventually. Or possibly? Death stroked his living scythe to calm it, then paused to cast a glance back along the almost empty street. And then he nodded to himself.

For apart from a small dust devil where it collapsed close to the wine bar's entrance, and the dirty naked foot protruding from a shop doorway, the street *was* empty, yes.

And the old, old man moved on...

■ ■ ■

Tele- (Gk. tele: 'far'.) Telescope: An optical instrument enlarging distant objects.
Micro- (Gk. mikros: 'small') Microscope: An optical instrument making small objects visible to the human eye.
Necro- (Gk. nekros: 'a corpse') Necroscope: a human instrument which permits access to the minds of the dead.

The first two perform physical, one-way functions. They are incapable of changing anything.

Harry Keogh is a Necroscope. He knows the thoughts of interred corpses. His talent works both ways. The dead know he knows their thoughts — and they won't lie still for it!

◙ ◙ ◙

Brian Lumley is the author of the bestselling *Necroscope* series of vampire novels. An acknowledged master of Lovecraft-style horror, Lumley has won the British Fantasy Award and been named a Grand Master of Horror. His works have been published in more than a dozen countries and have inspired comic books, role-playing games, and sculpture, and been adapted for television. When not writing, Lumley can often be found spearfishing in the Greek islands, gambling in Las Vegas, or attending a convention somewhere in the US. Lumley and his wife live in England. First published in *Necroscope: Harry and the Pirates*, TOR Books, 2009, "Old Man with a Blade" features the protagonist of his *Necroscope* world, Harry Keogh, maybe the *only* character that can unnerve Death!

POPULATION
─MANAGEMENT─
By Tom Dullemond

Formless formless formless!

Brandon scrabbled at his desk, knocking over his foot-wide fossil Ammonite paperweight as he pulled drawers open and dug through their contents — blank sheets, sticky notes, stationery.

Not the right forms. He needed the right form!

His Death stood motionlessly beside him, oval head at waist-height, humanoid plastiform face serene.

Half a minute or so passed over that stoic translucent face while Brandon continued to sift through his desk.

"My condolences," Death repeated, assuming Brandon hadn't heard it the first time. "On your death."

"Listen, I … uhm … I need to requisition the *Intent to Confirm Death Notice* form."

"That is form D-12, and any 'intent to confirm' form requires four working days to process. I am afraid you are dying this Friday morning, so there is not enough time to acquire the form."

"I need to post the *Expedited Request* at the same time, that will give me a—"

"Congratulations!" Brandon's Death stood a little straighter, and its eye LEDs glowed greener. "I have expedited your request for the *Expedited Request* and the requirement has been waived!"

Before Brandon's expression had time to shift from panic to relief it added, "Your *Intent to Confirm* has been expedited and your Death has been confirmed. My condolences on your death!"

Something in its simplistic logic circuits tripped on that *non sequitur* and its green eyes faded apologetically back to sorrowful orange.

Brandon wasn't consoled. "I'm twenty four! And I process death forms, I'm supposed to—" But it didn't matter. The confirmation had come through so there wasn't much point in filing a counter notice of intent to reconfirm the confirmation of the *Intent to Confirm Death Notice.*

He sank back into his thousand dollar ergonomic chair and closed his eyes, struggling for some of the inner peace he achieved each morning on the commute in his little one-person cablet.

"My condolences on your death, but I'm pleased to tell you that the department is actively recruiting a replacement bureaucrat as of this morning. I'm told they're having some trouble finding a person with your experience and dedication. You're quite a unique individua—" it hiccupped briefly "—Brandon Somerset."

Brandon held up a hand, stared off past the Death's rounded plastic shoulder and beyond his small cubicle across the otherwise empty office.

"Is this because I wouldn't take the job down-state?"

"Oh, I'm not privy to HR decisions, Brandon."

"I emailed them this morning that I wouldn't take the job, and now I'm being served with a Death. This is bullshit."

"I'm sorry you feel that way Brandon, but the lottery doesn't discriminate or favor. I'm simply here to help you through this difficult time. I have a list of affairs the department thinks you need to tidy up. They've taken the liberty of updating your public PeoplePage status to 'Dying'. You should probably prepare some replies. Your mother is very worried about you."

"Gah!" Brandon spun in his chair to face the terminal and flicked virtual windows aside until he saw his profile page. Condolence notices clogged his inbox. He pulled a few apart then realized most of them were just templates.

Sorry to hear about your loss. That was from an ex.

Damn, sucks to be you right now. Four of those from various acquaintances and from friends he'd lost real-life track of over the years.

His mother seemed the most upset, but even her handful of grieving paragraphs held an overtone of restrained effort, like she wasn't sure how much grief was appropriate.

He dashed off an *I'll sort this out* blanket response, but the reality was there wasn't much to sort out. His Death would help him wrap up his earthly affairs, accompany him to the government hospital on Friday morning, and pat him on the head while they gave him his lethal injection or whatever. Maybe they'd drop a piano on his head on the way, to give the newsies some filler.

"Is this some kind of trick?" he asked the robot. "Are they teaching me a lesson?"

"I wouldn't know about such things, Brandon. I'm your personal Death, ready to help you finalize your affairs. You should take a break and let yourself get used to the idea."

Brandon didn't need to get used to the idea. He'd seen this plenty of times. Most of his work involved allocating appropriate resources to the dying. He just figured that that gave him some kind of special immunity, so he'd grow old like in the movies, live his life out on a grassy hill somewhere. Not that he'd ever seen a genuine grassy hill with his own eyes.

Dammit! He was twenty-four! He only had twenty-four tickets in the lottery.

"What do I die of?" he ventured.

"Heart failure, in your sleep," the Death said. "It won't be any trouble. Thousands of people die of this every day."

"And you're sure this isn't some kind of elaborate prank? I have two notices on my file about being obstructive."

Notice one was the old lady who'd died of a heart attack when Brandon had messaged her that her husband had died of a heart attack. That little fiasco ended up costing the department a kidney transplant, after they had to account for the unexpected death and tweak the statistics back. He still got an email from that kid every year, on the anniversary of his free life-saving operation. Very messy business. Lots of accusations.

Notice two was from trying to tweak a Death for personal reasons. That hadn't worked out so well. But Brandon thought the department would have moved past that now, since the lady in question was dead despite his best efforts.

He made a sudden decision and grabbed his phone, stabbing a finger at his mother's number.

She picked up and ... it was the answering bot. Somehow it was always the answering bot.

"Hey ... hi. I was just wondering... Can you guys make it to the hospital on Friday morning? I'd really appreciate it. No ... no, I just need to talk to ma. No, I'm not ready to talk to her shrink about it. I'm fine ... yes ... yes. No. No I don't have time right now. I'm dying. Bye." He slammed down the phone. Roboassists were getting far too personal.

"I'd be happy to listen to anything you might want to talk about, Brandon," the Death said.

"Well I really think we ought to—"

"But first, I have a suggested list of people with whom you need to make amends, drawn up by the department to maximize your well-being."

"Uh ... o ... kay, then. Sure, what's on the list?"

"The lottery distributes death fairly, but it is always a shock for the winners. As part of your winding down, the department ensures that you attempt to make amends with those you have upset in your life. For you, Brandon, the list is longer than average."

"Yeah, well I grew up around a lot of jerks."

The Death paused and blinked its tiny LED eyes.

"It's why you aren't dying until the day after tomorrow, Brandon. You have a lot of relationships to mend."

"Well, first maybe you should mend *this*," said Brandon, and he put the spiral Ammonite paperweight through Death's faceplate.

■ ■ ■

He was still sitting in his chair, staring, when the new Death rolled in. The lift *dinged* and when he looked up, there it was, pretty much identical to the first, which still lay in pieces at his feet. It had been about five minutes. Not bad.

Brandon sighed.

"Alright, let's get started, Death." He began packing up his belongings. The Ammonite was barely scratched by the broken Death's head. He placed it flat on top and paused with the cool stone under his fingers.

"The very first person on your list is Bettina Grayling, a young girl who—"

"Seriously? I didn't ask her out after Junior High. That's it."

"She was very upset and remained single for three whole years. She bears you a grudge, and we'd like to cheer up her life."

"Oh, man, this is ridiculous. That's *her* issue. It was a kid's promise."

"Since it's my job to ensure each lottery death is a net gain for societal happiness, I would like you to contact Bettina and apologize for disappointing her."

"You're joking, right? Is my piano teacher Mrs. Andrews next? I remember I skipped out on a few classes my mom paid for." He laughed.

"Mrs. Andrews is third on the list. You also need to apologize to your brother for taking credit for his creative writing assignment in the eighth grade."

Brandon blinked at the Death, speechless.

"And it would be a nice personal touch if you handwrote each letter." Death handed him a gold-filigreed fountain pen.

By the time his Death explained that they had completed enough apologies for the first day, Brandon was emotionally exhausted and his concerns about how petty and ridiculous each offence was had been drowned out by the cramping pain in his hand. Who still wrote things by *hand*? In the end he had nine painfully handwritten apologies, black ink on marbled grey paper. The Death provided matching gray envelopes, addressed in machine-perfect cursive.

"That's lovely work, Brandon. Shall we go home?"

"Uhm, well…"

"I've requisitioned a two-person cab, so you'll have some company for a change."

"Suuure… Thanks, but—"

"Let me accompany you."

"Yeah, I was going to go to a bar instead. Just on a whim. Just the kind of day it's been, you know?" He lifted the box of work possessions and headed for the door.

The Death didn't notice his sarcasm. "I will accompany you, Brandon."

▧ ▧ ▧

Brandon stared at his whiskey. He'd not been in this particular bar before but this was as good a time as any to establish new habits. The other booths were empty. Quiet Muzak trickled through concealed speakers.

The autobar next to their table waited politely for him to hold out his drink. Two perfect, chilled ice cubes landed in the glass and the autobar rolled silently out of sight.

Brandon turned to his Death. "So ... so I can't have my job back?"

"That's right!" Death said. "I'm glad to report HR found someone with the right skills to replace you. It was close, you certainly are a unique individual."

"But I'm not dying today."

"It would be cruel to expect you to complete your apology letters as well as turn up to work in the last days of your life."

"This is all a big joke, isn't it? You're making me a better person, and if I pass the test I get to take that job down-state." He paused. "Does this count as bullying? Is this some kind of departmental bullying?"

"Not that I've seen," said Death.

That didn't make much sense but Brandon let it slide and sipped at his scotch. He could afford to try the more expensive single malts. Maybe he'd down a whole bottle.

He thought of the cramping in his writing hand and how utterly unpleasant that would be with a hangover. *Or maybe I'll just stay drunk until Friday morning.*

■ ■ ■

The twincab ride back home was deadly silent. The Death said nothing, staring into space. Brandon looked out his window at the other opaque bubbles moving alongside through dark sleet and had the oddest sensation that he was the only person left alive. When was the last time he'd spoken to someone in person?

He thought about it for a moment, realized he'd had an almost-real-time conversation over email with his supervisor, and felt a little better. Maybe next week he might—

Brandon stopped. That's right, there was nothing to look forward to. He'd always defined his life by having things to look *forward* to: finishing his studies so he could leave the damn boarding school and get a job, the holiday he was going to have when he finished accruing leave at work, the next episode of *Darius Grey: Resource Pirate*. And how was he going to watch all those classic episodes of *Arcblazer* he'd bought last week? Was even a single episode worth watching, given how little time he had left?

"The odds of me winning the lottery were pretty small," he said into the silent cab.

"It's unfortunate, but that's the reality of a lottery, Brandon."

"But how many tickets could there be, realistically? What's the average human age these days?"

"In the low 50s. The lottery program has helped ease the mid-century population pressures significantly, but with birth rates under control we expect the global average age to trend higher for another decade or so."

"Sure, uh… Okay." He'd never really understood statistics. "But basically that means most people have at least twice as many tickets as I do."

Death didn't reply.

"So there must be a billion tickets in there just in this sector, maybe even two." That was forty million people in the entire country, though, which seemed high. He thought maybe the Indian sub-continent and New China were allowed that many. Maybe.

"The lottery ticket count is obviously confidential, but there are thousands of draws a day. It's just bad luck, Brandon. If it makes you feel better, I'm personally very sorry. You are a good person. We're just making sure you leave behind the legacy you deserve."

The cab pulled off the road near his house, and Brandon flipped his wallet over the charge-pad. It blipped denial at him.

Death put a gentle plastic hand on his, pushing it back. "The department pays for your transport in this trying time, Brandon. It's the least we can do."

Brandon stepped out of the car, his box of possessions under his arm. "You're not coming in with me, that's for sure."

Death was already outside, on the cold permacrete.

"I need to make sure you don't do anything drastic, Brandon."

"Right…" Brandon looked out over the road. Cabs flitted over the sidewalk, mostly singles but with the occasional double cab shooting past. Was there a lottery winner with a personal Death in one of those twin cabbers, too?

"Well you can stay in the laundry room while I sleep."

He collapsed onto his bed five minutes later then spent another hour staring at the ceiling, trying to hear the sounds of life from his neighbors' apartments and failing. From his kitchen he heard the occasional tap of metal or plastic on wood as Death positioned itself amidst the laundry soaps and fabric softeners.

Eventually the silence around him faded away and he slept.

■ ■ ■

"Good morning, Brandon."

"I told you to stay in the laundry!" he said crankily. This was the last full day of his life.

"We have to spend the morning finishing your list, Brandon. There are only a few more letters to write, and I think you did a marvelous job already."

"And then?"

"Then you need to think about what you want to do with all … this." Death looked around the bedroom, waving blunt articulated fingers at the handful of movie posters, his clumsy bookshelf, not quite top-of-the-line chip equipment.

Brandon's stomach flipped for the briefest moment, but then he managed to latch back onto his suspicion that this was all a part of the department's efforts to improve his attitude and ship him down-state. The world refocused enough to let him climb out of bed and stumble into the shower.

"Go wait in the kitchen!" he shouted through steam. The hot spray clarified the world. Brandon pressed barely trembling hands flat against the tiled wall and scalded himself awake.

Death was waiting calmly beside the breakfast table when he walked out, refreshed and calm. It had laid out the fountain pen and several sheets of paper beside a bowl of breakfast flakes soaking in milk. Brandon was too polite to explain he didn't take his cereal with milk, and prodded the limp flakes half-heartedly while he looked over his list of grievances.

"Michele from *payroll?* Because I muted her PeoplePage account?" He'd never spoken to anyone at the office directly. The local department offices were mostly empty during the day and inter-office comms came through email.

"It's an unfortunate case. She heard about your efforts on the Sandra Cunningham Death lottery case and began to idolize you. When you stopped following her status updates she became depressed and tried to embezzle money from the department. Eventually she needed to be medicated."

"I knew you'd bring Sandra back into this."

"Sandra never knew you. There was no reason to try to fake her death."

"I saw it on the news. She was gorgeous, and she had a little daughter. If we can't make exceptions, what's the point of working in population control?" It didn't matter, because Sandra was dead anyway, and his current between-jobs-predicament might very well be related to his attempts to game the system on her behalf.

The Death paused for a few seconds, some sort of pre-programmed social affectation. "It's important that we keep human intervention out of the death lottery, Brandon. That's why robots manage lottery entries and why robots carry out the draw and robots help lottery winners like you. Robots like me, Brandon. We're the friendliest sort. I like what you did with your hair, by the way."

"You... What?"

"Please write that letter to Michele; she'll appreciate it."

▦ ▦ ▦

At noon, Death folded the last of his letters and slipped them into their named envelopes. Brandon cracked a beer can from his fridge in lieu of lunch and stared at his hands for a while.

Were they really monitoring world citizens in case a few of them died and needed a list of aggrieved people to apologize to? Really? Monitoring the whole world like that?

"No need to dwell, Brandon," Death said. "You did a great job. Now we should go through your possessions. The department doesn't have a Will on record but you have some savings, as well as accrued departmental benefits. I happen to have a list of recorded assets here. It won't take long, and afterwards we can have the rest of the day off together."

"Sure. I have a pretty tight schedule. Let's see... Last day today... Tomorrow is Friday. We're going to the hospital where I die but instead you're going to tell me the truth about what's happening?"

"That sounds perfect, Brandon."

Just hearing that from Death made him feel a little more in control.

"Hey, actually I do have something to say."

"I'm here to help. If there's anything you need to talk about, I'm here for you."

"I'm ... I'm sorry I took you out before. You know ... back in the office yesterday. I knew it wouldn't matter but I guess it was just my nature, fighting back."

"That's understandable, Brandon. These days when people die, they know they're doing so for the greater good, but even knowing this isn't always enough to overcome base human instincts of survival. For what it's worth, I forgive you."

"Uhm, sure. So..."

Death slid his list of assets across the table.

"You're a child of the new world, Brandon. The resource crunch is a thing of the past and you have no grandiose wasteful assets, and most of your wealth is in your bank account."

"I guess—" He ran his finger down the itemized list. "—these books can just go to charity. My clothes … well, sure, the same. Make things better for the rest of us, right?"

Death did not respond.

"And then I suppose the furniture can go to… Screw it! It can all go to charity. My mother doesn't need any of it."

"Personal items?"

Brandon looked at the list. A few drawings he'd done in early college art classes. Lots of digital music and films that anyone with a half-decent job could afford to buy for themselves. He was about to shrug it all into the recycle bin when he saw, 'Personal note — Mother' and stopped. What was that? He *remembered* that. It was a letter ma had sent him in high school, so where would it be?

Somewhere in the shoebox, of course.

"Are you alright, Brandon?" Death had noticed him jolt.

"Oh yes, of course. Just remembering." That feeling curled back in his guts again. He hadn't thought of his mother's letter for years. Sixteen-year-old lonely Brandon had really appreciated it, the old world charm of handwriting a letter when email would've reached him quicker…

He stood up suddenly and rushed to his desk, where his box of personal items from work sat forgotten. The spiral of his stone Ammonite felt like a glaring, accusing eye. In a desk drawer, underneath old magazines and bills, he found his shoebox, flipped it open, dug through some old digital camera chips from his youth. He stopped at an actual print photo someone had created of little Brandon and ma at a kids' birthday party in the city park. When had he last gone to a park?

He found his mother's letter at the bottom, flattened and smudged a little, still in the original torn marbled gray envelope. Death rolled closer behind him, where he crouched over the little treasure.

"Did you find what you were looking for?" Death said.

"It's … yeah, I just remembered it. I was having a tough time, you know how it goes for ∴.. actually, I guess you don't. Ma really helped, I don't even think she knew what was going on with me. Just apologizing for stuff, little things I barely remembered but, yeah, I guess they just sat inside me for…"

He paused as he folded open the letter, skimming the neat cursive writing. "You know, if it wasn't for this letter I would have killed myself. It arrived at just the right time and… Wait, a second!" He bit his lip, looked up at the robot. "This is the same kind of paper I've been writing on. And … and the envelopes…? This is a five year old letter! Is ma dead?"

Death said nothing. "You're very attached to your mother, Brandon. I wouldn't try to over think these things. Remember you spoke to your mother last week?"

"But that was via email. I … I'm not sure the last time I actually *spoke* to her. We keep missing each other, leaving voice messages…" His voice cracked. "What kind of sick game is this?"

Brandon stood up and placed the letter onto his desk. "I need a moment."

He walked back to his living area, found where he'd left his wallet and access card, and took a step towards the kitchen just as Death rolled into sight, then sprinted towards the front door.

"Brandon? Where—?"

He swiped the door open and threw himself through the gap and didn't pause as his eyes adjusted to the gloom of the stairwell and—

Ten small white cleaner bots crowded at his feet, all leaning backwards in surprise as he ploughed into them, felt his foot hook on a smooth plastic scrubbing brush and lost his balance. His wallet and keys went flying, and Brandon crashed headfirst down the stairs, spinning in a cloud of plastic shrapnel and tiny wheels, the plaintive cry of Death following behind and up and around and—

Permacrete punched him into the black.

▨ ▨ ▨

The blackness split into bright sunlight and Brandon blinked his eyes, gathering his wits. Something tight wrapped around his head and he tentatively explored bandages with his fingers. He was lying in a hospital bed.

Death stood beside him, plastic face at eye-height.

"What … what happened?"

"You tried to fly down the stairwell, Brandon. You hit your head. I was worried it might be a skull fracture."

"I… Hey, is that…? It's bright outside. Is it *Friday?*"

"Yes, unfortunately. I brought you to the hospital just in case. It seemed efficient."

"Uhm, thanks, I guess."

"That's what I do."

Brandon said nothing for a little while, blinking at the white wall.

"I was trying to escape."

Death waited patiently.

"But ... I think it was all part of this whole test, right? It was that letter from ma, reminding me how those few words just at the right time convinced me to hang on to life. I was really depressed."

"I know, Brandon, I saw it in your file. All the signs were there in your correspondence to your peers."

"I didn't kill myself back then. Life had promises still and ma showed me that, and then last night ... I thought if I keep following you around, isn't that just like killing myself? So I decided I wouldn't go quietly. I ... I was running away." He looked around, shrugged. "So... Yeah... That didn't work out so well."

Death remained politely still.

"Why were all those cleaner bots outside my apartment?"

"They don't see lottery winners often, Brandon. I wouldn't worry about those things. It won't matter soon."

"What did the doctor say?"

"The autodoctor says you are concussed, but you've been provided with anti-emetics and there should be no further problems."

"Except I'm supposed to be dying today."

"That's a separate issue. I'm very sorry about that."

Brandon paused again then grinned.

"Okay, okay. So are we done now? This was all just to mess with me, wasn't it?"

"Oh." That artificial pause again. "Oh! Oh yes, of course."

"Ha, I knew it!" A brief flicker of doubt, then, "Are you sure?"

"Yes, I am sure, Brandon. You were right all along, it was all a clever plan to motivate you, so that you would become a better person."

Brandon lay back in his bed, sighing. "That's such a relief, Death. I'm only twenty-four. I'm too young to die."

"I know."

"When will I see my mother?"

"Your mother is outside, in the waiting room. There are just some formalities to complete." Death rolled a little closer, placing a smooth hand on his shoulder.

"You've had a long day, Brandon. You should rest."

"When do I see my mother?"

"Soon. After you've settled in a little. Here, drink this to calm your nerves." Death handed him a cool glass of water.

Tired, Brandon pulled himself up a little and sipped at it.

"Thanks. I'm so relieved. I really thought it was the end."

"It'll be fine, Brandon. Everything is fine now. Finish your drink. Just close your eyes and rest."

"All that talk about lottery numbers, that was just to keep me guessing, right? Ha ha!"

"Just a part of the ... exercise, Brandon. You were very clever to work it all out. I'm very proud of you."

"Right ... well... We'll talk about that later, okay? When I look into that new job. But first I'll rest, and ... then I'll see some visitors?"

"Yes. Trust me. And we'll talk about it all later. I promise. But first... Just ... close ... your ... eyes..."

And Brandon did.

▩ ▩ ▩

Tom Dullemond is an Australian-based writer of speculative fiction and the occasional prize-winning literary piece. He works primarily as a software developer and juggles a day job, home projects, writing and family — not necessarily in that order. Tom has previously published work in anthologies such as *AustrAlien Absurdities*, as well as co-editing *The Complete Guide to Writing Fantasy* and writing regular flash fiction for the national Australian high-school science magazine, *Helix*. "Population Management" was originally inspired by trying to imagine what a bureaucratized death process might look like, but developed in a slightly different direction from there.

—ADDENDUM—

Danse Macabre reflects a religious tradition which postulates that the soul or spirit departs the body at the last moment of life. Consequently, the classical artwork appeared in religious settings. Here are a few examples of the types of places the art can be found, including some specific works from the less than 50 Danse Macabre tableaux still extant:

— church, monastery and nunnery exteriors — *Chiesa di St-Vigile, Pinzolo, Italy (1539)*;
— chapel and ossuary interiors — the ceiling of the *Friedhof Chapel, Wondrub, Germany (1670)*;
— cemeteries — the grotto in *Petersfriedhof, Salzbourg, Austria (1770)*;
— building carvings — the vault ribs in *Rosslyn Chapel, Rosslyn, Scotland (1459)*;
— stained glass — the only surviving panel in the UK in the window of *St. Andrew's Church, Norwich, England (1510)*;
— museums — panels rescued from the St. Ann's chapel and housed in the *Museum der Stadt, Füssen, Germany (1620)*;
— other structures — painted ceiling of the covered bridge (*Spreuerbrucke*) - *Luzern, Switzerland (1408)*.

As well, many Danse Macabre images can be found on coffins and tombs throughout Europe, and occasionally in North America.

The following Internet links include the artwork listed above as well as links for sites devoted to the subject of Danse Macabre art:

> — *Patrick Pollefeys' Dance of Death (listed by country):*
> http://www.lamortdanslart.com/danse/dance.htm
> — *Hans Holbein the Younger's Danse Macabre woodcuts*:
> http://www.godecookery.com/macabre/holdod/holdod.htm
> — *Dance of Death images and poetry:*
> http://www.danse-macabre.net/
> — *A scholarly perspective, Dr. Sophie Oosterwijk:*
> http://www-ah.st-andrews.ac.uk/staff/sophie.html
> http://www.ice.cam.ac.uk/components/tutors/?view=tutor&id=344&cid=377
> — *Danse Macabre images from Italy:*
> http://www3.sympatico.ca/tapholov/
> — *On Facebook, the Danse Macabre wall:*
> https://www.facebook.com/groups/19471035904/
> — *Danse Macabre composed by Camille* Saint-Saëns *in 1874*
> http://www.youtube.com/watch?v=YyknBTm_YyM

◼ ◼ ◼